A SECOND KISS

Sophie glanced at the mantel clock. "Even by the most generous interpretation of taking but a few minutes of my time, you have overstayed your welcome."

East acknowledged her point with a slim smile. "Touché."

"Will you leave by the usual route or do you prefer a window exit?"

"The door will do."

She nodded, stepping aside, her arms still crossed in front of her.

East studied her for a long moment. Resolve set nicely on her face. East supposed there were an infinite number of choices available to him, but only one that would not leave him with regrets. It was probably true that her sweet mouth would always tempt him now that he knew the taste of it, and equally likely that another kiss would never be enough, but Eastlyn decided for better or worse, he wanted another bite of the apple.

"Sophie?"

"Hmm?"

"I am going to kiss you." If she was startled by this intelligence, she did not show it, and Eastlyn did not give her further opportunity. One arm caught her at the small of the back and the other at her nape. He drew her close so that her head was angled toward his, then lowered his mouth to hers.

The taste of Sophie's mouth was a feast for the senses. Sweet. Tart. A hint of tang. Warm and honeyed. The suggestion of someting like mint. Her lips parted and fashioned their movement in a way that mirrored his, and there was something extraordinarily powerful in teaching her to kiss. . . .

Books by Jo Goodman

The Captain's Lady
Crystal Passion
Seaswept Abandon
Velvet Night
Violet Fire
Scarlet Lies
Tempting Torment
Midnight Princess
Passion's Sweet Revenge
Sweet Fire
Wild Sweet Ecstasy
Rogue's Mistress
Forever in My Heart
Always in My Dreams
Only in My Arms
My Steadfast Heart
My Reckless Heart
With All My Heart
More Than You Know
More Than You Wished
Let Me Be the One
Everything I Ever Wanted
All I Ever Needed

Published by Zebra Books

ALL I EVER NEEDED

Jo Goodman

ZEBRA BOOKS
KENSINGTON PUBLISHING CORP.
http://www.kensingtonbooks.com

ZEBRA BOOKS are published by

Kensington Publishing Corp.
850 Third Avenue
New York, NY 10022

All Kensington titles, imprints and distributed lines are available at special quantity discounts for bulk purchases for sales promotion, premiums, fund-raising, educational or institutional use.

Special book excerpts or customized printings can also be created to fit specific needs. For details, write or phone the office of the Kensington Special Sales Manager: Kensington Publishing Corp., 850 Third Avenue, New York, NY 10022. Attn. Special Sales Department. Phone: 1-800-221-2647.

First Printing: October 2003
10 9 8 7 6 5 4 3 2 1

Printed in the United States of America

Prologue

1796, Hambrick Hall, London

"There's a toll to be paid."

Gabriel Whitney slid to a halt as an arm was stiffly extended to block his path. Hambrick Hall's cobbled courtyard was still slick from an unexpected morning shower, and Gabriel's balance was not only threatened by the abrupt command to stop, but by the large parcel he held in front of him. The parcel was bobbled but not squeezed. He was scrupulously careful about that. Scones and biscuits and sweet raisin muffins would not be so tasty if they were reduced to crumbs. Crumbs were acceptable as evidence of a delicious repast, but hardly what one wanted as the main course.

With his balance and his parcel secured, Gabriel looked away from the water-glazed cobbles and toward the owner of the extended appendage. "There's a toll?"

"I've just said so, haven't I?" Young Lord Barlough looked to his two friends who stood ready to perform the same turnstile function as their leader. They were already levering their forearms in anticipation of Gabriel making a dash around the human gate he had become. He dropped his outstretched arm to demonstrate that he was unconcerned by such an action. "He can't really run, can he? He has the parcel, and we know he won't risk damaging it. It would never do to ruin his cakes and custards."

"Scones and biscuits and muffins," Gabriel said helpfully. "If the toll's for cakes and custards, then it doesn't really apply." It was a reasonable enough objection to raise, though Gabriel was not terribly surprised when Barlough made him out to be foolish.

"Scones and biscuits and muffins." The timbre of Barlough's voice rose and fell in the singsong cadence peculiar to childhood mockery. It also emphasized the rather uncertain pitch that sometimes visited Gabriel at odd moments. Barlough had no sympathy for anyone on the cusp of puberty now that he had moved past it himself. "The toll's for sweets," he said plainly. "Any sort of sweets. You have scones, you say?"

Gabriel nodded. A spiraling lock of chestnut hair fell forward over his brow. With his hands occupied securing the brown paper parcel close to his chest, he couldn't push back the offending curl, and it tickled him each time he bobbed his head. He thought he might not have noticed it at all if he'd had a free hand to absently scratch, but he could not deny that the tickling was becoming devilish annoying. He considered tossing his head back but suspected it would elicit some comment from the others about his resemblance to a horse. He shouldn't mind if they called him a great black stallion, but Barlough was certain to compare him to a brood mare. It was rare that anyone missed an opportunity to point out that he was of a certain size around his middle owing to his appreciation of cakes and custards.

Gabriel pushed his gently rounded jaw forward and tried blowing upward to shift the fallen curl. It fluttered once and fell back, tickling him far more than it had done previously.

"You look like a girl when you do that, Master Whitney." Barlough's brow kicked up as he once again looked for affirmation of this observation from his compatriots. "Didn't he look like a girl?"

Gabriel kept his eyes steady on Barlough, but Harte and Pendrake were still in the field of his vision. He saw them nod in unison, and his face flushed at the grave insult. It would have been a lesser slight for Barlough to make the inevitable horse analogy. Gabriel knew girls. He had an older sister and four female cousins. Girls were soft and round and rosy-cheeked. They had rioting curls and pouting mouths and were prone to fits they liked to call the vapors or worse, a strenuous bout of tears.

It occurred to Gabriel that he felt somewhat like crying himself. He sucked in his lower lip and bit it hard. The pain helped stiffen his resolve.

"He's blushing," Pendrake said. He made to nudge Barlough, but that worthy adroitly sidestepped the contact. As the Archbishop of the Society of Bishops, Barlough was not to be casually elbowed as though he were a chum. Respect for his position in the Society demanded that certain formalities be observed. Realizing his error, Pendrake made to cover the breach by quickly pointing his finger at Gabriel. "Blushing," he repeated. "Like a girl."

Gabriel felt the heat in his cheeks and knew it was true. He almost dropped the parcel to bring up his hands to cover them. If the color had been ruddy, it might have been acceptable. Old salts at sea were imprinted with ruddy color from the spray of water and the constant press of the wind. No one ever accused them of blushing. Gabriel's color, though, was as pink as a baby's bottom. It was humiliating. If he was going to drop the parcel, he thought, it would be to bring up his fists. The thought of it was already making his fingers curl. If he wasn't careful, he would not only ruin all the good things his mother had sent him, but he would ruin the plan as well.

Naturally there was a plan. His friend South had insisted there must be. Gabriel was more inclined to simply use his fists. It was as God intended, he had argued, when men were given knuckles and an opposable thumb. But South had been blessed with a brilliant head for debate and had managed to convince their mutual friends Brendan and Evan of the superiority of his thinking. Outnumbered three to one, Gabriel had conceded that perhaps fisticuffs was not the best way to challenge the Society of Bishops. He had, in turn, suggested slingshots, then cudgels, both of which had a certain appeal, slingshots because they were the weapon of choice when David faced Goliath, and cudgels because Gabriel liked the sound of them, even if he wasn't entirely clear on what manner of weapon they might be.

Gabriel Richard Whitney, known as East to his best friends, was one-quarter of the Compass Club. It was not a recognized institution at Hambrick Hall. Certainly it did not have the prestigious lineage and history of the Society of Bishops. The origins of the Compass Club were not steeped in vaguely mysterious circumstances, nor was there a long oral history to pass on to generations of new initiates. In contrast to the Society, the Compass Club had only recently come into existence. They had not once considered the idea of future generations, and although they had recently adopted a charter, it was merely bad verse penned by South. They all liked it well enough, but no one, not even South, denied it was bad verse.

Still under rather heated discussion was the matter of a blood oath. There was no disagreement concerning the oath. To a man they were in favor of being *sworn enemies of the Society of Bishops*. It was the issue of blood that cleaved them squarely down the middle.

Brendan Hampton, North to his friends, and Viscount Southerton, addressed familiarly and affectionately as South, were in favor of a bloodless oath. Evan Marchman, the one they called West, and Gabriel were of the opinion that blood shed over an oath was not only highly desirable but perhaps even necessary. The outcome was yet to be decided, but Gabriel suspected in this matter he and West would prevail. North and South could not maintain their position too fiercely lest it be mistaken for missishness. Gabriel knew he was not the only one who did not want to be compared to a female.

This last thought brought Gabriel around to face his predicament. He'd agreed to not using force to settle this dispute with the Bishops, and for all that he was only ten, he was still a man of his word. With some effort, he allowed his fingers to unfold and settle lightly around the parcel again. The smell of the baked goods was tantalizing. His mother had wrapped the package herself, he knew, but the contents were Mrs. Eddy's. At his mother's behest, their cook had been preparing all manner of special desserts for him for as long as he could remember. He was particularly partial to custard pie, but that confection did not travel well from their country home in Braeden. The Bishops would have been suspicious of custard, or at least they should have been if they'd read Hufeland's "Macrobiotics, or the The Art to Prolong One's Life." There were certain foods one should take pains to avoid, especially if they were three days old.

"How much is the toll?" Gabriel asked. He felt the heat in his cheeks recede as he put his mind to the mission at hand. If his composure in the face of their teasing wasn't enough to end it, he would simply have to ignore it. A certain amount of diplomacy was required here, and although it sometimes pained Gabriel to engage in such reasoned discourse, he also understood the necessity of it.

Barlough dismissed Gabriel for a moment to eye the package. He wondered about the scone-to-muffin ratio. He was not partial to muffins because there were often raisins, though he liked them plain well enough. Perhaps he would pick out the raisins for the others to have and keep the muffins for himself. There would be a mild protest from Pendrake and Harte, but they would accept his leavings because he was the archbishop and there was no higher authority in the Society. His decision would be the final word. "Your parcel," Barlough said to Gabriel. "Hand it over."

"All of it? I say, that's rather steep, don't you think?" It was tantamount to robbery, though Gabriel refrained from saying so. It was also not unexpected. For three weeks the Compass Club had been observing Society members exacting tribute from their Hambrick Hall classmates. Boys in an-

ticipation of receiving posts from home were their targets.
Society members followed their hapless classmates until an
opportunity presented itself to make the demand of payment. Usually the collection involved money, but exceptions
were made. Young Master Healy had paid with his favorite
commander from his army of tin soldiers. Reginald Arnout
had been required to hand over a slim leather-and-gilt volume of Blake's poetry. The coup de grâce was the payment
they received from Bentley Vancouver: a dozen cards illus-
trated with heretofore unimaginable acts of sexual depravity.
They were French, of course, a gift to Bentley from his older
brother on the eve of his thirteenth birthday. After only a
fleeting glimpse of the promised land as he walked from the
post, Bentley had been accosted by the advance guard from
the Society. He had had to produce the cards that he had just
tucked away and give them over. Poor Bentley was incon-
solable.

It was then that Gabriel decided they must act. Once he
was convinced that thrashing Barlough was not a sound
strategy, he had offered his own dependable parcel from
home as the best means of exacting retribution.

"I don't think I like giving you all of it," Gabriel said.
"Perhaps a few of the scones will do."

One of Lord Barlough's eyebrows arched dramatically.
"You're a cheeky brat, aren't you?" He looked around the
courtyard. It was all but deserted. The few boys that were
visible were hurrying to class and knew better than to take
an interest in what was transpiring under the stone archway.
As long as there had been a Hambrick Hall there had been a
Society of Bishops. They remained in existence because
they went about their business without fear of reprisal. "Are
your friends hiding nearby? Is that what makes you so brave?"

Friends. It made Gabriel smile to be reminded that he had
friends. It was a relatively new experience for him and one
he'd discovered he quite liked. He'd been more lonely than
he knew, solitary in his room except for the cakes and tarts
and biscuits he kept hidden under his bed, in his desk, and at

the bottom of his armoire. No one except his mother seemed to understand how much he missed being at Braeden, and although it was a poor kind of comfort to eat one of the pies when he was all alone, it was better than not being comforted at all.

"My friends aren't around," Gabriel said, schooling his features quickly. "They have important matters to occupy them."

"Is that so?"

"Yes."

"It was a rhetorical question I put to you. That means it does not require an answer."

"Oh."

"Your brain is a bit fat, isn't it?"

"I beg your pardon?" Gabriel's fingers were tightening again. To keep from throwing the first punch, he repeated the promise he'd made like a mantra. His lips moved around the words he could not utter aloud.

"Fat clog your ears, too?"

Gabriel's cherubic features remained very still, though his eyes—an almost exact match for the polished chestnut color of his hair—were watchful. It was no good to try to look menacing. He hadn't developed the countenance for it yet, what with his defining bones still softly molded in a perfectly round face, his jawline lost in the fold of a small second chin. He was unafraid to physically take on these members of the Society, even though he knew he would ultimately lose. Their numbers alone would defeat him. The well-deserved reputation he had as a thrasher would not serve him when the tribunal counted three and he was but one. The realization that perhaps what the Society wanted was more than what he carried in his arms helped Gabriel manage his temper this time.

"Let me pass," Gabriel said evenly.

On either side of Barlough arms were immediately raised. The young lord nodded approvingly at Pendrake and Harte for their quick response. "Your parcel, Feast."

Gabriel frowned. Had Barlough truly just called him *Feast?* "East, m'lord. My friends call me East."

"It matters not a whit to me since I am in no way your friend. I shall call you Feast. You look as if you regularly eat one." Barlough held out his hand, palm up. "Now, your parcel. I admit to a partiality for scones, and I suspect from the look of you that these have much to recommend them."

"I don't think you'll like these."

Barlough did not ask for an explanation. He was weary of the haggling and more than a little sorry that Gabriel could not be stirred to some ill-considered action. In a fluid motion that put everyone who witnessed it in mind of a cobra striking, Barlough snatched the parcel from Gabriel's hands by neatly slipping his fingers under the binding twine. He tossed it into the air when Gabriel made a lunge for it. Pendrake, the tallest of them, easily caught it. He held it out of Gabriel's reach by simply holding it overhead.

Belatedly aware of the ridiculousness of his position, Gabriel let his arms drop to his sides. He had an urge to hang his head but wisely chose not to overplay his hand. Instead he made a swipe at his eyes and brushed away the pitiful tear he had managed to squeeze out.

With a derisive smile that spoke more eloquently of his thoughts than any words he could have summoned, Barlough stepped aside. He made a show of graciousness by bowing slightly and using his arm in a sweeping gesture to indicate that Gabriel could now safely cross the courtyard.

Wishing he had a black eye and a few scraped knuckles to show for this encounter with the Bishops, Gabriel nonetheless knew that there had been a victory of sorts here. He had not only chosen his battle, but he had chosen a strategy that did not involve violence. He wondered if he was on his way to becoming a tinker after all.

All four members of the Compass Club were standing in the darkly paneled upper corridor of Yarrow House when

Barlough bounded out of his room and skidded into the hallway. The door behind him might have slammed shut if Pendrake and Harte had not been following so closely on his heels. For a moment they looked around, their movements frantic, eyes darting, arms swinging. Their feet danced in place while they considered what to do. Occupied by the problem that pressed them, they did not notice the small gathering at the far end of the hall. Even if they had, sunlight streaming through the stained-glass arched window put the individual faces of the Compass Club in dark relief and concealed the immediate identity of North, South, West, and most particularly East, who was standing at the forefront.

Trying first one door, then another, finding each one locked in turn, they hurriedly made their way down the hall in search of the very thing that would give them respite. Pendrake and Harte were startled to find they could not enter their own rooms. "Now what do we do?" Harte demanded. Bent awkwardly at the waist, his legs pressed tightly together, he gripped a brass handle to yet another door that would not open to him.

Pendrake's bowels rumbled uncomfortably. It was the only reply he could make, and it echoed so loudly inside his body that he was certain the others could hear it. They might have, but their own bowels were engaged in similar activity. At the end of the hall, the sound of so much digestive thunder gave the Compass Club their first unrestrained smile since East had been accosted that morning. Their patience had been borne out.

Barlough saw them first. His manner changed immediately as he strove for some measure of dignity. He walked stiff-legged, his buttocks clenched tightly. "You!" he said, patently astonished by East's presence in the private quarters of the Society's residence. "What are you doing here?"

East merely smiled.

Barlough looked at the others. "All of you! Out! You're blocking my way."

"Oh?" East asked as Pendrake and Harte came up behind Barlough. "And which way is that?"

Harte groaned softly and clutched his stomach. "The water closet," he managed. "It's the last door on the left."

"Is that so? I didn't realize." He stepped aside, and the rest of the Compass Club followed suit.

Pendrake lunged at the door, shouldering it when it resisted his first efforts to open. Since there was no lock, the only explanation for its refusal to open was that it was barricaded on the other side. Swinging around, Pendrake stared at the four young intruders. "What have you done to it?" He didn't wait for a reply. He fairly screamed at Barlough, "They've stoppered the door! We can't get in!"

Barlough's fair complexion was reddening now, and there was a faint sheen to his brow and upper lip. The restraint he was placing on his body's natural functions was beginning to show. He stared pointedly at Gabriel. "What is it you want?"

"The toll, if you please."

Barlough gritted his teeth but he persisted. "Name it."

"Sign this." From behind his back Gabriel produced a neatly drawn-up treaty. "Would you like to read it or shall I?"

Afraid that Gabriel would draw out each word of the document until the Bishops were writhing in pain or soiled themselves, Barlough grabbed it out of his hands just as he had the parcel. It was in that moment that he realized what Gabriel's intent had been all along. "The scones," he said.

"And the biscuits," Gabriel said helpfully. It was clearly a struggle for Barlough to talk now. "And the sweet raisin muffins."

"You poisoned us."

"Oh, no. Nothing like that. That is, there are no lasting effects." He spared a glance for Pendrake and Harte. "At least I hope not. I was most particular on that account."

Harte groaned again. His knees buckled a fraction, but he didn't drop to the floor. "Do something, Barlough, or I swear I shall explode on the spot!"

Barlough's thinking was not so foggy at this point that he disbelieved his friend. He felt as if he might explode himself. The humiliation of it would drive him from the school.

He would be the first archbishop of the Society to leave disgraced. Holding up the treaty that Gabriel had carefully penned, he read through it quickly.

"You don't intend I should sign it in blood, do you?" Barlough asked.

Gabriel grinned. It certainly had occurred to him. Without a word, he produced a quill and inkpot and placed them on the sill below the window.

Barlough dipped the quill and centered the paper carefully on the sill for his signature. He scribbled it quickly and passed it back to Gabriel who formed his letters with deliberation. It was then duly witnessed by all those present.

"The door," Barlough said. "Open the bloody door."

"That will take far too long," Gabriel said, letting the treaty flutter between his fingertips as the ink dried. "And I don't believe you can wait. There is, however, a solution."

At these words, South and North hopped up to the windowsill and opened the transom in the stained glass. Hooked to the latch was a rope, and attached to the rope, dangling from the outside of the prestigious Yarrow House at Hambrick Hall, were three slop buckets. Hand over hand, they pulled them up and in and presented them without ceremony to the three upper classmates whose bowels were fairly bursting.

"Odd how they came to be there," Gabriel said. He folded the treaty neatly and placed it in his pocket. "I imagine they were what you were looking for in your rooms."

The Compass Club did not wait to see if the Bishops used the buckets for relief in the hallway or managed to answer nature's most urgent call back in Barlough's room. They had East's treaty in hand. The low groundswell of laughter from the commons as the slop buckets were raised was an unexpectedly pleasant addition to the experience, though it seemed bad form to dwell on it.

"It was a good piece of work," North announced much later that night. "You are to be commended, East."

West nodded and bit deeply into a cherry tart that had arrived by express post after they had retired from the dining hall. "You were right to want to do something about the Bishops and their bloody extortion schemes. It was well done of you."

Viscount Southerton sat cross-legged on the floor while his hand hovered over the selection of desserts in the wicker basket. "That's why he's the tinker, you know. He has a good heart, East does, and it's in his nature to fix things."

East passed the basket on to North after South made his choice. He did not take anything for himself. "I suppose it is," he said slowly, coming to terms with the fact of it. Reaching in his jacket, he extracted the treaty. He unfolded it and laid it on the floor between his splayed legs. They all craned their heads to read it again.

Be it known to all and sundry that the Society of Bishops will collect no tariffs, taxes, tolls, or tributes for—

"Alliterate," South said to no one in particular. "That is always a good touch."

—traffic in any of the common areas of Hambrick Hall. Common areas are defined as those places where anyone may gather without invitation. The Society of Bishops further acknowledges it has no privilege, right, or responsibility to collect money, goods, or services for entry into any private domain not expressly controlled by the Society under their charter with Hambrick Hall.

"The Society has no charter with Hambrick," North said around a mouthful of tart. "They're a secret society."

"A society of secrets," said West. "There's a difference."

They all agreed it was so. Without a charter at Hambrick the Bishops could not lay claim to any area of the school as their private domain. Even Yarrow House was not strictly theirs. It was one of Gabriel's best ideas and one they were fairly certain Barlough had not clearly understood when he had signed. In defense of Barlough's thick-wittedness they accepted the fact that he had been under rather severe duress at the time of his signing. That had also been Gabriel's idea. South had insisted they proceed with a plan, but the plan had ultimately been Gabriel's.

Finally, for money, goods, or services already yielded to the Society of Bishops, the archbishop and the undersigned tribunal agree to make full reparations within a fortnight of the ratification of this treaty.

Picking up the treaty, Gabriel scrambled to his feet and went to his bookcase. He carefully placed his finest work to date between the pages of the essays of William Paley, specifically the "Principles of Moral and Political Philosophy." He hadn't read Paley's work yet, but he fully intended that he would.

It was just the sort of thing a tinker should know.

Chapter One

June 1818, London

Sophie imagined she could hear their laughter. She could not blame the heat of the day for the color that crept into her cheeks. It was their laughter that had done it, just the thought of it. There was something faintly disrespectful in the sheer release of so much good humor. The deep, rolling tones of it, reverberating as they did like a series of cavernous echoes, could garner attention from every corner of a crowded ballroom. It was the sort of raucous amusement that had an energy and boisterousness that quite took a listener's breath away.

That hard, spontaneous laughter nearly always inspired envy—except if one was the point of it as Sophie imagined herself to be.

She closed her journal without bothering to mark her place. Writing was not holding her attention the way she had hoped it might, and when it ceased to be a respite, she had learned to put it aside. She laid the journal down, then stoppered the inkhorn and returned her pen to its stand. She idly smoothed the blanket she'd thrown haphazardly across the grass. Sunlight sifted its way through the apple tree behind her and dappled the book's dark green leather cover to give it a spotted emerald hue. She turned her head away and leaned back against the tree trunk, closing her eyes as she had been wont to do since coming to the garden. It was foolish convention that made her think she shouldn't invite sleep out here. Where else, she wondered, was she to find some few minutes of respite if not in the relative privacy of this walled sanctuary? Her own room did not permit her so much peace as this place, not when it was so easily accessible to the children. They were encouraged to seek her out before pressing their concerns on their own mother. Sophie was the first to hear about scraped knees and spilled milk and the spider that had crawled under Esme's pillow, compliments of that rascal Robert. It was Sophie's duty to sift through the high drama of their childhood and inform their parents of those particulars that were deemed sufficiently important.

Today the children were confined to their rooms for the afternoon because of an unfortunate mishap involving a regiment of tin soldiers on the stairwell and the housekeeper's hard tumble from the uppermost step all the way to the first landing. It was Sophie's fault, of course. It did not matter that she was not at home when the incident happened, nor that the reason she was away from Bowden Street was due to her ladyship's insistence that she go immediately to the apothecary for a packet of megrim powders. There was nothing to be gained by pointing out that Lady Dunsmore had not had a megrim at the time she'd sent Sophie out, but merely that she had been in expectation of having one directly.

The tin soldiers had been purposely placed out of the children's reach by Sophie because of an earlier unfortunate mishap with the cook in the pantry, but no one speculated on how Robert and Esme had come to have them once again in their possession. Lady Dunsmore did not have the grace to look at all abashed. She dismissed the children to their rooms, dispatched a runner for the doctor, and laid the re-

sponsibility for it all at Sophie's feet. Her work done, she retired to her bedchamber with a megrim.

Sophie breathed deeply of the garden's redolent scents.
She supposed she should feel a shade guilty for enjoying the
children's incarceration, but she could not quite summon
that feeling. It had not passed her notice that she was in
some small way answerable for the end to which they had
come. She could have, after all, taken Robert and Esme to
the apothecary with her. Keeping them in eyesight seemed
to be the order of the day—and most days this sennight past.
There was no predicting what tricks they might get up to,
only that they would inevitably get up to some.

Even this new penchant they had developed for planning
and executing pratfalls among the servants was not entirely
their fault. Oh, it was not that anyone had encouraged the behavior; it was just that the children were not proof against
the mounting tension at No. 14 Bowden Street. Robert and
Esme were merely responding to what they felt all around
them. Among the adults civility was palpably strained. It
was little wonder that the children had acted upon it. Sophie
knew it was not their desire to see her dismissed from their
home, but just the opposite, to prove how very necessary she
was to them. Without her constant vigilance, they were determined to be no better than young ruffians. Sophie,
though, was the only one to interpret their actions in such a
benevolent manner. For her cousin Harold and his lady wife,
the children's behavior was further evidence that Sophie
made a poor sort of governess. She must leave them, Harold
counseled her, for her own good if she would not think first
of his dear children.

Naturally enough, there was a rub, because the good
Viscount Dunsmore could not simply send his homeless
cousin out into society unprotected. Marriage was the logi-
cal solution most frequently offered to Sophie, though until
a sennight ago there had been no suitors at the ready.

That was changed now. The Most Honorable Marquess of

Eastlyn was rumored to have made a surprising declaration. It seemed that from among all the young women counted as suitable to be his wife, Lady Sophia Colley was the one he had chosen.

Which brought Sophie back to the laughter she'd imagined. It required no special talent to call it to mind once again. The sound simply resonated within her, heating her cheeks a deeper, rosy hue than previously. It was not just the laughter that put embarrassed color in her face, but the fact that she could not doubt the laughter was directed at her.

It would be all four of them, she thought. How could it be else? They rarely seemed to be so deeply diverted outside of their own company. It was not that Sophie had never seen them smile or demonstrate a measure of amusement when they were left to their own devices; it was just that the smiles seemed tempered, the line of them vaguely derisive, and the laughter was subdued, perhaps wry. She had always supposed that they saved their abandoned and occasionally ribald humor for the moments when they were together, when they could share their individually collected observations of society's foibles and absurdities.

Surely, Sophie thought, if not precisely one of the ton's foibles, she was one of its absurdities. Regarding her as a suitable mate must have provoked the marquess into fits of laughter, or quite possibly his friends had pointed out the humor inherent in his situation. If it weren't for the fact that she was feeling rather sorry for herself, Sophie might have been able to rouse some sympathy for the Marquess of Eastlyn. There were many suspects as to the source of her rumored engagement, but the one person Sophie knew to be blameless was the marquess himself. He would not attach himself to her, even for the amusement of his friends. Eastlyn had never struck Sophie as a man given to petty cruelties, and she allowed that it was unfair to judge him as enjoying a laugh at her expense when the sound of it existed only in her own mind.

Something fluttered across the tip of Sophie's nose. She

batted at it idly, too weary to open her eyes and identify the cause. If it was one of Robert's spiders, she'd confound his plan to frighten her by ignoring the crawly thing. A moment passed before the tickling visited her again, this time between her honey-colored brows. She frowned slightly, creasing the space just above her nose. When it came a third time it fluttered across her cheek. It was when the sensation finally flickered along her jaw from ear to chin that Sophie was roused to action.

She slapped herself lightly on the side of the face and was rewarded for her effort, not by trapping the offending insect, but by the last echo of oddly familiar laughter. It struck her with more force than her hand had against her cheek. She *knew* the deep, throaty timbre of that laugh. Even when heard in concert with his friends' it had always been distinguishable to Sophie which thread of sound was his.

Lady Sophia Colley blinked widely and stared up into the amused countenance of Gabriel Whitney, the eighth Marquess of Eastlyn.

"May I?" he asked, letting his hand sweep over the expanse of blanket where Sophie sat. "It is a tolerably fine day for being out-of-doors and settled in the heart of nature's bounty."

The garden at No. 14 Bowden Street was hardly the heart of nature's bounty, but Sophie felt certain the marquess knew that. She wondered if he thought she was unaware of the same. Perhaps he believed her naiveté extended to all manner of things. Sophie rose as far as her knees, quickly pushing the rucked hem of her dress to modestly cover her ankles. "You might find the bench by the wall more to your liking."

East glanced over his shoulder to the heavy stone slab supported by two frighteningly plump cherubs. He raised one eyebrow. "I don't believe so, no. I would not find it in the least comfortable." The eyebrow relaxed its skeptical arch. "But if you are opposed to sharing your blanket, I will avail myself of this patch of grass."

Before Sophie could protest that she had no objections, or rather that she would voice none, the marquess simply dropped to the ground, folding his legs tailor fashion and resting his elbows lightly on his knees.

"Please, m'lord," Sophie said quickly. "Your trousers will be stained."

"It is good of you to warn me, but it is of no consequence."

"You will allow that your valet's opinion might be contrary to your own."

He smiled. "You are right, of course." East moved to the blanket where he repositioned himself in the same manner as before. He pointed to the book at Sophie's side. "What were you reading?"

Sophie could hardly make sense of the change of subject. She had to glance at the book to find some recollection of it. "It is my diary."

East saw the ink bottle and quill when she shifted her position to reveal them. "A worthy endeavor."

"Some think so."

"Though perhaps more of a strain on one's upperworks than simple woolgathering. Deep contemplation beneath an apple tree has much to recommend it. Or so North says." His rich baritone voice softened to a confidential tone. "I believe he has been inspired by Sir Isaac Newton's success."

Sophie's eyes darted into the boughs. Was it too much to hope that an apple would fall directly on the marquess's head? Barring that event, was it too much to hope one would fall on hers?

Following the direction of her gaze as well as her errant thoughts, Eastlyn casually remarked, "They're puny green things now, but if you will invite me to return in the fall when they're beautifully ripened and it takes no more than a hint of wind to nudge them from the branches, I can promise you that one of us will be most satisfyingly thumped on the head, thereby putting a period to all awkward moments between us."

Sophie was sure she did not like having her thoughts so

easily interpreted by this man. On the other hand, it was somehow reassuring that he also found this encounter awkward.
She eased herself back against the rough bark of the trunk and
let her legs slide to one side. Strands of softly curling hair
the color of wild honey fluttered as she moved. She lifted her
face and regarded the marquess with a certain solemn intensity. If the eyes that returned his amused gaze could arguably
be described as too large for her heart-shaped face, there was
no argument from any quarter that they were remarkably
sober.

"I've been in anticipation of your visit, my lord."

He nodded, equally grave now. How like Lady Sophia to
place her cards before him. She did not dissemble or play
coy as most young women in the same circumstances would
do. Even as her lack of pretense raised her in his estimation,
he was also reminded that she was not so very young, at
least not by the standards that were often set for a marriage-
able age among the ton. She was more of a certain age, one
somewhere after *la jeune fille* and before ape leader, mayhap
in her twenty-third year. He was heartily glad of it, if the
truth be known. Had she been younger he would have had to
tread more carefully, taking special pains not to trample a
heart already foolishly attached to him.

Lady Sophia was hardly foolish. On short acquaintance,
it was perhaps the thing he liked best about her—if he was
taking no note of her singularly splendid eyes. It was not
their studied seriousness that had drawn his attention on
their first meeting, but their coloring, which was in every way
the equal of her hair. He supposed the color they approxi-
mated was hazel, but it was far too dull a descriptor to be
leveled at these features. If her hair was honey shot through
with sunlight, then so were her eyes. Sophia's radiance,
though, came from within.

This last was what made her so totally unsuitable. She
was very nearly angelic with her too perfect countenance.
The heart-shaped face, the sweetly lush mouth, the small
chin and pared nose, the large and beautifully colored eyes,

and finally the softly curling tumble of hair that framed her face like the Madonna's halo . . . It was all rather more innocence than East believed he could properly manage. In principle he was in favor of innocence in females. In practice he found it tedious.

He waited for Sophia to gather the threads of her thoughts, loath to interrupt her now that she was earnestly giving him her full attention.

"I have heard the rumors," she said. "And I want you to know that I recognize they have no truth as their source. My cousin has admitted that you have not been in correspondence with his father, nor had any meeting with him in which you might have sought permission for my hand. Harold and Tremont would be happy if it were otherwise, but wishful thinking on their part cannot make it so. I am afraid they did nothing to dissuade people from believing as they will, and for that I am heartily sorry. The earl would count himself fortunate to have such a marriage arranged for me. I hope you will understand and go gently with such remarks as you might make to others. If they have caused you embarrassment by failing to deny any link between my name and yours, I apologize."

A crease appeared between Eastlyn's brows. He let his chin drop forward and rested it on his steepled fingers. "Surely it can't be your place to apologize, Lady Sophia."

Since she did not think either Harold or the earl had the stomach for it, even if they had the vocabulary, Sophie couldn't imagine who else was in a position to make amends. "I am not without responsibility, m'lord. I did not deny the rumors, either."

East raised his head and let his steepled fingers fall. He plucked a blade of grass and rolled it absently between his long fingers as he leveled Sophia with his thoughtful gaze. "You had many opportunities, did you?"

"I . . . that is, I . . ." Sophie was unaccustomed to fumbling for words. She did not thank the marquess for having that effect on her. Of late her conversations were primarily with Robert and Esme, who at five and four respectively were somewhat limited in their topics. Still, she had not considered that she'd lost her ability to speak intelligibly, if not intelligently.

"I am not mistaken, am I?" East continued. "You are not often away from home."

He was scrupulously polite. Sophie could allow him that. He was kind to couch his observation that she was not the recipient of many invitations. "I am away as often as I need to be," she said.

"I see." A hint of a smile edged his mouth. "Almack's?"

"On occasion."

"The theater?"

"When there is something worth seeing."

"The park?"

"When there is some*one* worth seeing."

He laughed. "Which is to say that you rarely take your constitutional there."

Distracted by his laugh, Sophie nodded faintly. She looked past his watchful eyes and focused on a point beyond his shoulder. A swallow alighted on the stone bench behind him and paced the length of it looking for crumbs. Since Sophie had permitted the children to take tea there only yesterday, the swallow was fortunate in his choice of picnic spots. "Perhaps I am about town more often than you suspect and it is only that I am outside your notice."

Eastlyn started to deny it but caught himself abruptly when she held up a hand. Her smile was slight, but genuine.

"You must not be gallant, my lord, and deny such a thing is the most reasonable explanation. I am fully aware that I am an unlikely female to command your attention. It will ease your mind to know that our initial introduction aside, you are not the sort of someone I would go to the park to see."

It did *not* ease the marquess's mind. In point of fact he was not insulted; but she had tweaked him rather sharply, and while he thought he should avoid hearing her explanation, he simply could not. When he had left the Battenburn estate this morning, he had been in expectation of a wholly different meeting with Lady Sophia. Though he had cringed at the possibility, he had forced himself to consider the prospect of tears and how they might be dealt with swiftly but with some compassion. The exercise had been a waste of gray matter, he realized now. Far from being near tears, the eyes that met him were frank and reasonable. Except for one brief lapse, Lady Sophia remained composed. Perfectly so.

"You would not go to the park upon hearing I would be there?" he asked. "Even if I were driving my new barouche?"

"Do not feign disappointment, my lord. It is badly done of you. You can be naught but relieved that I bear you no affection."

He was. Or at least he thought he was until she placed it so baldly before him. He wondered if she was entirely correct in assuming his disappointment was feigned. "There you have me," he said slowly, regarding her with new interest. "But you must allow that I am curious. What makes me so beneath your notice?"

"Oh, no." She shook her head, and the brilliant halo of hair waved softly about her face until she was still again. "You misunderstand. It is not at all that you are beneath my notice, only outside of it."

"There is a difference, I collect," he said dryly.

"Certainly. The former suggests you are not worthy of my attention. I meant to say that you simply do not fix my attention."

"You are not making it more palatable, you know. I cannot recall when last I was so deftly cut to the quick." He could, but it had been at Hambrick Hall, and he had planted the boy who had done it a facer. It was scarcely the tack to take with Lady Sophia. If she dealt blows with her fists as well as she did with words, he would be the worse for it in the end.

Sophie searched Eastlyn's face for some sign that she had indeed done him an injury. His finely cut features remained impassive during her scrutiny, giving nothing of his thoughts away, no hint of amusement or distress. Still, it was Sophie's conclusion that he was teasing her. Any other outcome would have been difficult to imagine, no matter what emotion he affected. Her words could not have truly pricked him. The Marquess of Eastlyn must know he was recklessly handsome.

How could he not be aware of heads turning when he came upon a room? Though she was not out often in society, Sophie still had had occasion to witness the phenomenon. For the marquess's part he seemed supremely unconcerned by the attention he received, which only reinforced Sophie's opinion that he held himself as deserving of it. At the Stallworths' ball to open the Season past, she had observed him in conversation with his friend Viscount Southerton in front of an indecently large mirror in the grand hallway. Only a man as confident in his appearance as the marquess could have avoided a sideways glance at his person. Even Southerton, who was very well turned out himself, was not above darting a look in the mirror to check the line of his perfectly starched chitterling or the fit of his waistcoat.

The Marquess of Eastlyn did not require the use of a mirror for affirmation of his fine countenance. His mirror was every approving look cast in his direction, every warm smile that greeted him. Society was favorably disposed to him, and it was a circumstance unlikely to change no matter what sort of nonsense he perpetrated with his friends.

He was not so different from her father.

Sophie received that thought as though taking a physical blow. It caught her just below the rib cage, and she actually stiffened with the pain of it. Her mouth parted, and she drew in a short breath, making every effort not to gasp.

"Are you quite all right?" Eastlyn asked. It seemed to him that Lady Sophia had become several degrees more sober, if such a thing were possible. The wash of pink in her cheeks was gone now; even her mouth was pale. He was moved to look behind him, suspecting that whatever had caused this change in her countenance must be at some distance beyond his shoulder. East saw nothing but the garden wall and the stone bench, neither occupied by any member of her family likely to induce such alarm. "Shall I get you something? Water? Spirits?"

His offer of assistance forced Sophie to collect herself. It required rather more effort than she wished it might. "I am all of a piece," she said calmly.

One of Eastlyn's brows kicked up, and he made a survey of her face, flatly skeptical. "You are certain?"

"Yes." Sophie watched him draw his fingers through his hair, leaving it furrowed until each burnished strand fell back into place. Clearly he did not believe her, yet he had no choice but to accept her at her word. She forced herself to return his steady, inquiring gaze, hoping he could not see past the lie. He could not truly want to be burdened with the truth; it was only his innate civility that prompted what appeared to be genuine concern.

She thought of all the ways he was different from her father and started with the physical, coloring being the most obvious. Where her father, the late Earl of Tremont, had been fair-headed and fair-skinned, the marquess was much darker, with hair the color of chestnuts and eyes that were only a shade more warmly polished. Sophie's father had shunned the out-of-doors, preferring gaming hells to pastoral pursuits. In contrast, there was a touch of sun caught in Eastlyn's complexion, lending him the look of a man who had interests beyond the gentleman's clubs he frequented. Eastlyn was of a height with her father, though he cut a trimmer, more athletic figure. Sophie allowed that perhaps it was not a fair comparison because her clearest memories of her father were toward the end of his life, when drink and dissipation had left their mark at his thickening waist and heavy jowls. The portrait of Frederick Thomas Colley still hanging in the gallery at Tremont Park showed the younger man, the one who had difficulty with the serious pose he affected and whose quicksilver smile hovered like a poorly kept secret at the corners of his mouth.

When Sophie captured that portrait in her mind's eye, it was much harder to see how Eastlyn might be different.

She did not know a great deal about the marquess, although she would have had to have lived abroad these last three years not to know something of the man he was. He played at cards, she knew, and wagered often with his friends. He was a member of several clubs and kept a box at the theater. He was welcomed at Almack's, though it was not his habit to attend, and he was invited to every function of note by every hostess who desired her gathering to be well attended. The particulars about his life were unexceptional, including the fact that like so many of his peers, he kept a mistress in town.

Sophie doubted anyone intended she should know this last thing about him; it was not the sort of detail one discussed in front of the rumored fiancée. Even had the engagement not been fiction, Sophie still thought she would want to know about a mistress.

There was nothing to be gained by not understanding the place she would have in her husband's life. If he meant to regularly commit adultery, it was something worth coming to terms with, no matter that it might cause her some distress in doing so. On the other hand, if she did not love her husband, a mistress might serve her very well, keeping her husband occupied while she was engaged in the activities that gave her pleasure.

Eastlyn regarded Lady Sophia's perfectly cast features with some consternation. Her expression was now one of absolute serenity, yet East had the distinct impression she was no longer aware of him in any substantive way. It was just as she had said earlier: he was unable to fix her attention.

Devil a bit, but it bothered him. It was not an admission he particularly wanted to make, and having made it, not one that he wanted to dwell on overlong. In what way could it possibly matter that Lady Sophia Colley was as uninterested in him as he was in her? Surely that was the best of all circumstances. Everything was made so much simpler by her easy acceptance of their situation. She did not blame him for any part of it, though she must suspect it was someone he knew who gave the rumor its sharp teeth. She was not in anticipation of a real offer of marriage, or even a sham engagement to satisfy the rumor mill until one of them was in a position to make a dignified exit. He would have insisted that she be the one to cry off, of course, and lay the blame for their dissolution at his feet. His reputation would not suffer unduly. Lady Sophia would not be so fortunate if she were cast as the one doing the injuring.

It was all moot. There would be no engagement, in truth or in fiction, and that was certainly as it should be. Eastlyn did not welcome the prospect of carrying out his work while observing all the tedious conventions that an affianced couple must needs endure. There might be less pleasurable ways to pass part of one's life, but they didn't come immediately to East's mind.

That was why it surprised him when he said, "You know, Lady Sophia, in some quarters I am considered a desirable partner."

She did not so much as blink. "At cards, you mean."

"At marriage."

"But you play cards."

"Well . . . Yes, I do." Eastlyn wondered at her point, for it seemed to be completely at odds with his.

"And you make wagers."

"Yes."

"You drink to excess."

"I may start soon."

Her mouth flattened rather primly.

"Very well," East said, entertained by her disapproving mien, but not proof against it either. "I admit to being foxed on occasion."

"You have called men out."

His amusement vanished. "One man."

Sophie gave no indication that she was in any way intimidated. "You shot him."

"Yes."

"And killed him."

"That was the purpose of shooting him, yes."

There was a brief pause as Sophie considered the necessity of her next words. She had not conceived that she might have cause to say these things to Eastlyn, but the remembrance of things past had shaken her. Mayhap the marquess did not deserve such a setdown, yet Sophie felt compelled as if by some force outside herself to deliver it. "So," she began with a gentle matter-of-factness, "by your own admission you are a gambler, a drunkard, and a murderer. With so much to recommend you, it is little wonder you are sought by mothers in want of a husband for their daughters. These qualities have a certain cache among the ton, do they not? Gaming indicates a willingness to risk, drinking to excess, a surfeit of confident recklessness, and—"

"And murder?" he asked.

While Sophie suspected he was out of all patience with her, she went on as if there had been no interruption. "Murder suggests a resolve to act. In your particular case, a regard for principles and the necessity of upholding them."

Eastlyn pretended to weigh her words carefully. "It is your estimation, then, that I am embraced by mothers and their daughters, indeed, by all of the ton, not because I am regarded as a model of rectitude and good sense, but because I am the very opposite of those things?"

"That," she said, "and the fact that you are rich as Croesus."

"Richer."

"Just so."

Eastlyn dusted off his palms, erasing all trace of the blade of grass he had ground between them. He leaned back so that his weight rested on his braced arms and extended his legs, crossing them casually at the ankle. His boots were layered with a fine coating of dirt from the long ride from

Battenburn, and a similar dusting had attached itself to his jacket and trousers. He had not stopped at his town house to bathe or change his clothes, not because he did not think Lady Sophia deserved that measure of respect, but because he believed that it was more important to have this misunderstanding behind them. In hindsight, Eastlyn allowed that he had been more anxious to relieve himself of responsibility than he had been strictly sensitive to Lady Sophia's feelings.

It was clear he had offended her in some way, though how he had managed to accomplish it—and so decisively—remained a poser. Perhaps she cared more for appearance than he had considered. It did not recommend her to him, for he often found too much was made of how one was turned out and little enough attention paid to what was turned in.

"I fear I must apologize for the poor state of my attire," he said. "I came here directly from Battenburn."

Sophie stared at him. It was no easy thing to follow the line of his thinking. "My lord," she said with some emphasis, as though speaking to one thick-witted. "It cannot have escaped your notice that only a few moments ago I called you a gambler, a drunkard, and a murderer. What sort of maggot do you have in your brain that would make you think I care a whit for your fashion?"

Eastlyn sighed. He thought rather fondly of the pistol lying snugly between his stockinged calf and the soft leather of his dusty boot. He had a mind to use it—on himself. It would put a period to the maggot. "You are not a restful sort of companion, Lady Sophia."

"I should hope not."

"I had thought quite differently," he said. "Even said as much to South and Northam."

"You spoke of me to your friends?"

He was fairly certain he had stepped into it once again, but since he had never quite managed to extricate the first misplaced foot, Eastlyn was comfortable having them both in the same place. His situation might be less than ideal, but at least he had regained his balance. "Of course. I speak of many things to my friends. Nothing would be served by making an exception in your case, and they were curious about my engagement. I had said nothing of it at all to them, you see, because I had not known I *was* engaged. They learned of it from some of the guests at the baron's estate, just as I did. It is quite an experience to be congratulated for something one knows nothing about."

Sophie nodded slowly. Her experience had not been so different. "I had not imagined the rumor would have traveled so far."

His shrug was indifferent. "From town to country. It is the usual way of these things. With so many parties dedicated to the third anniversary of Napoleon's defeat at Waterloo, it was inevitable the tale would spread as quickly as the plague."

"It is not a pretty metaphor."

"But it is apt."

Sophie did not deny it. She fingered the material of her dress just above the knee, pressing a fold together, then smoothing it out. It was an absent gesture, one she engaged in when she was neither as composed nor as incurious as her placid features might suggest. "You told them you were not engaged, of course."

"Of course."

"They believed you?"

"I should hope so."

"Then it was not your friends who first raised the story of our engagement?"

Eastlyn looked at her sharply. "Did you think so?"

"It occurred to me." She paused, waiting him out. Patience had always been her strong suit, but she was learning the limits of it with the marquess. When she could tolerate his silence no longer, she asked, "Am I wrong?"

"Yes." He waited now, anticipating her next question, though he could see that she was loath to put it to him. When she artlessly caught her lower lip between her teeth and worried it gently, Eastlyn found his eyes drawn to the line of her mouth. She did well to show some reticence, he thought. Her angelic looks be damned, the most surprising things came out of that perfectly sculpted mouth.

Aware of his scrutiny, Sophie released her lip, touching the teeth marks she had pressed to the soft underside with the tip of her tongue. She was made further self-conscious by the small crease that appeared between Eastlyn's brows and the darkening of his eyes. "You are scowling at me."

He wasn't, but he was not unhappy that she thought so. She was perhaps as innocent as he always thought her to be. That would prove to be her best defense should he imagine an attraction toward her. Eastlyn relaxed the line of his brow and returned his attention to her faintly accusing eyes. He was coming to understand that in Lady Sophia's company his balance was a rather precarious thing. If he was not stepping where he shouldn't, then she was knocking one leg out from under him. "I beg your pardon," he offered with clipped politeness.

Which brought Sophie back to the matter at hand. "About your friends," she said carefully. "Do you believe their denials?"

"You are assuming I asked them if they began the rumor. I did not. I think I know their character well enough to know this type of trick is not done by them. You may believe me or not."

"I believe you."

Both of Eastlyn's brows rose slowly. "Why? Can it be you have changed your estimation of my character? Gambler? Drunkard? Murderer? Am I absolved of all these things?"

"Not at all," she said with disarming frankness. "But I never imagined you to be given to untruths. If I had entertained such a notion, you would have put it quickly to rest when you answered my questions with such forthrightness."

He grunted softly, thinking of his pistol again. There was an odd sort of logic to her thinking that he couldn't quite grasp and wasn't certain he wanted to. "So the fact that I have admitted the flaws in my character also makes me an honest man."

"Yes."

Eastlyn simply collapsed back on his elbows and briefly closed his eyes. Slim beams of sunlight through the parted branches warmed his face and eased the set of lines across his brow and at the corners of his mouth. He breathed deeply, finding the small ache that had begun behind his left eye could be suppressed if he did not overtax himself.

"My lord?"

Her voice was proof that she had not disappeared. He opened first one eye, giving her a long, considering look, then the other, doubling the effort. "You are certainly a perverse creature, Lady Sophia. Have I mentioned that?"

"I believe you said I was not a restful person. There was no mention of perversity."

His mouth crooked to one side. She was having fun with him now, and the marquess found he did not mind. Still, there was the coil of this false engagement to settle and his desire to make certain Lady Sophia emerged unscathed by any scandal. Eastlyn pushed himself upright, then drew himself to his feet. He held out a hand to Sophie, who regarded him with some surprise. "A walk, if you will," he said. "After so long a journey on horseback, it cannot help but improve my thinking."

Sophie felt compelled to point out, "It is but a very small garden, m'lord."

"Yes, but then I have a very small mind."

This last did not raise Sophie's smile. Slipping her hand into his, she allowed herself to be helped to her feet. She accepted the crook of his arm, keenly aware that from somewhere in the house they were being watched. Eastlyn could not help but know it himself. It was not fear of impropriety that dictated there be a modicum of supervision. Sophia was of an age where it was not unseemly for her to be alone with a male acquaintance in a setting such as this. The reason she and Eastlyn were being observed was exactly the opposite. Within the house at No. 14, there was the most fervent hope that matters would proceed in a most improper manner and that Sophie could be forced to change her mind about marriage.

Eastlyn and Lady Sophia stepped onto the narrow path of crushed stone. Sophie's fingertips grazed the velvet petals of a pink rose as they walked through the lattice arbor. For a moment their features were shaded from the sunlight.

"You are going to say it, aren't you?" she said, feeling his steps slow.

"I must."

"It is not necessary."

"I think it is." It was a matter to which he had given a great deal of thought on his return to London. He had not, however, arrived at a solution that satisfied. When last he had considered it, he had been leaning toward the opinion that opposed the very position he meant to take now. It was interesting to him that Lady Sophia was adamantly opposed to it, but he did not want to hear the course of her thoughts or how she had arrived at such an end. It would only make his head ache.

Sophie drew a deep breath and let it out slowly. With considerable calm, she told him, "Then have it done quickly, m'lord. Afterward I will call for refreshment so you can wash the taste away."

He stopped completely and drew her toward him, taking both her hands in his. He gave them a small shake. "You must look at me, Sophia, else how will you judge the truth of my words?"

She lifted her chin and looked up at him. He was a full head taller than she, and his shoulders half again as broad. It would be an easy thing to always stand in the circle of his arms, but she couldn't think of one reason why it would be the right thing to do. "Go on," she said. "Now. For both our sakes, have done with it."

She was not making it easy for him, which was precisely

the tactic she had chosen to avoid just this end. It had been her strategy all along, he realized, as if she had known from the moment he breached the walls of her garden sanctuary that he would want to speak these words. Odd that she had believed he would make the honorable gesture when he had been uncertain himself.

Eastlyn narrowly avoided clearing his throat. The effect would have added weight to the moment that the moment simply did not require. "Lady Sophia, it is my fervent wish that you will acquit me of being presumptuous. Although our acquaintance has been brief and, based on our previous encounters, I would not have judged that we might suit, I have had reason to revise that opinion this afternoon. I am sincere when I say you will make me a most happy man if you would do me the honor of becoming my wife."

Sophie merely stared at him, saying nothing.

Eastlyn waited. A fine sheen of perspiration attached itself to his upper lip.

Sophie cocked a perfectly arched eyebrow and remained silent.

No coward by anyone's definition, the marquess now had reason to believe his knees might buckle.

Taking pity, Sophie said, "I will see to those refreshments now, my lord. Please, excuse me." She withdrew her hands from his and presented him with her back. She was halfway to the rear entrance of the house when she heard him call after her.

"That is no answer! I would have your answer!"

She paused, but did not turn, and Eastlyn was not privy to the sad, uncertain smile that cut across her features like an open wound.

Harold Colley, Viscount Dunsmore, stepped into the hallway immediately upon hearing Sophie's entry. He did not apologize for the start he gave her but went straight to the point. "Well?" he demanded. "Is it done? Has he come up to snuff? The two of you looked to be having quite a coze."

"You were watching." It was no question, but a statement,

and disappointment quieted her. She had expected that he would observe her meeting with Eastlyn but not that he would be so bold as to admit it. Harold really had no shame.

"Of course I was watching. You are living under my roof and therefore my responsibility. How else could I be assured Eastlyn would mind the proprieties?"

"Then you saw he was a gentleman." She turned to make her way to the kitchen belowstairs but was brought up short by her cousin's fierce grip just above her elbow. She did not try to shake him off, and neither did she look pointedly at his fingers pressing whitely into her flesh. Instead she waited him out calmly, holding his narrow, disapproving gaze until his hold eased. She would bear the imprint of this brief encounter for days, she knew. In spite of the summer heat, long sleeves would be in order. "I have promised our guest some refreshment," she said.

"In a moment." Harold let his hand fall to his side. He worked his lower jaw back and forth as he weighed his words carefully and reined in his anger. His fingertips tingled as the blood returned. "I have no liking for losing my temper," he said. "You would do well not to provoke me, Sophia."

There was no response that satisfied in these circumstances, at least none that she had been able to discover. It was difficult, perhaps impossible, for Harold to accept that she did not set out to nettle him. These moments of intemperance galled him because he liked to view himself—and have others view him—as a reasoned, thoughtful man. When he made decisions they were considered ones, if not considerate, and he perforce had the expectation that they would be met with agreement. His opinion on any matter was so sound, so commonsensical, he believed that others must follow it as proof of their own good judgment.

"Pray, forgive me," she said softly, no longer meeting his gaze. Since coming to live with Harold and his family upon the death of her own father three years past, Lady Sophia had learned a certain amount of contrition was required to place the peace before them again. In most instances it was not difficult for her to do because there was so little of consequence at stake. She was not opposed to offering an apology to placate her cousin even if it attached some fault to her. "It is only that you startled me."

Harold grunted softly, thereby communicating his acceptance of her regrets. He was a trim, but slightly built man, given to carrying himself stiffly as though this bearing might compensate for a lack of physical presence. It had pained him to be forced to observe the small drama unfolding in his own garden from a position in the house, his nose pressed to the glass like a beggar at the baker's window. "I should like an answer," he said.

"My lord Eastlyn is waiting for one as well."

Harold thought he heard a hint of impertinence in Sophie's tone, but he chose to let it pass for now. He had remarked to his father only last month, when the earl had made his perfunctory inquiry into Sophia's welfare, that she was a sensible female, perhaps more so than most of her sex. Biddable was how he had described her, an unexceptional companion to the viscountess, a proper influence on the children. It was no hardship to have her under his roof, he'd reported to his father, and surely Sophie would prefer the activity of London to rusticating with the earl at Tremont Park. As he had little interest in having Sophie underfoot for much longer than a single fortnight, the Earl of Tremont was easily persuaded to extend Sophie's stay in town. There was still the matter of a suitable match for her, a situation that could be more easily remedied, the earl agreed, if Sophie remained available to the London bucks.

Which was why Viscount Dunsmore found himself so vexed by her recalcitrance in regard to the Marquess of Eastlyn's suit. Not only was her refusal to do as she was told an affront to his sensibilities, but she made him appear a poor judge of character. There was no aspect of this last that set well with Harold.

"Please, cousin," Sophie said. "His lordship will wonder

what has become of me and if I mean to return to the garden."

Harold led her into the rear parlor where he had posted himself to observe Eastlyn's suit. He rang for the butler and permitted Sophie to request lemonade for herself and her guest. As soon as they were alone again, Harold pounced. "What precisely did the marquess say?"

"He said he was sincere in his suit and that I would make him most happy by agreeing to be his wife. That is the standard, is it not? It is much the same as Lord Edymon said to me when he pressed his suit. Also Humphrey Bell. Is it something men learn at Eton and Harrow, do you think?"

Harold was unamused by what he thought was an unseemly attempt at humor. "I was not aware there were previous applications for your hand, Sophie. You have never mentioned it." Perhaps if she had, he thought, he would have been prepared for this small mutiny with Eastlyn.

Belatedly, Sophie realized that Harold had probably used a similarly unimaginative proposal when he sought Abigail's hand. She had doubtlessly offended him again, a state of affairs she seemed to be unable to avoid these days. Even treading carefully, she managed the thing with tiresome regularity. It did not bear thinking how accomplished she might become if she actually applied herself to the task. "Edymon came to me before Father died, though I suspect his lordship knew there was not much time left. Mr. Bell came afterward, when it was still uncertain where I would go." She would have told Harold she had no regrets about her answer to either man, but a servant appeared with a tray, glasses, and a pitcher of lemonade. "Take it to the garden," Sophie said. "And tell his lordship that I will join him directly." It surprised her when the maid did not remove herself immediately, but looked to Harold for direction. She saw her cousin hesitate a moment, staring at the tray as if contemplating the necessity of offering this small hospitality. His agitation was clear, and when he finally gestured that the maid should go on, his direction was impatient and churlish.

Sophie made to excuse herself again. "You would not have me be rude to our guest."

"Indeed not," he said tightly. "How little unpleasantness there would be left to share with me."

Sophie charitably supposed her cousin meant to suggest sarcasm with his tone. To her ears he merely sounded spoiled, and it was borne home to her anew how little liking she had for him. "I must go," she said when he continued to block her way. "Please, Harold, you must see that it is required of me to speak to his lordship. You cannot expect me to tell you first what I mean to tell him." In point of fact, she had told Harold repeatedly what she intended to tell Eastlyn should he make a proposal. Her cousin simply refused to believe her or, more accurately, believe he could not change her mind.

While Harold was forming another carefully crafted objection, Sophie used the distraction to turn sideways and slip neatly past his jutting elbow and the doorjamb. She was already in the hallway when he realized she was escaping and at the door when he began cursing. Although Sophie understood all too well that she would be made responsible for that curse, she didn't pause on the threshold to the garden. Instead, she flung open the door and hurried from the house, slowing her steps only when her feet touched the crushed-stone path.

In spite of the calm she affected by the time she reached Eastlyn, she knew her face was flushed. It required some effort on her part not to press her palms to her cheeks. If she was fortunate, Eastlyn would merely conclude that it was her eagerness to return to him that forced the color on her complexion, not that it was brought on by her cousin's latest effort to intimidate her. She was more embarrassed for Harold than frightened, or even angry. She doubted he would ever understand how his grasping, rapacious nature offended *her*.

"My lord," she said in the way of greeting as Eastlyn came to his feet. "Please, do not trouble yourself. I beg you, sit." Sophie saw he had a glass of lemonade in his hand. The pitcher and extra glass were on the bench. "Is it to your liking?"

"If you mean has it washed away the taste of my proposal," he said, "I fear that will require something fermented, preferably for twenty or more years in an oaken cask."

Sophie marveled at the perfect aridness of his tone and wondered that he did not eschew his glass and drink directly from the pitcher. "My comment stung, did it?" she said softly, the merest smile lifting one corner of her mouth. "I cannot even apologize because it was my intention that it should."

"I never doubted it."

Sophie slowly sat down. Wishing she had indeed asked for something stronger, regardless of the hour, she poured herself a glass of the lemonade. "I did not want you to make your proposal."

"You were clear on that point."

"Yet you made it anyway."

"It was a matter of honor."

Sophie wasn't certain she understood why he thought that was true, but she did not ask. Wrapping both hands around her glass, she drew in an uneasy breath and released it slowly. "Have you truly considered the consequences, my lord, if I were to accept?"

Chapter Two

Eastlyn wondered if he had ever been so discomposed as he was in the presence of Lady Sophia Colley. He had negotiated terms of surrender between entire countries that were less troubling to him. But then, he acknowledged, this was about his *own* surrender, and in all those other situations he had been dealing with levelheaded men who were well versed in the nuanced language of diplomatic relations.

Sophie's faint smile hinted at her amusement. Though Eastlyn's fine features remained imperturbable, his silence in the face of her question spoke most eloquently of his feelings. "I collect you are happy to have this bench under you," she said.

Her perceptiveness did nothing to ease his mind. He did indeed imagine he would be on the ground without the support of the stone cherubs, but did not thank her for pointing it out. How she managed to unsteady him was a thing worth considering, though he doubted he would intimate as much to her. In the event there were future encounters, Eastlyn acknowledged that he would do well to be prepared, and that perhaps the better course was to simply avoid her altogether. At this moment, however, there was still the matter of the question she had put before him and her expectation of his reply.

"Naturally I have considered the consequences of your acceptance," East said. "Did I not say you would make me most happy?"

Sophie's amusement slowly faded while her slight smile remained fixed. "I should say yes, you know, not to this last question, but to your proposal. It would go a very long way to proving how wrong you are. It is my opinion, however, that that sort of lesson has import for me as well. I find I am selfish enough not to trade the prospect of my own happiness for the certainty of ruining yours. You surely have acquitted yourself admirably today, making your proposal when you could not be certain of my answer. It was wrong of me to tease you with the anticipation of my acceptance when I knew you hoped for precisely the opposite outcome, and while I acknowledge the wrongness of it, never think I regret it. You deserved it, my lord, for placing your need to discharge yourself honorably above my express wish that no proposal be offered."

Sophie watched the marquess's eyes darken at the centers and wondered that he did not flinch or move to strike her. Although neither would have had the effect of silencing her, she would have understood those responses. His calm in the face of her censure was outside her experience. "You spoke of your happiness," she said quietly, "and not of my own. Indeed, how could you when you have not the least notion of what would bring that elusive thing about? As you said yourself, we have only had benefit of a short acquaintance. It is inconceivable to me that anything that has passed between us this afternoon has altered your true opinion that we would not suit. More to the point, my lord, it has not altered mine."

East observed the high color in Lady Sophie's cheeks slowly recede, leaving her eyes to sustain the passion her words had aroused. She had more than pricked him this time with her words, yet she seemed to take no satisfaction from it. The rather odd framing of her fixed smile suggested something more than regret, something mayhap closer to sadness, though whether it was an emotion prompted by his ill-conceived proposal or the necessity of taking him to task for it remained unclear.

Returning his empty glass to the tray between them, Eastlyn considered what reply he might make. She would not find it in any way flattering that he was once again having to revise his opinion of her. There was no good way to say that she was possessed of more resolve than he had ever supposed was possible. Far from being as serenely insipid as her sainted looks might suggest, Lady Sophia could brace herself quite firmly to deliver the direct setdown. "You are right, of course," he said at last. "I was not considering your feelings in the matter of marriage, but only in the matter of this rumored engagement. The fact that we have become the latest nine-days' wonder cannot have any appeal for you."

"It doesn't," Sophie said. "But you must admit that a hasty marriage will do nothing to quell the speculation surrounding us."

"At the risk of offending you anew, I never suggested that we bring the thing about quickly."

"A prolonged courtship? I think not. It would be an agony for you."

He smiled a little, one of his dark brows edging upward. "An agony? That is perhaps overstating it, don't you think?"

"An agony for me, then."

"Pray, do not spare my feelings."

Sophie realized that he was not entirely put out with her, but rather more amused. "You are still laughing at me," she said quietly, averting her eyes lest he see that she was hurt by it.

"Still?" Eastlyn tried to catch her glance as she turned away, but she would not meet him. Her assertion did not have the sting of an accusation; it was simply a statement of her perception. "I have never laughed at you. In fact, it is quite the opposite. You make me laugh at myself. There is little chance that I should be puffed with self-importance with you ever at the ready to deflate me. My friends would heartily approve, you know. They never pass an opportunity to do the same."

She looked at him sharply, wondering at the truth of his words. "Then you must be regularly in need of pricking, m'lord, for you are always laughing in their company."

Eastlyn thought about that. "Not always," he said. "But often. You must know it is the way of old friends."

She didn't, but she nodded anyway. To do otherwise would have prompted him to make an inquiry or a comment about her friendships, and she was loath to explain that she had none. Given the fact that he derived such satisfaction from his own, he would find her lack of the same pitiable, and Sophie found the thought that she might elicit pity from him unendurable.

"Did you think they were amused upon learning of this engagement?" Eastlyn asked, watching her closely. When she nodded again, he noted the hesitation in her response, as though she were giving something away in this small confession. "They were," he said softly and saw that his admission elicited some surprise. It was then that he understood. "It was amusement at *my* predicament, Lady Sophia. Not yours. They had only the utmost sympathy for you."

"I do not think I believe you."

He shrugged lightly. "Does this mean you are no longer disposed to think of me as an honest man?"

It did present a conundrum, Sophie realized. "Very well," she said finally, "but I cannot help but point out that their response is hardly flattering to either one of us."

"Ah," he said, unperturbed. "There you have me."

Sophie felt the corners of her mouth twitch and resolutely resisted the urge to smile. "And I am not in want of their sympathy," she said somewhat coolly, her chin lifting a notch.

"I shall tell them you are certainly in need of none. They will learn the truth of it quickly enough for themselves."

"Whatever can you mean by that?"

Eastlyn could not miss the immediate change in Sophia's demeanor. The defensive tilt of her chin vanished, and there was no longer the brittle edge of frost in her words. "Perhaps I should not have given you such full marks for your perspicacity," he said pleasantly. "I did not think interpretation was required."

"But surely you do not intend that I should become acquainted with your friends, nor they with me. To what purpose?"

"To no purpose. It is done all the time in society. Introductions are made. Certain rote courtesies are exchanged. Perhaps there is conversation on a topic of mutual interest. Dry stuff, all of it. In the main nothing comes of it, but one is given the sense civilization will cease to exist without the effort." He regarded her steadily. "Never say you mean to put a period to civilization. It's a fragile thing, you know. A small misstep in one direction and . . ." Eastlyn let his voice trail off while he held up his hands, palms out in helpless appeal.

"You are shameless," Sophie said.

"Yes."

"And provoking."

He smiled. "You are very kind to say so."

Sophie shook her head slowly, exasperated, but not undone. "I cannot decide what to make of you, my lord." She added quickly, "And, pray, do not say again that I could make you a happy man. I should likely be as successful making you a pigeon."

"Tell me again," John Blackwood said, giving his guest the benefit of a second wry appraisal while he tried not to laugh aloud. "The lady said she would as likely make you a pigeon?"

"It was perhaps amusing the first time I told you," Eastlyn said dryly. "On successive recitations I am finding it less so."

The colonel's slim smile grew infinitesimally wider. "For-

give me if I disagree. If anything, it strikes one as more deftly
comedic. She has a certain talent, this Lady Sophia, that bears
watching. I think you would do well not to let her slip so easily from your grasp."

Eastlyn sank into the wing chair opposite the colonel.
Upon leaving Sophie he had traveled directly to his town
house in Everly Square and availed himself of a bath and
fresh clothes. There was some consternation exhibited by his
valet regarding the state of his person, most particularly
what his person was wearing, but East was too tired to pay
heed, knowing all the while Mr. Sampson would put everything to right. Now East stared down the length of his long
frame as he slouched low in the chair and stretched his legs
before him. His boots had been polished to a reflective sheen
and the tops turned down to reveal the soft brown leather underside. His buff breeches were pressed. The brass buttons
of his waistcoat shone. The line of his jacket lay just so over
his broad shoulders, and the loosely tied cravat gave the appearance of careless grace when in fact upward of ten minutes of his life had been surrendered to Sampson to achieve
that look. It still astonished him that he had had the patience
for it.

The marquess was no Brummel. He gave the matter of his
wardrobe little enough heed, leaving the particulars to his
valet. That he wore his clothes with such indifferent elegance owed much to trusting Sampson to turn him out in a
satisfactory manner. It was not the usual thing for him to tolerate fussing over the knot of his cravat, yet he had given
over to it because of Sophie. It was not that he had been
thinking of her precisely; it was simply that she had worn
him out.

"Do you see your future there?" the colonel asked.

"Hmm?"

Blackwood cocked one eyebrow as he considered the problem of East's preoccupation. What was required was the
younger man's full attention, not this diversion, especially as
it was unplanned—and therefore entirely unpredictable. The

colonel, priding himself on knowing many things about many people, knew little about Lady Sophia Colley. "I say," he repeated, more firmly this time. "Is it your future you see there?"

East looked up. "Pardon?" he said, still somewhat vague as to the colonel's meaning. "Oh, you mean the contemplation of my boots."

"Precisely. One might suspect you saw in them some glimpse of the future."

"Like a crystal ball?" He grinned crookedly, shaking his head. "No, not at all, though my valet has buffed them to that perfection. How does he manage it, do you think?"

"I hope you do not mean for me to answer that." The colonel could only imagine East was more in the way of exhausted than he had first let on.

"No," Eastlyn said.

Blackwood wheeled his chair closer to the marquess. The colonel's physical strength was tested by the wasting disease laying siege to the long muscles of his arms and legs, but there was nothing wrong with his mental acuity. From behind gold-rimmed spectacles, he regarded Eastlyn thoughtfully. Not one to rush to judgment, he let his gaze slide over the marquess's face, taking note of the fine lines at the corners of his mouth and eyes, then lower to the slope of the shoulders and incline of the posture. East might have taken the time to turn himself out, but he was bone weary. Even as he thought it, he watched Eastlyn try manfully to stifle a yawn.

Amused, the colonel shook his head. "Give me your drink, lad. Another sip and you will surely take your slumber here in my library."

It was true enough, Eastlyn thought. He leaned forward and passed his tumbler to Blackwood, noting the fine tremor in the older man's hand as he made to grasp it. He didn't think he had allowed his eyes to linger long, yet the colonel had noticed and did not let the moment pass.

"Bah! These hands." He waved the one not holding the

tumbler in a dismissive gesture. "Don't give them another thought. I find that whiskey calms them."

Eastlyn smiled as he was expected to. Like Sophia, the colonel had no use for his sympathy or anyone else's. "Mayhap it is that drink makes you insensible to the tremors."

"Now you sound like my physician. Frankly, it is but two sides of the same coin." He knocked back what remained of East's drink, set the tumbler on a nearby table, and held out both of his hands, fingers splayed and rock steady. "There. You see? It is done. The tremors are gone or we are both unconcerned by them. It makes no difference." He laced his fingers together in a loose fist and rested his elbows on the curved arms of the chair. "I think it would be prudent to discuss the particulars of your assignment later," he said. "I had not thought to see you so soon. I believed I would have to send for you at the Battenburn estate, and I fully intended to do that on the morrow; yet here you are, and not because of a summons from me, but because you desired to see Lady Sophia. Perhaps an opportunity will present itself so I can thank her."

"Perhaps," Eastlyn said slowly. "But I will not arrange it. You would not thank *me*."

The colonel's slight shoulders shook as he chuckled, the sound rumbling deeply from his chest to his throat. His body might no longer be robust, but his laughter was. The assignment he had for Eastlyn would not suffer by waiting a day or more to discuss it. Of more interest to him now were details of Eastlyn's return. "She is a termagant?" he asked.

"Termagant?" Eastlyn shook his head, thinking of Sophie's serene countenance, the perfect line of her lush mouth, the solemn expressiveness of her eyes. He did not recall that she had ever once raised her voice or given him reason to believe that she was possessed of a nature that could. His dressing-down had been accomplished in a completely reasonable tone of voice. "No, Lady Sophia is no shrew, but I defy you to name a woman who can deliver a more cogent argument."

"On what subject?"

"On any subject, I fear, though marriage and my character were the main points of discussion."

"She was disinclined to see the merits of either, I take it."

Eastlyn's half smile was disarmingly self-effacing. "Called me to task for wagering."

"I see." The colonel raised one hand to his chin, massaging it thoughtfully to rub out his growing amusement.

"Drinking, too," East added.

Blackwood cleared his throat. "Is that right?"

"She pointed out that I was a murderer."

The colonel was immediately sober. "A murderer? What would make her level that charge at your head?"

"She has apparently heard about the Hagan affair. We know it is a very old business, but there is always someone willing to repeat it. Her cousin perhaps." Eastlyn shrugged. "It hardly matters. I *did* shoot the man."

"You did not kill him."

East said nothing, plowing his hair back with his fingertips instead. A small puff of air parted his lips, the passing of a weary sigh.

"Aaah," Blackwood said. "You did not clarify that point. You allowed her to think just the opposite."

"It seemed important to her. I endeavor not to disappoint."

The colonel wheeled himself to the sideboard where he poured himself two fingers of whiskey. "You are an odd one, East," he said over his shoulder. "After all these years, you are still something of an enigma."

"It is not by design."

"Isn't it?"

Eastlyn realized he should have known the colonel would not permit him so easy an exit. "Perhaps it is," he said finally. "But it is also true that you know me better than most."

"As well as the Compass Club?"

East considered that and decided the colonel was in the right of it. "Yes. Every bit as well as they do."

"Then it follows that you are still a puzzle to them."

"I suppose I am, though they are kind enough not to refine upon it in front of me."

The colonel laughed shortly and wheeled himself around. He sipped his whiskey. "Your point is taken."

It did not seem odd to him that it was as if he had known Eastlyn and his friends for a lifetime. This was not the case at all; indeed, the years of his acquaintance with each member of the Compass Club were varied. It was Brendan Hampton, now the Earl of Northam, who had made the introductions. Blackwood had first heard of the Compass Club when young Hampton, then a second son with no expectation of inheriting the title, served under his command in India. The stories his lieutenant told of his Hambrick days were harmless enough, mischief really, of schoolboy tricks and intrigues, and yet there was some bit of cleverness in the schemes of these particular boys that stayed with him. Later, when illness forced him to leave his post in India, he returned to London and accepted a position in the Foreign Secretary's office at Wellesley's request. In very short order he had cause to elicit North's special talents as a soldier and strategist. When it was a sailor's specific skills he required, he asked North about Matthew Forrester, Viscount Southerton. Evan Marchman, West to the others in the group, came to his attention next, and finally it was the tinker, Gabriel Richard Whitney, now the Marquess of Eastlyn, whose expertise was required to make an unusual and sensitive repair between a certain Austrian archduke and a former mistress of the Prince Regent.

It was not always possible, the colonel had learned, to achieve even a fragile peace with customary diplomacy. Eastlyn often had an imaginative way of striking a balance.

"Balance," the colonel said, plucking the thought from his head to test it aloud.

Eastlyn frowned, wondering if he had briefly fallen asleep. It seemed he was having difficulty following Blackwood's conversation of late. "Pardon, sir?"

"Balance," he repeated, more firmly this time. "It occurs

to me that you have lost yours." The creases at the corners of his dark eyes became more pronounced as he made a thorough examination of Eastlyn's person. There was a deepening of the slight downward curve of his mouth.

Having little choice, East waited for the colonel to finish his assessment. It was not the first time Eastlyn had been virtually held immobile by the strength of that black gaze, but there was no likelihood of ever becoming accustomed to it.

"Yes," Blackwood said after several long moments. "It is most certainly true that you have managed to lose your equilibrium."

"It is true now," East said. "For I haven't the vaguest notion what you mean. I had it when I came in here."

The colonel snorted, the nostrils of his hawkish nose flaring slightly. He raised his glass of whiskey and took a drink. "Look at yourself," he said, gesturing with the glass. "You are sprawled across my wing chair as if it were a chaise longue. Your appearance would suggest you are either boneless or were raised without benefit of civilizing influences, quite possibly in the Americas."

Eastlyn's half smile was not a proper smirk, but it edged very close to that disrespectful line.

Blackwood noted the look but made no comment. To his way of thinking it was further proof that the marquess was no longer in command of his faculties. "Perhaps it is sheer weariness that makes one eyelid droop a definite degree below the other or your head list to the side, but I have known you to go two full days without sleep and still be able to negotiate a settlement. At the moment I doubt you could negotiate a path to the door."

East turned his head slightly and eyed the exit with his hooded glance. "I could make it."

"It was not a challenge, though you are welcome to try. I was speaking metaphorically."

"I'll stay where I am, then, if it's all the same to you."

The colonel's eyes narrowed at the faint slur in East's speech. "When did you last eat?"

"Haven't." His eyelids fluttered briefly, then closed.

"Nothing at all?"

Eastlyn managed to shake his head, but it was with noticeable effort.

Blackwood's brow furrowed with considerably more than avuncular concern. He was charged with the care of the men under his command, and he took this obligation seriously. In the case of East and the rest of the Compass Club, it no longer felt like something dictated by duty. He had long ago acknowledged his genuine affection for them. "What have you had to drink, East?"

The marquess made to reach for the glass of whiskey that was no longer on the table at his side. His fingers closed around air before his arm fell heavily to his side.

The colonel put his glass down and rang for his butler. It wasn't possible the whiskey had put East in this state. He hadn't had sufficient libation to hammer his senses.

"Lemonade," East said.

At first Blackwood could not make sense of what he'd heard. He pushed himself closer to Eastlyn's chair and leaned in. "How is that again, East?"

"Lemonade . . . with Lady Sophia."

"Of course," the colonel said dryly. "Lemonade. I could more easily credit the lady herself with doing this to you."

East roused himself to offer up a lopsided smile. "She made me lose my balance."

"Indeed." It was satisfying to know East had not lost his sense of humor. "Then all is explained." The colonel watched Eastlyn drift into a sleep that had more in common with a drugged state than exhaustion. When the butler appeared, Blackwood directed Eastlyn be made comfortable in one of the bedchambers and his own physician sent for.

Sunlight slipped through a part in the heavy velvet drapes and slanted lengthwise across the four-poster. Eastlyn looked down at the bar of light lying against his wrist like a golden shackle. It had been a near thing yesterday, he thought. Had Lady Sophia not exercised some remarkably good sense in turning down his proposal, he might have found himself shackled to her in a permanent fashion.

Groaning softly, East pushed himself upright. The pillow that had been behind his head slipped to the small of his back. Eastlyn plumped it once for a better fit and responded to the scratching at the door.

One of the colonel's servants entered the bedchamber carrying a breakfast tray. She bobbed a curtsey as soon as she settled the tray on the bedside table. "Colonel Blackwood was most particular that I bid you good morning, your lord-ship, and inform you that he selected your food himself. He will see you in the library once you have broken your fast."

Eastlyn nodded. "Prettily said."

She bobbed again, and bright yellow wisps of hair fluttered around the ruffled trim of her cap. Her eyes darted between the covered dishes on the table and the marquess. "Do you require assistance, m'lord?"

"Did the colonel suggest you inquire or are you improvising?"

She frowned, uncertain of his meaning.

Watching her befuddlement, Eastlyn sighed. "It is of no importance. Please tell the colonel I will join him in short order."

"Very good, m'lord."

Eastlyn waited until the pleasant rustle of crisp skirts passed into the hallway and the door was closed before he pulled the tray onto his lap. He had never been one to dally with the servants, even when he was a much younger man. It had been a critical part of his father's instruction that one did not use one's position to take advantage of others. If position came with certain privileges, then it also carried the equal in responsibilities. Influence could be brought to bear, but only when the other party was truly free to choose. Had Eastlyn closed his eyes just then, he could have easily brought the exact nuance of his father's tone to mind, instead of the young maid's agreeably husky voice. It was an unfortunate truth, Eastlyn supposed, that the privileges of his title did not relieve him of responsibility to the servants, even when those servants were not in his employ. The colonel's coquettish upstairs maid might give the appearance of one able to make her own choices, but Eastlyn could never be certain that he had not subtly forced her hand.

Far better, then, to stay in one's class in matters of the flesh. In matters of the heart . . . well, it was only commonsensical that one simply stayed away.

Eastlyn uncovered the dishes Blackwood had chosen for him: a soft-cooked egg, toast, two thin slices of tomato, and a single strip of blackened bacon. The selection was exactly right in content and quantity, and East imagined that his disposition—and his rumbling stomach—would be much improved after he'd eaten.

He had a vague memory of last evening's ending; the question of balance that had been put to him by the colonel echoed faintly in his head. He recalled the overwhelming pressure of weariness, but something more than that also, the intuitive awareness that he was not only weary, but weak. There was a slippery difference in the two that he could not quite define, yet he knew it was so. It did not bear thinking what Blackwood would make of it, so East applied himself to his meal instead.

The colonel was waiting in the library as promised. In spite of the warmth of the day, a rug covered his thin legs, and a small fire had been laid. His chair was situated close to the fireplace, and he held a poker across his lap. Eastlyn dutifully stepped inside the room when he was gestured to do so and shut the door behind him, also at the colonel's prompting.

"It keeps the heat in. Deuced warm for you, I'll wager, but I find I'm often cold these days." Blackwood pointed to the same chair Eastlyn had occupied last evening. "Sit. We'll see if you can manage the thing without sliding to the floor this time."

Eastlyn raised an eyebrow but did as he was told.

The colonel's soft grunt was approving. "You seem to be all of a piece."

"And I was not last night?"

"You were *liquid* last night."

"Foxed? I confess I don't remember anything beyond a single drink."

"You had hardly more than a single swallow. You were not foxed, East."

"Then tired beyond my experience and feeling every one of my two and thirty years."

"I doubt that your journey from Battenburn explains what befell you last evening. Until my physician assured me otherwise, I was in fear that you had some seizure of the brain."

Reflexively, Eastlyn touched the side of his head with his fingertips. "Not a fit, then?"

"No. Nothing like that. Doctor Keeble suggests you were drugged."

Eastlyn smiled crookedly and allowed his hand to drop to the arm of the chair. "You should not allow the quack to treat you."

Blackwood did not mirror East's good humor. "Belladonna, he says. It would explain your symptoms. Perhaps a tincture of opium. Your pupils were dilated and your muscles were inordinately weak."

"But I didn't eat yesterday. There was quite a row at Battenburn before dawn, and it was every bit loud enough to rouse me from my bed."

"Pistol at the ready, no doubt."

"Of course." Eastlyn made no apology for it. "The baroness was in quite a state because her bedchamber had been invaded by the Gentleman Thief, and it was her very shrill contention that the scoundrel had taken his leave with her favorite necklace. I joined North in a search that came to nothing, except that it deprived me of a decent breakfast. I took my leave soon after and came straightaway to London."

"And?" The colonel drew out the single word, making it a question that prompted Eastlyn to continue.

"And I went to Number 14 Bowden Street," he said. "That is where Lady Sophia resides with her cousin and his family."

"There is nothing more?"

"Well, she told me she'd have more success making me a pigeon than a happy man."

"I believe you mentioned that."

"Did I?" He tried to recall, but his conversation with Blackwood was still blanketed in fog. "I left her shortly after that, on civil terms, I thought. I went home, bathed and changed my clothes, then came here. I admit things are not entirely clear after that."

"The belated effects of the drug. Apparently you did not take it in sufficient strength to cause you immediate distress. Doctor Keeble surmises that your symptoms were magnified by your fatigue and mental confusion."

"I was confused?" Eastlyn sifted backward through the snippets of conversation he could recall and found himself once again squarely set in Lady Sophia's garden. "The lady, you mean," he said, his half smile edging upward. "I suppose I cannot disagree. She was completely diverting."

The colonel allowed that this was an understatement. "She offered you lemonade, I believe."

"Yes. How did you know?"

"You mentioned it last night."

He must have, he thought, for there was no other way the colonel could have happened upon that information. What Blackwood was making of it, though, Eastlyn had no liking for. "You think Lady Sophie drugged me?" The absurdity of it was rife in his voice. "It was presented to me in a pitcher, and we both poured from it."

"And drank?"

Eastlyn remembered eventually draining his glass. He could not say if the same was true for Lady Sophia. In his mind's eye he could see her replacing her glass on the tray, but could not sharpen the image to know whether it was still full, half full, or empty. "We both drank," he said at last, unwilling to cast suspicion on the lady when his memory was at fault.

The colonel considered this as he tugged absently on a forelock of black hair. He swept it back with his fingertips as he came to a decision. "I did not think it was possible that the lady could be at fault, but it is the sort of thing that bears investigating. I will also make appropriate inquiries regarding the state of her health." He held up a hand as Eastlyn made to interrupt. "Never fear. It will be done discreetly. No one in the family will know they are being questioned. It's her cousin, did you say? Colley is the family name?"

"You will not make inquiries."

Blackwood's glance narrowed, and his brows rose a fraction. "I won't?"

"No. What is between Lady Sophia and me is of a private nature, Colonel. It has nothing to do with any assignment you have ever given me. She is no threat to the peace or dignity of society—any society—and I do not want her treated as one. It is not possible that she was in any way responsible for my regrettable condition last night."

The colonel's dark hair was liberally salted with gray, and the line of it was receding. These things could be explained by the natural progression of age, except that Blackwood preferred to blame Eastlyn, Northam, Southerton, and West. This moment was one of many supporting that view. "I cannot persuade you?"

"No."

Blackwood picked up the poker in his lap and used it to stab at the fire while he considered another approach.

"I am set on this," Eastlyn said. He understood his mentor's silence and knew that he could expect a change in tactics. In point of fact, Eastlyn realized he could not stop Blackwood from doing as he wished, yet something between them would be altered if the colonel made his inquiries. "Can we not leave it?"

The poker went still in Blackwood's hands. "If you are wrong about the lady, then your life may be forfeit. Do you expect that I should make no effort to protect you?"

"I am not wrong," East said with quiet conviction.

"Who is she, East?"

"No part of my life. And it is better that she remain so."

The colonel reset the poker with the other fireplace tools. "Can you not humor me in some small way? Tell me at least how this engagement came to be. I heard of it, you know, but you had already left for the Battenburn estate when the news came to me."

"You were surprised?"

"I was skeptical."

Eastlyn felt himself relaxing. His fingers eased their grip on the arms of the chair, and he offered up a small smile. It was so very like the colonel not to accept the town gossip as gospel. "I took quite a ribbing from the others."

Blackwood nodded. "I should be something close to astonished if they passed on the opportunity."

"So would I." He rested his head against the back of the wing chair, and his chin came up slightly. "There is no engagement, sir."

"I am beginning to appreciate that, yet it has become what passes for common knowledge among the ton."

"I believe Lady Sophia's family encouraged the rumor once they heard of it. At the very least, they did not deny it."

The colonel rubbed his chin as he considered this. "Her family?" he asked. "Not the lady herself?"

"I accept that she is without blame in this." Eastlyn did not expect Blackwood to be so easily convinced. It was in the man's nature to probe at all aspects of a problem. "I heard nothing about my supposed engagement while I was in London. I imagine the rumor was just taking substance and strength as I was taking my leave for the Battenburn rout. I first learned of it from some of the baron's guests." He sighed, remembering the confusion he was forced to mask as he was congratulated for his good fortune. "They were tripping over themselves to wish me happy."

"Then you did not deny it either."

"Only to North, West, and South. To let it be acknowledged as a falsehood would have cast Lady Sophia in an unfavorable light. She did not deserve to be treated so shabbily. The trick that was played was meant to make things uncomfortable for me."

The colonel's eyes narrowed as he considered Eastlyn's assertion. "I take it you have a suspect for the source of the rumor."

East nodded. The tips of his steepled fingers tapped lightly together. "I have had no opportunity to confirm it yet. My first responsibility was to Lady Sophia."

"She has absolved you?"

"She was everything gracious."

"How fortunate for you. It could have been difficult to extricate yourself if she had been in expectation of a proposal."

Eastlyn's gaze fell to his hands, and he stared at them a long moment, saying nothing. "Yes," he said finally. "It was as you say, fortunate." He looked up and caught the colonel still watching him closely. He smiled easily, stretching his long legs before him. "I suppose I've always been lucky that way, haven't I?"

Blackwood was struck by the tone that was a bit off the mark for one reveling in his luck. It made him more curious about the lady. "I do not believe I am at all familiar with her," he said. "How long have you been acquainted?"

The question forced Eastlyn to recall again the circumstances of his first introduction to Lady Sophia. "It was at one of Lady Stafford's musicales. Mozart, perhaps. Or Bach. I don't know. It was a tedious affair, but then they often are. Dunsmore was in attendance with his wife and—"

"Dunsmore?" the colonel asked, interrupting. "Dunsmore is Lady Sophia's cousin?"

"Yes. A second or third cousin, I think. I'm not certain. I have never made a point to inquire."

"Then Tremont is—"

"Her cousin also. The earl is Dunsmore's father."

"Of course." The tumblers fell into place in the colonel's steel trap mind. "Lady Sophia is the daughter of the late earl. Francis . . . Franklin . . ." He held up his index finger to stop Eastlyn from supplying the correct name. "Hah! It was *Frederick* Colley. A thorough bounder if there ever was."

"I take it you were acquainted with him."

"No. Good heavens, no. My acquaintance was with his reputation. You're familiar, no doubt."

"I am not," Eastlyn admitted. "My knowledge of Lady Sophia's family is slight."

"You should have found out more before you got yourself engaged to her."

"Amusing," Eastlyn said sarcastically. "I hope you do not mean to entertain me with your wit this morning. My headache of last night will most certainly return."

The colonel apologized easily. "Forgive me. As you noted, it was a poor attempt at levity." He adjusted his spectacles, pushing them down the bridge of his nose so he could peer at Eastlyn over the gold rims. "I suppose the particulars of the late earl's life are unimportant now that you have settled this matter with Lady Sophia." He fell silent, his features perfectly neutral, while he waited to see if Eastlyn would take the dangled bait.

East did not. What he did was find the humor of the situation and offer up a slim, slightly mocking smile. "How little I would have learned from you if I snapped at that. Confess, you would be disappointed."

Blackwood sighed. "Hoisted with my own petard."

Eastlyn's smile widened a fraction. It was not often that he could catch the colonel out so neatly. "Tell me about the late earl, or not," he said. "But I will not inquire because it is of no consequence to me. I doubt I will have reason to seek Lady Sophia's company again. After speaking with her yesterday, I am free to deny the rumors without causing her distress. She, of course, has always been free to do the same."

"Her family might be of a different mind."

"They are. But I believe she means to rein them in."

"You are highly eligible. Tremont has—"

Eastlyn shook his head, interrupting the colonel. "Lady Sophia doesn't think so."

"What?" Blackwood pushed his spectacles back up over the bridge of his hawkish nose and regarded East intently. "How is that again?"

"Lady Sophia doesn't think we would suit, though I think she means I would not suit her. I have a vague recollection of telling you that she called me a murderer. And a gambler. A drunkard also."

"Then you were serious?"

"Completely. So was she."

The colonel's frown deepened as he considered this. "But you are quite wealthy."

"I believe she was the one to point that out. It did nothing to make my character flaws more palatable."

"Dunsmore cannot like that," Blackwood said. "There are debts, I believe. Heavy ones. Bad investments also."

It did not surprise Eastlyn. It was not an unusual circumstance with inherited titles and lands, especially ones that were entailed, as he surmised was the case in Sophia's family. Although the colonel had not offered the information yet, East gathered that the late earl was the reason for the empty pockets. "Lady Sophia does not seem to be of a mind to lay the problem of her family's finances at my door."

"Someone was," Blackwood reminded him.

"Yes. But she was not the one. Dunsmore, perhaps Tremont as well, might not be above trying to take advantage of the rumor, but as I mentioned before, I most sincerely doubt they are the source of it."

The colonel had his own idea who was responsible for starting the gossip, but he did not test his hypothesis with

Eastlyn. He'd make a wager, he thought, with South or perhaps West. They were also likely to be privy to some information that he was loath to ask East. "When do you mean to confront this individual?"

"Soon."

"I have an assignment for you," Blackwood said. "If there is to be blood shed, I would be obliged if you would make certain it is not yours."

"I have always been heartily grateful for your concern," East drawled. He sat up straight as his mind turned to the matter of his business with the colonel. "What is it you would have me do?"

"There has been serious discussion of establishing a settlement in Singapore. The East India Company would like to see it happen as early as next year, and I don't have to tell you how important a settlement would be to the Crown. If such a thing could be accomplished without an excess of political posturing, we would all be better served for it. You will see to it, won't you, East? You know the stage and the players. The Prince Regent's announcement that he is in favor of the settlement has had the unfortunate consequence of merely raising suspicions. There are more questions in Parliament about the soundness of the venture, and the East India Company wants to be assured of wider support."

"Military support, you mean."

"If it comes to that."

East was silent for several minutes as he applied his thinking to the problem. For all of that time it was as if he were alone in the colonel's study, every sense concentrated on the task before him. "It will mean negotiating with Helmsley and Barlough. They are among Prinny's most vocal detractors. I suspect something of substance will have to be offered to bring them around. Shares, perhaps, in the Company."

The colonel nodded once. "I trust you to know what is best. You have had dealings with Barlough before, as I recall, and been quite successful in reasoning with him."

"Stealing his chamberpot is always a good beginning."

Blackwood chuckled; the story was a favorite of his. "Liverpool has given his approval," he added. "He envisions this as a victory for the Tories if the naysayers can be brought around."

The prime minister was in need of a feather in his cap, Eastlyn thought. Liverpool's leadership during the Napoleonic wars had been crucial in bringing about a successful end, but the restrictive policies he had enacted during wartime were still in effect while the people's tolerance for them no longer was. Eastlyn was not in agreement with any plan, prescribed by government or demanded by the people, that suppressed freedoms of speech and the press. "The minister has his own detractors," East said evenly, his opinion of no importance here. "He must be aware of the mounting opposition."

"How could he not be? His life is politics." He cocked one dark brown. "You will see to this? Speak to Helmsley and Barlough?"

East did not immediately agree, his mien still contemplative. "When you conceived of this assignment, had you already heard of my engagement?"

The colonel saw the direction of East's thinking before the figurative corner was turned. "Yes, but it is of no account because I did not make any connection between Lady Sophia and Tremont." The Earl of Tremont, Blackwood knew, would loom as large an obstacle to the establishment of the settlement as Helmsley and East's childhood tormentor. "If you are in expectation of problems because of it, you can pass on the assignment. I will speak to South when he returns from Battenburn."

East felt no urgency to rush his acceptance because the colonel suggested Southerton. He and his friends might compete at racing bloods through narrow London streets or wager who would be the first to nod off over his cups, but there was no rivalry for the colonel's work. "South will not make too fine a mess of it," East said equably. "I do not think he would be bothered a whit at the prospect of leaving Battenburn."

"South is *on* assignment at Battenburn," the colonel said. "And you are purposely being difficult."

East laughed. It was a charge that was often leveled at his head, most consistently by his own mother. "Very well. Of course I will do it. Tremont presents no conflict for me, though you should know at the outset that I will not sacrifice myself to marriage in order to secure a British settlement in Singapore."

"I never thought it."

"I am not remotely inclined to believe you," Eastlyn said without rancor. "You think of everything."

Blackwood was not offended in the least; rather he accepted it as a compliment. "It would be more accurate," he said, "that I considered and dismissed it."

"Just so." East rose to his feet. "I regret that I have to take my leave, sir. I have not yet spoken to my mother or father, and they are sure to have an opinion about the engagement-that-is-not. As to the Singapore matter, I will make all the appropriate contacts. I cannot say how long it will take to influence the outcome in favor of the Crown and the Company, but you may be confident that I will do whatever is required."

"Oh," the colonel said softly, "I am never so certain of anything as I am of that."

Eastlyn made a slight bow of his head, acknowledging the remark. "I am most grateful for your hospitality last night and again this morning. It was generous of you to look after me."

Blackwood dismissed East's thanks with a wave of his hand. "Pray, extend my best regards to Sir James and your mother. It has been an age since I've seen them about."

Since his parents were in society with a frequency that tired Eastlyn when he thought of it, he knew that it was the colonel who had become more confined. "I will certainly do so," he said. "They often inquire after you."

The colonel made no reply to that, but wheeled his chair forward to see Eastlyn out. At the door he raised his eyes and regarded East with affected innocence. "You will keep me informed, won't you, in the event that you speak to Lady Sophia again and find yourself in need of either a physician or a special license."

Chapter Three

Lady Francis Whitney Winslow looked up from her embroidery as the pocket doors to the drawing room opened. Her eyes brightened as she took in the fine figure of her son standing on the threshold. "Aah! So you have come at last. And there's a good boy you are for not making me wait overlong. I heard that you had returned to London, but I thought the wags could not be in the right of it since you meant to be at Battenburn for a fortnight." She patted the space on the settee beside her and proffered her cheek at the same time. "So here you are, but as it is already past the noon hour, I collect I am not your first call of the day."

Grinning, East bent and kissed his mother's cheek. As scoldings went, it was a mild one. "But you are, Mother. Today's first call, that is. However, I arrived in town yesterday, so if you mean to split hairs . . ." He sprawled on the settee and turned slightly to one side to better gauge her reaction.

Franny Winslow had only affection for her son today. Perhaps later she would be out of sorts with him—not that it would last long—but this afternoon she was feeling most generous toward him. "I have decided to forgive you," she said.

"That is good of you, though I suspect it is premature. You have not heard the whole of it."

That was when Franny looked more closely at her son. His eyes, often remarked to be much like her own in shape and color, were not as lively as they might have been. The smile, offered so easily to her upon his entry, showed some signs of strain at the corners. "Then it is as I first thought," she said. "There is no engagement."

He nodded. "Where is Father?"

"He has gone to his office and then to the bookseller's. He is most particularly excited about a manuscript that has come into his hands. I simply cannot rein him in. I'm afraid we cannot expect him soon. You will have to make do with me, Gabriel, and I will give him every detail. He cautioned me not to place too much credence in the rumors, and I can tell you, I was very torn. It is no easy thing to learn of your son's engagement from a friend, and one is bound to wonder at the truth of it; but a mother does have certain hopes for her children." She put her embroidery hoop aside and rested her hands in her lap. "Shall I ring for tea? Mrs. Eddy will have cakes for you. Your favorites, I am sure. She always does."

Eastlyn knew the futility of trying to refuse this offer and accepted it because it gave his mother so much pleasure to coddle him. In truth, at times like these he was not entirely opposed to it either. "I could not call on you until I had spoken to Lady Sophia," he said as she rose to ring for refreshments. "I did so immediately upon arriving in London, and there is now agreement between us as to how we mean to go on."

Franny looked over her shoulder and favored her son with an arid glance. "Separately, I take it."

"Yes, Mother. Separately." He thought her subsequent sigh a tad dramatic, but he supposed it was in proportion to her disappointment. "I must needs point out that Cara has presented you with three grandchildren, two male, all of whom are hale and hearty, though Simon does drool overmuch. The line shall continue, so there is no justification for pinning the whole of the responsibility on me."

Franny arched an eyebrow. "My, you *are* out of sorts."

"I beg your pardon."

"I should like to see you settled. I will not apologize for that."

Eastlyn closed his eyes briefly and rubbed the bridge of his nose with his thumb and forefinger. "You have been conspiring with Lady Redding. Southerton reports his mother has been preaching from the same text."

"It is hardly a conspiracy. We are of similar minds."

"And the Dowager Countess Northam?"

"The same." She laughed delightedly when she heard her son's soft groan. "You should surrender to the inevitable, you know. We will have our way." The butler arrived at the door, and Lady Winslow requested tea and cakes. She returned to the settee and patted her son's knee lightly. "Tell me about Lady Sophia. I confess I know little enough about her. Is it true she is Tremont's niece?"

"A cousin," East said. "Second, I think. That would make Dunsmore a third cousin."

"Oh, yes. Dunsmore. He is not an agreeable sort."

"More so than his father." While they waited for tea Eastlyn shared what he knew about Sophie's family.

Bloodlines and family intrigues were not so important to Lady Whitney Winslow as they were interesting. She did not have to look farther than her own son to see what could be wrought when events conspired to reshape a family tree. She thought of her husband who was gone from home and what he would make of Gabriel's predicament; then she thought of the husband who was long gone from her life and what she would make of their son.

Gabriel was a man, she thought, but it was not so easy to always see him in that light. The vision of him as he was as a child in the aftermath of scarlet fever—frail, thin, his complexion mottled by sickness—was never completely absent from her mind. His beautiful eyes had been made unnaturally bright by the fever, but their gaze was unfocused. He cried for her and was too delirious to know that she came. That haunted her, the needy cry of her child and her inability to comfort him. She had already lost the battle to save her husband from the fever; she would have made any sacrifice demanded of her not to lose her son.

Walter Whitney was only thirty-five when he succumbed. He was the third son born to the Marquess of Eastlyn by that worthy's third wife. There had never been any expectation that Walter would inherit his father's title, and indeed, his premature death had insured it could not happen; yet his older brothers were similarly unsuccessful in attaining the longevity of their common sire, and the title and lands eventually came to Gabriel.

It had not passed Franny's notice that the title had passed through an entire generation of Whitney heirs in not much above a decade. Walter's oldest brother had breathed his last in his mistress's bed, a fact that was never mentioned in the family, but was well known it often seemed, to everyone outside it. His son inherited next and upon reaching his majority promptly took a drunken spill from his thoroughbred's back and broke his neck. Having naught but a sister, and entailment being what it was, the title then went to Walter's second brother. While Samuel did his best to make certain the line continued through him, he sired only daughters, and upon his death (he shot himself examining his hunting rifle) it was Gabriel's.

Franny was not overjoyed by what some would say was her son's good fortune. It seemed to her that the title was more curse than blessing, and her inclination to protect her son from life's harsh turns could have easily become an obsession. It was Sir James, the man she had married after her mourning was at an end, who saw to it that she tempered her maternal instincts. He was, for all intents and purposes, Gabriel's father, and she did not believe the bond they forged could have been stronger had it been a bond of blood.

She wished her husband were here now because his presence could be counted on to provide calm and reason. Gabriel was, of course, both calm and reasonable, but Franny required the reassurance from someone who loved her son as well as she did. Sir James had done so from the beginning, taking Cara under his wing first, knowing all the while that Gabriel would follow his much admired sister's lead. It would not hurt, Franny thought, if Cara were here as well. For all that Gabriel seemed to have the matter of his false engagement well in hand, it could not hurt to hear other opinions.

"What do your friends say?" Franny asked, pouring herself a second cup of tea.

"They have made a point of wishing me happy."

Franny pursed her lips, but her disapproval was mostly feigned. "Fell all over themselves making the jest, I'll wager. Laughing too hard to voice an opinion or offer their help."

"Their opinion is that Lady Sophia has been poorly used." His voice dropped, and he added gently, "And they did not offer help because none is needed. It is all being dealt with."

"I trust that is so, Gabriel, yet it occurs to me that the understanding you have reached with Lady Sophia might be inadequate to halt the rumors."

"I have thought of that. There is one more call I will be making today."

"Oh." Franny fell silent, wondering what she dared say. Keeping her own counsel did not sit well with her, but there were also matters that one did not properly discuss with one's own son.

"Mother?" Eastlyn said.

She did not quite catch his eye, preferring to study the pattern of dainty blue flowers on her teacup. "Hmm?"

"You are biting your tongue, I can tell. You may as well say what is on your mind. It will save you from going to Father and putting him up to broaching the subject with me."

Franny placed the teacup on the silver tray at her side and fussed for a moment with a loose thread on the fringe of her shawl. "I can think of only one person who would want to cause you this sort of discomfort among your peers, Gabriel. It *is* Mrs. Sawyer that you intend to visit, is it not?"

Eastlyn had no one but himself to blame for the turn in this conversation. What other mother, even prompted to speak freely, would accept the invitation to discuss her son's mistress? He would wager Southerton had never had this dialogue with Lady Redding, and Celia Worth Hampton, for all that she was unafraid to speak her mind on a variety of subjects, quite possibly drew the line at the topic of North's paramour. West was spared the ignominy on two counts: one, because his mother had *been* someone's mistress and, two, because she was dead. True, none of them were keeping a mistress at the moment, but the same could also be said of him.

"You are distressed, are you not, that I have mentioned her?" Franny said. "It is not the done thing, to be sure, but it cannot be avoided. She is an evil woman."

This genie was not going to return to the bottle, so Eastlyn resigned himself to the inevitable. "She is hardly evil, Mother. It is truer to say that she is unhappy."

"She is a woman scorned."

Although his mother made this announcement in a tone that brooked no argument, Eastlyn could not let it pass. "I did not turn her out. Mrs. Sawyer chose to look elsewhere for protection."

"Because you would not come up to snuff."

There was an inkling of an ache behind his left eye that Eastlyn thought he would do well to suppress. He massaged his temple with his fingertips and said calmly, "You seem to know rather a lot about it."

"One hears things."

"You will never tell me how. Promise me you will never reveal how you come by your intelligence. I am certain it would be lowering to know that my life is grist for the mill."

"We discuss South and Northam, too."

Eastlyn groaned softly, both amused and resigned, and the ache behind his eye became a throb.

Franny saw the flicker of pain in her son's eyes and understood what was at the source of it. "Shall I ring for a compress?"

He shook his head. "It will pass." At least he wanted to believe it was so. He needed all his faculties when he confronted Annette. "More tea, perhaps." He said this not because he wanted any, but because he knew his mother would need to fuss. It was better to direct her in a fashion he could tolerate. His patience was not infinite by any means.

Franny poured and passed the cup and saucer. "There is one thing I do not understand," she said.

"Oh?"

"Why did Mrs. Sawyer choose Lady Sophia as your intended? It seems to me that this was most particularly done, not happenstance at all. But why? For all that there is some notoriety associated with her family name, there are no pariahs. She herself is not often about, at least that I have been cognizant of; but she belongs to a younger set, and I might have missed her debut. How well were you acquainted with her before your names were linked?"

It had not taken his mother long to arrive precisely at the heart of the matter. "Barely of any acquaintance," Eastlyn said quietly. "There is no recounting that I can give that will improve myself in your eyes. I am not proud of my part in how the thing is likely to have come about." He set his cup in its saucer and regarded his mother over the rim. She was determined to be of an open mind, but he suspected she would ultimately defend him. This time her protection was unwelcome for he knew he was in the wrong of it.

"Mrs. Sawyer asked me about the sort of woman I would someday marry," he said. "You see, Mother, it is not a subject that is outside of my thoughts."

"Nor hers, unless I miss my guess," Franny interrupted in wry tones. "Pray, go on."

"I had been introduced to Lady Sophia some hours earlier—a musicale at Lady Stafford's—and her name came to my mind when Mrs. Sawyer posed her question. You might well believe that this was because she made a favorable impression on me, and I suppose it is true in some regard, yet it is passing strange that I recalled my introduction to her at all. The encounter was so brief and with so little to recommend it as to be eminently forgettable. It was badly done of me, but I offered up Lady Sophia as the opposite of all I should wish in a marriage partner."

"I see. It *was* badly done of you."

Eastlyn nodded. "Lady Sophia did not deserve my ridicule."

"True, but what Mrs. Sawyer has done with your thoughtless remarks is beyond the pale. Your mistress was angling for a proposal, Gabriel. That did not escape your notice, did it?"

"No. I knew what she was about. I saw the trap and thought I had neatly avoided it."

"What? By describing to her the sort of woman you would *not* marry? You cannot be serious. It merely made her more confident of her appeal. She would see herself as having nothing in common with someone like Lady Sophia."

"She doesn't."

"That is my point. The comparison gave her hope, Gabriel."

"It was not my intent."

"As if that matters. You are well rid of her."

Eastlyn was compelled to point out, "I did not put an end to the arrangement, Mother. She refused my protection."

"That is because she thought it would prompt your proposal. Thank God it did not. I should despair of your good judgment had she been able to bring the thing about. What will you say to her now? She *is* a woman scorned, you know. It is exactly as I said. It occurs to me that if mothers were more prepared to discuss situations of this nature with their sons, the sons might not make such a muddle of them. The Mrs. Sawyers of the world have a leg up on the rest of us because there is nothing they hold as sacred."

Eastlyn actually slid lower in his corner of the settee and put one hand to his head. Squinting slightly, he regarded his mother with the eye that did not have the ache behind it. "Never say you mean to share that view with your friends. You will ruin me, Mother. Every time a man is forced to listen to his mother's opinion of his mistress, my name will be invoked in the blackest way possible. I will probably be called out so often that I shall have to hire someone to manage the dawn appointments." It would be worse, he thought, than his first days at Hambrick Hall when he was regularly thrashing one or another of his classmates because of the steady arrival of all those cakes. "I cannot depend on Southerton or North to act as my seconds, for I suspect they will be at the forefront of those challenging me, and West will not want to choose sides."

Franny's mouth flattened, but it was only in aid of checking her laughter. She was not proof against his arguments when he used absurdity to make his point. "Oh, very well," she said. "I would not want to stand accused of challenging the tenets of the ton. You may depend on me to keep my opinions to myself, at least on the matter of what can be properly discussed with one's offspring."

East pushed himself out of his corner and gave his mother's hand an affectionate squeeze. "You are very good to me," he said, meaning it. "You will tell Father all, won't you? I really cannot remain longer."

Franny nodded. "And I shall write your sister directly. Cara did not think the rumor could possibly be true. She was certain you would have told us if you had made Lady Sophia an offer of marriage."

Before his mother spied something in his features that would give the truth away, East bounded to his feet. Cara was only marginally less his champion than his mother. If they learned he had proposed to Lady Sophia, neither of them would comprehend that he had also been refused. That information would not likely endear them to Sophie, and she was no more deserving of their misplaced censure than she was of Mrs. Sawyer's. "The colonel sends his best to you and Father," he said by way of taking his leave.

Lady Winslow did not miss a beat. "Aah, so you did pay him a visit before coming here. I cannot like being third on your list of duty calls behind Lady Sophia and Blackwood, but I suppose it is something to be ahead of Mrs. Sawyer."

Eastlyn's lips twitched. "You will never change, Mother, and I count that as a good thing, indeed. Were you to pass on an opportunity to scold, I should probably expire from the shock of it." He kissed her cheek while she was still mustering a reply. "Do not trouble yourself to get up. I will see myself out."

Watching him go, Franny absently picked up her embroidery hoop and drew out the needle. Stitchery presented her with no distraction to her thoughts. She was perfectly able to consider what course she might take to make Lady Sophia's acquaintance without tangling a single thread.

"Your refusal is not to be countenanced." Tremont's complexion was florid, and one had to look no farther than Lady Sophia to find the cause of this condition. The earl's journey from Tremont Park to No. 14 Bowden Street had been remarkably without incident, and his coloring was not influenced by the heat of the late afternoon sun. The windows in the drawing room at the rear of the house were opened to the garden, and a pleasant enough breeze ruffled the curtains and occasionally the chitterlings on his shirtfront. No, it was Lady Sophia who had become the bane of his existence, a position heretofore held by his late cousin, her father.

Sophie sat perched on the edge of a damask-covered chair. She wished she had chosen something other than the apple green calico to wear this afternoon; something in ecru would have been a better choice, for it would have blended splendidly with the chair. She was not nearly as prepossessed as Tremont and Harold believed her to be. The earl had always cut an imposing figure, and it was difficult not to shrink from it. While Harold was trim and athletic, taking pleasure in gentlemanly pursuits like boxing and racing, his father looked as if he worked on the docks all day, hefting crates without benefit of nets or pulleys. Tremont had a robust voice and broad mannerisms. He often emphasized his speech with abrupt gestures, from time to time even shaking his mallet-sized fists.

It was an effective performance from the pulpit. Sophie remembered visiting the church where Tremont had his living when he was still the vicar at Nashwicke. She could not have been more than seven when her father had first taken her to hear his cousin preach. She sat in the very first pew and actually felt the bench tremble beneath her. Her father did not stop her from crawling onto his lap, and that was where she remained until the Reverend Richard Colley gave the benediction. She was no longer afraid of the fire and brimstone sermons that he was wont to deliver, even without benefit of a pulpit, but that experience was not easily forgotten. It would have been sufficient reason to be uncomfortable in his presence, but it was no part of the reason she despised him.

She waited him out and was rewarded for her patience when he focused his sharp attention on his son.

"I thought you said she could be brought around, Harold. Is that not what we discussed?" The earl's eyes did not absorb heat the way his complexion did. The look he had for his son was glacier blue. "This is not at all what I expected from you."

The tips of Viscount Dunsmore's ears turned red, but he held his ground. To give up even a fraction of the space he held would be interpreted as acknowledging his failure. "We knew at the outset that it was unlikely that Eastlyn would make a proposal, Father. It really was not incumbent upon him to do so."

"Then you promised that Sophie could be made to agree because you believed she would never have the opportunity to do so? Is that what you are telling me now? You were merely being patronizing?" As so often was the way with

Tremont, the questions were strictly rhetorical. He had often challenged his congregation in a similar manner and would have been heartily surprised if anyone had considered speaking out. Questions of this nature were meant to stir self-reflection, and he saw that this was certainly the case with his son. "Well, he did propose," Tremont said, slapping the flat of his hand on the mantelpiece for emphasis. A pewter candlestick jumped in place, and the candle it supported was set askew. "And she has most churlishly refused."

"I was not churlish," Sophie said. The words were not meant to be spoken aloud, but when the attention of both men turned to her as one, she knew what she had done. Steadying herself for a reply that was neither tremulous or impudent, Sophie added, "The marquess was acting contrary to his own judgment. He did not want to marry me, and I would have been most unkind to have preyed upon his honor."

"His honor?" Tremont said, his voice rising a notch. "Have you so much fine feeling, then, for his honor and none at all for your family's? Eastlyn is as rich as Croesus."

"Richer."

Tremont was so struck by Sophie's cheek that he actually gaped.

Sophie decided she may as well be hanged for a sheep as a lamb. "The marquess said it himself when I remarked similarly on his fortune. I said he was rich as Croesus, and he said he was richer."

A muscle jumped in the earl's square jaw. He looked from Sophie to his son. "Do you permit her to say whatever comes to her mind? I am thinking now that she should have remained at Tremont Park with me and not had such free rein under your roof."

Again Harold demonstrated his good sense by not responding. Silence was all that was required to shift his father's attention back to Sophie.

"Have you considered that I could turn you out, Sophia?" Tremont asked. "You would not be the first young woman, nor daughter of a peer, to be sent from home for such willful disobedience. Where would you go? Must I point out that you have no one save us to support you?"

Sophie drew a shallow breath and said carefully, "I thought the idea of shackling myself to his lordship was in aid of supporting you."

Tremont's hand came up again, this time stiff-fingered with his thumb at attention. He sliced the air with it, causing a disturbance that ruffled the curling tendrils of hair at Sophie's forehead. It was not his intention to strike her, but to make her think he meant to. What he considered noteworthy was that she had not flinched. "You would do well to modulate that defiance," he told her. "It is not an attractive quality."

Sophie had not remained still because she was unafraid of being struck, but rather because she was unafraid of being struck in the face. She was of no use to the family if she was damaged goods, and her appearance was determined by Tremont and Harold to be her only asset. "I believe, my lord, that there are other means besides marriage for me to contribute to Tremont Park. I know something about the management of the estate and making the farms productive again. I have studied the latest techniques for improving the land, and I believe with only two good harvests we can realize an increase in the rents. If we were to practice even a measure of frugality or make a pledge to live within our means, there would be funds to pay the creditors and no new debts to dodge."

Harold crossed his arms in front of him and regarded his father with his head cocked slightly to one side. His entire posture communicated that Sophie's little speech was something he had heard before. "*This* is the refrain she has been singing since her arrival in town. As a governess for the children she has been unexceptional, and my wife finds her fit enough as a companion, but this . . . this insistence that we should manage the household with no regard to our social responsibilities, well, frankly it is wearing on all of our nerves.

She would have Lady Dunsmore burn the same tallow candles the servants use and make do with fewer servants altogether. She thinks there is no necessity in replenishing our wardrobes when the fashion is not significantly changed from last Season."

"It is only that—" Sophie fell silent, cut off by Tremont's quelling look. She kept her feet flat on the floor to restrain the tremor in her legs.

"Mayhap you do not understand our position," the earl told her. He made an attempt to temper his voice. Tremont was incapable of cajolery, but he could be less severe when it served his purpose. "The current state of our finances has very little to do with tallow tapers or a bolt of Belgian lace. We are come to this point—and you will forgive me for speaking plainly—because of drinking, whoring, and gambling. You will recognize these vices, mayhap, as your father's *raison d'être*. My cousin had no regard for the responsibilities of his station, and he was in every way subservient to his baser instincts. After your mother died there was no limiting his licentious behavior. No matter what you think you know to the contrary, your father's weak character certainly influenced the untimely end of his own pitiable existence. With the possible exception of your care, Frederick did little that was not motivated by his own pleasure-seeking."

Tremont was perfectly aware that the color had drained from Sophia's face. He imagined that if he grazed her with his fingertips, he would find the touch of her to be quite cold, perhaps capable of burning him with its iciness. It did not stop him from continuing. There were things that must be said, and he was a firm believer in being cruel to be kind. "The reason any funds remain in the family coffers, Sophia, owes much to the fact that Providence finally cornered your father. I have no quarrel with the God who struck Frederick down and made him bedfast. No less compelling a tragedy could have kept him from squandering what was left of his fortune."

Sophia felt the numbness around her heart spread to other

internal organs. She no longer noticed the queer little tightness in her stomach or the constriction in her lungs. The effects were carried quickly by the coursing of her blood so that in moments it was no easy thing to feel the tips of her fingers or toes. When a dark veil fluttered at the periphery of her vision, Sophie thought she might faint. It was contemplating the very ignominy of that event that made her struggle to draw air.

Tremont was still not finished. He clasped his hands behind his back and rocked slightly forward on the balls of his feet. "You are to be commended for nursing your father in the final years of his life. No one can fault you for the care and devotion you gave him; yet it is also true that the estate fell further into disrepair during that time, the rents decreased, and there was even less income than before. I have seen the accounts, Sophia. If you had so many fine schemes for the management of the land and the farmers and the crops, the time to put them into practice would have been then, don't you think? That you upbraid us now for looking for another solution seems rather ill-considered. We had no part in creating this opportunity with the marquess, but it would be foolish in the extreme if we were not to seize it. You would do well to reflect upon your refusal, m'dear, and think how such a marriage might benefit you."

Harold sensed that Sophia was of no mind to defend herself now. That she was an easy mark did not bother him in the least. "What can be your objection to the fine things that Eastlyn can bring to your life? You can be certain he will be generous. You will never be able to spend the allowance he will give you. You will be chatelaine of his great country homes at Braeden and Easter Hill, and there is his town house here as well. You will be in demand as a guest at every affair of importance, and there will be carriages and fine clothes and a box at the theater."

There will also be his mistress, Sophie thought, and this time she had the good sense not to say so aloud. What she said was, "I should like to go to my room if you please."

Over her head Harold and his father exchanged glances. It was Tremont who answered. "Of course. And you will think on what was said here, won't you, dear?"

Sophie nodded, doubting that she could think of anything else.

"Very good," the earl said, satisfied. "Someone will inquire from time to time as to the direction of your thinking."

That was when Sophie understood that she would not be leaving her bedchamber anytime soon.

The widow Sawyer was apprised of Eastlyn's presence in her home as she was making preparations to leave for a ride in the park. It was rather late in the afternoon for such an outing, but she had it on good authority that the Viscount Dunsmore often made his way along the shaded paths at this hour, and Mrs. Sawyer was of a desire to make his acquaintance. Eastlyn, however, could not be gotten rid of if he was not prepared to go, and he had already been informed that she was at home. To punish him for the effrontery of calling upon her without notice of his intention, Mrs. Sawyer decided he should cool his heels in her drawing room while she exchanged her riding habit for more suitable attire.

The ruby silk was chosen specifically because she knew he admired her in jewel-toned colors that offset her ebon hair and white skin. Her maid carefully redressed her hair with ivory combs so that the loose strands around her face softened her features with their casual disarray. She wore silk stockings, red leather slippers, and no jewelry except for tiny pearl studs in her ears. She pronounced herself ready to see him after dabbing her throat and the pulse points of her wrists with rose water.

Eastlyn stood upon her entry to the drawing room. He noticed that she paused on the threshold long enough to be attractively framed in the doorway. He had always been diverted by these entrances of hers, though kind enough not to say so. She would not have found his amusement in any way complimentary of her efforts. He waited patiently for her to disengage herself from the affected pose and appreciated the view as she intended he should.

"Annette," he said by way of greeting. "You are looking well."

One dark eyebrow rose. "Only well? I meant to look delicious. Tell me, have I failed?" She closed the door behind her and crossed the room, offering her hand to him. She knew he would not refuse the overture. His reliable manners were the chink in his armor. She watched his lips touch her knuckles, and the sight of it, more than the act itself, caused the most delicate sensation to ripple down the length of her spine.

"You are exquisite," he said, meaning it. "As always." But delicious? he wondered. No, it was not an adjective he would ever associate with her. It implied a certain warmth that was not in her nature, not that he had been bothered overmuch by the lack. But delicious he knew, and it was a buttered scone. Annette was a petit four.

She made a small curtsey, pleased by his compliment but careful not to preen. "Won't you sit?" she asked, gesturing to the sofa. "Shall I pour you a drink? I still have the whiskey you like."

Eastlyn passed the sofa in favor of the wing chair. "Nothing, thank you. I do not intend to remain long. You are, after all, under another man's protection."

Annette sat and smoothed the splash of scarlet silk across her lap. "Yes," she said. "I am. I wondered if you knew. It is not at all the done thing for you to visit me. It is Lord Brownlee who has set me up, and he is reckoned as a superior marksman."

"I have spoken to Brownlee," East said. "I found him taking an early supper at White's." He took what was perhaps an immoderate amount of satisfaction in seeing he had surprised Annette. "He will not countenance a lengthy interview, but when I explained my purpose he was most amenable."

"I see."

"I wonder if you do, Annette. I cannot help but notice that you have not wished me happy. With so many other people it is the first thing to cross their lips after the usual courtesies are concluded. Is it that you do *not* wish me happy or that you know very well that there is no engagement?"

"It is rather awkward, isn't it, for me to express felicitations on the news of your engagement? We were intimates, after all. Perhaps I have fonder memories of our liaison than you do. I can admit to harboring the green-eyed monster."

Eastlyn gave her full marks for schooling her features, and her eyes, far from being shaded with the green cast of jealousy, were an unusually clear shade of gray. "You chose to look elsewhere for your bread and butter, Annette. I made no demands to that effect."

She shrugged. "If you say so, Gabriel. Perhaps I misread the handwriting on the wall."

East leaned back in his chair and tapped the tips of his steepled fingers together. "I want you to do nothing else to perpetuate the rumor you began," he said flatly. "You will not involve yourself in gossip about Lady Sophia Colley, either by giving it your passive support because you have listened to it, or by your active participation. I care not at all what you choose to say about me. Tell what truths you know or what lies you can imagine, it is of no importance. But hear me well, Annette, I will not subscribe to you using an innocent to get some of your own back."

Annette fanned herself with her hand. "My! I had no idea you were given to such heated discourse, Gabriel. Would that you had shown the same passion in my bed."

Eastlyn caught himself before he made an ill-considered reply. There was nothing to be gained by permitting their exchange to become a critique of his sexual prowess—or the lack of it, if she was to be believed. Neither would he turn the tables. Finding fault with her performance after so long an absence from her bed was boorish. Perhaps the most unkind thing he could say about her accomplishments between the sheets was that she was exquisite, not delicious. He doubted that she would have the good sense to be offended.

When East made no reply, Annette lowered her hand to her lap. "Really, Gabriel, are you accusing me of creating a fictitious engagement for you? And with Lady Sophia Colley? She is not your taste at all. Who would believe me?"

"Most of the ton."

"I think not, but what can it matter? You have never cared what they think. Indeed, did you not just invite me to say anything about you that I wished? I really do not understand you."

"I care what they think of Lady Sophia. She will be made to look foolish when it is revealed there is no engagement."

Annette made a dismissive gesture. "Then marry her. That will still wagging tongues, and I suspect it will be agreeable to Lady Winslow."

If Eastlyn had been discomfited by discussing his former mistress with his mother, that unhappy state was increased tenfold by the prospect of discussing his mother with his former mistress. He wisely chose to avoid it. "May I have your word, Annette, that you will cease to use Lady Sophia in such a poor way?"

"Hardly, Gabriel. Giving my word would be tantamount to admitting I bear some responsibility in this matter. I assure you, I do not. You can accept that or not, but it is all I am willing to offer."

"I had hoped you would be reasonable."

"I believe I am."

Eastlyn could not imagine that more could be accomplished here. Annette's position was firmly held, and he did not think she would give ground. This standing fast made him think of Sophie and her equally flat refusal to be swayed by his presentation of the facts. For reasons he did not care to examine too closely, that thought made him smile.

"You are amused," Annette said wryly. "Pray, is it something you can share?"

"No, not at all. I do not believe you would understand." It was not an entirely fair assessment since he did not understand it himself.

"That smile is the very worst thing about you, Gabriel. The amusement that no one else is privy to. It is annoying in the extreme."

"It is perhaps just as well, then, that you realized so long ago that we do not suit."

"Yes."

He thought she might have caught the tip of her tongue on the word, so sharply did she bite it off. "You never cared for my friends," he said, goading her to draw blood this time.

"I do not suppose you thought to level your accusations at their heads. Any one of them is a more likely candidate to start such a rumor than I am. I imagine Mr. Marchman would find it entertaining to see you squirm under the pressure of an impending marriage."

"West did indeed have a laugh at my expense. Northam also. Southerton, I believe, choked on it."

"He recovered?"

"Yes."

"Pity."

One of East's brows kicked up. "The gloves are off, I collect. No matter. I like you better this way, Annette. It is infinitely more entertaining when you say what you think. The tolerance you affected for my benefit must have been wearing."

She regarded him coolly. "You cannot imagine."

He smiled slightly and got to his feet. "Oh, but perhaps I can." As a parting shot it had the sure aim of one of his pistol balls. Eastlyn was already streetside when he heard the unmistakable tinkling sounds of shattering glass. He imagined the delicate porcelain figurines that populated the mantel in Annette's drawing room had become the latest victims of her temper.

* * *

Sophie closed her journal and placed it on the bedside table. She had written very little this evening and only marginally more the night before. She could not ignore the fact that with the passing of each day in confinement her concentration suffered.

Gutting the candle stub in its dish, Sophie slipped lower into the bed and turned on her side. She slid one arm under her pillow so her head was raised at just the right angle to appreciate the starshine. The drapes had been deliberately left parted so she could enjoy this view, and tonight there was but a slim crescent of a moon to detract from the stars.

It was an old habit of hers to count the number visible at her window, a nighttime ritual she had once enjoyed with her father. If she closed her eyes, Sophie could imagine the depression in the mattress as he sat on the edge of the bed and held her hand. His warmth was almost tangible. And the scent of him . . . tobacco and peppermint . . . If she breathed hardly at all, it would come to her, and she would be comforted.

The ache at the back of her throat, that lump of unshed tears, was not so easy to ignore. She swallowed hard and blinked rapidly and assuaged herself with the brilliance of the light that for a moment seemed to collect into a single beam of remarkable beauty.

A month had passed since she had been permitted to leave her room. Thirty days. She knew because she had marked each one in her journal, sometimes convinced that it was only this simple ritual that kept her from going mad. It occurred to her that she could not decide which description of the passing of time seemed shorter, thirty days or a month, and it suddenly was important that she make that distinction. The waste of even a single day was appalling to her; this confinement of a month had been nearly unendurable.

Sophie knuckled her eyes, and her vision cleared. She stared at the window again and the stars framed in it.

"How many do you see, Sophie?" her father would ask.

"Fourteen."

"As many as that, eh? I did not know you could count so high."

In time she had learned to count much higher, and if she exaggerated the number she could see from her bedchamber, her father never called her to task for it.

"Which one are you, Sophie?" he would say.

"Just there, Papa. At the corner of the sky."

Her father would bend his head and search for the same view of her star as she had. "And so you are. What do you see from there?"

"All of heaven."

"And what do you see from here?"

"The same, Papa."

"Then heaven is everywhere," her father said.

"I think it must be," Sophie whispered. "It was very good of God to make it so."

She remembered how her father had smiled then, the bitter-sweet nature of that particular placement of his lips, like a man who had known perfect joy once and had not the hope of knowing it again.

Sophie did not think she had yet achieved the same depth of melancholia that she had observed in her father. It was his companion every day of his life that she could recall and was always more noticeable to her when he was being most determinedly happy. No, she had not reached that same sad place, but she thought it was in sight.

Self-pity did not sit well on her shoulders, but neither was it effortless to shrug off. Sophie considered that Tremont might be correct when he had announced again today that she was unconscionably selfish. The earl had convinced himself that she could change the family's fortunes through a well-made marriage to a generous husband. Sophie could no longer deny that what he was proposing was not as disagreeable as it had been. Not that the generous husband should be the Marquess of Eastlyn; she could not countenance that. Still, if she were to permit Tremont to make her a suitable match, someone who was not the marquess, would it really be a surrender of her very self?

She was losing her resolve, she realized. It was slipping away, taking the same course as her concentration. She would never be as brave as she wanted to be. It was not hard to fool herself into believing she had the courage of her convictions when her convictions weren't challenged. She had been so full of herself for turning away Eastlyn, not for the refusal precisely, but for what it would prove about her principles to Tremont and Harold. Now, a mere month of being confined to her room had shown her how unremarkable her stand against the marquess had been. Tremont had announced two days ago that she would be returning to the country with him. No doubt there was a genial squire nearby, comfortably plump in the pockets, someone the earl had determined would do for the nonce.

Sophie settled more deeply against her pillow. There were twenty-four stars framed in her window. Somehow she had managed to count them while contemplating her inevitable capitulation. It was distressingly clear to her that the attempt to divert her thoughts had not been successful. She missed walking in the park with the children and taking them to the bookseller's. She missed going downstairs for breakfast and quieting Robert and Esme as they swung their legs hard enough to make the table shake. She had even come to miss Abigail's nervous chatter while reading the *Gazette* and Harold's long-suffering sighs while he hid behind it.

Her visitors had been Tremont and Harold. They never lingered long, and they rarely argued. It was as if they recognized she gathered her resolve by fighting theirs. The less they pressed, the more she felt like giving in.

The stars beckoned her, and she searched out the one that would be her view from afar, the one that would open up the heavens to her when that aspect from her room was not so clear.

One. Two. *Ping.* Three. *Ping. Ping.* Four. Five. Six. *Ping.*

Sophie sat up and cocked her head to one side to catch the origin of the sound. *Ping. Ping. Ping.* She scooted to the edge of the bed as a shower of gravel from the garden path bounced off the window. Hurrying from the bed, Sophie threw open the sash and ducked to avoid the next scattering of shot from below.

"I beg your pardon."

There was no mistaking that voice, and in any event there was also that smile. Eastlyn's teeth gleamed whitely. Sophie stared down at him, transfixed. Several moments passed before she collected she should say something. "What are you doing here?"

"Enjoying your garden."

"It is gone midnight."

"Much later. Did I wake you?"

She shook her head. "You must go." Her whisper was husky with urgency. "You will wake everyone."

"You are the only one with a room at the rear. And Tremont and Dunsmore are gone from the house. No one will hear unless you raise the alarm. Are you going to raise the alarm?"

"No." There was no point in lying. She thought he was the sort of man who would know a lie for what it was. Sophie wondered about the earl and Harold. She had not known they were not at home. It seemed odd that Eastlyn should be privy to that fact when she was not. "I should like it if you would leave, just the same."

"I want to speak with you."

"You are."

"Privately."

"Here? In my room?"

"In the house. I promise that I require only a few minutes of your time. The drawing room will be suitable. It doesn't have to be in your bedchamber."

It did, though, because she couldn't move herself anywhere else. "I cannot let you in."

"I will let myself in."

Sophie hesitated. His presence here below her window

was so out of the common mode that she had no way to make sense of it. Thus far he had refrained from calling her his fair Juliet. She counted that as a good thing. "Very well," she said. "But you will have—" She stopped because he had already disappeared.

Sophie closed the window and secured it. A piece of gravel lodged itself under her bare foot, and she swore softly at the inconvenience of it. She lighted the lamp on her writing desk and carried it with her to the adjoining dressing room, carefully avoiding the stones that still littered her carpet.

She slipped into her robe, belted the sash, and was on the point of lacing her slippers when she heard the door handle to her room being turned. It did not seem possible to her that he had come so far in such a short time. Electing to forego the slippers, Sophie went quickly to the door. He must have sensed her presence because there was a pause in the turn of the handle.

The first full twist did not give Eastlyn entry but proved to him the door was locked. It required less than a full minute with the proper picks to make it turn effortlessly in his hand. When he pushed open the door, Sophie was there waiting for him. He stepped inside when she beckoned him and closed the door quietly. The lamp bobbled in her hand so that shadow chased light across the wall and ceiling.

Eastlyn pocketed his picks and leaned one shoulder casually against the door. He studied her face in the flickering light. "I think, Lady Sophia, that you had better explain to me why you are a prisoner in your own home."

Chapter Four

"A prisoner?" Sophie asked. She surprised herself by having the wherewithal to remain calm. "That is a rather dramatic description, don't you think?"

East decided then that he would not be moved off course by a question of semantics. He took the lamp from Sophie's hand and crossed the room to set it on her writing desk. He noticed the open journal and the neat copperplate hand but did not permit his eyes to linger on the exposed pages. Instead, he turned away, and lest he be accused of prying, chose the fireplace to make his stand. "Your door was locked to me."

Sophie offered a slim, ironic smile. "Never say I am the first woman to deny you entry to her bedchamber. In the event you discover your luck has turned in this regard, you must endeavor to take it on the chin, m'lord."

He thought he might actually like to shake her. She was not precisely defiant in her manner and posture, but her degree of self-possession in these unusual circumstances was something to be reckoned with. It begged the obvious question. "Do you have many visitors to your room at this hour?"

It was his sincere curiosity that kept Sophia from taking offense, though she did not deign to answer it. "Why are you here? You promised you needed but a few minutes of my time."

Eastlyn ignored her. "It is only that you remain all of a piece," he said. "Composure of the sort you are showing me now is not so easy to affect. Either you are an actress of considerable skill, the very equal of Miss India Parr, say, or these conditions are not unfamiliar to you and your preternatural calm is the result of experience."

Sophie's features remained perfectly serene. "There is a third possibility, m'lord."

"Oh? I should like to hear it."

"You must consider that I am calm because I *am* calm. I have not an excitable nature."

Eastlyn pretended to consider this, pausing a beat before announcing his own view. "No. That is definitely not the way of it here."

She blinked. "I beg your pardon?"

Leaning his shoulder against the mantel, East crossed his arms in front of his chest and regarded Sophie thoughtfully. Her face was bathed in the golden glow of the lamp. The light brightened the halo of her wild honey hair and softened the definition of her cheekbones and the line of her nose. "I entertained just such an opinion of you upon our first introduction," he said. "You were so lacking in animation on that occasion that one could be forgiven for overlooking you among the hothouse flowers. An orchid is a pleasant enough thing to cast one's eyes upon, yet one does weary of so much still perfection."

Sophie was quite certain that if he were not making her dizzy with his reasoning, she would have the resources to be insulted. Her eyes widened marginally as she absorbed his observation.

Eastlyn's chin came up slightly to indicate the window and the garden beyond it. "But on the occasion of our meeting there," he said, "I was persuaded that you have more to recommend you than the otherworldly beauty of a cultivated flower. I am not mistaken, am I, Lady Sophia? Your nature is

not in any way as composed as you would have me think."
He chuckled softly when she merely continued to stare at
him, neither challenge nor surrender in her eyes. "You must
go on as you see fit, of course, but as for convincing me that
you are so imperturbable, you should know it is unlikely that
I will ever come to believe it."

Sophie was silent for several long moments. Her eyes
strayed to the window, then measured the distance back to
where Eastlyn stood so casually at her fireplace. He was
making no effort to temper his grin as he clearly interpreted
the gist of her thoughts. She sighed. "I would do it, you know.
Toss you out on your ear if I could decide how it might be
managed. Then there is the matter of keeping you out. It is
significantly more problem than I can apply myself to at the
moment. This is not at all the usual thing."

Eastlyn's soft chuckle did nothing to settle Sophie's
nerves. Belatedly she realized she had answered the question
he had put to her, admitting in a rather backhanded fashion
that she was more actress than unruffled by natural disposition, and that entertaining visitors in her bedchamber was in
no way a common occurrence.

"Come," Eastlyn said. "Won't you sit? There is no reason
why you should not be comfortable."

There was every reason, Sophie thought, and the marquess was clearly a bedlamite for pretending it was otherwise. Still, she dropped like a stone into the chair that was
pressing at the back of her knees. She noticed he did not
seek out a seat for himself, although her room offered him
the spindle-backed chair at her writing desk or the bed. Both
choices would have made further conversation awkward, the
writing desk because her back would have been to him, and
the bed . . . well, because it was her bed.

Sophie pressed the sash of her robe between her index
and middle fingers, laying out the ribbon of cool silk on her
lap. "You promised me," she reminded him. "A few minutes
only."

"Yes," he said. In truth, he thought he would be gone by

now, but her locked room had startled him and immediately presented a different line of questioning. "But first, I want to know why your door was locked."

"The most obvious answer is that I reconsidered the wisdom of letting you in and locked it myself."

"You might have reconsidered your invitation," he said, "but the rest of your obvious answer is a fabrication."

She flushed a little but held her gaze steady.

Eastlyn thought Lady Sophia might make a worthy opponent at cards if it were not that dissembling raised a pale wash of color in her cheeks. He called her bluff. "Produce the key."

Sophie shrugged lightly. "I merely presented you with an obvious answer, m'lord, not necessarily the factual one."

East's eyes narrowed slightly. "Sophie."

She was startled when he addressed her so familiarly. It was the custom of her family to give a full accounting of all three syllables of her given name, as though the diminutive were common or vulgar. Coming from Eastlyn, it sounded nothing of the sort. She shied away from describing it as intimate and settled for the less threatening term of friendly. Still, she was not disposed to give ground. "The condition of the door does not concern you, and as it presented you with so little an obstacle, it can be of no consequence."

He was having none of it. "You have been nowhere in society since we spoke in your garden. By my count it has been more than a month. I believe that represents a withdrawal of some proportions, even for you."

"How can you possibly make such a statement when you have made it abundantly clear that I have never been one to draw your attention? You have not the least notion of how often I appeared in society."

East hesitated, wondering what he should tell her. In the end he decided upon the truth, believing no sacrifice was made by it. "I have since learned something of your habits," he said, "and I know it has been almost your daily practice to take Dunsmore's children walking. In the past you also accompanied Dunsmore and the viscountess to dinner parties or poetry salons. You were occasionally seen at Almack's or in the audience at the Drury Lane Theatre."

Sophia's lush lips flattened into a thin, disapproving line, and her eyes became markedly cooler. "You will understand that I am not complimented by your interest."

"It is one of the few things I *do* understand, and I apologize for discomfiting you; however, the inquiry was made necessary when you simply disappeared."

"Not attending a reading of Byron's verse or choosing to entertain the children indoors is not the same as disappearing."

Eastlyn made a slight bow of his head. "I stand corrected."

"In making your inquiries, your lordship must have learned that I was most often called upon to round out the numbers at dinner parties or that I went to the theater with Lady Dunsmore when Harold was unavailable. That I have not been out these past weeks has everything to do with Abigail's poor health and a dearth of invitations. You mayhap thought it was in aid of avoiding you?"

"What I think is that you would rather give me the cut direct. It is the sort of thing done better with an audience so it would not behoove you to avoid me." He watched Sophie fold the sash of her robe lengthwise and begin pressing the crease between her thumb and forefinger. "I am teasing, Sophie. I do not flatter myself that you have given me a moment's thought since I last took your leave." His slight smile faded, and his expression matched hers for gravity. "For my own part," he said, "I have been gone again from London, so I was not immediately aware of your absence. You might have heard that my friend Northam was recently married."

"I had not." The depth of the isolation to which she had been subjected struck her anew. "Surely that is good news."

Eastlyn was slow to comment. "Yes," he said finally. "I think it is."

Sophie raised one eyebrow, waiting for the rest of his

thoughts on the matter of his friend's marriage. It seemed to her that Eastlyn was a man most uncertain of its wisdom.

"It happened very quickly," he told her, feeling his way. He had no wish to perpetuate the gossip surrounding North's hasty marriage to Lady Elizabeth Penrose. He judged that Sophia was unlikely to repeat anything he might tell her, but he felt vaguely disloyal to Northam in putting the entire truth before her. "A love match, they say. They should deal well together."

"Aaah." Sophie did not point out the incongruency between his words and his delivery of them. "A love match is always to be desired."

East frowned a little at the suggestion of sarcasm in her tone. Unsure whether he was asking her or making a statement of fact, he said, "You don't believe that."

"Of course I do. I am a romantic, m'lord."

The ironic inflection was still in her tone, and East was not a whit closer to comprehending her true sentiments. "I like Lady Elizabeth," he said, "and I know North will do well by her."

"Lady Elizabeth?"

"Penrose," he said. "Do you know her?"

"We have been introduced." Sophie did not add that given Eastlyn's estimation of her social aptitude, she was hardly likely to have made a lasting impression. To say so would merely have pointed out how much his comment had stung. "A dinner party at the baron's house in town was the occasion. I believe she is often in the company of Lord and Lady Battenburn. I would like to think your friend is most fortunate. There is much to recommend her."

"Indeed," East said. "She is a bruising rider."

"Yes, of course. That is of paramount importance in choosing a bride." The fact that Elizabeth Penrose rode at all surprised Sophia, though she did not reveal it. Elizabeth's gait was quite uneven owing to some accident, the origins of which Sophie had been too polite to inquire about. "I must point out, m'lord, that I am not." She caught his mild confusion.

"A bruising rider, that is. I can hold my seat, but I have been told my form is unconventional."

East took that information in stride. That she was bent on showing herself in the poorest of light was still more intriguing than tiring. "North and his lady were married at the Battenburn estate," he said. "I returned to witness their union and then remained away for several days to attend to some personal affairs."

"There is no reason you should explain this to me. I was not making inquiries of my own."

All too aware of how Sophie could distract him from his purpose, East ignored her comment. "In my absence there were at least two invitations extended most specifically to you," he said. "I had nothing to do with either; indeed, I only learned of them upon my return. It is my understanding that you refused both." While the colonel had kept his word not to make any overtures, his mother had not shown similar restraint. Not only had she put forth an invitation to Lady Sophia, but she had enlisted South's mother to do the same. The Dowager Countess of Northam might have been persuaded to follow with a third if not for the inconvenience of her own son's wedding. "I can accept that you refused my proposal for sound reasons, but to decline the invitations of my mother and her friend was not what I expected of you."

"What should I have done, m'lord? To answer them favorably would have merely given more credence to the rumor. I did not think it wise to be seen at your mother's home. It would have been the same with Lady Redding. Everyone would know what prompted the invitation. How could I know you would not be there, and really, what difference would it have made? People would be moved to make too much of my visit."

"Then it was your choice?"

She nodded. She had been roundly lectured for her obstinacy in declining the invitations, but Tremont had not been able to force her to give any other answer. It had been early yet in her confinement, and Sophie was not at all certain she would respond in the same manner if Lady Winslow or her friend were prepared to ask again.

Eastlyn studied Sophie's serene countenance, looking for any faint shift that might indicate that all was not as it seemed. "You are well?"

"Yes."

He could not dispute her words. She appeared in good health, though perhaps paler than he remembered. It was difficult to tell in the lamplight. "Then why have you not been away from home?"

"I do not choose to be."

"I do not understand why your door was locked. It seems as though someone means to keep you in."

"I cannot say. You woke me from a sound sleep. Perhaps Harold always locks the door when he is gone from home. I shall ask him, m'lord, though of a certainty if he takes such a precaution, it is for my protection."

Eastlyn's gaze dropped to her hand. The sash was neatly pressed now, the crease as permanent as if it had been put to a hot iron. East uncrossed his arms and straightened. "I do not think I believe you, Lady Sophia."

She didn't flinch. "That is your prerogative."

"I think you are being punished."

"I have no means to persuade you otherwise."

East pushed away from the wall and came to stand just a foot in front of her. "Stand up."

The long line of Sophie's throat was vulnerably extended as she lifted her eyes. Standing now would put her toe-to-toe with him. "I am comfortable, thank you."

"I did not ask after your comfort. Stand up." When she gave no indication that she meant to obey, East leaned over, grasped her by her elbows, and hauled Sophie easily to her feet. "Show me your arms."

Beneath her, it was as if the floor was shifting. A tremor started in her toes and worked its way up her frame. "I don't—"

East's grip fell from her elbows to her wrists. He raised

her arms so the silken sleeves of her robe fell backward. The light was too poor for him to see properly, but the faint markings on her forearms made him want a closer look. He released her to get the lamp, and when he turned around Sophie was hugging herself tightly. He regarded her resolve and said equably, "If you scream, it is almost a certainty we will be married within a sennight."

"I most assuredly will not scream."

"Good." He approached with the lamp and held it at the proper angle for inspection. "Show me your left arm."

What she did was show him her right hook. It caught the hard edge of Eastlyn's jaw before he could dodge it, and the contact of knuckle and bone made a surprisingly solid sound in the quiet room. East managed to hold onto the lamp long enough to set it down on the writing desk. In almost the same motion he clamped his hand hard over Sophie's open mouth.

"You said you wouldn't scream," he whispered against her ear. Her reply was muffled by his palm, and East carefully lifted his hand a fraction. It was just enough for her to gasp, and Eastlyn could not properly temper his smile when he saw the tears in her eyes. "Hurt your hand, did it?"

She nodded.

"If it's a consolation to you, it was not without discomfort for me."

Discomfort? Sophie wanted to *howl* with the pain of it. She tried to shake her hand out, but the movement brought her fingers in contact with Eastlyn's hard thigh. The pain became a tingling that she felt all the way to her toes. The sensation was worse than her jammed knuckles, and she was suddenly completely still and thoroughly mortified.

"Here. Permit me to see." East turned her in his arms and lifted her hand for his inspection. He simultaneously worked his jaw from side to side.

In spite of his words, Sophie saw that he was indifferent to both her assaults. The solid punch and the accidental touch, neither were of import to him, and except for the slight flexing of his jaw, he appeared immune. Distracted by this realization, and not a little in awe of it, Sophie lent herself to his examination. By the time she realized it was more than her hand he was in want of seeing, it was too late. Her arm, below and above her elbow, was being scrutinized. The bruises were not so faint in better light, and with their telltale shape and the distance separating them, there was but one conclusion.

"Tremont?" Eastlyn asked.

"No."

"Dunsmore." He did not make it a question this time. East continued to study her arm and saw evidence that the most recent bruises were not the only ones. He doubted that any he could see were even the first. "The viscount has a penchant for treating you roughly."

Sophie shrugged lightly, not because it was of no consequence to her but because it was.

Eastlyn frowned. "Why, Sophie?"

"Because I am unreasonable, I suppose." She did not look at East now, but kept her eyes averted. "And disagreeable."

"You are both those things," he said, matter-of-fact.

Sophie's face lifted sharply, and her mouth parted, though speech deserted her.

She really had a very lovely mouth, Eastlyn thought, and there would be precious few opportunities to kiss it. He bent his head quickly and touched his lips to hers. She stared at him, perfectly wide-eyed as he did so. It made him smile, this look of naked astonishment, and the tip of his tongue tickled the underside of her lip as he straightened. He thought she might have leaned into him as they separated, mayhap reluctant to end the kiss. "You are shockingly impractical," he whispered, cupping her chin. "And of such a singular intelligence that you are bound to be made irritable by the impoverished minds around you. Even so, it is insufficient reason for you to be mauled."

Sophie could still sense the shape of his mouth on hers, and the urge was upon her to raise one hand to her lips to keep it there. He should not have done that, she thought, and then to follow it up, not with endearments or an apology, but with an accounting of her shortcomings (though an incomplete list), well, it was truly the outside of enough. The full effect was to render her speechless.

"I will speak to Dunsmore," East said. "It can—"

"No!"

"No?"

She supposed Eastlyn was unused to being opposed. "No. You mustn't." Lest there was any misunderstanding, Sophie shook her head for emphasis. "It cannot help but make things worse. You would not approve of interference in your affairs; it is the same for Harold."

"I am not in the practice of abusing women. Protection is one's duty to them, not rough treatment. If I were engaged in the latter, I hope someone would feel compelled to set me on a better course."

"You are muddled in the upperworks, though I don't suppose you can help it. It seems to be part and parcel of a chivalrous code. Like any knight, you are bent on making the noble rescue and have not asked if the right thing will be the most helpful thing. Oh, pray do not cock that eyebrow at me in just that superior manner. I am giving you the benefit of my singular intelligence, and your impoverished mind would be improved by listening." Having said this, she raised one honey-colored eyebrow and mirrored his rather lofty expression of moments ago. Eastlyn was no longer arrogant, but something approaching amused.

"If you were to speak to Harold," Sophie went on, "how would you explain coming by your knowledge? If you merely reported to him that you have my word of what was done to me, he would counter that I was given to exaggeration, or more likely, that it was an outright falsehood. If you give him the evidence of your own eyes, he will naturally want to discover how such a thing was possible. He believes that we last spoke a month ago. I think you will agree that it is better he remains under that misapprehension."

Eastlyn might have rocked back on his heels if he were given to such overt expressions of surprise. Years of negotiations and diplomacy had taught him that little was gained by putting his every emotion on display. "But I don't agree," he said calmly. His words had the effect of moving Sophie a fraction off her toes. She had not his years of experience to fall back on. "From my perspective it seems the surest way to offer the full measure of my protection would be through marriage, and the most certain method of bringing that end about would be to let your cousin know I was here this evening."

Sophie paled as all the blood in her body seemed to pool in her feet, rooting her where she stood. "You would not . . ." But her features showed the full measure of her uncertainty. "Pray, do not . . ." Her voice trailed away when she saw he was unmoved by her distress.

"It begs the question of why you allowed me to come here in the first place."

She frowned, not comprehending his point. "I could not have kept you out, it seems to me. You all but walk through walls."

In other circumstances, Eastlyn would have smiled at this ghostlike description of his skills. Diplomatic missions being what they sometimes were, he had indeed acquired a happy talent for unconventional entry that had served him well. "I asked permission to come inside," he reminded her, "and you gave it."

"You were standing below my window, conducting yourself in a manner that was certain to draw attention to the both of us." Her tone was pitched with exasperation now. "You cannot put me between Scylla and Charybdis and pretend I could have made a better choice."

The sound that came from Eastlyn's throat was something between strangled laughter and a suppressed cough. Between Scylla and Charybdis was precisely how Northam and South had described his predicament when they first learned of the engagement. The allusion still held, East thought, because his former mistress was much in the way Southerton saw her: *a seething whirlpool, the kind of female monster that could suck a man into her vortex and—*"

"Are you all right?" Sophie asked. "Shall I fetch you a glass of water?"

East raised his hand, indicating that such was not necessary, though he could not quite gather words. He was recalling how Southerton had expanded his point, as he often did, in spite of East's protests that he was familiar with Homer. "*And Scylla . . . Wasn't she a nymph or something equally naughty before her appearance was changed?*" North, naturally enough, had been moved to offer his opinion: "*It does seem more fitting that Lady Sophia should be Scylla.*" They had stopped their ribbing only when he removed the pistol from behind his back and threatened to shoot them both.

A pity he could not make the same threat now. "I will take that glass of water, if you please," he said instead.

Sophie removed herself to her dressing room where she poured fresh water from the porcelain pitcher on the washstand. Thinking the marquess did not know his own mind, Sophie nevertheless did not give him a piece of hers. She handed over the glass and watched him carefully as he drank, afraid he might come to choke again. When he had downed the last of it, she removed the glass from his hand and set it on her writing desk. "Better?" she asked.

"Infinitely. Thank you." He could not explain where his thoughts had taken flight. Lady Sophia did not strike him as one who would appreciate South's depiction of her as a nymph turned monster. In point of fact, he knew of no woman who would. It was the sort of observation best kept between men, he decided. There were so few secrets left to safeguard from women, it seemed prudent that this should be one of them.

"You will say nothing to Harold?" Sophie asked. "It shall be our secret?"

For a moment Eastlyn believed Sophie had plumbed his mind and plucked his last thought. "Secret?" he repeated in want of a moment to tidy his thinking. "Oh, yes. Yes, of course, I will say nothing to Dunsmore now, though you cannot depend upon my discretion always."

Afraid he would renege immediately, Sophie did not press for a more thorough promise than the one he gave her. She nodded faintly in acceptance.

Eastlyn knew she was in expectation of him leaving, but he was not done. "I would have the truth, Sophie, from your own lips. You are being confined here, are you not? A punishment, perhaps, for refusing my proposal?"

She hesitated, uncertain what she wanted to tell him that he had not already concluded on his own. "It is a confinement," she said, "but not precisely a punishment. More an attempt at coercion. My cousins think that you will still be amenable to marriage if I can be made to change my opinion of it."

"I see. And your opinion now is . . . ?"

Sophie knew she could not afford to show the slightest indecision. No matter that this last month spent almost entirely by herself had weakened her resolve, if she communicated this to Eastlyn, he would bring his own pressure to bear. Her defenses were not impregnable against so many assaults. "I am unchanged," she said. "A marriage between us would not suit. Any pretense of an engagement to satisfy the wags is unnecessary. I hope you will not concern yourself with my confinement. It is soon to be at an end. The earl is returning to Tremont Park, and I am to go with him. It will be a good change for me to rusticate in the country. If I am confined there, at least it will be on hundreds of acres."

Eastlyn had heard nothing about Tremont's plans to return to his country home and wondered if he could believe Sophie's assertion. Because of North's wedding and the necessity of returning to Battenburn, East had not yet taken Colonel Blackwood's assignment fully in hand. While he had studied the East India Company's proposal of a Singapore settlement, and spoken to several representatives from the Company, he had not arranged to meet with either Helmsley or Barlough. He had put off speaking to Tremont because of the man's desire to see Sophia married for financial gain; it was certain to be a factor in negotiations. The meeting, however, with the prime minister had proceeded well enough, with Liverpool reiterating to Eastlyn what the colonel had said: the settlement was a most desired outcome for the Crown.

But Sophie in the country? East thought. He was not as reassured by this turn of events as he considered he should be. It had been rather foolish of him, he supposed, but his imagination had been wandering in Sophie's direction upon seeing North and Elizabeth exchange vows. He had not been made so feeble-minded by the ceremony that he shared his thinking with anyone. There would have been wagers made immediately, and Eastlyn decided he should spare Sophie becoming the subject of one. Although the amounts the Compass Club risked were always absurdly small, they took the ventures if not quite seriously, then with humor that had a competitive edge.

"You will be gone long?" East asked for want of something better to say.

"I don't know. I expect Tremont will cast his net for other suitors."

"A landed gentleman, mayhap," East said, careful to keep sarcasm out of his tone. "No title, but income from rents to spare."

Sophie's eyes darted away. She nodded briefly and found that she was suddenly hugging herself as though cold. "You have always known, then, that it was about finances."

"It came to my attention, yes."

Sophie imagined the queue to inform Eastlyn had organized itself quickly. She wondered who had been at the forefront. Tremont had done a credible job of keeping the state of the family finances a private matter, but there were always people who knew the truth, and people who took particular relish in repeating what they thought they knew. "You can comprehend that from Tremont's perspective it is a desirable match."

"You have said as much before," East reminded her. "And you offer it as if it excuses his behavior. It does not. Your confinement here is every bit his doing. Dunsmore is nothing if not a dutiful son."

Sophie had no reply to that. She was not in disagreement with his assertion.

"Will you be safe there?"

"I am safe here," Sophie said softly.

Eastlyn looked pointedly at her left arm which was once again covered by the silken sleeve of her robe. "Your definition of what is safe is in want of revision."

Sophie glanced at the mantel clock. "Even by the most generous interpretation of taking but a few minutes of my time, you have overstayed your welcome."

East acknowledged her point with a slim smile. "Touché."

"Will you leave by the usual route or do you prefer a window exit?"

"The door will do."

She nodded, stepping aside, her arms still crossed in front of her.

East studied her for a long moment. Resolve set nicely on her face, defining the slim line of her jaw and the unwavering brightness of her wild honey eyes. Her lower lip protruded slightly, not in a way that gave her a soft pouty look, but in a manner that lifted her chin and firmed her position. The faint lift of a single arching eyebrow and the fractional tilt of her head completed the picture that was at once as determined as it was provocative.

East supposed there were an infinite number of choices available to him, but only one that would not leave him with regrets. It was probably true that her sweet mouth would always tempt him now that he knew the taste of it, and equally likely that another kiss would never be enough, but Eastlyn decided for better or worse, he wanted another bite of the apple.

"Sophie?"

"Hmm?"

"I am going to kiss you." If she was startled by this intelligence, she did not show it, and Eastlyn did not give her further opportunity. One arm caught her at the small of the back and the other at her nape. He drew her close so that her head was angled toward his, then lowered his mouth to hers.

Like the fruit first offered by Eve, the taste of Sophie's mouth was a feast for the senses. Sweet. Tart. A hint of tang. Warm and honeyed. The suggestion of something like mint. Her lips parted and fashioned their movement in a way that mirrored his, and there was something extraordinarily powerful in teaching her to kiss, for that was precisely what Eastlyn knew he was about.

It was not that Lady Sophia Colley had never been kissed before, but that on so many occasions it had been done inexpertly. Timothy Darrow had been the first when he ran her to ground behind the stable at Tremont Park. She could have raised a hue and cry because he was only a young groom, not yet in his fourteenth year, and she was the daughter of the earl and three years his junior. She had never told a soul how he had pinned her to the rough stone wall and dared her to call for help. He had been angry, of course, and more than a little frightened or he would not have attempted such a transgression. Sophie blamed herself for her predicament because moments before she had been spying on him from the loft. He and Katie Masters had been covered with hay, but not so much of it that she hadn't been able to get her fill of his bare arse pumping up and down between the scullery maid's open thighs. It had not seemed to Sophie that there was an abundance of fun to be had in this sport; but the kissing looked nice enough, and so when Timothy had trapped her, she had permitted him to put his mouth to hers.

She decided then and there she had been wrong about the kissing. It had nothing to recommend it.

Sophie hadn't been kissed again until Harold had done it on the occasion of her thirteenth birthday. They had both heard rumors that there might someday be a match between them, thus uniting the fortunes of the family. That had been when her father still possessed a substantial amount of his wealth and Harold's father had considered the title lost to his descendants if not secured through marriage.

The kiss had been mercifully brief. Harold's tongue had been thick and sour, and Sophie was quite certain she did not want to have it in her mouth again, no matter that he seemed to like the taste of her well enough. When she grew weary of him trailing after her skirts in anticipation of another opportunity, Sophie gave it to him—and drew blood when he tried to thrust his tongue past her bared teeth.

Harold's father had taken her in hand then, but her punishment had not been so terrible as that kiss.

Lord Edymon had taken the liberty of placing his mouth upon hers immediately after his proposal. If Sophie had had any doubts as to their unsuitability, they were put to rest when he ground his lips so hard against her that she winced. Humphrey Bell, her second suitor to come up to snuff, kissed so wetly he created sucking sounds that echoed in Sophie's ears long after she had pushed him away.

Too hard. Too wet. Too loud. Too thick. All of it too silly. The poets were wrong, Sophie had decided. There was no rapture in the ritual, no matter that there were hundreds of sonnets dedicated to the practice.

It was odd, then, that she was reexamining that premise.

If only this kiss had been as brief as the first teasing brush of his lips. Although it had seemed complete enough to her at the time, that kiss had been but a promise. What he was doing to her now was all about fulfilling it.

His mouth worked over hers slowly, as though her lips were a thing to be savored. She felt herself ripening under his gentle assault and never questioned the peculiarity of this being true. There was a heaviness, a swelling in her breasts and a succulence to her open mouth, and the change was alarming; and yet she could not deny that she felt safe.

Eastlyn's embrace kept her steady, but not secure. She sensed the space between them was deliberate, an act of consciousness exercising restraint. It made her aware of him in a way she had not been before, of his strength held in check, of his broad shoulders curved forward to shelter her. He was taller than she, significantly so, and yet it was no strain to reach his mouth, such was his ability to accommodate the disparity in their heights. She did not realize then that he had moved to lean back against her writing desk or that she had come to stand between his slightly splayed thighs. What Sophie knew was that this kiss was effortless, as natural and as thoughtless a response to life as breathing.

She held the front of his open frock coat in her fists, bunching the brushed wool so that creasing was inevitable. He was not so fierce with her. The hand that cradled the back of her head was gentle in its hold. His fingers were threaded through her hair, the pad of each one a separate point of light pressure on her skull. Just below her belted sash, at the curve of hip and bottom, rested his other hand, unmoving, steadying, there to support her when she lost her balance, as she was certain she would.

The heat was unexpected. And the damp. She felt them both in the suck of his mouth and the matching, steady pulse between her thighs. His lips nudged hers softly, taming her response when her breathing grew rough and her heart surged. He feasted on her mouth, tugging on her lower lip, running the tip of his tongue along the sensitive underside, flicking her skin as though capturing sun-drenched droplets of dew.

In the first moments of contact, Sophie's eyes were opened wide and searching, but what followed was an intoxication of the senses, and the soporific effects of East's drugging kiss weighted her lashes and darkened the centers of her eyes. It was sleep, and yet not sleep, the clarity of wakefulness in the unreality of a dream.

She kissed him back, measure for full measure, matching the tension of his mouth, the insistence. There was hunger here, and Sophie had not known she was starving. She sensed urgency for something when she had not realized there was a need. She was unfamiliar with the ache between her thighs or the heaviness that seemed to define the empty space.

Restless, uncertain, she leaned into him. There was the slightest increase in pressure at her back, a suggestion only that she could move closer still. She did, and it was this small movement, and East's deepening kiss, that unwound the tightly coiled spring inside her.

It seemed to her that she became liquid in his arms. The shudder was like a concentric ring of ripples across the surface of a pond, only this tremor had its source somewhere deep inside her. He held her upright because she could not have managed it herself. It was not so easy a thing to remain standing when muscle tone had been replaced by a flood of sensation.

She might have gasped, she thought, but the sound was swallowed by him. He stole her air, leaving her light-headed and heavy-lidded, and helpless in a way that she could not thank him for. Sophie had no name for what had happened to her, but it never entered her thinking that it was outside Eastlyn's experience.

It was, though. To not put too fine a point on it, she had come in his arms, not while they were joined in intimate coupling—which he might have expected—but from naught but kissing. Perhaps it was a very good thing, he decided, that Sophie was confined to her room at No. 14.

East drew back a fraction, kissed her lightly on the lips, rested his forehead against hers, and took a steadying breath. His smile came slowly to the forefront as he straightened completely; his eyes remained watchful. Holding Sophie at a point just below her elbows, he noticed her silk sleeves were no longer cool to the touch, but imbued with her warmth and her scent.

Sophie stared at him. Her lips were damp and remained parted. She sucked in a short, shaky breath and said quietly, "We will not do that again."

Eastlyn heard no demand there, and while her words did not have the inflection of a question, there was the nuance of an appeal. "No," he said. "We will not."

As one slightly dazed, Sophie nodded slowly. "You should leave now."

"I suspect you're right." He made no move to do so, though. How could he? he wondered, when her eyes looked as if they might swallow him whole. "Sophie?"

"Hmm?" The murmur tickled her lips, and she found the sensation almost unbearable. The line of her mouth flattened as she suppressed this last vestige of unexpected pleasure.

East's eyes darted to her mouth. The temptation was to linger there, perhaps kiss her again, but he did not reveal any part of that thought. "You never told me why you permitted me to see you tonight."

Sophie had not anticipated the question would be put to her again. He would not let a thing go, she realized, until he was satisfied on all counts. She suspected he hadn't the capacity for forgetting what was of importance to him and was very likely to bedevil her until he had his answer. "Am I mistaken?" she asked. "Did you not ask to see me?"

"I did."

"Then you wanted me to turn you down?"

"Not at all. I wanted you to see me. I *expected* you to say no."

She nodded. "Well, there you have it, for I am truly weary of doing the expected thing. I have lately come to the lowering realization that I am faint of heart, my lord. No one likes to believe cowardice is a substantial feature of one's character, yet I have had to accept that it is at the very core of my nature. I am now determined to act contrarily. My life cannot help but be changed because of it."

Eastlyn knew himself to be frankly fascinated. He could not have taken his leave just now if Sophie had put his own pistol to his head. "So you have chosen to test your mettle with me?"

She did not answer immediately, but gave the matter some thought. "Yes, I believe I have. Do you find that objectionable?"

There was a distinct possibility, Eastlyn decided, that she might actually render him speechless. Her question had been posed with the utmost sincerity. "I suppose that depends, Lady Sophia, whether I am merely at the forefront of a very long parade to your bedchamber, or if I am the sole participant in the march."

"What an utterly ridiculous thing to say. Did you not just agree that we would not do this again? What can it matter if you are one, or one of many?"

East let her go because it seemed to him she no longer needed his support, and his hands should be free in the event he decided to place them around her neck. "I think I will go now."

Sophie made a small nod of encouragement and hoped that she did not seem too eager. It would be shaming to her if Eastlyn suspected how very close to tears she was. He could not appreciate what it was like to be subjected first to his scrutiny and then to his questions. She had abandoned good sense for adventure when she had agreed to allow him to see her, and she was right that her life was changed for it. It did not follow that he should be privy to all the particulars.

It was her most fervent hope that she would see none of him again.

Eastlyn hesitated a moment more. It was unlike him not to act more decisively, especially on a matter so minor as taking his leave, but something kept him there that was not comfortably defined. He remained where he stood, drawn toward Sophie as a wave was to shore. It required more in the way of resolve than she could ever appreciate not to simply wash over her.

"Good evening, Sophie." Then he was gone.

Tremont Park was built on a gently sloping hill northwest of London. The approach to the Park was long and winding, and the great house was visible on three sides during the circuitous climb. There had been plans drawn up over the years to straighten the road and fashion a more direct route to the Park, but every earl had eventually abandoned the idea. Publicly they cited the cost as reason enough to put the plans to rest. While true that the effort would have been costly, it was more to the point that no one wanted to surrender the privacy of the Park to visitors who were wont to arrive without invitation. From almost every room in the house, except at the rear, one could see the approach of a carriage from as far off as five miles. Armed with a spyglass to help identify the markings on the side of an approaching coach, a succession of earls at Tremont were afforded the opportunity to make their escape. They had managed to avoid creditors, hangers-on, mothers-in-law, and on one notable occasion, the queen's advance guard.

Sophie sat at a small table placed outside for her luncheon. It was covered with a white linen cloth and a gold damask runner. Large tassels hanging from each end of the runner were sufficiently heavy to keep it and the tablecloth in place. A plate of thinly sliced cucumbers and tomatoes had been prepared for her as tiny sandwiches, each one hardly more than a mouthful. Sophie appreciated the effort Mrs. Beale made to present the fare as enticingly as possible, but it was not enough to nudge her appetite. She sipped her tea instead and fed the sandwiches to the birds.

The summer days were shortening now, and September would soon be upon them. Sophie judged there would be few opportunities to sit so comfortably outside while she wrote in her journal. She sat back in the wrought-iron chair and drew her knees up so she could rest her book against them. Sunlight filtered through the umbrella spread of the nearby chestnut tree and dappled the pages. She read what she had written before the interruption of food and drink and found it to be in need of only small revisions.

She tapped the end of the quill against her lips while she considered the wisdom of describing Tremont's blustering at breakfast only that morning. To those looking on, which included only herself and the footmen, the earl had begun the meal in an agreeable state. He had been presented with yesterday's *Gazette* along with his eggs and tomatoes and expressed none of his usual complaints about the news being as stale as the air in the smoking room. He folded the paper neatly into quarters and read while he ate, largely without comment. If there was an occasional grunt, it generally brought a footman to the table to replenish his coffee or offer bacon from the sideboard.

For her part, Sophie had been glad of the quiet. She was most comfortable not drawing attention to herself and would have been content to take her meal in her bedchamber if the earl had not insisted on company. He rarely engaged her in conversation, so Sophie came to understand very quickly that his insistence was about exercising his will over hers, and not because he was seeking her opinion.

The fact, then, that the earl had slapped the paper hard enough on the edge of the table to make it shudder had caused Sophie *and* the footmen to come to attention. Tremont actually came out of his seat. "The bounder!"

Sophie stared at him.

"Jackanapes! We had an agreement!"

There was twisting just below the region of Sophie's heart. She placed the flat of her hand against her mouth as she hiccuped.

Tremont rolled the *Gazette* into a tube and shook it at her. "You will be pleased, I'll wager, for I know you had little liking for him."

Sophie tried not to appear or sound hopeful. "What has happened, my lord?"

"You may very well ask. I would not be at all surprised if it was a scheme concocted between you." The earl rounded the table and tossed the *Gazette* on top of Sophie's plate. "Read for yourself. He has made a fool of me, and if I discover you conspired with him, I will see you turned out of this house."

Sophie carefully lifted the paper and shook bits of egg and tomato seeds from the back side before she attempted to open it.

"And do not think you will be able to apply to my son for help. Harold will not take you in after this further example of your perfidy."

Having no idea in what manner she might have betrayed either of her cousins, Sophie wisely remained silent. She skimmed the paper for the item that had caught Tremont's eye and pushed him dangerously close to apoplexy.

"There!" He poked the offending column with his fingertip when she was slow to discover it. "There! Read what the whoreson has done!"

Sophie read. She read it twice, in fact, just to be certain there was no mistaking the matter. Tremont hovered near her shoulder, his hot breath coming in small gusts as he followed along with her study.

The whoreson, Sophie discovered, had married, and he had done so only two days past. The timing was particularly interesting because the jackanapes had made his vows a mere three days after Sophie had finally agreed to make him a most happy man.

In retrospect, it seemed clear to Sophie that Tremont had been made a good deal happier by her promise to marry than either she or the bounder had been.

Yes, she decided, dipping her pen into the pot of ink. She would put it to paper in just that way.

Chapter Five

Annette Sawyer picked her way carefully through the crush inside Lord Helmsley's salon. She had spied Eastlyn's entrance some thirty minutes earlier but had carefully bided her time. It would never do to seem purposeful in her approach. If Eastlyn did not remark on it, certainly his friends would. They were all with him this evening—or he was with them—one was never sure of the distinction, or if there even was one.

Northam had arrived first, accompanied by his bride of only a few months. They looked well enough together, though the new countess had a regrettable limp which was noticeable in every observation except when she was engaged in a waltz. Mr. Marchman had been announced soon after Northam and his lady, and while he seemed perfectly at his ease in conversation with those around him, Annette knew from her association with Eastlyn that he hid his discomfiture well. Mr. Marchman—she never referred to him as West as Eastlyn and the others were wont to do—kept himself at the room's periphery as though escape were never far from his mind. Viscount Southerton entered with Lady Powell on his arm. Like Annette, the lady was a widow who enjoyed a certain amount of freedom in her personal life as a consequence of that status. Similarities between the two of them could not be stretched much beyond that point. Lady Powell's husband had been a respected member of the peerage who had left her quite well off, while her own husband had been a captain in the regiments and left her with a pension so small she would have starved soon after if not for the sympathies of the men he had commanded.

Southerton did not linger at Lady Powell's side, Annette observed, but released her to a clutch of guests gathered near the salon's open entrance to the garden. She was immediately in animated conversation with the Baron and Baroness of Battenburn and did not appear to notice the viscount's defection, though Annette could scarcely believe this was the case. It was far more likely that the lady did not want to lay overt claim to Southerton, as that would surely cause him to bolt for parts unknown. Annette applauded the strategy, for it was one she often employed with a restive male. When a man did not know the bent of his own mind, someone must take him in hand. The thing required some subtlety, of course, and sure knowledge of the man's particular Achilles heel, but it could be accomplished. Annette's current status as a war widow with a narrow entree into society was directly attributable to her success at leading men about by their . . . noses.

The one she counted as her most disappointing failure was the last to be admitted to the salon. Annette thought she had glimpsed his carriage earlier, but when he didn't arrive in a timely manner she assumed she had been mistaken. She was no longer certain that was the case as Lord Helmsley reappeared moments after. Annette immediately suspected an intrigue. Her understanding of what Eastlyn did for the government was limited by his irritating discretion, but Annette counted herself astute enough to know when something was afoot. While Eastlyn gave nothing away as to the nature of his meeting with their host, Helmsley had a certain tightness about his mouth that had not been in evidence earlier. Some might suspect he had just been snookered at cards, but Annette knew that was unlikely. She would make a point to discover more, she decided, for it was this sort of knowledge that would serve her when her fair appearance no longer could.

It was not with this in mind that she made her way to Eastlyn. She had no expectations of learning anything from him. If he could not be made to talk about his political schemes in the aftermath of lovemaking, he could not be induced to give anything over now. If she was going to learn something of import, it would have to come from Helmsley, and how that might be accomplished would require some planning. Of more significance to her now was taking advantage of this opportunity to remind Eastlyn of what he had allowed to leave his bed.

The presence of Northam's wife at this affair made the timing of Annette's approach a delicate matter. She could not expect an introduction to the countess from North. Among the very few strategic blunders she had made in the course of campaigning for protection, the earl was perhaps the most egregious example. When she had sensed that Eastlyn was distancing himself from her, months before he knew it himself, she had gone to Northam with a proposition of her own. He had been flatly disapproving as only the truly priggish could be, and Annette had too late seen her error in thinking he had expressed an interest in her. She had made an enemy there, not precisely because she had sought him out, but because she had still been attached to Eastlyn when she'd done so. It was not her boldness that made him think ill of her. It was the betrayal of his friend that he could not forgive.

Annette was certain Eastlyn knew naught of it else he would have put an immediate end to their arrangement. Northam's own code meant that he would never inform East directly of what she had done, but this did not mean she could acquit the earl of sabotage. She knew firsthand that it was possible to communicate a dislike for someone without ever once stating it in plain terms, and she came to understand that North was as skilled a player in that arena as she.

Waiting for Lady Northam to be asked to dance tried Annette's patience. It meant exchanging more inane pleasantries than she wished with Lady Macquey-Howell while her husband hovered nearby. Lady Macquey-Howell was in the middle of an interminable discourse on the merits of the new play at Drury Lane when Annette spied North's wife being escorted away by the fastidiously turned out Baron Battenburn. Annette quickly fashioned a plausible excuse for herself and inserted it when Lady Macquey-Howell paused for breath.

"H.M.S. sighted off your port stern," Southerton informed East.

The marquess did not look over his left shoulder. "How is that again?"

"Her Mistress Sawyer."

Eastlyn winced, though North and Mr. Marchman did not know whether it was because of Mrs. Sawyer's approach or South's impoverished humor. "You are certain she means to come here?" he asked.

"I, umm, yes, I do believe—" South stopped midsentence and inclined his head as his gaze moved past Eastlyn. "Why, it is Mrs. Sawyer come to grace us with her singular beauty, and how fine she is looking this evening. May I say that emerald is a particularly flattering color?" He stepped forward to take her gloved hand and raise it to his lips. "Will you take a turn with me in the dance?"

Annette did not betray her annoyance. Now that she was here, she would not be so easily removed from Eastlyn's side. "Perhaps another time," she said pleasantly. "Although I believe Lady Powell would welcome your attentions."

Southerton's eyes darted to where Grace Powell was deep in conversation with the baroness. It did not appear that his presence was missed in the least. "She is satisfied, I believe, to exchange the latest *on dit* with her friend."

"As you are with yours, no doubt."

"Precisely."

Annette smiled coolly at Northam, then Mr. Marchman,

and felt herself flushing slightly when Eastlyn still did not turn in her direction and address her. A cut direct from him would do serious harm to her reputation. The ton knew she no longer enjoyed his protection, but that signified nothing in its own right. Arrangements of the sort she had had with him were changed all the time, and often as not the partings were amicable and did not arouse comment. Such had been the case when she broke it off with Eastlyn, though it was not accomplished without some attention on her part. East was, after all, a marquess, and the fact that she was immediately set up by a peer with a lesser title and a fraction of the wealth seemed to fly in the face of how things should be done. But for Eastlyn's innate decency, it might have looked for all the world as if she had been the one sent packing. He had allowed her to keep her pride intact by letting it be known that she had left him. It was perfectly true, of course, but that had never influenced rumor before and would not have done so now without his help. He had also perpetuated the notion of his own heartbreak by not taking another mistress.

Annette had never made a misstep by depending on East's good manners. She fought off her inclination to panic that this was not the case now.

Eastlyn turned slowly and made a polite bow. "Mrs. Sawyer."

"M'lord." She lowered her eyelashes in faint acknowledgment of his greeting and felt her breathing ease. "You have scarce been in attendance at any functions this month past. I have come to inquire as to the state of your health."

"I am well, thank you." There was an awkward pause as he steeled himself to return the amenity. "And you?"

"I enjoy very good health," she said. "It is the daily ride in the park, I think, that helps. It is my opinion that taking a turn in the fresh air promotes one's constitution."

"You take the phaeton?"

"Yes." It was the equipage he had presented to her soon after she became his mistress. They had later gone to Tattersall's where he had chosen a pretty black mare to pull it. "I am judged to be an extraordinary driver, you know."

"Yes, I've heard."

Keeping her smile intact, Annette's gaze swiveled to Mr. Marchman. "I saw you not above a week ago, racing your gray up the center path. You were in the lead, of course, though I cannot say whether you finished at the head. Did you?"

"I am crushed that there is the least question in your mind."

She tapped him playfully on his arm with her closed fan. "That is no answer, Mr. Marchman."

West gave himself full marks for not flinching from her coquettish assault. His friends were no doubt expecting him to brandish his knife. "I won the race," he said evenly. "It was a narrow victory. Barlough pushed his beast hard in the end."

"That was Lord Barlough following so closely? I confess I did not recognize him."

"It was. You know him, then?"

"Oh, no. By reputation only. We are not acquainted." She let this information hang there to see if Marchman would take it in hand and offer to make an introduction. The bastard did not. Annette dismissed him as of no use to her and offered a cordial smile in Northam's direction. "My lord."

"Mrs. Sawyer."

She noted his greeting was considerably cooler than her own had been. "You were not in the race, I collect."

"No, I was not."

"Has marriage curtailed your amusements, then?"

North did not want to respond to any question concerning his marriage, especially one put to him by Eastlyn's former mistress. He was grateful for Southerton perceptively inserting himself back into the conversation.

"Come, Mrs. Sawyer, you know Northam has never had any amusements. How could one hope to measure what influence marriage has had?"

As expected, Annette smiled. "You are right, of course. He is too serious by half." She glanced at Eastlyn. "Is that not what you always said?"

It was Marchman who answered. "Which is only East's way of pointing out the rest of us are too easily diverted."

Annette marveled at the way they instinctively closed ranks to protect one of their own. Was it a trait of all Hambrick schoolboys, she wondered, or these four in particular? She decided she would persevere. North's wife would be returning to his side soon, and Annette was aware she would do well to take her leave before then. She chose to address Eastlyn directly and ignore the wall the others erected around him.

"I suppose I am late in offering your lordship my condolences," she said. She did not pause to allow Eastlyn to feign a lack of interest. "I have only this morning learned that Lady Sophia Colley is promised in marriage to one Mr. George Heath. I trust this will put an end to any residual speculation that she is your intended."

"If it is true," East said carefully.

"I had it from Dunsmore, who had it from his father. I believe the earl's correspondence can be trusted."

Eastlyn wondered what a proper response would be. He was acutely aware that his audience was not limited to Annette and that her timing was deliberate. She knew he would not accuse her of anything untoward in front of his friends. "I was not aware you knew Dunsmore."

"I know many people," she said simply. "It is good news, is it not? She can return to London on the arm of her intended and put a period to this gossip that she is gravid with your child. Unless, of course, she has become gravid with his. That will complicate things, I believe. How will the truth ever come to light?"

Eastlyn was unaware of taking a step forward until he was pressed against Marchman's restraining arm. Mrs. Sawyer was already turning away, her exquisite smile firmly in place.

"East?" Southerton moved to block his friend's view of

the departing widow. "You do not want to look as if you mean to do murder. Not with so many witnesses present." He nodded in West's direction to encourage that worthy to lower his arm. "North, you will want to present some obstacle to your wife's arrival here until we can remove East from the premises. If nothing better occurs to you, you might ask her to dance. It has not gone unnoticed by us that you have yet to do so this evening, and we do not find it at all encouraging."

"I have not danced with my wife," North said in arid accents, "because she has ever been at the call of my friends."

"Well," West said, "we insist you take her now. Battenburn is escorting her directly toward us, and East does not yet have himself in hand. He is bound to thrash someone, and you know how badly that can go if you are in the way."

North put two fingers to the slightly crooked bridge of his nose. "You broke this, not East."

"Yes." West continued in reasonable tones, "But I did *not* break his nose, did I? When you recall how often I went after him, that is evidence enough that he is the better fighter."

Eastlyn felt his mouth twitch. "Have off, all three of you. Your methods of diversion are unorthodox but effective. I am all of a piece and will find my own way out." He had to suffer their scrutiny for several long moments while Lady Northam approached ever closer. The proof that they were satisfied with his control came when Southerton stepped aside and let him pass. He heard North's wife inquire after him just as he was slipping through the squeeze at the hall entrance. He did not hear North's reply but depended upon it to be a convincing excuse for his hasty retreat.

It was much later that Southerton found him at the club, but not yet so deep in his cups that he could not be counted on for lucid conversation. "I thought you would be for home at this hour," East said. "What are you doing here?"

"You are here, aren't you? It seems to me you shouldn't be compelled to drink alone." South motioned to a steward and requested a whiskey. "You do not mind if I join you?"

"No."

South accepted the terse reply at face value, choosing not to dwell on the tone. "You will never credit it, but Helmsley was robbed this evening. It happened not long after you left. It was good you were gone, for the wait to give statements to the runners was interminable."

"The Gentleman Thief?"

"Yes. And North once more in the thick of it. He will come under suspicion again, and Elizabeth's defense of him will not be heard in the same light as before. It was all very noble when she sacrificed her reputation to prove his innocence, but now that she is actually married to him, her protests do not have the same weight. Something will have to be done."

Eastlyn studied South over the rim of his glass. "I suspect North is already doing it."

South took up the drink that was brought to him and sipped from it as he considered what East meant. "The colonel?"

Eastlyn nodded. "I think it is North's assignment to catch the thief. I've thought so since the rout at Battenburn this summer past. You know how Blackwood despairs of us tripping over one another in the course of our work, so it's no good applying to him for information, but I suspect that he's set North on the trail of the thief. We are out of it, I'm afraid, until our services are requested."

It was a reasonable supposition in the light of the events at the Battenburn estate, South thought. Lady Elizabeth's startling announcement that North had been with her on the night he was alleged to have committed a theft had diverted suspicion from North and created the circumstances upon which a marriage of convenience was formed. "You could be right," South said slowly, letting the idea take shape in his mind. He ran one hand through his bright helmet of yellow hair and regarded Eastlyn with his light gray glance. "Well, that is something, is it not? And me with so little to do of late that I fear I shall expire of boredom."

"It is infinitely preferable to you pushing the rest of us to that end."

South chuckled. "Do you think I might avail myself of your box at the theater, East? I am of a mind that a comedy at the Drury Lane will provide suitable distraction."

"Of course. Is it the play that interests you or the talented Miss India Parr?"

"I have seen neither so the answer must be both." He eased back in his leather chair and took another swallow of his whiskey. "Is she as talented as they say?"

"I do not know what *they* say. I say she is gifted, but please, use my box and judge for yourself." Eastlyn suspected South had not come to the club to discuss the thief who had been bedeviling the ton or his own need for a diversion to boredom. "Why are you here, South? Did you pull the short broomstraw?"

"Actually, we cut cards for the privilege. I showed the four of spades."

"Rotten luck."

"Yes." His grin removed all possible sting from his reply. "There is no gossip about Lady Sophia carrying your child, East. We would not have kept you in the dark if we had heard of it. Not only did it not come to our attention, but North's mother has been everywhere of late showing off Elizabeth, and she was unaware of any such gossip."

That information pushed Eastlyn perfectly upright. "Bloody hell, South. You *asked* her?"

"North's wife or his mother?"

"Either. Both. It doesn't matter. Even repeating it in the form of a question will start tongues wagging."

South slumped lower in his chair. "If it doesn't matter, then it was the dowager countess we asked. She will be perfectly discreet."

"Hah! That means she will only make the same inquiry of her closest friends, your mother and mine chief among them. How is it possible that we can be depended upon to keep our counsel on the colonel's business and have so little regard for our own affairs?"

"I suppose it is in the very nature of our friendship."

"That is not a good answer. You would not brook this interference. You would not even ask for help."

"You would force it on me anyway."

Eastlyn sighed because it was no good being angry. South was right; they *would* force it on him. He finished his drink and set his glass aside. "Mrs. Sawyer divined what would happen if she spoke her nonsense aloud. That is what bothers me most. We were manipulated by her, South. Never think that she is not quick-witted or that we are too clever to be used in such a fashion. Standing toe-to-toe with the Society of Bishops did not ready us for dealing with the female sex. We are woefully ill-prepared. Woefully. And that is my considered opinion."

South eyed Eastlyn's empty glass for a long moment, then gave his friend equally careful study. Shaking his head, amusement edging his mouth upward, he asked quietly, "Precisely how many drinks did you have before I came to your rescue?"

Sophie leaned forward over her mount's neck, urging him with her posture, not her crop, and let him *fly* between the banks of the meandering stream. Apollo made the distance easily and never broke stride as he started across the open field. Sophie wished she might lie across his back and let him take her where he would, so much a part of him that he would not recognize her weight and form as something separate from his own being. She wondered if the sun-baked desert sands were in her Arabian's blood, whether his dam and sire had pounded across shifting dunes the way he did across this golden English field.

The lowering sun was in her eyes, and for a moment she closed them and let Apollo run with his instincts. Would he take the stone wall? she wondered. Or head into the stand of trees where it was dark and cool? He might circle round to the stream again and balk this time at the breadth of the jump. That would send her sailing over the top of his head and put her squarely in the drink. Apollo was an intelligent animal, Sophie thought, with sense enough to laugh at her for blindly trusting him.

Amused but not foolish, Sophie opened her eyes and regained her proper seat in time to assist Apollo's leap over the crumbling stone wall that marked the edge of the road. Sheep grazing on the hillock waited until the last possible moment to scatter, and then they bleated loudly as Apollo thundered past. Sophie laughed when she heard their intemperate cries. They did not sound so terribly different from Tremont of late.

A sennight had passed since the earl had seen the *Gazette* announcement that the Honorable George Heath, youngest son of Viscount Dryden, had married Miss Rebecca Sayers, politely referred to by Tremont as a Nobody. For her part, Sophie was glad for Miss Sayers and only a little sorry for herself.

Mr. Heath impressed as a man with a kind disposition and even temperament. He was steady and reliable, of moderate intelligence, and given to short discourse in the plainest of speech. He knew a modest amount about many things and almost nothing substantive on any subject, but at least he seemed to be cognizant that this was so and was not given to prattle on in ignorance. Mr. Heath confessed to possessing few talents, and this admission was not prompted by his innate humbleness, but rather because he was agreeably truthful. He did not paint or compose or read novels, and he had not many interests outside of hunting and breeding livestock.

In short, he was wholly unimaginative.

It did much to recommend him to Sophie, rather than the opposite. When she pledged to marry him it was because she meant to embrace the mediocrity of his character. There was no wildness in Mr. George Heath to cause her even a moment's inconvenience. He would not drink to excess, play at cards until dawn, or arrange for his seconds to meet him in some lonely field. There would be no passion between them, only duty, and to Sophie's way of thinking it was an agreeable arrangement. What she might have with her husband would be sufficient for an unremarkable life.

There was also eight thousand pounds per annum.

The money was what had made Tremont in support of the match, and the loss of it was what had sustained his black mood. Though she knew she was quite innocent in how events had taken a turn, Sophie was in favor of staying out of the earl's line of sight. She refrained from stating the obvious: Mr. George Heath was not so easily led to water as he had appeared to either Tremont or his own family. The viscount's youngest son was not willing to settle for a marriage of obligation, even if Sophie was. It made him more courageous in her eyes, though of necessity this was another view she kept to herself. Sophie admired Mr. Heath for seizing his opportunity for happiness with Miss Sayers. The man had had a passion after all, and he had only needed the proper circumstances to provoke its expression.

Sophie had nothing but kind words for Mr. Heath, and she would have told him so if there had been opportunity to correspond. Tremont would permit her to post only what he had approved, and there was little chance that he would sanction the admiration she was wont to convey.

It was not that Mr. Heath's defection was of no consequence to Sophie. Rather the opposite was true. She was certain Tremont would again cast his net in aid of finding her a proper partner, and she doubted she would be as largely fortunate as she had been with his last choice. Tremont had but one measure of suitability for her intended—the depth of his pockets—while Sophie's yardstick gauged a man's character. Her cousin might have chosen someone much less fitting than George Heath, and still could. Worse, he might return to the place of his earlier failure and set himself the task of bringing the Marquess of Eastlyn around. Sophie was not at all certain he had put that idea firmly behind him.

Apollo veered toward the woods, and this time Sophie did not give him license to do as he pleased. She guided him with the reins and the pressure of her thighs and heels to skirt the perimeter of the trees. He flawlessly executed her commands, just as if he had intended to go in that direction all along, and she praised him for it. He would prance and preen later, quite full of himself for having given her such a good run, and she would tease and admonish him by turns, promising him treats when he was fit to have them.

There was probably an application here, Sophie thought, for how all males might be managed, but since Apollo was a gelding she could not believe it would win wide acceptance.

Sophie slowed the Arabian as they approached the stream again, and this time she let him pick his way down the bank and splash through the brisk run of water. Droplets sprayed her face, and she did not bother to wipe them away, choosing instead to tilt her head so that she might catch one on her lips.

From his vantage on the road above her, Eastlyn watched Sophie's antics with something akin to wonder arresting his features. He had first caught sight of her when she and the Arabian had taken flight over the stream. It had occurred to him that she might not control the landing, but the thought was fleeting when he saw her form and the animal's response to it. It was the same when she urged her mount over the stone wall. She had lied to him, he realized. She had said she was on no account a bruising rider. There had been truth, though, in her assertion that she could hold her own but that her form was considered by some to be unconventional.

It was a proper understatement, for Lady Sophia's seat on her Arabian defined unconventional. She was riding astride.

He had followed her progress across the field and up a

verdant slope where she had permitted her mount to bedevil
the grazing sheep. Eastlyn had lost sight of her then as she
took the far side of the hill. He did not urge his own horse
forward on the road, but remained where he was, waiting for
her return. He glimpsed the crown of her bare head first and
the flutter of her windswept hair. She was skirting the edge
of the wood, darting in and out of the shadows made by the
towering oaks and slimmer beeches.

She shared nothing in common with the young lady he
had first met at the Stafford's musicale. He could not have
imagined that the quiet, reserved innocent of that short acquaintance would ever *conceive* of riding hell for leather across
the countryside, much less execute that conception. Nor could
he have fathomed that she would take to the course with
such abandon and defy the strictures of society by riding
astride. This woman had a passing similarity to the one he'd
met in the garden at No. 14. There had been some spirit
there, though constrained by her own common sense. What
had been suggested to him on that occasion was that Sophia
was possessed of a certain confidence and resolve that was
not unattractive.

He had glimpsed a version of the reckless passion he witnessed now when he had stolen his way into her room. It was
what had prompted that first brief kiss and made certain
there would be a second, but even then he had not understood the totality of her restraint, only the sum of his own.

Eastlyn lifted his hands from their at-rest position on the
leather pommel and snapped the reins lightly. He did not
look away from where Sophie splashed in the stream.
Tempest, his Irish thoroughbred whose name was indicative
of his customary humor, carried him along the steadily rising road. East knew the moment he was spied by Sophie because she went still as stone. He supposed that her immobility
was not merely in response to the arrival of a guest, but that
she had immediately identified him. It confirmed his thinking that he would not be entirely welcomed at Tremont Park
in spite of the earl's assurances to the contrary.

There also seemed to be a distinct possibility that Tremont had said nothing at all to Sophie about their correspondence.

Eastlyn's carriage followed some distance behind him, bringing his valet and belongings enough for a month, though he anticipated his visit would be much shorter than that. He wondered at the wisdom of speaking to Sophie before announcing himself formally at the house. It seemed likely that his arrival could have been noted miles earlier, as far back as when he and Tempest crested the hill rising out of the village of Loveridge, and that now the earl might be expecting him. Positioning himself in Tremont's good graces was a consideration, given the fact there was the colonel's work to be done, but it was not of sufficient importance to Eastlyn that he would decide to pass on this opportunity.

"Bloody hell," he whispered, for it seemed that a curse was in order as he turned Tempest off the road. He could not recall the last time he had taken so precipitous an action. His friends would not recognize him, and Blackwood would despair of his judgment. "Bloody, bloody hell." And then he committed his mount to taking the steep downward path to the stream.

Sophie urged Apollo up to the near bank and held him fast as Eastlyn approached. She was uncertain that remaining here was a good choice, yet running from him seemed a ridiculous response when she had no hope of avoiding him forever. Apollo shook out his damp black mane and pawed the ground. He was in anticipation of a race, and Sophie's control was tested to keep him in place, especially when Eastlyn brought his mount abreast of her.

It was unfair, she thought, that he could have traveled from London and looked no worse for the wear. His polished hat remained at the angle approved for rakish charm, and his short frock coat showed only a fine layering of dust from the road. He was much as she had seen him upon his first visit to Bowden Street, from the polished brass buttons on his coat to the turned-down tops of his boots. He had been unbearably handsome then, and Sophie noticed that he had not seen fit to alter his appearance. It was left to her, therefore, to steel her spine for yet another assault on her senses. She was not inclined to thank him for it.

"You're glowering," she said. It was an improvement of sorts over his fine looks because it added a deep crease between his brows and a downward twist to his mouth. Her mood was immediately lightened by these indications that his handsome features were subject to change, and further bettered by the thought that he was unhappy to see her. "It has probably escaped your notice that I did not invite you here. Let me assure you, that is the case." She pointed up the hill to the house since that had been his direction, though she would have liked better to have shown him the road out. "I give you leave to go."

Sophie noticed her imperious tone and churlish manner had exactly the opposite effect she was courting. Eastlyn's glower vanished only to be replaced by a gleam of amusement that she felt certain did not bode well for her. When he didn't move, she said, "I prefer that you glower, you know."

He made a faint bow with his head. "I shall keep that in mind."

"Why were you? Glowering, that is."

Eastlyn liked the way her chin came up just so when she meant to provoke him. She had a delicate heart-shaped face that undermined her efforts to look fierce or threatening, though she seemed unaware of it. Nothing would be improved by bringing it to her attention, he thought. She made up for the lack of sharp features with the finely honed edge of her tongue. "I was not glowering at you," he said.

"You were looking at me."

"Yes, but the scowl was meant for me."

"I didn't know you could do that."

"Under the right circumstances."

Sophie considered this. "Then, pray, continue to do so."

Eastlyn laughed. "It is good to see you again, Lady Sophia."

Sophie glowered.

"Aah," he said. "You are of a like mind."

"And you are a fool." She noticed that he did not take the least offense, though she doubted it was something he was accustomed to hearing. "Why are you here? You have not come for me, have you? That is, you are not in expectation of . . ." She stopped because she hardly knew how to finish the thought. "Pardon me. I did not mean that you could not have some reason other than . . ."

"Other than you?" Eastlyn watched the pale pink roses in Sophie's cheeks deepen in color. She did not avert her glance, though he thought it must have pained her to remain so directly under his study. She seemed uncomfortable with confrontation but determined not to avoid it. His eyes were drawn to her mouth where she had sucked in a portion of her lower lip and was now worrying it gently. He did not believe she would want to know how often he had thought about her mouth, or what precisely he had been thinking about it. He dragged his eyes away from the lush line of it and met hers again. "I am here to speak to your cousin about matters of politics."

Sophie was suspicious, but she could not find fault with his answer. Since inheriting the title, Richard Colley applied himself to politics the way he formerly applied himself to religion. There was an unmistakable fervor to his arguments that he had honed at the pulpit. Not every member of the House of Lords was receptive to his impassioned speeches, but it was not because he ever lacked for facts. It was his interpretation of them that raised the brows of the ruling party and the knowledge that he held sway over others. "At Tremont's invitation?" she asked.

"Not precisely. That is, it was my inclination to speak to him here rather than wait for his return to town. I proposed that if it suited him, I would come to Tremont Park. He was graciously amenable."

"I see."

"You do not believe me."

"You are very good, you know, at interpreting the bent of my mind. Can you tell what I am thinking now?"

He laughed outright as her bright, wild honey glance narrowed so that only the most pointed barbs escaped. "You should not use such language, Sophie. It is ill-becoming of a lady."

"Actually, I am restraining myself. I know many more colorful phrases, and I shall be thinking all of them directly."

Eastlyn grinned. "I believe you."

She nodded, satisfied that he did. "Come, I will escort you to the house. Is that your carriage on the road?"

East followed the line of her arm to where a cloud of dust was rising just above a row of spruce trees. "Most likely." The road opened between two hillocks, and he had a clear view of the coach in the dip. His driver had kept the horses at a good pace since leaving the inn at Weybourne and would arrive before he did if he did not go now. He turned, prepared to suggest a race, but Sophie had anticipated him and was already moving full-out in the direction of the house.

Eastlyn gave chase, but he knew at the outset he would not be able to catch her. She was too fine a rider, and she had not disadvantaged herself with a lady's saddle. Her complexion was glowing from the exertion and excitement of the ride when he finally reached her. She was also not able to temper her wide smile. "You are gloating," he said.

"Not at you."

"You are looking at me."

"True, but the pride is strictly for my own accomplishment."

Grinning at her tart accents, East dismounted and gave his horse over to the waiting groom. He moved to help Sophie down, but she had already swung around and was giving instructions to a second groom. "They will provide excellent care for your animal," she said. "My father was a good judge of horseflesh and an even better judge of the sort of men who care for them. You have a fine thoroughbred. Did you raise him yourself?"

"No. I purchased him on a visit to Ireland a year ago. Go on. Introduce yourself to him. His name is Tempest."

Sophie laid her hand on Tempest's lathered neck and stroked him. "My," she said softly. "Aren't you magnificent? Eighteen hands high if you're an inch. Long and leggy." She glanced at Eastlyn. "He knows he is a handsome beast, m'lord. Observe how he postures for me."

It was just the sort of thing Eastlyn thought he might do himself if it would make Sophie put her hand on his neck. "He does like to be admired."

Sophie smiled and gave Tempest a final pat. She motioned to the grooms to take the animals away. "Apollo is Arabian," she said, mounting the steps to the front door. "I trained him myself."

"You broke him?"

"I gentled him," she corrected. "There is a difference." Sophie paused and looked over her shoulder to where East was still standing in the drive. "Are you coming, my lord?"

He caught her by taking the steps two at time, his long legs making the climb effortlessly. The door was opened to them just as East's coach arrived. Servants hurried from the house to take his trunk and bags and direct his driver and valet. The butler accepted East's hat and gloves and gave them over to a footman.

"Where is his lordship to have a room, Huntley?" Sophie asked.

"The east wing, my lady."

"How appropriate," Eastlyn murmured dryly.

"That won't do," Sophie said. "You must prepare something else."

Huntley's already drawn face was suddenly stretched more tightly over his sharp features. He regarded Sophie with some confusion. "Lord Tremont was most particular. He chose the room himself."

"I'm certain he did, but it will never do." Sophie had no liking for having this discussion in front of Eastlyn. If Tremont had apprised her of the marquess's arrival, she would have instructed the servants on the arrangements. The preparations certainly would not have included a bedchamber in her wing of the house. She turned to East and saw that he was regarding her closely, a polite smile on his features that made her think he had already surmised too much. "The east wing is considerably drafty, and your lordship will find the fireplaces do not draw as they should. I think you will be more comfortable elsewhere. I will see to it."

"You must do as you think best," East said, his tone perfectly neutral. The gleam, though, was back in his eyes, and he didn't try to shield it from her. "I am certain I will find the accommodations to be more than adequate." His eyes swept the wide entry hall with its green-veined marble floor and gracefully curved staircase, following the path of the ornately carved railing and spindles to the upper floor before his glance came to rest again on Sophie. "Drafts do not bother me overmuch, and the nights are not so cool that I will require a fire."

Sophie addressed Huntley as if Eastlyn had made no reply. "Please see that his lordship is made comfortable. I will speak to my cousin. Is he in the library?" She excused herself when Huntley confirmed Tremont's presence in the library and hurried away.

Eastlyn watched Sophie go, her manly riding attire doing nothing to dissuade him that she was gloriously female. The fashion was perhaps outside the common mode, but the fault might lie entirely with the mode, he thought. Tweaking it now and again could not be entirely bad, especially when the results looked so fine from every conceivable angle. He appreciated the view a moment longer, vaguely aware that Tremont's butler was clearing his throat, a rather pointed suggestion in terms of allowable comments by the servants.

"I will take the room that has been prepared," East said.

"Very good, my lord. Whatever is not to your liking, you will permit us to make right for you."

The bedchamber Eastlyn was shown was actually a suite with an area for dressing and bathing on one side and a sitting room on the other. The furniture was all functional pieces, with freshly polished surfaces and gleaming brass fittings. Crowded in the dressing room were a wardrobe and a chest of drawers, a commode, a cheval glass, and a large copper tub already lined with linens and ready to be filled. The sitting room contained an assortment of chairs, including a rocker and a cherry wood escritoire set out with writing paper and a freshly filled bottle of ink. The bedchamber held a four-poster with forest green velvet curtains that had been drawn back to the headboard. Small tables flanked the bed, and a cedar chest sat just beyond the foot of it. The rooms were comfortably airy, not drafty, with tall leaded-glass windows whose individual square panes were set at an angle to suggest diamonds.

Eastlyn's valet appeared and directed the placement of the bags and trunk in the dressing room and the prompt filling of the tub with steaming water. There was nothing for East to do but let himself be turned out in a manner that would not embarrass Sampson. He sank deep into the tub while Sampson arranged his clothing in the wardrobe and chose the items that would require attention in the ironing room. The only time East's comments were needed was when Sampson could not decide which linen shirt to set out with the nankeen breeches. Eastlyn's contention that either would do did not settle the matter for his valet. Poor Sampson, East thought he would be in his element working for South, who actually made the effort to care about such things.

East closed his eyes and rested his head comfortably against the lip of the tub while Sampson answered a summons at the bedchamber door. The commotion in the outer room did not immediately register with Eastlyn; he was skirting the edge of sleep. He became aware of it only as the voices drew nearer to his place of sanctuary.

"It is no good trying to keep me out," Sophie was saying, "when I haven't the least intention of going in."

"But your ladyship is—"

Eastlyn did not hear the rest of Sampson's protest because water filled his ears as he slipped still lower into the tub. For some reason he recalled the colonel's suggestion that Lady

Sophia had drugged the lemonade she'd served him in her London home. It occurred to him now that she was changing tactics and intended that he should drown. How clever that she should make it seem the deed was done by his own hand.

Sophie presented herself on the threshold of the dressing room. She had a glimpse of Eastlyn's raised brows just above the surface of the water before she shut her eyes. "You will drown," she said. "And there really is no need. I am not coming any closer, and even if I were, you should know that I have seen a naked man before."

Eastlyn heard that well enough. He exerted himself sufficiently to raise his head and blink water from his eyes. Sophie had not changed her riding clothes, and she was looking moderately more disheveled than she had upon dismounting. Her face was flushed, perspiration marked her forehead, and her hair was still a cascade of slightly damp and unruly curls. If not for the presence of his valet, he might have asked her to join him in the tub. He took the gentleman's approach, however, because it seemed that one of them should behave with sense. "You are speaking of museum pieces, and it is not the same thing at all. Sampson, remove her immediately."

Sophie braced herself in the doorway, holding tightly to the frame on either side. "It is not only museum pieces," she told him quickly. "I have seen a man in the flesh." She sensed Sampson's presence behind her, and her knuckles whitened with the strength of her grip. "Please, I must speak to you. Do not send me away."

Eastlyn finally heard what he had not caught before, and it made him hold his reply a fraction longer. It was not Sophie's words that arrested him, but the manner in which they came from her. Here was panic. "Very well," he said quietly. "Sampson, it is all right. Stand aside and I will call you if your services are required."

More relieved than disturbed by Eastlyn's decision, Sampson nodded over the top of Sophia's head. He retreated into the bedchamber out of the line of their sight, but not of his hearing.

"You can relax your hold," Eastlyn told Sophie.

She let her hands fall to her sides, but her fingers did not easily lose their curled shape. "I most humbly beg your pardon," she said. "You must believe that I have never—"

"I thought not," he drawled in dry accents. "And I did not invite you to open your eyes now."

She shut them quickly. "I have never done a thing so bold as this. That is what I was trying to say. The other is quite true."

"Concerning the naked man, you mean."

"Yes."

"You will not apprise me of the details now."

"No." Sophie shook her head to emphasize that it would be forgotten. "No, I never intended that you should learn of it at all."

Eastlyn was quite certain that was true. "Perhaps you should make your reason for being here evident, Sophie. The water grows cold."

"Tremont does not want to consider that you will be more comfortable elsewhere." There was a small rush of air from Sophie's lungs as she finished the words before she finished the breath. "You must suggest other accommodations."

"But I *am* comfortable here."

"You cannot be. Do you see that door?" She raised her hand and pointed blindly in the general direction of the door that stood on the opposite side of the room. It was situated between the chest of drawers and the wardrobe. "My dressing room is on the other side. This was my father's suite during the time that he was ill and I cared for him. Of necessity I was required to be close, and the adjoining rooms were ideal for that. But not now. You must see that. My cousin is constructing a situation in which we might be compromised."

Eastlyn said nothing to that. He called for his valet instead. "My headache powders, if you please. Step out of the doorway, Sophie."

She did so and stumbled when her foot caught the edge of one of Eastlyn's valises.

"Oh, for God's sake, open your eyes when you move about."

Sophie could not mistake that Eastlyn was finally out of patience with her. She stared at the floor while Sampson entered with a packet of powder and made the preparations at the basin. She was still contemplating the border design in the carpet when Sampson slipped out again.

Eastlyn drained his glass and set it on the floor beside the tub. He took in the slope of Sophie's shoulders and the angle of her head and wondered if he could believe what he was seeing. "Am I to suppose by your posture that you are experiencing some measure of contrition?"

She looked at him now, and her features were set gravely. "I regret that I have caused you distress, my lord. I did not know what else to do except to come here to warn you away."

Frowning, Eastlyn raked his fingers through his damp hair. "What is it that I do not understand, Sophie? You do not want me in the room adjoining yours because you say Tremont means to affect a compromising situation, yet by coming here you have set up the very circumstances you insist you want to avoid. I confess to more than a modicum of confusion."

Sophie could appreciate his perspective, but it was more important that he appreciated hers. "My cousin knows I have no wish to marry you. I proved that to him with a month-long confinement in which I never wavered aloud from my position. He is not so certain of you, however, and there is your reputation to influence him. Tremont has not the imagination to permit him to think I would come straightaway to your room, or that I would refuse to remove myself when I found you . . . that is, when you are . . ."

"Naked?"

"Indisposed." Sophie regained her faltering composure. "He is in his library awaiting your arrival and has no reason to rise from his chair. But later, not tonight perhaps, but often during your visit, he will be watching you and searching out his opportunity. You must not make it so easy for him. You must not remain in my father's rooms."

Eastlyn heard it again, not Sophie's words precisely, but the thing she *wasn't* saying, and a chill that was not to be blamed on the cooling water raced up his spine.

Chapter Six

Tremont regarded Eastlyn over the rim of his glass of port. He gave the younger man full marks for carefully biding his time. So many of the marquess's generation—and Tremont included his own son here—approached every problem as if it required an immediate solution. Few of them seemed to comprehend that there was seldom a crisis. Tremont appreciated that Eastlyn had not pressed for a political discussion over dinner. It would have made for a deuced uncomfortable meal with Sophia hanging on every word, quite possibly thinking she had something of import to add to the conversation.

"You think this Singapore colony is a good idea, then," Tremont said, settling back into his chair. The soft leather upholstery held the faint aroma of cigar smoke, and the seat had taken shape around his figure, making the chair as comfortable as an old slipper. "The Chinese government will support the trade?"

East kept his response neutral. "My own thoughts have no bearing. The reports indicate the Chinese will not be adverse to the Company's settlement."

"But they did not seek it out."

"No."

"I see." Tremont sipped his port. "I continue to have reservations about the wisdom of this plan. There is the opium trade to consider. No one is saying aloud the traffic will be increased tenfold, and yet everyone knows it."

Eastlyn had not considered he might share a concern in common with Tremont. The East India Company's toehold in Singapore would surely lead to a tidal wave of trade, with opium being a most profitable commodity. "I have not heard you raise this particular objection before."

"I have not judged it to be the proper time to make a public statement about the drug trade," Tremont said. "There are many who will be enriched considerably by it, and that is something to note when standing in opposition to the Company's plans. I do not believe all the decisions I make must be popular ones, but I am cognizant that one must choose one's enemies as carefully as one's friends." He paused, rolling the stem of his glass in his fingers. "How widespread do you make the support for this settlement?"

Eastlyn's faint smile was a trifle mocking. Tremont was being disingenuous. The earl knew his opinion for or against could have a great influence on the outcome. "I think my presence here speaks to that."

"So it does." He remained silent, thoughtful. "What is it you would have me do, Eastlyn?"

"Think on it. Give the matter your full consideration. Nothing more than that. It is little enough to ask, I believe."

"Indeed. So little, in fact, that I wonder you traveled so far and with such dispatch to request it."

East shrugged lightly. He sensed that Tremont was treading carefully, not wanting to appear too eager in stating the conditions that might influence his thinking. "I find that London does not have as much to recommend itself to me as the country." He made a point of allowing his eyes to wander around Tremont's large library with its comfortable appointments and floor-to-ceiling bookshelves. The room appeared to be well used by the earl. The writing desk was the site of carefully stacked papers and an assortment of pens, and the drinks cabinet was stocked with decanters that were not entirely filled. This last suggested that Tremont availed himself of its use rather more quickly than the servants could replenish it. "You are of a like mind?" Eastlyn asked.

Tremont rose to fill his glass. "Actually I have come to appreciate London and now find that the country is only tolerable. The house and lands, however, require my attention. After years of neglect by my cousin, I am discovering that a firm hand is needed here." He glanced over his shoulder as he poured the port. "I am remiss in inquiring about your accommodations. You are satisfied with your room? Sophia seems to think it will not do."

"It is where her father slept, I believe," Eastlyn said. "She is perhaps uncomfortable with the idea of it being occupied again."

"It's been three years." Tremont returned to his chair and brought a measure of his impatience with him, sitting down hard enough to make the claw-and-ball feet ripple the Aubusson rug. "The gel needs to stop dwelling on what's done. It was God's will that my cousin should go when he did, and Sophia would do better not to question His divine plans."

Eastlyn thought Tremont's contention was somewhat harsh, but he did not take issue with it directly. Coming to Sophie's defense could only have a complicating effect on the time he spent here. "If it is all the same to you, Tremont, I should prefer another room. I have no desire to be the cause of Lady Sophia's distress."

"As you wish."

Eastlyn could not help but notice Tremont's agreement was reluctantly given in spite of his words to the contrary. "Thank you." He finished his port and set the glass aside, in no way inclined to have another. "You will think about East India's proposal, will you not? I look forward to discussing it further tomorrow."

"Of course. There is much to consider." Tremont rested

his chin on the knuckles of one hand while he studied his guest in a most open manner. "We have had no conversation between us regarding your own proposal."

East did not hurry his response. He wasn't entirely certain what Tremont meant. "My proposal?" he asked. "To what do you refer?"

Tremont merely smiled. "Mayhap you should think on it. I am eager to hear more on that subject on the morrow."

The night air was cool, but Eastlyn took no notice. He walked through the terraced gardens at Tremont Park at the same leisurely pace he would have set for the full light of day. After excusing himself from Tremont's presence, he had wandered outside rather than avail himself of the opportunity to explore the house. There would be ample time to do that in the morning. With Tremont well into his cups by evening's end, Eastlyn suspected the earl would not quit his bed early. Any discussion about the Singapore settlement would necessarily come later in the day. There was the more disturbing possibility that Tremont would want to discuss Sophie first.

Eastlyn was actually surprised by Tremont's restraint. Sophie's presence at the table was reason enough not to raise certain questions over dinner, but once he and the earl were alone Eastlyn had been prepared to be cornered. Tremont had not struck East as a patient man, let alone a tactician. It was an opinion in want of revising if he was to hold his own with the man. Tremont had been quite willing to hear him out in regard to the settlement. It had laid the foundation that his support was necessary to the interests of the Crown. It was in Eastlyn's own best interest not to overstate that point and give Tremont too much leverage over him, yet it was difficult to strike just the right balance. Several rounds of cards had done nothing to encourage East that he had made a good job of it. Tremont's spirits seemed to be set a notch too high, and his mood was unchanged whether he won or lost at the table. East interpreted that to mean that Tremont believed he was already in complete possession of the high ground.

What concerned Eastlyn was that Tremont might be right.

Occupied by the problem before him, he did not immediately see Sophie at the periphery of his vision. It was only when she moved that his attention was caught by the shifting shadows. He hesitated, wondering if he should pretend she had escaped his notice, then decided she did not deserve such gentle treatment. She had not been disposed to give him consideration when he was in his bath. A certain amount of retribution was in order.

Too late, Sophie realized her mistake was in trying to avoid being seen by moving out of the way. There was nothing for it but to stand her ground as he approached. Moonshine cast Eastlyn in its blue-gray light, lending his features the cool perfection of marble sculpted by a master's hand. He was smiling at her, not in a way that was openly amused, but secretly so, and his eyes were black now, both penetrating and predatory. Sophie had the odd sensation, not easily suppressed, that his advancement bore less resemblance to a greeting than a hunt.

Eastlyn was bareheaded this evening and unable to tip his hat. He inclined his head instead. "I had not expected to come upon you again tonight. It is rather late, is it not, for you to be out?"

"I was going to say much the same thing to you. I would have thought your journey would have prompted you to retire early."

"Yes, well, I have had my fill of cards and port and cigars and find none of it conducive to sleep. You?"

"Contrary to your contention that this is a late hour, I do not find it so. I am often about. There is a small lake on the other side of that stand of pines that I like to visit. On a night such as this one it holds the moon and is pleasant to look upon."

Eastlyn regarded Sophie more closely, taking in her posture and the small tremor that made her seem to shimmer in the moonlight. She had her hands clasped behind her back, a pose that made him suspect she was hiding something. It occurred to him that her hair was darker than the night could account for, and it prompted him to reach out suddenly and touch a spiraling tendril at her temple. His fingertips came away damp. He grinned openly at her, quite sure now that he knew what she held at her back. "Why, Lady Sophia," he drawled, "I do believe you took a spill in the lake."

Sophie let her hands fall to her sides and revealed her towel. "Oh, you know very well I did not. I was swimming."

East did not try to suppress his chuckle. "The water must have been . . . um, bracing."

"It was freezing."

He decided to take pity on her. "And now you are, too. Come, let me escort you back to the house where you can find warmth." Without waiting for her assent, East tucked his arm under hers and brought Sophie around to the path. Once on it, he took the towel from her unresisting fingers and made a fashionable turban for her hair. "It might not win approval in London salons, but it could gain wide favor here in the country." He removed his frock coat and placed it around her shoulders. "Better?"

In spite of Sophie's wish that it were otherwise, it *was* better. She had never gone swimming so late in the year and had been seduced by the warmth of the day and a restlessness that could not be satisfied in the confines of the great house. It was not until she dove under the water that she realized how little heat the lake retained below its surface. Striking out hard for the opposite side did nothing at all to warm her blood. Indeed, Eastlyn's arm linked in hers and the touch of his fingertips in her hair had done considerably more to remove the chill from her marrow. "Thank you," she said, glad that her teeth did not chatter. "You are most kind."

"Just practical," he said. "It occurs that Tremont will not deal well with me if I cannot thaw you."

Sophie came close to stumbling then. There was a second

meaning to Eastlyn's words that she did not think she was mistaking. She shot him a look that would have told him how out of sorts she was if he had bothered to glance in her direction. He did not, however, choosing instead to remain sublimely unconcerned, and Sophie was forced to tell him. "You are speaking nonsense, my lord. What I think about you can be of no importance to my cousin. He cares nothing for my opinion on any matter, and this can be no different."

"If you choose to believe that, I will not try to persuade you otherwise."

Sophie actually ground her teeth together. In the still night air the sound of it carried so that Eastlyn could not mistake it for anything else.

"You have something on your mind, I collect." He waited but she did not answer, and he chose to change the subject— after a fashion. "I learned in London of your engagement to Mr. George Heath. I was remiss in not mentioning it when I encountered you this afternoon."

"Hardly remiss," she said. "Rather more circumspect than you are being now. You must have heard also that Mr. Heath is now married to Miss Rebecca Sayers."

"Yes." He paused and looked at her, regarding her profile as they walked. "Was your heart bespoken for as well?"

"No."

East considered this. "So you agreed to marry Mr. Heath when you bore him no great affection, yet would not answer my proposal in a similar way. I do not understand that, Sophie."

"No, I suppose you do not, and I am of no mind to explain it to you. You will have to accept it, I'm afraid." She pulled Eastlyn's coat more tightly about her shoulders. The scent of him was in the fabric, and it was all she could do not to breathe deeply of it. "I am glad that Mr. Heath expressed himself so convincingly in the end. He deserves to be happy, and it seems to me that is more likely to be accomplished with Miss Sayers at his side than with me."

"I think you underestimate your influence."

"No," she said flatly. "I do not."

"I find myself quite happy at your side."

Sophie turned her head, her mouth set disapprovingly. "I wish you would not give voice to that sort of flattering drivel. I have always been able to depend upon your honesty. I should like that to continue."

They were at the edge of the garden, not much more than twenty yards from the rear entrance to the manor's solarium. Several lamps had been left burning there, each shedding enough light in its respective circle to indicate the room was unoccupied. Eastlyn held Sophie's elbow fast, halting her advance to the house. He did not turn her toward him, but stepped around himself so that he was facing her. "That is unfair of you. I did not mean to flatter you, only to express what I know to be true. You not only belittle yourself but my feelings as well."

Startled and not a little ashamed, Sophie averted her glance, then her head. Eastlyn cupped her chin and tilted her face toward him, though getting her to raise her heavy lashes required more in the way of verbal manipulation than physical.

"Look at me, Sophie." He might have missed the small shake of her head if it had not been for his fingertips against her skin. "You cannot be so shy of a sudden. Is it because you know I mean to kiss you if you do not look up?"

That announcement had the desired effect. Sophie's glance flew to his, and she stared at him with darkening eyes.

"I mean to kiss you anyway, you know."

She did know. It was so very hard not to lean into his mouth as he lowered his head, so difficult not to press herself against his chest or grip his shoulders and hold him to her. Her swim tonight had been in aid of avoiding this exact end. She had not meant to provoke a confrontation with Eastlyn, but rather circumvent one. The water should have chilled her blood and put a period to the restlessness that plagued her all evening. The effect was not quite what she had wished for, not when he had the capacity to nullify it so easily.

Eastlyn's mouth was warmer than his hands, infinitely

more tender than his touch, and yet it was substantial and sure and held her so firmly that she might have been cradled in his arms. Sophie's eyelids fluttered closed, and she sucked in a small breath when he parted her lips. She remembered this kiss, remembered her promise and his that it would not be repeated, and still it was happening. Sophie wished that she might be the one to draw back but acknowledged that she was more selfish than he and possessed of as little good sense.

East rested his forehead against hers and whispered her name a hairsbreadth above her mouth. It was part endearment, part curse, and she did not take issue with either. "I asked Tremont to arrange another room for me."

"I didn't know. Thank you."

Straightening, drawing in a steadying breath, East added, "I didn't do it for you, Sophie. I did it because that door was too great a temptation." He watched her open her mouth, hesitate, then close it again. "You know I can get into your room by any means that I wish, but to have it so easily accessible was a challenge of a different nature. It occurred to me that I did not want to be tested in that manner."

"But—"

"I would fail, Sophie, and you would be compromised, and we would be married. That is the truth of it."

"You are assuming I would allow myself to be compromised."

One of Eastlyn's brows lifted. "At the risk of being overly confident . . ."

Sophie placed both palms flat on his chest and gave him a solid push. "Out of my way, my lord."

Chuckling quietly, Eastlyn stepped aside and permitted her to pass. "I could not fail to notice that your clothes are dry," he said as she walked by him. He saw her step falter and knew he had her attention even when she kept going. "And that you are not carrying any wet garments." He did not look away when she turned her dark glare on him. "The next time you choose to swim in your wherewithal, Sophie, you will want to keep in mind that my tub is a great deal warmer."

Sophie made a point of not avoiding Eastlyn the following day. There was nothing to be gained by pretending he wasn't underfoot. She broke her fast with him in the family dining room and noted to herself that Tremont was conspicuously absent. She thought it was quite intentional on his part until Eastlyn casually informed her that her cousin most likely had a sore head.

"He drank rather a lot over cards," East said. He tucked into his eggs while he watched Sophie push hers around her plate. "You have no appetite?"

She did not, but was too proud to allow Eastlyn to assume it had anything to do with him, or her impulsive decision to take a swim the night before. Ignoring the uncomfortable roiling of her stomach, Sophie gamely swallowed a forkful of her scrambled eggs and followed it with a bite of toast. Aware that Eastlyn was watching her, she hoped that settled his concern. "Did Tremont beat you soundly at whist?"

"He did."

"You do not sound as if you are at all put out by it."

"It does not sit well," he said. "But then I haven't yet lost."

The enigmatic reply brought Sophie's head up. Her brow creased. "I do not suppose you will explain yourself."

Eastlyn pretended to consider it, then said, "No, I do not think I will."

Sophie wished he would not look at her with that perfectly agreeable smile when his words were to the contrary. She imagined he had been able to say all manner of outrageous things because of that roguish charm. Worse, she did not think he had ever consciously practiced it, but that it came to him as naturally as drawing air. She could not very well insist that he stop breathing, could she? "Tremont cheats, you know."

"Indeed. He is rather good at it." Eastlyn speared a thin slice of tomato. "I confess that I am surprised you realize it. Do you play cards with him?"

"No. He has never invited me to do so because it would place him in the untenable position of having to explain his hypocrisy. He would have me believe that cards are the devil's tools and games of chance have no place in a house where religion is practiced." Sophie realized she had said more than she meant to and that Eastlyn's interest was considerably piqued. She was cautious in her tone as she continued. "My father told me long ago that Tremont plays cards. He also told me I should avoid sitting at a table with him because he cheats. I have always been thankful I have never been placed in a position of having to refuse him. It would be awkward to explain what I know."

"Would you?" asked Eastlyn. "Refuse him, I mean."

Sophie did not answer immediately. There were certain ramifications to consider if she were to do such a thing. Defying her cousin by refusing to marry Eastlyn was a minor rebellion when compared against calling Tremont a cheat and a hypocrite. "No," she said finally. "I don't think I would." She was not entirely surprised when Eastlyn's eyes dropped to her bare arms. The short puffed sleeves of her simple muslin day dress left most of her arms exposed, and if there had been bruises, he would have seen them. Sophie pretended not to notice the direction of his gaze and therefore did not comment on his intent. "My cousin would find my playing to be poor entertainment for him. It has been quite some time since I held cards in my hands."

"You played with your father?"

She nodded. "Often."

Eastlyn sipped from his coffee cup. "If it does not distress you, I should like to know more about him."

"How he died, you mean."

"How he lived."

Sophie's eyes flew to his. Eastlyn's request was one that had not been made of her before, and her reflexive response was to flatly refuse. He had given her a reasonable excuse to do so. All she had to say was that it *did* distress her, and he would put the subject behind them. But then where would his curiosity take him? Would he apply to Tremont for information, or mayhap Harold? It was a certainty that Eastlyn was not in complete ignorance of her father's failures, as public as those had been, but where else could the marquess apply to hear an alternate account of her father's life, the one that was both bitter and sweet and could only be related through a daughter's perspective?

Sophie placed her fork on the table and her hands in her lap. Her fingers pleated the linen napkin instead of the fabric of her dress. Her chin came up slightly as her decision was made, and except for the steady movement of her fingers, a stillness settled over her. "My mother died when I was not yet three," she said quietly. "That is the place to begin, you understand, for there are those who believe my father killed her. I would say it is truer that he died with her. She was trying to bear him a son, you see, an heir, and it remains a fact that she was advised after my birth not to have another child. I do not know this from my father—he would never speak a word against my mother—but the snippets I have collected over the years from the servants make me think she was strong-headed and would not be denied. I know my father was very much in love with her, so perhaps it is no lie that by his weakness he had a hand in her death. He certainly considered it was so."

Eastlyn thought Sophie's eyes appeared brighter than usual, though it might have been only that her face had become so pale. He wondered that she had not chosen to beg off when clearly this was no easy subject for her. He understood there was pain here, but was not prepared for the rawness of it. It seemed to him that he was witness to a wound that had never once healed. Questions occurred to him, and he let them pass, loath to interrupt her.

Sophie smiled a trifle crookedly. "It is hard to know about love, I think. That emotion has consequences that are too often outside the province of happy endings." She thought that Eastlyn looked at her oddly then, but he made no comment and she continued. "My father was rarely in residence at Tremont Park after my mother died. When he visited he was hardly ever alone. He came with an entourage of friends, acquaintances, and hangers-on. You cannot imagine how this place came alive at those times. The rooms were full, the staff moved with heady purpose, and laughter spilled into the halls and stairways. There were card games and entertainments, fortune-tellers, musicales, poetry readings. There was dancing far into the morning." Sophie felt her breath catch as a memory grabbed her by the heart and squeezed. She went on because it seemed suddenly right that she do so; the opportunity to speak without fear of contradiction might never present itself again. "I would fall asleep sometimes on the stairs, just below the landing. I always meant to go to bed, of course, before I was caught out; but my intentions were rarely so strong as my curiosity, and Papa would find me in my hiding place and carry me to bed. I was never scolded for spying on the guests, though perhaps that had less to do with me and more to do with my father's guilt."

Eastlyn suspected that her father's guilt had nothing to do with spending so little time with Sophie. Indeed, the late Earl of Tremont probably had made more effort to see his daughter than was the habit of most fathers. The guilt, then, Eastlyn surmised, must have had at its source the earl's own belief that he had denied Sophie her mother. "He indulged you?" Eastlyn asked.

"Indulged? That hardly describes it. He spoiled me most terribly." She saw in Eastlyn's polished chestnut eyes the clear light of skepticism. "You do not believe me? You must apply to my cousin for confirmation. Tremont will be most happy to inform you of the truth of it."

East had no difficulty accepting that. He also knew he would not broach the subject. "I take it he does not countenance the spoiling of children."

She shrugged. "I am not so certain. He is tolerant of his

grandchildren in a way I could not have predicted. I only know that he did not approve of my father's easy manner toward me. In time, I think, he no longer approved of me."

"So there is no love lost there."

Sophie nodded slowly, unwilling to share the whole of it. "You must appreciate that his lordship and I are often at loggerheads. You have only to examine my recent opposition to your proposal—and his response—to understand how it is between us." Sophie saw that Eastlyn shifted slightly in his chair. "Am I speaking too frankly?" she asked. "It was not my intention to discomfit you."

"I admire your forthrightness, Sophie, even when it tweaks my pride. I cannot say that you were wrong for refusing me. I have certainly come to understand that you paid a price for it, though I think I do not yet fully appreciate what that cost was."

Sophie did not find that his compliment or his understanding offered her any ease. Embarrassed, her eyes slid away from his as she picked up the threads of her story. "My father found amusements that diverted his attention from Tremont Park. I think that if I had not been in residence here, he would never have visited. I cannot say when he stopped thinking of it as his home, only that he did. I traveled with him to London on occasion, more so when I was much younger. You will know, of course, that my father was a frequent patron of the gaming hells, and being with him in town did not mean I was in his company. I preferred when he brought his friends to the Park, for at least I saw him then. We were never so distant as when we were residing together at Bowden Street."

Eastlyn had not realized the house at No. 14 was the same one where she had lived with her father. To have the house taken over by Dunsmore and his brood must have been lowering in its own right, but to have been confined to a room and residence where she had once been free to come and go could have been naught but a searing humiliation. He remembered how Sophie had tried to keep him from making his proposal and how he, in his need to acquit himself honorably, had disregarded her wishes. He began to comprehend how well she had understood the effect his proposal would have and how blithely ignorant, mayhap arrogant, he had been.

"Forgive me," Sophie said quickly, interrupting Eastlyn's introspection. He looked as if he meant to make an apology, though the purpose of doing such eluded her. There was no reason he should, yet she could not believe she had mistaken the glimpse of something akin to guilt in his eyes. She had seen it often enough with her own father to know the look of it in someone else. "I am being maudlin, and I have no use for it nor on any account wish to subject you to the same."

"I did not—"

Sophie pushed her plate away and stood abruptly. "If your lordship will excuse me, there are matters that require my attention elsewhere."

Eastlyn knew she was running from him, but he had no wish to say as much. He nodded once, rising as she quit the room. Her exit was not as hasty as he suspected she wished it might be, and his admiring glance followed her until she disappeared into the hall.

Sophie had not lied when she said there were matters in need of her attention, though the urgency was rather less than she had suggested by her tone. None of the tenants she visited that afternoon were ill, and while they all welcomed her into their homes, Sophie felt as if she were intruding instead of being helpful. She used the time to cast her glance surreptitiously about the homes and make a mental list of items the tenants were in want of. She could no longer trust that anyone would voice even a single need to her. If it were stiff-necked pride that kept them silent, Sophie would have known how to make it easier for them to accept her help. After all, what she would do for them was not charity, but an obligation, or at least she had always thought of it in that light.

Still, it was not pride that kept them quiet. It was resignation. They had surrendered to the idea that Tremont would do nothing to improve their lot, and more disturbingly from Sophie's point of view, they saw her as powerless to change that.

It was true, after a fashion. From the outset she had had no influence on her cousin's manner of tending to the estate. He placed his trust in Mr. Piggins, who was no less inadequately skilled to his position of manager than Mr. Beadle had been before him. She had no one but herself to blame for Mr. Beadle, for she had hired him soon after her father had been confined to his bed. She knew she had been slow to understand what damage had been done by her poor choice and her own neglect of the estate's affairs. She also never offered the steady decline of her father as an excuse for her misjudgment and lack of attention. If the tenants understood that she was trying to make amends now, it was never mentioned aloud.

It was Sophie's opinion that her efforts thus far had been largely ineffective and the tenants were right to greet her overtures with reservations, if not outright suspicion. They were entitled to that stance until she could prove to them, and to herself, that she was not so impotent as she seemed.

To that end when she returned to the manor she raided the larder for foodstuffs, the infirmary for medicines, and the linen cupboards for sheets and blankets. This was not done without the assistance of certain trusted house servants, including the housekeeper, cook, and first butler, for there were inventories to be kept and appropriate adjustments to be made. The fact that Mr. Piggins was a thief himself was both a hindrance and a boon to Sophie's plans. She had to be more clever than he was since he oversaw the household accounts himself, but it was also quite possible that Tremont would eventually find Piggins out and dismiss him for his spurious record-keeping.

The items she collected were carefully carried off to the stable where they were stored in the tack room with the permission of the head groom. It was not only a measure of how much Tremont was disrespected and Mr. Piggins was despised that Sophie was able to enlist the aid of the servants. She had long ago been taken under their wing. Her upbringing had occurred as much belowstairs as above it. A succession of governesses and tutors had not been able to keep her out of the larder and lamp room and laundry. She was as familiar with the kitchen at Tremont Park as she was with the library, and she knew the location of the basil leaves and mint in the same way she knew where to find Blake's *Songs of Experience*.

Sophie was returning to the house from the stable when she was confronted by Eastlyn on the same path. "Is Tremont not yet about?" she asked by way of greeting.

"He is still unwell," Eastlyn said. "And means to stay abed for the remainder of the day. That leaves me at sixes and sevens. I wonder if I might press you to accompany me on a tour of the Park?"

"Tremont is not unwell," she said. "Or at least not so unwell that he cannot be a more genial host. It is yet another attempt to make us companions."

"That had also occurred to me, but I believe I can moderate this urge I have to seduce you. Can you say the same?"

Sophie stared at him for a long moment. "You are given to saying the most outrageous things."

He nodded, unrepentant. "Come. I should very much like to see this lake of yours."

Rolling her eyes, Sophie turned and fell in step with him. She tucked several windblown strands of hair under her straw bonnet and refastened the blue satin ribbon. It was not possible to be angry with him, she decided, not in any real or lasting fashion. "Are your friends as even in their temperament as you?" She glanced at him sideways and saw that he appeared much struck by her question.

"Is that what you think? That I am of an even disposition?"

"Well, yes, of course."

Eastlyn grinned. "I shall have to tell West and the others. It will amuse them, I think, for they are of another opinion entirely."

"How can that be?"

"I suppose because their experience with me is decidedly different than your own. At Hambrick Hall I was given to venting my spleen." Eastlyn remembered how South and West had been moved to keep him from throttling Annette at the Helmsley affair. "They would say that not much has been changed since those days."

Sophie couldn't imagine. She knew she had put his tolerance to the test, but he had invariably been gentle, if unconventional, in his response to her. "What did you do?"

"I fought everyone. Everyone. All the time. I should have been expelled except for the influence my mother and father brought to bear." He chuckled at her suspiciousness. "If you are thinking that influence equaled money, then you are in the right of it. Quite a lot of money, actually, because I did inflict the occasional serious injury."

"Lord Northam?" she asked. "He has had his nose broken, I believe."

"I cannot take credit there. That was West."

They reached the stable, and Sophie asked for their horses to be made ready for them. In deference to her attire, she was forced to use a lady's saddle. While Eastlyn looked on, she made a point of apologizing to Apollo for the inconvenience of carrying her in such a manner.

"He would not mind so terribly," she told East, "if I were more skilled. It is a sad truth that I am not. I hope you are only in want of a tour, as you said, and not another race."

Eastlyn assured her that he was not eager to be soundly beaten again; then before she knew what he was about, he had his hands neatly fitted to her waist and was lifting her onto the back of her horse. She was very nearly insubstantial in his hold, so effortlessly was she lifted onto the saddle. East suspected it was not solely the presence of an interested pair of grooms that kept Sophie from taking him to task. It seemed to him that he caught her so completely off guard that she was without words at the ready. She looked eminently kissable in her surprise, and he was immediately sorry he had put her outside of the reach of his mouth.

She made it easy to forget all the reasons why kissing her was not a good idea.

They rode away from the stable in silence until Eastlyn broke it with his refusal to apologize. "I am not sorry, Sophie, so there is no point in entertaining thoughts that I will say I am."

Sophie looked over at him, amused. "I was not in expectation of an apology," she said. "Indeed, I should be insulted if you delivered one. I was enjoying the quiet of the Park, not withholding conversation."

Eastlyn marveled anew at her ability to put him so firmly in his place. He was very nearly insubstantial in *her* hands, he decided, and when that thought made him grin he had enough sense left to make himself appear abashed.

"Why did you fight?" Sophie asked, ignoring his smile and whatever foolish notion that had prompted it. "At Hambrick, I mean."

So they were back to that. Eastlyn wished that he had not mentioned Hambrick. He should not have been so quick to correct her impression that he was evenly tempered. He told her, "For all the usual reasons schoolboys fight, I suppose."

She offered a single raised eyebrow as proof that she was not satisfied with his answer.

"Very well," Eastlyn said. "Sometimes it is a matter of defending one's honor, or that of a family member or a friend. There are slights, both real and imagined, that must be attended. There are accusations and rumors and sly games of the kind that boys like to get up to. At Hambrick there was also the Society of Bishops."

"The Society of Bishops?"

"A means of organizing cruelty."

Sophie glanced sideways at Eastlyn. He was staring straight

ahead, and in profile he looked as if he were cut from stone. "Did you want to be a member of the Society?"

Eastlyn smiled a little then. "No. Never. They were adversaries from the first day."

"And your friends? Was it the same for them?"

"They weren't my friends until later. In the beginning we each made our stand alone." Eastlyn slowed Tempest to a walk as they reached the wood. The trees grew close together, and he judged they would have to proceed single file along the narrow path made by Sophie and Apollo's successive visits to the pond. He waited for Sophie to move ahead and permit her mount to lead the way.

"Then it was your mutual dislike of the Society that brought you and the others together?" she asked.

"No. Not at all." He regarded her with a slight frown between his brows. "What is your interest in the Compass Club?" East saw his question did nothing to temper her curiosity, and he anticipated where she would go next. "It is the name we eventually gave ourselves. West's idea. Northam. Southerton. Eastlyn. You see how well it fit. We swore ourselves enemies of the Bishops. It was all dramatically accomplished."

"Blood oaths?"

"No, more's the pity. North had no stomach for bloodshed. South either, now that I think on it."

Sophie laughed. Eastlyn sounded so young just then that she could easily imagine him pressing his friends to open a vein to seal their alliance. She gave Apollo a kick and started him along the path. The air grew immediately cooler in the deep shade of the tall pines, and Sophie raised her shawl so that it covered her shoulders. The sounds of their horses' hooves were dampened by the thick bed of pine needles under them, making conversation with Eastlyn easy to continue. "If it was not the Society that effectively brought you together," she asked, "was it the nature of your names? Though I confess, I do not understand about Mr. Marchman."

"It was not our names. There was not a title among us when West made his observation. It was his contention that we might all inherit one day if only enough people were to conveniently pass on before us." Eastlyn did not miss Sophie's perfect astonishment at this ghoulish revelation. For a moment he thought she would unseat herself. He shrugged a trifle sheepishly when her head swiveled around so that she might stare at him. "Boys must find something to talk about," he said by way of explanation. "It was all very innocent, you understand. West only meant to make a point. No one among us considered ways to bring the thing about. Well, perhaps West did contemplate murder, but he never acted toward that end. His father is still very much among the living, and there is a brother, a legitimate son of the duke, who will inherit first."

"Then Mr. Marchman is a bastard?"

"Yes, but he allowed us to be his friends anyway."

When Sophie turned away to regard the path she was smiling at Eastlyn's easy defense of his friend and his friendship. She suspected it was always thus with them, that they would rally in the face of any threat. "Your lordship is fortunate, I think, to still have such friends as you made in your youth."

"East," he said. "I wish that you would call me East. And, yes, I am fortunate." As they broke through the trees, Eastlyn came abreast of Sophie. "Your friends have all scattered?"

"No," she said. "They still live at the Park."

Eastlyn did not immediately give chase when Sophie allowed Apollo to break into a hard gallop. Instead, he removed his polished beaver hat from his head and raked his thick hair with his fingers. He was sufficiently struck by what Sophie had revealed to him that he addressed his mount. "What do you make of that? She counts the servants as her friends." Eastlyn gave Tempest a smart smack on the rump with his hat and let the thoroughbred fly. Clods of rich earth were dislodged behind them as Tempest raced across the open field. They caught Sophie and Apollo some thirty yards before they reached the lake and passed them in time to skirt the water's edge.

Sophie dismounted without assistance and let Apollo wander away. Eastlyn stayed in his seat for a time, surveying the length and breadth of his surroundings from the vantage of this higher perch. The late afternoon sunshine glanced off the smooth surface of the lake, reflecting ribbons of gold and orange light across the top. A family of ducks, disturbed by the intrusion of horses and riders, wandered off into the high grass. Their departure rippled the water so that the mirrored light shifted and sparkled. In the distance the fields were laid out in a patchwork pattern so neatly defined they might have been the work of seamstresses rather than farm laborers. Behind them, Eastlyn noted, the stand of trees was not so tall as to entirely block the view of the manor's roof and uppermost turrets.

"I suppose Tremont can see us from the house," Eastlyn said, dropping to the ground beside Sophie. She had already removed her shoes and stockings and was raising her muslin gown to a modest level just below her knees. He dragged his eyes away from her small bare feet as she lowered them into the water. "Do you think he will trust his own eyes or make use of a spyglass?"

"Neither," Sophie said, kicking up a spray of water. "He will not rouse himself. It is Mr. Piggins that you should be looking for. That is Tremont's spy."

"Piggins? The estate manager, you mean? I believe I surprised him in the gallery after breakfast. A rather curious looking individual and unfortunately named, I think. Stooped shouldered and round of face. His nose even turns up in a most awkwardly familiar manner. It rather invites comparison to the animal, does it not?"

"That is very bad of you," she said, casting East a sideways glance. "He cannot help how he has grown into his name. I have no liking for the man, but it is his disposition I find offensive."

Eastlyn drew his legs toward him tailor fashion. "You are

right, of course, though I have often observed that appearance is the thing by which we are first judged."

"I do not disagree, but we would be poor sorts of creatures if we made no further inquiries into the qualities that distinguish a person's character."

In spite of his own experience, Eastlyn thought, it was exactly what he had done to Sophie. Was she telling him that she knew that, or speaking only in the most general terms? "When I was at Hambrick," Eastlyn said quietly, "they called me Butter-rump." Beside him, he felt Sophie's surprise as a palpable thing. This time when she turned her eyes in his direction, she kept them there. East continued to face front and stare out over the glassy pond, a slight, self-mocking smile lifting the corners of his mouth. "I was considerably . . . um, round, shall we say, in my first year at Hambrick. Butter-rump was not such a bad moniker as these things go. I did have a fondness for butter rum cakes, so it was appropriate on that count as well. In retrospect, it was clever of the Bishops to actually nail the thing so cleanly, though I suspect it was more accidental than well considered."

Sophie recalled what he'd told her about all his fights at Hambrick and understood now that he had given her partial truths at best. She swung her legs more slowly in the water as she considered how often he must have struck out against the pointed teasing of the other boys. What was it he had said about the Society? *A way to organize cruelty*? That was the gist of it, if not the exact phrasing.

Eastlyn rested his elbows on his knees and lightly tapped his steepled fingers together. "You must not make too much of it, Sophie. Your sympathy would be misplaced. I gave as good as I got, usually much better. I fought when I heard the name and sometimes when I only thought I did. And I was selfish as well. I regularly received treats from my mother that I didn't share with anyone. I stayed in my room and ate every crumb and then flattened the face of the next boy that called me Butter-rump."

"It is difficult to know who delivered the sweeter come-uppance."

He glanced at her, his look letting her know what he thought of her humor. "You can give me more sympathy than that," he said dryly.

"I am sorry." Sophie untied her bonnet and set it aside in the grass. She leaned back, bracing herself on her arms. "What about Lord Northam and the others? How did they become your friends?"

"It was West's doing, actually. Being a bastard he had his own battles to fight and something to prove as well. Because of my reputation for fighting, he challenged me one day, right in the upstairs corridor of Danfield House, and hadn't the good sense to back down. There was quite a tussle in the hall, and it brought the other boys running. Northam and Southerton were the only ones foolish enough to throw them-selves into the fray. We all fought then, rolling on the floor as one, trading blows at such close range the damage was not so great that we required more than a score of stitches be-tween us. West had a black eye, I think. North managed to protect his nose this time, though he had a badly staved thumb. South nursed a lump at the back of his head for sev-eral days."

"You?"

"A cut lip and a bruise on my chin. After we left the infir-mary I invited them to my room for cakes."

Sophie laughed, delighted. "Did you really?"

He nodded. "I was certain we'd be put out of school for the fight, so it only seemed fitting that I shared my last good meal with them. Becoming fast friends was surprisingly simple after that."

"So none of you were expelled?"

"No, though after the caning from the headmaster we all came to wish that it had been otherwise. North's grandfather attended Hambrick, so there was virtually no possibility of him being removed. South's parents had influence of a political nature. My mother opened her purse strings yet again on my behalf, and Marchman they kept on as an example of sorts, proof that a bastard was no better than he ought to be. West's situation at Hambrick was more difficult after that, not less, and there was no objection from his father. His grace barely acknowledged his existence."

"Then he needed you."

East said nothing for a moment. "It was more the other way," he said quietly. "We might have simply flailed around like so many fish out of water if not for West. I always think he would have survived in any circumstances, while we required more in the way of purpose."

"Sworn enemies of the Society of Bishops?"

"Precisely."

Sophie lifted her face to the sun and let it bathe her complexion. She closed her eyes and raised her feet so that just the tips of her toes were above the water. "After so many years as their opponents," she said lightly, "it must have been a disappointment to surrender that calling."

"Why do you assume we have put it behind us?" Eastlyn asked.

She roused herself enough to open one eye and regard him with patent skepticism. "You are no longer schoolboys."

"True. But there is still a Society of Bishops."

"At Hambrick."

"It merely begins there."

She looked at him with both eyes wide open now. "What are you saying?"

"Only that it exists outside of the school's cobbled courtyard." He shrugged as if it were of no import. "I thought you might have known that, Sophie. At one time Tremont was their archbishop."

Chapter Seven

"Tremont?" Sophie asked. "In the Society? Are you certain?"

"Quite." Eastlyn plucked a blade of grass and rolled it lightly between his fingers. "It is not an impossible thing to discover if one knows where to look." And the colonel, Eastlyn learned long ago, had resources to look anywhere he liked. It was not entirely surprising that Tremont was a member of the Society, but the fact that he had risen to the highest rank within the Bishops was certainly of import.

"I did not know he went to Hambrick. My father was at Harrow. I suppose I always thought Tremont attended there, too." Sophie reached over and took the blade of grass from between Eastlyn's hands just as he meant to make a whistle out of it. She tossed it into the water. "I require your full attention," she said in quelling accents.

Eastlyn very nearly saluted her, so definite was her order. He squashed the impulse when he saw how completely in earnest she was. This intelligence that Tremont was a member of the Bishops had struck a chord with her, and Eastlyn wanted to know more about that. He regarded her, waiting.

"What does it mean to be archbishop?" Sophie asked.

"He is their appointed leader. It is not a position necessar-

ily given to one of the oldest boys. Barlough was the archbishop for most of the years I was at Hambrick." He saw
Sophie stiffen. "Do you know him?"

"Barlough. Yes, I am acquainted with his lordship."

He waited to see if she would explain the nature of this
acquaintance, but she offered nothing further. "Once elected,"
he went on, "the archbishop stays at the head of the Society
until he leaves school. A new boy is then elected from
among the Society members. The exiting archbishop will
enjoy certain privileges for the remainder of his life because
he once held that position. It is one much to be desired
among the members."

"What sort of privileges?"

"Well, when he goes to university there will almost certainly be students there who were Bishops at Hambrick.
They will help him achieve honors and distinguish himself
to the dons. Afterward there will be assistance with entree
into the same society the rest of us occupy, assuming such
assistance is required. A good marriage can be helpfully
arranged, for instance, or gaming debts made to disappear.
Political influence is part and parcel of the arrangement.
That is but a short list of the kind of things the Bishops will
do for one of their own, and most especially for a former
archbishop."

Sophie raised her feet out of the water and drew up her
legs until her knees were close to her chest. She clasped her
arms around them, hugging them to her. She felt cold in a
way that could not be explained by the lowering sun or the
light breeze that rippled the lake water and made the grass
bow in successive waves. "These things," she asked, not
looking at Eastlyn now. "Are they done in secret?"

"I suppose that depends on the nature of what is being
done," he said. "At Hambrick much of the Society's business
is conducted in secret, but then they usually acted in a way
that brought attention to themselves. I do not think I knew
every member of the Bishops while I was at Hambrick, but
by the time I left I had ferreted most of them out. The Bishops

have been around almost as long as there has been a Hambrick Hall, Sophie, but they are still only boys there. It is after they leave that their influence can be more widely felt. The older members shepherd the young ones so that discretion is the rule, not the exception, and while they are known to each other, their existence beyond their membership is not commonly understood."

East found it was not so easy to determine the bent of Sophie's thoughts. That she was troubled was clear. What the source of it might be was not there for him to grasp. "It is curious that it never came to your attention that Tremont attended Hambrick."

"I don't know why you think that," Sophie said. "You have cousins, I collect. Can you tell me where they went to school?"

"My cousins are all female," he said. "But I take your point. Do you know where Dunsmore attended?"

"He did not leave Nashwicke. That is where Tremont had his living. He was the vicar there and had a comfortable arrangement under the patronage of Lord Glen Eden. Harold was tutored with his lordship's son for a time, I believe; then the task was taken up by his mother and father."

"You have never mentioned Tremont's wife before."

"She died some six years past, not long after Harold married. She was very different from her husband and her son, and I had great affection for her, though it was not often that our paths crossed. She was kept very busy with the duties of her station as the wife of a clergyman." Sophie blew upward as a strand of hair was twisted free of its mooring pins and fell across her forehead. When the light breeze lifted it a second time the curling end came to rest at the bridge of her nose. Her eyes crossed.

Chuckling, Eastlyn leaned over and brushed back the curl himself, though he was not the least offended by its waywardness as Sophie seemed to be. Her hair was like liquid beneath his fingertips, as smooth and as thick as its wild honey color suggested to him. His smile faded. He wished that she might have kept her eyes comically crossed rather than look at him as she did now, with that mixture of uncertainty and near-panic. Eastlyn let his hand fall away while Sophie quickly refastened her hair with the pins. "Are you afraid of me?" he asked.

"No." She wondered if she had given herself away by telling him the truth, and she waited with a breath trapped in her throat for his reply.

"It seems sometimes as if you are."

Sophie said nothing, but she finished drawing that breath, then let it out slowly. It was just as well that he was suspicious of her reply. She was uncomfortable with the notion that the person she was afraid of was herself and had not meant for him to discover it.

Eastlyn studied her expression a moment longer. It was fixed now, in that mask of perfect serenity she used to hide herself away in plain sight. Sophie's public face was very much a private one, he thought. It was as maddening to him as it was intriguing.

Sophie pressed her chin to her knees for a moment, thoughtful again. "What is it that you have come to discuss with my cousin? And, pray, do not merely say again that it is a matter of politics as if I could not understand. It is patronizing."

"You are right," he said easily enough. "My sister has said the same. Also my mother. My female cousins—all four of them. Even North's bride has taken me to task. I do not mean to give offense."

"I know. It is the stupefying arrogance of your gender." She smiled politely. "But I do not mean to give offense."

Eastlyn had a mind to check himself for wounds. Rather than give her opportunity to sling another arrow at him, he set the parameters by which he could answer her question. "I should like to have your word, Sophie, that what I mean to tell you is not to be shared. If Tremont reveals it to you, you may act on it in any manner you wish, but if I am your only source it must remain between us. Do you understand?"

"Yes."

He nodded once. "It is not generally known that the East India Company is looking to make a settlement—"

"In Singapore," she said.

"At the risk of patronizing you again, how did you know?"

"It is simple, really. Tremont often practices the speeches he means to give. He is always looking for the right inflection to affect or the pause that will enhance the gravity of his words. You have heard him speak. Can you not imagine how those stentorian tones carry past the library doors? I suspect most of the servants at Tremont Park have heard snippets of his discourse in the act of carrying out their duties. I mention this most especially lest you come to think I have shared your information with them."

Shaking his head, Eastlyn stretched his legs out and lowered himself back on his elbows. "Bloody hell," he said softly. "Bloody, bloody hell."

"If you are thinking the secret is compromised, you could not be more wrong. The servants have little interest in what happens half a world away, and it is of as little import to their families. If they attend to what Tremont says, it is only with the intention of mocking him later. He is not widely admired by anyone belowstairs." She added quickly, "Not that it keeps them from performing their duties in an exemplary fashion."

"Their loyalty is to you. I understand."

"Their loyalty is to Tremont Park. That is considerably different. The Park has been home to many of them for a lifetime. They would not do anything to compromise their positions here." Sophie leaned back as Eastlyn had, her posture mirroring his. "China could prove as important to the Crown as India," Sophie said thoughtfully.

"The potential is certainly there."

"The Company would perhaps want some assurances they would be protected."

East glanced at her. "You also listen at the library door?"

"Some things," she said wryly, "I can conclude on my own."

"Forgive me. Go on."

"The military might be required. That would understand-ably make the Parliament more cautious, what with so many good British soldiers already committed to India and our in-terests in Africa. We are only recently released from fighting Napoleon on the Continent, and it cannot yet be half a dozen years since we were also fighting the Americans. It makes me wonder if there is perhaps not some sentiment of opposi-tion to this settlement plan."

"And if there is?"

"Then perhaps Tremont's opinion has become a matter of some importance. I know he is not without influence. In light of what you have told me about the Bishops, it may be he is taken more seriously than I credited." Sophie turned on her side toward Eastlyn. A blade of grass tickled her cheek as she laid her head on her extended arm. "On which side of the fence are you hoping he will fall? That is why you are here, is it not? To garner his support for your cause?"

"It is not precisely my cause. My opinion in matters of this kind rarely is of import, though I will tell you I am not entirely opposed to the settlement. In any event, I am charged with communicating the wishes of those who would see this thing accomplished."

"But you have reservations."

"They are of no account."

"Still," she said, "I should like to hear them."

He sighed. It seemed she could not be dissuaded. Eastlyn had found it far simpler to turn Tremont from this course. "My reservations are actually quite similar to your cousin's. The Company's settlement would indeed be a boon for the Crown. It would open up trade and broaden our sphere of in-fluence. Each of us would be improved by the other."

Sophie greeted this last with skepticism. "That is most definitely *not* Tremont's thinking. He resists the idea that other cultures might have something to teach us. Rather, he takes the opposing view, that our arrival in any part of the

world must be warmly greeted and that only the most ignorant of people would not embrace our manners and mores."

"And our God?" Eastlyn asked.

"Certainly. Tremont has a missionary's zeal."

"It was odd that he never mentioned that. I thought he
would announce his support for the settlement because of
the opportunity it presents for converting the natives to
Christianity."

Sophie did not comment on this, though she found it curious herself. One of Tremont's favorite discourses concerned how one might best persuade a heathen people to
adopt his God. "You have not yet explained your own reservation."

"You are relentless."

She smiled. "That is the pot calling the kettle black."

He could not fault her for stating what was so obviously
true. "It is the opium trade," he said. "I fear that we will
force it upon them with even greater ambition than we are
doing now because it is a profitable venture for so many.
There are few in opposition to it and even fewer who will say
so publicly. To my mind I cannot think of a more reprehensi-
ble way to subjugate the will of a people. Once it begins I
imagine the Crown will be reluctant to monitor itself with
any real zeal. It cannot help but come to a bad end."

A small vertical crease appeared between Sophie's eyebrows, and the tiny gold shards in her eyes darkened as she
considered what Eastlyn had just revealed to her. "And you
say that my cousin shares this same reservation?"

"He does not know my own thoughts on the matter, but
yes, he has stated that the opium trade makes him reluctant
to lend the settlement his full support. He is also concerned
how he might raise his objections. It would be an unpopular
reason for not supporting the settlement."

"What would be a popular one?"

"Politics," East said flatly. "Opposing it simply because
the Prince Regent has let it be known he is in favor of it.

Liverpool has also lent it support. There are always those seeking to pull out the rug from under the minister. If they can remain standing themselves, all the better. If they trip over him, perhaps he will cushion their fall." He also turned on his side and propped himself on an elbow. "It is the way favor is curried, Sophie. If the opposition can gather enough support for their thinking, then certain favors can be asked for to win over their assent."

East saw that Sophie was not pleased by his answer but that she accepted it. Perhaps she had imagined that matters of government were influenced by high-mindedness. He could think of many times when that was the case and half as many again when it was not. "Your cousin's opposition is predicated on the opium trade, however, and appears to be principled. To the extent that his opinion can be changed, he will require concessions from the Tories."

"And you are their emissary?"

"After a fashion."

"Harold told me you are attached to the Foreign Office in some way. I suppose it was in aid of providing me with yet another reason why I should marry you. He did not use these words precisely, but I gathered from him that you enjoy a considerable sphere of influence. Is that right?"

"I would not say so, no."

"Because you are modest?"

He grinned. "Hardly."

But he was, she thought. He could be arrogant in manner and tone, yet it always seemed in support of some purpose. It did not exist as an abiding part of his character. About the qualities that were intrinsic to who he was, he was largely quiet and unassuming. Amusement simply deflected inquiry into his nature. Sophie did not return his grin, but that did not mean she was unaffected by it.

Lying here in the grass, her arm tucked under her head, Sophie was visited by the sensation of being abed in her own room and the comfort of counting the stars framed in her

window. She regarded Eastlyn with a like intensity and heard
her father's voice coming to her as if from a great distance.

"What do you see from there?" he asked her.

"All of heaven."

"And what do you see from here?"

"The same, Papa."

"Then heaven is everywhere."

Looking at Eastlyn, Sophie was more certain than ever
that her father had been right. She was unaware of her eyes
growing perceptively brighter or of a light flush coloring her
complexion. She did not know that her mouth was slightly
parted now or that her breath had hitched. The strands of
hair that fluttered against her forehead and temple went unnoticed. She was aware only of the distance that separated
her from the man at her side. It seemed at once too far to
cross, then again not far enough.

Sophie leaned into Eastlyn and placed her lips lightly on
his. As kisses went it was a fleeting thing, almost without
passion, yet it was warm and soft and erotic, not for what it
gave but for what it held back.

Eastlyn reached for her, but Sophie rolled away and scrambled to her feet, grabbing her bonnet as she rose. She whis-
\led for Apollo; Tempest also came at her beckoning. Behind
her, she heard Eastlyn grumble at what he considered his
mount's defection. "Do not follow me," she told him, glancing over her shoulder as she began to lead Apollo away.

He started to speak and then held himself quiet when he
saw that she was not only serious, but that she was also
pleading. He nodded shortly and took up Tempest's reins. He
mounted without inquiring if she needed a leg up and swung
around in the direction opposite of hers.

From the uppermost turret of the manor there was a flash
of light at the window. Eastlyn studied the small rectangle of
glass a moment, but nothing occurred again to catch his eye.
The setting sun was winking from behind a cloud. It was
probably only that, he thought. Just a reflection.

* * *

Sophie announced herself at Tremont's room while he was having dinner. She noticed that he was having the same meal she and Eastlyn had shared not above an hour earlier. Apparently his appetite was not diminished by his malaise. For her part, Sophie had found sitting with Eastlyn in the vast dining room to be awkward at best. She could not look at him without recalling her impulsive kiss, and she could find no means of putting it behind her. She remained composed throughout the interminable courses because she must, but Sophie believed it could not have escaped Eastlyn's attention that she had eaten very little.

"Your lordship is no longer feeling ill?" Sophie asked, eyeing the array of covered dishes set before Tremont.

"I am feeling tolerable." He spoke around a mouthful of boiled potatoes. "What business do you have here, Sophia?" Using the point of his knife to gesture at her, Tremont indicated that she should sit in the chair to the left of the fireplace. "Do not hover so," he said when she did not move quickly enough to suit him. "It is disconcerting."

Sophie sat and immediately felt her disadvantage, which was, of course, Tremont's intention. "I came to inquire when you will conclude your business with Lord Eastlyn?"

Both of Tremont's dark brows lifted. "That is an impudent question."

"Yes, my lord."

Tremont unerringly speared a thin slice of roast beef while his eyes remained narrowed on Sophie's gravely set features. Her calm countenance struck him anew as wholly unnatural and provided further proof that she had been raised in a godless house. "You are already tired of entertaining our guest?" he asked.

"He is not my guest."

"You are splitting hairs, my dear. He is here at my invitation, and some of the burden of making him welcome must necessarily fall on your shoulders."

Sophie kept her gaze steady on Tremont, afraid that looking away would give him evidence of her uncertainty. "I understand that you have told his lordship that you oppose a settlement in Singapore."

"Is this what young people talk about when left to their own devices? It is hardly something that concerns you. You would do well to confine yourself to matters that do." Tremont expected that to effectively put a period to Sophie's discourse. He was visibly annoyed when she continued.

"I further learned that your objection is predicated on the fact that it will increase the opium trade. You can understand my confusion, then, knowing that you have a rather large interest in the success of that trade. I know you have invested heavily in the merchant ship *Aragon* and that her captain is a known trader in opium."

Tremont set his fork and knife on the table. "You have taken rather a lot upon yourself, Sophia. I believe your facts are somewhat confused."

"There is no confusion, my lord. I have overheard you making the arrangements myself."

"You dare!"

Sophie saw that her cousin kept his seat by great force of will. It hardly mattered because she felt herself shrinking in place anyway. She was on less firm ground once she had begun to lie, and admitting that she had been party to the arrangements was a complete fabrication. Her source of this information had given it unwittingly but was no less deserving of protection because of it.

Sophie had already determined that she must bear the consequences herself. "It is a transaction filled with risks," she said quietly. "As I am certain your lordship is aware. If it fails, we will be plunged so deeply in debt that we may never satisfactorily recover. You have hinged what remains of the family fortunes on an enterprise so fraught with danger that it confounds good sense."

Tremont's complexion turned ruddy as Sophie made her

last pronouncement. "You speak to me of good sense when you have little enough of it yourself. It is not against the law to trade in opium."

"It is," she said. "In China."

"That is of no consequence to us. They would deny free trade with tariffs so high that no profit can be made by our merchants. The sale of opium merely balances the accounts."

Tremont's ability to justify his position no longer alarmed Sophie. "Have you considered what will befall us if *Aragon* fails to make port or sell her cargo?"

"I am admitting to no such arrangement, but if I were, I would point out that you have to look no farther than yourself to account for it. You were given a great opportunity to assist your family and firmly refused it. Indeed, it seemed to me the opportunity was heaven sent, so unexpected and timely was it. It makes little difference that I have since learned that Providence's angel was in fact Eastlyn's mistress. She had in mind some sort of revenge, I collect."

Tremont could not be certain, but he thought Sophia flinched. He definitely saw it in her eyes. "We were handed a spiteful mistress's poor trick on a platter and could not make use of it. That is no one's failure but your own. Whatever has been done, has been done since you made your adamant refusal to have Eastlyn as your husband. That you come here and suggest I am engaged in any enterprise that might bring ruin to this family shows a particular hypocrisy, Sophia, that is wholly unattractive." He picked up his fork, jabbed hard at several golden medallions of squash, and thrust them into his mouth. "You may leave," he said, gesturing toward the door when she didn't move.

"There is only one reason I can imagine that you have insisted you are opposed to the opium trade," Sophie said. "And that is to promote yourself as a man of high morals who rests his judgment on matters of principle. I am given to understand that by pretending to take a strong position in this matter, it is possible for you to negotiate certain concessions from the minister."

Tremont pushed the table away. It was a more decisive movement than simply sliding back in his chair. Silver covers rattled in their dishes, and a serving spoon clattered to the floor. He finally had the response from Sophie that he was in want of: she ducked her head and shoulder in anticipation of a blow. What Tremont did was pull her out of her seat and bring her to stand squarely in front of him. "Have no doubt that I should strike you," he said tightly. "Your father left you undisciplined and wild, and if I were in need of further proof of what you try to conceal from others, you obliged to provide it this afternoon. Aaah, I see you know very well to what I am referring. You were seen lying with the marquess at the lake, more indecently attired than you were yesterday when you greeted him. At least on that occasion you were fully clothed. Today, I understand, you removed several articles."

Sophie did not defend herself. She was careful not to provoke Tremont further by staring up at him. She kept her face and eyes averted and all but held her breath until he was finished.

"You do not deny it, Sophia." Tremont gave her a small shake. "You kissed him also. Piggins was particular about that. You kissed the marquess. It was not something done to you." He took note of her flush but misunderstood its cause. Tremont could not know that Sophie was less embarrassed by the kiss than she was by allowing herself to be so simply caught at it. "At least you have the grace to be ashamed," he said. "That is something."

Sophie did not correct his misapprehension. She deserved censure from Tremont because she had forgotten her own warnings to Eastlyn. As for the kiss, he could scarcely say worse things to her than she had already said to herself.

"You will attend me in the chapel, Sophia. I believe that it is fitting that you pray with me."

She sagged a little in his hold just then, hating it that she should have to depend upon his strength to keep her upright. There was nothing to be lost by speaking now. Tremont had named his punishment, and she would be obliged to accept it on her own or be forced to do so. "You think you can coerce Eastlyn into making a second proposal," she said, "by with-holding your sanction of the Singapore settlement. It won't work, my lord, because I intend to tell him the truth about your own dealings with the *Aragon*. You will not be able to ask any boon of the minister's office. You will be exposed as a man of no principle at all."

Sophie lost her footing as she was pushed backward into her chair. Her hip caught the wooden arm before she grabbed it to right herself. "I would sooner be his mistress than have him for my husband," she said.

"How fortunate for you that he has one of those, then. A man may have a wife and a mistress, but not two of either." He bent low over Sophie's chair, bracing his palms on the curved arms. "You have taken rather too much upon your-self, Sophia, and your judgments of me are suspect. You have not mentioned once how your own father used the drug and would have killed you rather than let you interfere with his source of it. Do you think the marquess knows about that? Have a care what secrets you think to tell, for you may find your own are not so secure as you believe."

Sophie closed her eyes as Tremont's hot breath bathed her face and did not open them again until she felt him draw away. "It is because of my father that I must do something," she said quietly. The words were the right ones, she knew, but there was little fight left in her. She sat very still, waiting.

Tremont returned to his chair and sat heavily, ignoring Sophie for several long minutes while he served himself from the warm plates. "Wait for me in the chapel, Sophia," he said at last.

It was a dismissal, and this time Sophie chose to obey. She managed to keep her legs from folding under her as she left the room. There would be time enough for bended knees later.

* * *

Sophie was alone in the chapel when Eastlyn came upon her. He stood in the narthex by the marble font, watching her pray at the altar rail. Her slim back was ramrod straight, and her head was bowed. A square of linen covered the crown of her splendid hair, and she wore a tightly fitted, serviceable black gown better suited to Pilgrims or mourners. He could not see her face or judge her profile, but he suspected that he would find her features fixed in severe contemplation. Was she asking forgiveness? he wondered. Or praying for the fulfillment of something much desired? Eastlyn thought it was likely that if Sophie's prayers were answered, he might very well be struck down where he stood. As a precaution, he quietly moved into the nave and sat in a pew near the front. God would have to take careful aim, he thought with some irreverence, if He were not to catch Sophie as well.

East estimated that more than ten minutes had gone by without Sophie shifting from her position. Occasionally she swayed in place, leading him to believe she would rise, but she never made any real attempt to do so. He could not imagine that she had so many sins to confess. It occurred to him that she had heard him enter and was waiting for him to leave before she took her own. To make it easier for her, Eastlyn stood and stepped into the aisle. Candles at the altar flickered and drew his attention. He paused, glancing at the sweep of light across the polished walnut rail and then the floor. His eyes were caught by several small, smoothly rounded stones near the hem of Sophie's gown. They were clearly out of place on the granite floor of the chapel, but for the trick of the light and the contrast of their milky coloring to Sophie's severely black attire, East knew he would not have seen them at all.

He counted six at first, then spied another just peeping out from under a fold in her gown. Curious now, he approached the altar rather than turn away from it. He saw more stones scattered around her kneeling form, and his suspicions about the nature of her penance grew stronger. East placed the fingertips of one hand lightly on her shoulder.

"Come away, Sophie. You can have done nothing so grievous that you must needs do this to yourself."

"Go away."

Eastlyn had to strain to hear her words. She had not spoken them above a whisper. "Sophie. Please." He leaned forward a fraction so he might see her profile. Her lips moved around the words of a silent prayer, but nothing she said was meant for him. Without removing his hand from her shoulder, East hunkered down beside Sophie, careful not to drop his own knees on the pebble-strewn floor. He could see her face more clearly now, and the wash of candlelight outlined every one of the tears she had shed. The dark fan of her lashes was damp, and the sweep of them made violet shadows beneath her eyes. "Come," he said, more firmly this time. "Enough."

Sophie shook her head and repeated her soft plea for him to leave.

"Not without you."

"I cannot rise."

Eastlyn let his hand fall and slipped his fingers under the stiff material of Sophie's gown. He scooped out better than a dozen small stones. They were everywhere under her, he realized, and there could be little protection afforded her by the dress. "I will carry you if I have to," he said.

"No!" She turned to him then. "You must go before my cousin returns for me."

East frowned. "Returns for you?" he asked softly. "Do you mean he accompanied you here?"

Sophie turned her face away again and continued her prayers.

It went against Eastlyn's better judgment to leave Sophie as she was, but he remembered that she was privy to things he did not know, and if known, then things he did not understand. He stood slowly, letting the milky pebbles clatter to the floor. The sound of them falling, he noticed, made Sophie start. He saw her face contort in pain as the movement caused the stones to dig into her tender skin in places they had not before. He tried again. "Let me take you from here."

Sophie had no chance to refuse him a third time because approaching footsteps cut off her reply. She glanced quickly at Eastlyn, her eyes pleading, and saw that he had also heard and was already moving away. Sophie faced the altar again, wiped the tears from her face, and forced composure into her features. It was difficult to draw a breath as she waited for the inevitable confrontation between Eastlyn and Tremont. They could not fail to pass each other in the narthex. She wondered at the sacrilege of offering up a score of selfish prayers that would keep it from happening.

Tremont's footfalls echoed loudly in the stillness of the chapel. He walked briskly to the altar rail and stood beside Sophie. "It has been two hours," he said. "I told you I would come in just that time." He had also observed her at odd moments to assure himself that she was obedient of his instructions. He would have allowed her to remain in the chapel much longer if she had been less tractable. She expected his attention, he knew, and that was acceptable to him. That she depended upon him to make his observations also kept her compliant.

"I cannot rise," Sophie said. Except where the stones dug into her knees she could feel almost nothing. She wanted to turn around and see for herself that Eastlyn was gone from the chapel. He could not be, of course, unless he had been spirited away by Divine Intervention. "I require your help."

"How those words must stick in your throat," Tremont said. He extended his large hand and waited for Sophia to take it. Her hesitation in doing so galled him, but he did not withdraw.

Sophie placed her palm in his and tried to pull herself up. "I cannot," she whispered, hating her weakness, the pleading in her voice. The stones made new impressions in her flesh as Sophie sank to her knees again, and this time she could not help but whimper at this fresh pain.

Tremont's features showed no trace of sympathy. He bent and placed an arm under each of Sophie's and pulled her to her feet. She could not stand without his support and would have collapsed to the floor if not for the arm he hooked tightly about her waist. His strength was hardly tested when he hefted her against his side and carried her, shoes dragging, to the first pew. He set her down and allowed her to gingerly stretch her cramped muscles. An array of pebbles was embedded in the fabric of her gown. He leaned forward and plucked one out and examined it in his open palm.

"It is like a pearl," he said. "Should you like it better, Sophia, if you were to make your repentance on a bed of pearls?"

Needles of sensation pricked her calves and the soles of her feet. She pointed her toes, flexed her ankles, and began to remove the stones clinging to her gown. She laid them on the bench beside her, casting them before the swine, she thought, though they were nothing at all like pearls.

"You are very quiet," Tremont said. "It becomes you." When he deemed he had given her sufficient time to recover, he pointed to the stones still littering the floor. "You will gather those as well."

Nodding, Sophie came to her feet carefully. She used the arm of the pew for support until she was certain she was steady enough to stand, then walk. It took her several minutes to collect the stones which she in turn gave to Tremont. He slipped them into a leather pouch along with the ones on the bench and pulled the rawhide string closed.

"Take my arm," he said, holding out his elbow to her. "You are like a foal with your wobbly gait. Perhaps you will want a lie-in tomorrow. I will make your excuses to Eastlyn. You may be sure of it."

"Yes," Sophie said softly. "That is what I will do. Thank you."

Praying, it seemed to Tremont, had served to quiet his cousin's combative spirit this time. He marveled at the change in her, the submission, and was satisfied by what he observed. He would insist that she apply herself to prayer more often, for it appeared to him that her soul had at last been touched.

From his hiding place beneath the pew where Sophie had been seated and had protected him with the spread of her skirts, Eastlyn listened to the sound of the footsteps recede. When the sanctuary was quiet again, he rolled out from under the bench and sat for a time. When he finally rose, at first it was only as far as his knees. Head bowed, Eastlyn prayed, and found he could live with what was in his heart.

Sophie dismissed her maid before she was finished with her bath. Putney left reluctantly and only after Sophie was forced to have a harsh word with her. The servants all knew about her punishment in the chapel, Sophie was certain of it. She imagined it was how Eastlyn had found her, though she doubted she would find one of them willing to admit it. Whoever had informed the marquess of her whereabouts had done so with the best of intentions. They were helpless to assist her when Tremont meted out his discipline, but she understood why one of them would put so much faith in Eastlyn.

He had the look of a man who might accomplish anything.

Sophie did not permit herself to dwell on either the marquess or the humiliation she had known in his presence. To put her mind elsewhere, she eased herself out of the water and drew a towel around her middle. Stepping over the lip of the tub carefully, Sophie found her balance. Water dripped on the floor and pooled around her feet while she stood waiting for the ache in her knees to pass.

Putney had had the foresight to place a spindle-back chair close to the tub, and now Sophie sat on the hard seat. She rubbed her hair with a second towel until it was merely damp, not dripping, then gently massaged her knees before she stood again. Her nightshift and robe were hanging on the inside door of her armoire, and Sophie chose only her shift. She was for bed straightaway this evening, desiring only to lie there in the darkness and lick her wounds like any injured animal.

Sophie poked the fire several times, making it give up heat and light enough to keep her warm until she fell asleep. The covers were already drawn back for her, and she pulled them around her shoulders as she slid onto her side, facing the window as was her habit. Tonight there were no stars framed by the opening in her drapes, and even the moon had disappeared behind a thick bank of clouds. It was just as well, she thought. She doubted she would have found solace in the ritual this evening, or that she would again. Far better to put it behind her and accept what was. She was alone and she was afraid and following the drift of stars in the night sky was cold comfort indeed.

She slept without dreams.

Eastlyn lighted the stub of a candle at Sophie's bedside. Neither the small sounds he made in this activity nor the flame itself roused her to wakefulness. There was no longer any evidence that she had wept in earnest earlier this night; her features were softened to a Madonna's countenance in repose. Loath to disturb her, yet knowing there was nothing else to be done, East laid his hand gently on the slope of Sophie's shoulder. She was not covered there by either the comforter or the neckline of her gown, and the touch of his palm was against her warm bare skin. She moved then, not to avoid the cup of his hand, but rather to burrow herself deeper and try to nudge it with her chin. Eastlyn was reminded of a newborn kitten blindly snuffling for the nourishment and ease of the mother cat's teat.

"You will not find that here," he murmured, letting his fingertips drift to her neck. "Come, Sophie. You must wake."

She came to awareness of a sudden, and every instinct told her she must scream. The hand quickly clamped over her mouth prevented it. Sophie stared up at Eastlyn, recognizing him immediately but unable to make sense of his presence.

"I mean you no harm." He eased himself onto the edge of the bed while he kept his hand in place over her mouth. "There is no reason you should scream. Indeed, it would have the opposite effect that you would wish. I cannot think of a faster means by which we might land ourselves in the soup."

Sophie blinked widely at him. How was it, she wondered, that she knew the words he was speaking yet did not understand the language? It was utter nonsense that she heard, like the gibberish one might use to entertain an infant.

"Sophie?" Eastlyn was uncertain that he was understood, but he chose to lift his hand a fraction above her mouth anyway. All she did was release the breath she had been holding. That caused East to breathe more easily as well. "Will you sit up?"

Did he mean to have a conversation? The stare she returned in his direction was not so much blank as it was disbelieving. Sophie was slow in responding to his query as a result.

"Shall I assist you?" he asked.

She shook her head. Pressing the heels of her feet into the mattress, Sophie pushed herself upright and leaned against the bedhead. She withdrew the pillow at her back and hugged it to herself. It ill-afforded protection of her person, but as a weapon it might serve. Sophie could envision the need to clobber the marquess with it.

Eastlyn regarded her, taking particular note of the mutinous set of her mouth. "Are you quite awake?"

She pinched him.

"Ow!" Of necessity his exclamation of pain was subdued. He rubbed his forearm where she had managed to get more of him between her fingers than his frock coat. "What was that in aid of?"

"To see if I am dreaming. Apparently I am not."

"I thought the point was to pinch oneself."

"That would hurt, don't you think?"

He cocked an eyebrow at her, but his eyes were amused. She was indeed awake. "Point taken."

Sophie's butter-wouldn't-melt expression remained unchanged. "What are you doing here? You must have very little regard for me that you can so blithely ignore every warning I've given you."

"And you must have very little faith in me if you think I will be caught out."

"But my cousin—"

"In the arms of Morpheus, compliments of Bacchus. Which is to say he is sleeping off the effects of an entire bottle of the grape."

"One does not have to have attended Hambrick, you know, to be familiar with the Greeks."

"Forgive me. You were regarding me with a complete lack of comprehension."

"It has nothing to do with what you are saying," she replied dryly, now quite pointed in her regard. "There is still Mr. Piggins. He is—"

"Also deeply asleep. It is the medicine he takes at bedtime, I believe, which does the trick."

Sophie realized Eastlyn had learned of the habits of Tremont and Piggins in very little time. She suspected he had considerable assistance from belowstairs, beginning with intelligence gleaned from his own valet. "Very well," she said. "I am satisfied we are not to be disturbed. I remain in confusion about the necessity of your sojourn to my room." She glanced at the clock on the mantelpiece and saw that it was gone midnight. "There can be no good reason for it."

"Then I hope you will listen to this poor one." Eastlyn turned slightly on the bed, drawing one knee up so that he might face Sophie properly. "I wish to remove you from Tremont Park," he said. He held up a hand to stop her interruption, and her lips remained parted around the protest she did not utter. "I have no doubt that Tremont would quite properly refuse to allow it, so I have elected not to put the question to him, or even apprise him of my intent. I do not mean to take you to Gretna, Sophie. You may put that from your mind. I would not force a marriage upon you, and I do not seek to compromise you; rather I mean to take you to a place where you might be treated with more affection and goodwill than is your lot here or at Bowden Street."

That he had paused and was in anticipation of a reply made no difference now. Short of pinching him again, Sophie could only stare.

"Sophie? Have you nothing to say?"

She hugged the pillow more tightly, resting her chin on the plump end of it. "You are in earnest, are you not?"

"Completely."

"And you are considered to be an intelligent man."

"It has been remarked so, yes."

"In full command of your faculties."

"There are questions in that regard."

Sophie did not return his ironic grin. "I appreciate that what you saw in the chapel this evening has unsettled you, but I—"

"What I observed in the chapel caused me to be considerably more than unsettled, Sophie. It was a punishment thinly guised as penance. Nothing less. From Tremont himself I heard how long he left you there. After two hours on those pebbles it was a bloody miracle you could walk at all." He searched her face, looking for some sign that she was in agreement. She remained expressionless, not precisely calm, he thought, but numb. "I collect it is not the first time he has abused you in such a manner, for you seemed to understand too well all that was required of you."

When she made no reply, Eastlyn tugged at the comforter so that her arms were laid bare to him. His eyes immediately found the livid bruise above her right elbow. "It was not Dunsmore this time who did that to you." He swore softly. "That it should happen just beneath my nose, it is not to be borne."

"You must not blame yourself."

"I don't."

"I am responsible." Sophie lightly massaged her elbow where Tremont's fingers had left their purplish marks. Because of her downcast eyes, she missed the surprise in Eastlyn's own. "I ignored my own warning, you see. At the lake. I should not have—"

"Kissed me?"

"Kissed you," she finished. "It showed a regrettable lapse of judgment."

So they *had* been seen. That flicker of light at the turret window had not been the winking sun after all. "It was a kiss," Eastlyn said with a certain amount of impatience. "We were not caught *flagrante delicto.*" He witnessed her blank expression. "That means—"

"I *know* what it means," she said testily.

Eastlyn was rather more amused than offended by her tone. He counted it as a good thing that she was finally riled. "You are in no circumstances responsible for Tremont's manner of retribution. I think he takes perverse delight in subjecting you to his will. It is as if he wants more than mere obedience from you. He demands your agreement as well. Your sanction. You must needs communicate that he is in the right of it before he is satisfied. I do not pretend to understand it; it is only what I have very narrowly observed."

Sophie could find no fault with that observation. Eastlyn had clearly defined this aspect of Tremont's character. "What would you have me do?" she asked. "I cannot resist him and spend *three* hours on my knees. I am not nearly as brave as I want to be. There is an end, and I think I have come upon it."

Eastlyn did not believe it, even though he knew she believed it herself. "I would have you leave," he said. "Tonight. My sister Cara is currently in residence with her husband and children at their country house near Chipping Campden. I have written a letter for you to present to her explaining your need for sanctuary and secrecy. She will have many questions, for that is her nature, but none that you need answer against your will. She may apply to me for the particulars when I arrive."

"I don't understand," Sophie said. "You will not accompany me to your own sister's house?"

"Not immediately. I will meet you there directly. I must remain behind to explain to Tremont what I have done. Do not worry that I will tell him where you are. It is only my intention to assure him that you are safe and that I am culpable, not you."

"He will call you out."

"That is most unlikely."

Sophie was not certain she shared Eastlyn's confidence. She had learned that Tremont's actions were not entirely predictable. She was quiet a moment, thinking. "I have never once entertained the notion of leaving," she said at last.

"It is not proof that you are a coward, Sophie, but rather that you have too much courage. You continued to make a stand when reason dictated you should surrender or flee."

"I think you are giving me too much credit."

Eastlyn did not share her opinion. "You also thought you had no place to go."

"But I don't." Sophie met Eastlyn's eyes and took measure of his resolve. Could hers be any less than his own? "Or rather I didn't."

He released a breath slowly as her meaning was made clear. "Then you accept."

She hesitated, then nodded slowly. "Yes," she said. "Yes, I do."

Chapter Eight

The alacrity with which everything was arranged let Sophie know how much Eastlyn had relied on her agreement. She wondered if he would have used other means to persuade her had she not fallen in so easily with his plans, or if he could have accepted her refusal. The question had no bearing now, for she had no intention of testing him.

Eastlyn's valet appeared to pack Sophie's clothes. Sampson would brook no interference from her. He managed the thing with a speed and efficiency that made Sophie wonder if he had been put to this specific service before. It encouraged her to regard Eastlyn's offer with a slightly more jaundiced eye.

She was given time to dress but no choice in her attire. Sampson had emptied her armoire of everything but a single gown and its accessories. What was left was a plain muslin dress with a pale yellow ribbon trimming the hem. The valet could not have known it was one of her favorites, she thought, yet she could not acquit him of being as prescient as his master. When she presented herself outside her dressing room, she was summarily handed her navy blue redingote, matching bonnet, and fox muff.

Eastlyn was already gone from her bedchamber and so

was one of her trunks. Sampson hefted the other to his shoulder and sagged very little under its weight. Sophie was left to take a valise and close the door behind them.

The carriage was prepared and waiting outside the stable, but before Sophie would climb aboard she insisted on speaking to the head groom. The items meant for the tenants that were stored in the tack room were very much on her mind. She could not dismiss the thought that she was abandoning the families at the Park again. It did not assuage her guilt that they would not see it in that same light, for they had never put any faith in her to change their lot.

Eastlyn came upon her in animated conversation with the groom. "You must go now," he said. "It is wise for you to have the best of all possible beginnings. Rain is coming and it will slow your journey."

She knew he was right. One could smell the scent of the coming downpour on the back of the wind. "A moment, please."

He stepped aside but not so far that he could not hear her orders to the groom. She was most specific about what was to be done and how it might be completed without discovery. In spite of the urgency he was feeling to have her under way, East could feel a smile tugging at his lips. He could appreciate the courage this small act of kindness showed even if she could not.

Sophie turned to Eastlyn too late to glimpse his smile and finished fastening the tabs on her redingote. "I am ready, my lord."

"Very well." He made a sweeping gesture with his arm to indicate she should precede him, then assisted her entry into the carriage. He leaned inside to make certain she was situated. "Sampson will ride with my driver, and he will give you whatever assistance you require."

"He can have no liking for the position of lady's maid."

"Do not concern yourself on that count, though you will deal better with him if you do not refer to him as such."

She smiled, albeit a shade uncertainly.

"You are in good hands, Sophie. Indeed, I could not entrust you to better unless the Compass Club was here."

It was indeed a high compliment to his valet and driver, Sophie thought. "You are certain you will not join me now?"

"Quite." He removed a letter from inside his coat and handed it to her. "I did not seal it," he said. "That is so you may read it if you have concerns about its content. It will serve as an introduction to my sister and explain that I will arrive shortly."

Sophie sat forward in her seat so that she was very near the open door. "I think it would be better if you told my cousin that you are completely innocent here. You must say that you were abed when I left."

"And how do I explain that you took not only my carriage but absconded with my valet and driver as well?" He tapped the point of her nose with his fingertip. "It is better my way, Sophie."

She sighed. "If I had more time to think, I would arrive at a better plan."

He let his hand fall away. "Of that I have no doubt." Eastlyn leaned in and kissed her on the mouth before she could sit back. "If I had more time," he said, "I would make a better job of this farewell."

Sophie was entertaining no doubts on that score, and she was not proof against the roguish grin he gave her as he shut the door. Somewhat bemused, she felt him push the step into place and then heard his palm smartly slap the side of the carriage. She stared at him through the window until darkness enveloped his lone figure.

Sophie did not read the letter Eastlyn gave her. Instead, she placed it carefully in the pocket lining of her fox muff and was particular that she kept it close. The rain that Eastlyn predicted settled on them soon after they passed Loveridge. It slowed their journey considerably, causing Sampson to apologize several times for the poor accommodations of their first night's lodging. Sophie did not find as much fault as he, but supposed that as Sampson was used to traveling with the marquess he had come to have a higher standard. Her own family's finances being what they were, Sophie rarely elected to make a night's stay between Tremont Park and London. No one else denied themselves that comfort, but Sophie considered it an excess when the trip could be made in a day if necessity demanded it.

The second night was spent in a more commodious hostelry. The innkeeper and his wife were pleasantly accommodating and had no complaint about bringing food and drink to Sophie's room, even at the late hour of her arrival. Many of the guests were already abed, and those remaining in the taproom were not excessively boisterous.

Sophie ate roast lamb, boiled potatoes, and fresh greens for her supper, but she was considerably less hungry than the generous portions of her meal required. Rain had come again, and she watched the golden etchings it made on the windowpane compliments of the fire's reflection. When she at last set her knife and fork down it was pouring in earnest.

Storms had never frightened her. Nannies and governesses had pulled her away from the windows where she watched the lightning strikes, their own fears making them insist that she be mindful of the glass. She had been fortunate never to absorb their dread, finding places to hide from them instead of the storm.

Sophie stood at the window and pressed her forehead to the pane. She cupped her hands around her eyes to further her view of the yard. The first flash that followed nearly blinded her with its brilliance. She blinked rapidly in reaction and saw the trees across the muddy lane seem to march toward the inn.

A rider approached, his head bent low against the driving rain, the layered shoulder capes of his Carrick coat fluttering in the wind. Lightning marked his position first on the road, then the yard, and finally as he dismounted in front of the inn. Sophie knew him instantly by his measured stride to the door, and her heart turned over queerly in her breast. She stepped back from the window with an alacrity that would have been applauded by every nanny and governess she had known.

There was nothing to do now but wait.

Eastlyn was greeted with some suspicion by the innkeeper and his wife when he identified himself as one Mr. Corbett, recently come from Trenton Mews on his way to Chipping Campden. To explain his arrival without a single valise, East fabricated an unfortunate robbery along the road ten miles back. It was a story that was easily believed and led to a lengthy exchange with the innkeeper's wife about what the world was coming to. The innkeeper, though, was of a more practical nature, and to allay his most pointed concern, Eastlyn produced money enough from inside his cuffed boot to pay for his bed.

He was shown to a room abovestairs at the back of the inn and reminded how fortunate he was to only have to share his quarters with two others, both gentlemen themselves. Eastlyn thanked the innkeeper and began removing his sodden Carrick coat in the corridor. Being of no mind to become wet as Eastlyn shook off the coat, the innkeeper quickly excused himself. East waited until the man's heavy tread could be heard at the bottom of the stairs, then he counted off the doors in the poorly lighted hall until he found the one he wanted.

He rapped twice, lightly, and waited to see what would happen. He had not permitted himself to predict what might follow when he'd first spied Sophie at the window of the inn. There was no way of knowing whether she saw him or not, or whether seeing him was to be preferred over the other. She might ignore his bid for entry altogether or open the door in expectation of finding Sampson or the innkeeper's wife, and close it again when she viewed him on the threshold.

"Who is there?" Sophie asked from the other side of the closed door.

Eastlyn grinned. He had not anticipated that she would make inquiries. "Mr. Corbett," he said, not much above a whisper. "Late of Trenton Mews and on his way to Chipping Campden." He waited. For a time there was only the low rumble of voices from belowstairs and the steady tattoo of dripping water; then the handle turned, and the door opened a fraction. He stared at the single wide eye that Sophie put to the crack. It was more brown than gold in this poor light; but it was wonderfully familiar to him, and his heart eased to know he had not mistaken her figure at the window.

"Mr. Corbett?"

He shrugged. "It is as fine a name as any. Are you going to let me in, Sophie?"

"I should not."

"No, you shouldn't."

She did, though. She meant to be as straightforward as he. Opening the door far enough to permit him to slip inside, Sophie let her eyes make a sweeping assessment of his condition, and then she announced the obvious. "You are soaked to the marrow, my lord."

It was not so bad as that. Where his clothes were wet it was because he'd held his coat too close. He allowed her to take the woolen Carrick from him and place it over the back of a chair near the fire to dry. He removed his hat and shook it out. From Sophie's appraising glance he decided his person was not much improved. He raked back his damp hair with his fingers and looked around the room. "It is a pleasant enough accommodation?" he asked her.

Sophie took the hat from his hand and placed it on the seat of the chair. "I find it so. It is much improved from last evening."

"Oh? At Brideswort?"

She shook her head. "We did not make it as far as that. The carriage could not negotiate the muddy roads with due speed, and we found lodging in Coldwell. We stopped this

evening before the weather turned again. It was a wise decision. Mr. Sampson and your driver are taking very good care
of me." Sophie did not mean for her comment to invite his
glance; but it did, and she felt herself warm under his regard.
"We were not in expectation of meeting you on the road. I
suppose we only have to look to the skies for the reason.
Have you announced your presence to Sampson?" Sophie
could not miss East's slender, mocking smile. His faintly
hooded glance could not conceal either his wry amusement
or his deepening interest. "No, you could not have seen your
valet, could you?" she said. "He would not have allowed you
to leave the room in your present attire and smelling of
sheep."

"I think you are standing too close to my wet woolen
coat," he said. "You must come here if you mean to accurately judge me."

Her chin came up slightly as she crossed the room to
stand in front of him.

East's smile faded, and the cast of his features became
solemn. "It was not my intention to dare you, Sophie. You
have nothing to prove to me."

"I know," she said softly. "This is not against my will. It
has been very much on my mind."

"And mine."

She nodded faintly, searching his face. He did not look
away, and his eyes darkened until they were like black mirrors. "I am not entirely certain what must be done now," she
said. "Perhaps your wet clothes?"

It was the fact that she was not being disingenuous that
raised Eastlyn's low, throaty laugh. He tugged on the belt of
her robe and pulled her toward him until her raised mouth
was a moment from his. "In good time, Sophie. We will deal
with my clothes in good time."

It was not clear who closed the distance between them.
There was no importance in knowing the thing when there
was no blame to be attached to it. Sophie's arms lifted to
East's neck, and she wound them there, unmindful of the

damp curling ends of his hair. The sleeves of her robe fell back to her elbows, and she could feel the contrasting textures of his linen stock and the collar of his frock coat. She stood on tiptoe, pressing herself more fully against him, and could feel the stamp of his brass buttons through the thin material of her robe and nightshirt. The slant of his mouth changed, and she felt his hands wander from the small of her back to cup her bottom. She was pulled hard against him, and the impression of those buttons was forgotten by the outline of his erection between her thighs.

Eastlyn eased his hold when he felt Sophie slightly stiffening in his arms. His kiss gentled. He touched his lips to the corner of her mouth and then lifted his head just enough to let her draw air. He noticed she made a point of studying his neckcloth, not his face.

"You will think me missish," she said. She was aware of a peculiar shortness of breath and a racing tempo to her heart.

"Hardly missish."

"Unworldly, then."

"You *are* unworldly."

Sophie judged wisely that she should not continue in this vein. She doubted that Eastlyn, in spite of his rogue's reputation, was in the habit of taking virgins to his bed. He might very well have cause to reconsider his actions if reminded too often of her innocence. She determined that she would do better not to raise the subject again, especially when she felt a decided lack of innocence in her heart.

Her fingers pressed against the nape of his neck, forcing his head lower as she raised her own. She kissed one corner of his mouth, then laid her lips lightly at his jaw. She touched the sensitive point just below his ear and let her tongue tease the tip of his lobe. His throaty growl vibrated against her palms, and she was once again pulled tight in his embrace.

His arms around her, the shelter of his body was at once secure and dangerous. Sophie had not the capacity for unraveling that conflict. His mouth on hers was an assault on her senses that left her unsteady on her toes and requiring him for support. He kissed her closed eyes and grazed her temples with his lips. His breath was hot on her ear and against her brow, and he murmured words that she could not properly hear but seemed to understand anyway.

He kissed her throat and the underside of her jaw, and Sophie heard the small catch of a breath that she did not identify at first as her own. He came back to her mouth, and she opened it under his. His tongue swept the underside of her lip before plunging deeply. It made a pleasant rasp against her own tongue as she pressed it into play. The suck of his mouth sapped what was left of her ability to stand, or maybe it was only that he chose that moment to lift her off her feet and carry her to the bed.

Sophie was surprised when he set her on the edge and dropped to his knees in front of her. She had conceived a few notions of how things might proceed, and none of them accounted for this. She tried not to allow her uncertainty to show but knew she had not been successful when he smiled at her in that knowing manner of his.

Without looking away, Eastlyn lifted one of Sophie's feet and placed it on his thigh. He unlaced the soft slipper with an economy of motion that was most deliberate in nature. He watched her gaze fall to where his fingers worked and was satisfied when he saw the pale pink wash of color rise from her throat to her cheeks. Reaching under her nightgown, he found the top of her stocking at a point just above her knees and untied the ribbon that kept it there. He rolled it carefully all the way to her toes, letting the ribbon wound between his fingers slide silkily against her skin.

Sophie was breathing less steadily by the time Eastlyn raised her other foot. Knowing what he would do did nothing to settle her tripping heartbeat. Rather the anticipation of his searching fingertips was more than Sophie thought she should be made to bear. She almost raised her shift herself and told him to have done with it, yet she kept her silence because there was another part of her that could never want this thing to be hurried.

Sophie was learning something about herself that Eastlyn seemed to already know.

She glanced at him when he finished removing the second stocking. His eyes were more black than chestnut-colored now, and there was a faint flaring to his nostrils as he breathed deeply. He did not release her foot but began massaging it instead, first her instep, then the arch. The sky blue ribbons he had collected from above her knees were still wound about his fingers. The ends of them trailed along his thigh as his fingers gently kneaded the ball of her foot.

Sophie could not help herself. When Eastlyn did the same with her other foot she leaned back on her elbows and closed her eyes. She did not even mind when she heard his low, satisfied chuckle. It surpassed reason, she thought, that she should come to care not at all that he was laughing at her.

Eastlyn released Sophie's foot. It dangled a few inches above the floor, and she made no effort to draw it up. He slipped his hands under her shift again and found the backs of her knees. He pulled her so that her bottom rested close to the edge of the mattress and her knees were splayed by the breadth of his chest and shoulders. He felt every part of his body respond to the musky woman's scent of her.

The indecency of her position pushed Sophie upright as little else could have done. She made an attempt to close her thighs but was blocked by Eastlyn's body and his light grip on the backs of her knees. She relaxed when he merely held her still, and she noted a measure of indecision on his taut features. He grinned at her suddenly, though it seemed as if the line of that quick smile was a trifle pained. His brows lifted a notch, and the glint in his eyes mocked himself.

His voice was softly husky. "All in good time, Sophie."

It seemed to her that she should make a reply, but the proper response eluded her. She was vaguely disappointed when his palms slid along the length of her calves and reappeared from under the hem of her shift. He shook out the ribbons from between his fingers and reached for her robe's sash. The loose knot was undone easily, and he parted the material so his hands could rest at her waist. The lawn fabric of her nightgown was no barrier at all to the heat of his palms.

"Take off your robe."

Sophie shrugged, and the silky material simply slid off her shoulders. The neckline of her gown was cut wide and low, and one of the straps dropped past the curve of her collarbone. She started to lift it, but Eastlyn shook his head and she left it there. Her hand hovered a moment, caught between the act of righting her gown and doing nothing at all. When she lowered it, she let her fingertips graze the side of his face and her thumb touch the corner of his mouth.

He turned his lips into her hand and kissed the heart of her palm. Sophie felt it as a sudden heaviness in her breasts and a flash of heat between her parted thighs. She bit her lip to quell the sound that rose in her throat.

Eastlyn let his hands fall to either side of Sophie's waist as he stood. The small lighted candle she had placed at her bedside extinguished itself, and the room had only the glow of the coals in the fireplace to save them from darkness. "Do you require help turning down the covers?" he asked.

Glad for the shadows that lingered over East's face and her own, Sophie shook her head. She eased herself up the bed until she could turn back the blankets and then slipped under them.

"Do not become too comfortable there," he said. "I sleep on that side."

She could claim no such ownership of a particular side as she had never shared her bed before. She began to move over and was stopped by his hand on her shoulder.

"Stay where you are. I am not for sleep just yet."

"Oh." Sophie watched him begin to remove his frock coat. "I thought perhaps you had changed your mind."

East paused his fingering of the brass buttons. "No," he said. "Have you?"

"No." Though she was having some regrets now about the candle being gutted.

Eastlyn did not know if he should be as relieved as he was by her answer. He was not unmindful of using her to get what he wanted, yet he could not dismiss the notion that he was being used as well. In spite of the fact that he was the one experienced here, he continued to think that Sophie had acquired the upper hand.

He removed his frock coat and loosened his stock. Aware that she had not averted her gaze, Eastlyn said, "Tell me about that other naked man."

Sophie blinked, and her eyes lifted from where they had been leveled at the waistband of his trousers back to his face. "Naked man?"

"The one you swore to me you have seen before." He pulled the tails of his shirt free, then sat on the edge of the bed and raised one leg to remove a boot. "Or was it all a lie?"

"It was no lie. His name was Timothy Darrow, and he was a groom at Tremont Park."

"He is no longer there?"

She shook her head. "He was dismissed."

"Because you saw him naked."

"No. Because he was never good with the horses. No one save him and Katie Masters ever knew I saw him stripped of his breeches."

Eastlyn was beginning to get an inkling of what had happened. His erection was pressing painfully hard against his own breeches, and yet he did not think he had ever been so diverted as he was now. He let his boot thump to the floor which had the effect of bringing Sophie's attention back to his face. He served her an arch grin and began removing the other boot and stocking. "And who was Katie?" he asked.

"One of the maids in the scullery." Sophie jerked a bit as

he dropped the second boot and was a shade breathless as she explained, "I spied them *flagrante delicto.*"

Eastlyn's chuckle resided deep in his throat and gave sound to the perfectly roguish smile that still lifted the corners of his mouth. "I see. Then you are a great deal more worldly than I had thought."

"You are having fun with me."

"Yes, I am." East leaned over her and placed his hands on either side of her shoulders. "And I intend to have a great deal more." He lowered his head and fit his mouth to hers. Her lips parted immediately, and it was as if there had been no pause between what he had done to her before and what he was doing to her now. Her arms came around his shoulders, and she bore the weight of him against her breasts. He pushed at the blankets that separated them and felt her move to accommodate the same urgency to be closer.

Sophie whimpered softly as East's lips tugged at the curve of her neck. His tongue flicked her skin. She felt his mouth on her collarbone and his teeth pulling at the edge of her shift. He caught the tip of her breast in his mouth through the fabric and sucked. Her response was immediate. She arched under him as a ribbon of heat uncurled along the length of her spine, making her breasts swell and ache and turning her insides to liquid. The dampening of her shift around her nipple, the slight abrading quality of the material, made her feel even the most delicate touch of his tongue.

When he raised his head she shifted restlessly at the loss and was comforted to the point of madness when he applied the same singular skill to her other breast.

She was extraordinarily responsive in his arms, to his touch, and Eastlyn found a great measure of satisfaction in wresting those small cries from her throat and feeling the tension in her just beneath the surface of her skin. So pliant was she, so receptive to whatever was done to her, that he could scarce temper his own desire to feel her release.

Sophie drew a ragged breath as Eastlyn rolled away. He lay beside her with his forearm across his brow, and she noted that his own breathing was not much steadier. There was no part of her that did not ache with need. She remembered Timothy Darrow tumbling Katie Masters in the stable and how little she had thought there was to recommend that activity. Another opinion in want of revision, she decided.

"You are smiling," Eastlyn said. He was propped on one elbow now, regarding her mouth with particular interest.

"Hmmm?" She glanced at him. His eyes so darkly intent on the shadowed curve of her mouth made her stomach curl deliciously. "Yes. I suppose I am." When she was wrong—as she was about Tim and Katie—she was *very* wrong. Spectacularly so.

"Take off your shift, Sophie."

That order, summarily given and brooking no argument, collapsed her smile and quickened her heartbeat. Sophie reached for the hem of her nightgown, already rucked above her knees, and pulled it up to the tops of her thighs. At that point her fingers caught the edge of the patchwork quilt, and she drew it over her as she raised her shift. She managed to lift it as high as her breasts before she felt resistance.

"You must think you're very clever."

Sophie looked down at the fistful of quilt in Eastlyn's possession. "I am." She quickly pulled the shift over her head as she scooted under the blanket. He pulled it away from her, of course, but she was already turned on her stomach and unable to entirely restrain her laughter.

"You would not be so amused," he said dryly, "if you knew what a lovely target your bottom presents."

That brought Sophie's head up and effectively silenced her. She held her breath as he lifted his hand . . . and brought it down with infinite gentleness on the curve of her buttocks. He caressed the taut flesh until he reached the back of her thigh and then let his fingers trail up again so they came to rest at the small of her back.

"You're trembling." East could feel the tremor just beneath her skin. He let his hand wander the length of her spine, massaging her back just below her shoulder blades.

He watched her head bow as she relaxed until it finally came to rest on the pillow again. He felt her gaze on him as his fingers slipped into her hair. She made no protest when he re moved the anchoring pins, and when he actually sifted through the tumble of curls to touch her nape, she sighed.

Eastlyn sat up and removed his shirt and neckcloth, letting them fly over the edge of the bed to join Sophie's discarded shift on the floor.

"I only saw his bare arse," Sophie said as Eastlyn moved to unbutton his breeches. She offered this quickly in the manner of a confession most reluctantly given. "Timothy Darrow, I mean. It was only his arse."

"Bloody hell, Sophie. You do say the most singular things."

"Are you choking?"

East cleared his throat. "Quite possibly." He lifted a dark brow as his fingers returned to his breeches. "Unless you turn away you are going to see considerably more than my bare backside."

She sat up instead and pushed his hands out of the way. He watched her face as her fingers worked. The meager light from the fireplace could not explain the suffusion of warmth in her cheeks. He did not try to assist her until she had the drawstring of his drawers untied and her fingertips curled around the material at his waist. He rose up the few inches necessary to remove the last of his clothes. When he was done, Sophie pushed them out of the way and over the side, though her eyes never strayed from the proof of his arousal.

Eastlyn lay back and pulled Sophie with him. She fit herself neatly at his side with no urging from him, one leg raised against his thigh, an arm flung across his chest. Her lips were very near his shoulder, and he could feel her light breath on his skin. "You are very quiet of a sudden," he said.

"It's rather a lot to take in."

That gave him pause. "Is your meaning figurative or literal?"

"Both, I think."

East turned his face and found the top of her head with

his lips. He laid his smile in the sweet scent of her unbound hair. "You had better kiss me, then. You will find it more easily borne that way."

Without protest, Sophie allowed herself to be turned on her back. He found her mouth and kissed her deeply, and she gave herself up willingly to the pleasure of it. Her hands slid over his back, and she felt the bunching of muscles and the retraction of skin, sometimes in response to her touch, sometimes in anticipation of it. Exploring, she found two small divots at the base of his spine and a raised crescent scar on his shoulder. He shivered when her thumb tripped lightly down the length of his vertebrae, and the vibration of his body was felt by hers.

Sophie was aware of nothing so much as an ache of wanting. Her tender breasts felt heavy, the tips engorged to such sensitivity that even the lightest pressure hovered as close to pain as it did to pleasure. He seemed to know what she could bear and what she could not, and the trail of his hand went lower, caressing her hip and the curve of her thigh, then rising again to the flat of her abdomen. His fingers made a spiral around her navel and dipped low into the copse of dark honey hair on her mons. His knee insinuated itself between hers, and there was space enough now for him to slip his hand between her legs.

She gave a little start at this unexpected intimacy but did nothing to deny it. When he bid her open to him, she did, raising one knee slightly and lifting her hips at the first press of his fingers inside her. She pushed against the heel of his hand, and the movement gave her such intensity of pleasure that she immediately shied from it. Her grip on Eastlyn's shoulders tightened, and she drew a great breath of air which only seemed to lodge as a lump in her throat.

East's hand stilled, and he nudged her lips with his. "You are very quiet, Sophie. You don't have to be so quiet."

"I do," she whispered. "Else I shall scream."

He grinned because her beautiful distress was so clearly not from pain. Kissing her full on the mouth, his fingers moved again, and this time she tightened around him. She was warm and wet, so ready for him that he could have slipped a third finger inside her and she would have only welcomed the pressure of it.

He withdrew his hand instead, slipping it under her bottom as he moved between her thighs. The slightest urging of his fingers had her lifting for him. He reared back and pressed his entry.

Sophie let her hands fall from Eastlyn's shoulders and curl into the sheet instead. Her breath caught, and for a moment her body went rigid; then she found she was taking him, all of him, into her, and the size and length of him was not too much to bear. There was pain, not unexpected in its degree or duration, but not so much that she wanted him to leave her. She watched his face, the shadowed, tautly held features that were evidence of his effort not to hurt her. Where she gripped the sheet, her fingers slowly unfolded. She raised her hand to his cheek and caressed it with her knuckles. One caught the corner of his mouth. His lips parted on a soundless expulsion of air as she drew the knuckle across the lower curve.

"You are very quiet, Eastlyn," she said. "You do not have to be so quiet."

He wondered if she even realized that she had finally deigned to use his name. The intimacy of that seemed as substantial to him as the joining of their bodies. "I do," he said. "Else no one will hear you scream."

He pushed himself deeply into her then and heard the cry she could no longer restrain. Her body contracted around him: her arms, her knees, her thighs, and again where she held him in the most carnal embrace.

Sophie felt as if the beat of her heart was changing to match the rhythm demanded by East's body. Her hips rose and fell in a cadence that was unfamiliar to her but wholly natural. Her throat arched, and she felt his mouth on the curve of her neck, sipping her skin. He drew up again and thrust hard, pushing her back as he ground against her, and the ball of heat that was centered at their joining simply exploded.

Every muscle in her body that had been pulled taut was pulled tauter yet. She hovered on the edge of pleasure, seeking purchase, then gave in to it because no other possibility existed. She threw her head back and lifted her spine, and the scream she might have made was swallowed by his mouth hard on hers.

Eastlyn felt the same rush of pleasure a moment later, as if it were something that could be absorbed from her. He braced his arms, lifting, arching, his hips making a final thrust. Pinpricks of sensation skittered across skin that no longer seemed to fit him as it should, and he spilled his seed into her.

It was only then that Sophie felt the full import of what she had done. There was no sense in it, she thought, that she should be so aware of the consequences now when they had been in plain view at every juncture. She might have never opened the door, or upon opening it, she might have told him to leave. She could have remained at the fireplace when he entreated her to come closer or kicked him with her slipper rather than let him remove it. She could have said no each time she said yes.

Sophie let her breath out slowly and lay very still. Eastlyn's weight was not uncomfortable, and the steady thud of his heart gave her ease. He could have stayed joined to her much longer and she would have made no protest, yet when he left her to rise from the bed she did not protest that either.

She turned away as he poured water into the basin at the commode and washed himself. A cold gust of air swept the room when he opened the window to discharge the contents of the bowl. Sophie pulled the quilt up to her shoulder. She heard him pouring water a second time and then the soft approach of his footsteps as the floor creaked under him. The mattress depressed behind her.

"There will be some blood, Sophie," he said quietly. "And you will want to remove the—"

"Yes," she said, loath to let him finish. "I will."

East held the basin steady while she sat up. He noticed that her movements were awkward as she would not allow the quilt to fall below her breasts. Reaching over, he pulled the blanket free from where it tangled under her legs and effectively ended her tug-of-war. He made no comment, and she did not thank him.

"Will you turn aside?" she asked when he pushed the basin toward her.

"If you wish."

She said nothing, but simply waited.

East faced the fireplace. He heard her dip the flannel in the water and wring it out. He did not dwell on her ablutions after that. Leaning over the side of the bed, he picked up his drawers and put them on, cinching the drawstring at his hips. He gathered Sophie's nightshift and robe and laid them behind him on the bed, then took up the remainder of his discarded clothes and set them on the chair where his coat was drying. He stayed at the fireplace, adding tinder and coals to warm the room again, and waited for Sophie's approval to turn around.

He had not considered that she would leave the bed, but that was precisely what she did. Without an invitation to do so, East glanced over his shoulder at her first footfall. She had slipped into her shift, but not her robe, and was carrying the basin to the window. "Let me," he said.

Sophie did not look at him, but shook her head in firm refusal. She rested the bowl on the lip of the sill and pushed the window open. Rain spattered her arms as she tossed the contents into the yard. The wind pressed her shift against her breasts and billowed the fabric at her back. The chill that went through her went bone deep.

Eastlyn came up behind her and closed the window when she did not move away. He rested his hands on the curve of her shoulders. His chin nudged her hair. "I glimpsed you at this window upon my arrival. Did you know that?"

She shook her head. "I wasn't sure."

"It seemed that you were waiting for me, though I knew you couldn't be. We should not have met here at all. I should not be half this far, and you should be half as far again."

"It did seem unlikely," she said softly, closing her eyes.

"You believe me, then, when I say this end was not designed by me at the Park."

Sophie's smile was faint, a trifle plaintive. "I believe you."

His fingers tightened a fraction, and he drew Sophie back so that she rested against him. His arms slipped under hers and crossed beneath her breasts, cradling her. She laid her hands on his forearms and rubbed the back of her head against his shoulder. "I want you to marry me, Sophie."

The proposal was not unexpected, and she did not remove herself from his arms to refuse it. "No," she said. She tilted her head slightly so that he might look down and see the resolve in her eyes.

"Sophie."

She turned away. "No."

"Things are changed between us."

"Only if we allow them to be."

Eastlyn felt his patience being drawn taut. "You are unreasonable. How can you not see that you must marry me?"

Sophie made her wish known to be released now by tugging gently on East's folded arms. She sensed his hesitation in the brief tightening of his grasp; then he let his arms fall to his sides, and she was free. She stepped away from him and the window and turned again when she was out of his easy reach. "Must? Is that the ultimatum you had in mind when you came to my room tonight?"

"I told you, I did not plan this. I —"

"At Tremont Park," she said. "You did not set this plan at Tremont Park. It came to you here. When you saw me at the window, mayhap. Or when I opened the door to you." Her small laugh was without humor. "I cannot pretend that I was seduced, for I wanted to lie with you. I trusted you, you see, not to use it to force my hand. You made me that promise. Do you remember? When you invited me to leave Tremont

Park, you told me that your intention was not to force me
into marriage."

A muscle jumped in Eastlyn's lean jaw. "I also said I
would not compromise you."

"And you have not. I am only compromised if we are
found out."

"I should have let you scream."

She flushed a little at the harshness of his words and the
picture they presented in her mind's eye. She refused to look
away, however, and kept her gaze steady on his. "You are Mr.
Corbett here, are you not? Unknown to anyone except by
that name?"

"I used that identity so Tremont might not trace my path
to Chipping Campden."

"And Sampson announced me as Miss Barbara Hyde-
Jones expressly for that same purpose. You must see the convenience of it. You did not apply to Sampson for assistance
when you arrived, but came straightaway to this room. Much
as you might like to think otherwise, my lord, we are not yet
compromised."

Eastlyn fell silent a moment as he took note of the ache
beginning to make itself felt behind his eye. "Can the idea of
marriage to me really be so abhorrent?"

"It is marriage to anyone I find distasteful."

"Yet you accepted Mr. Heath."

Sophie wondered what she could tell him. "Mr. Heath did
not present the same temptation as you," she said at last.

"I cannot think how I am supposed to take your meaning."

"Any way you like." She hoped he would accept her words
in the most obvious way possible and flatter himself into
thinking she did not want to be forever beguiled by him. It
was not the manner in which she meant the words, but he did
not have to know that. His money was the temptation. Her
family would only let him live long enough to get her with
an heir. She would be a very rich widow, and he would be
dead. In the case of Mr. George Heath, she had judged him

of insufficient fortune to inspire such avarice, or at least she had hoped it was so. It was perhaps in every way for the best that Mr. Heath chose to make Miss Sayers his bride.

Eastlyn searched Sophie's face, but she had thrown up her guard, and he could not divine her thoughts. What he knew was that she did not yet trust him and that he could not accept her words at face value. "You say things that are the truth," he said, "and yet not the truth. It makes for peculiar conversation and certain misunderstanding."

"I will not marry you," she said. "That is plain, I believe."

"Indeed it is."

"Then we are settled."

Eastlyn thought that was the very last thing they were, but he did not disabuse her of the notion. Had North had such a time of it getting Elizabeth to agree to marriage? It seemed to East that once a lady was thoroughly compromised, even if it was not yet a nine-days' wonder, she should have the good sense to make a march on the altar.

There was one gambit left to him. "You have considered, have you not, that you might conceive a child by me?"

Sophie nodded and did not tell him how foolishly late she had been in arriving at that consequence. "Should it occur, you may depend that I will not hide the truth of it from you."

"That, at least, is gratifying."

She ignored the sardonic lift of his brow and his tone that was as dry as dust. "There are many places I can go where I am not known and live comfortably with my child. I believe it is done quite often. Clovelly, perhaps, in Devon might suit me very well, and you would not find the expense of a small cottage burdensome."

Eastlyn regarded Sophie for a long moment and spoke only when he knew he would not raise his voice. "You will remember this, Sophie: that as much as I am provoked by you, I have not once raised my hand or caused you to abase yourself by kneeling on a bed of stones."

Slapping her would have been less painful. Sophie almost reeled with the intensity of the quiet anger in his voice and his eyes. She watched him dress from where she stood, making no move to return to the bed or block his way. He did not speak again, not even upon leaving her, and when she heard the commotion belowstairs she knew he meant to quit the inn. To go to the window and throw it open was a temptation. She felt a light tremor in her legs and fingertips as she resisted the urge, and was only aware afterward that it was the slamming of the door beneath her that was its source.

She was alone again, still afraid, but perhaps not so much as she had been. Sophie returned to the bed and sat for a time, her mind empty of all thought. When she grew cold she lay back and found herself taking the side of the bed Eastlyn had claimed as his own. She breathed in the scent of him there, in the sheets, on the pillow. The heat of his body still lingered in the quilt.

Drawing it closely around her, Sophie finally surrendered to her need to cry, then to sleep.

Enough laughter erupted from one of the private theater boxes at Drury Lane to stop the lead actress from delivering her line. The loud prompt that was given to her from the wing brought silence from every quarter except that box. The audience's attention shifted from the stage to where the Marquess of Eastlyn was entertaining his friends.

"I know the line," Miss India Parr said without rancor. "What I cannot know is if I will be permitted to speak it." This had the effect of raising sympathetic chuckles among the largely male audience and finally wresting quiet from the Compass Club.

"Now you've done it, East. I believe she is speaking to us." North indicated the stage where Miss Parr was standing with her fists resting on the wide panniers of her gown and her elbows cocked sharply outward. Her painted lips were pursed in a perfect bow, and her darkly drawn eyebrows were arched so high they fairly disappeared into the fringed curls of her powdered wig. This exaggerated demonstration of impatience would have been more amusing if it had not been directed at them.

East turned and gave his attention to the actress. He made a good show of appearing much struck by this turn of events. He forced a carelessness into his voice that he had no feeling for. "Why, so she is. Odd, that. Doesn't she have a line?"

Sitting at East's side, it was Marchman who answered, *"You can't expect me to save you, Hortense."*

This prompt, offered as it was in dry, uninflected accents, lifted more chuckling from an appreciative audience. East saw that South was preparing to make amends for their unfortunate lapse of manners. It was Southerton's ribald aside that had put East into a paroxysm of laughter that had been as contagious as it was ill-advised and ill-timed. He did not blame them for being unaware that his laughter was strained or that it had gone on too long. He might apply, he thought, to the director of this Drury Lane production and see if there was a part at the ready for a fool.

He watched South stand and Northam grab him by the tails as if there was some fear he might pitch himself over the side of the box. East merely shook his head, a tad impatient now, and waited for South to speak the correct line to the actress.

"You cannot expect that I will always save you, Hortense."

On stage Miss Parr's eyes narrowed. "You have it exactly. Shall you go on or must we?"

"I must humbly beg your pardon," South said, inclining his head in an apologetic gesture to her, then the audience. "For myself and my friends. Pray, continue."

East remained with his friends for the remainder of the play, though he had little interest in it. Afterward he made the mistake of contemplating aloud what sort of retaliation Miss Parr was likely to make if they presented themselves at her crowded dressing room. "Polite slap, do you think? Or a blow?"

North saw where this would lead and decided that his recent marriage lent him certain insights into confrontations with the female sex. "Three shillings that it's open-handed."

East heard himself agree, but he imagined that in this same situation even the sainted Sophie would be moved to use her fist. After Marchman also agreed it would be a slap, South took the opposing view. It was then left to them to decide who would beard the lioness in her den and finally settle the wager.

North held up his hands palms out, eliminating himself from consideration. "I fear I cannot be the one. Elizabeth would hear of it before the night was over, and I am not up to explanations involving actresses. It is not the kind of thing that is generally well accepted."

Marchman snorted. "You have only to say that you were with us. She knows that any manner of things can happen."

"My wife is with my mother," North said. "I can appease one, but not both. It is the very devil of a fix when they join forces. Like Wellington and Blücher at Waterloo."

Eastlyn felt a tug of sympathy for his friend. His own situation was just as pitiable. "I'm afraid I must also refrain," he said with feigned lightness of feeling. "I'm in a damnable coil as it is. No sense in tightening the spring."

Marchman grinned wickedly. "You're referring, I take it, to your engagement."

"I am referring to my *non*-engagement, West."

"*Non*-sense. The announcement in the *Gazette* was pointed out to me by . . . well, by someone among my acquaintances who attends to such things. The wags have the story. There is betting at White's. There must be an engagement. Your mistress says it is so."

"My mistress—my former mistress—started that particular rumor." East actually felt his jaw tightening and the beginnings of a headache behind his left eye. "The only thing Mrs. Sawyer could have done to make it worse was to have named herself my fiancée."

God help him, East thought, he didn't know if that was true any longer.

Chapter Nine

"Oh, dear." Cara Trumbull caught her lip after this whispered utterance and looked down the table to see if she was overheard. Four pairs of eyes were turned expectantly in her direction. Two of those pairs she had some leverage over, and she glanced at their plates and saw they were near to being cleaned. "Go on, children. Mr. Barnard will be waiting for you in the schoolroom. You might astonish the man by appearing before the appointed hour."

Jon regarded his mother with patent disappointment and saw that she was quite unmoved by this ploy. His uncle had taken some pains to show him how pulling this particular face could be used to wrest sympathy from his mother. Jon decided he had not the way of it yet and more practice was in order. He took his sister's hand and helped her down from her chair. Julia did not seem at all put out by the prospect of attending Mr. Barnard in the schoolroom, which supported Jon's view that females were clearly not right in their upperworks. His father had begged him not to share this view with his mother if he wanted to see his ninth year out, so as Jon passed that worthy on the way to the door he merely winked.

Cara frowned and regarded her husband suspiciously. "What was that in aid of, Mr. Trumbull?"

"I couldn't say. Our son comes by peculiar notions from time to time."

Sophie sat quietly during the exchange that followed. Her hosts traded opinions as to whose side of the family was more burdened by eccentricities, and while Sophie did not keep a running tally, she thought the Whitneys might have a slight edge on the Trumbulls. It seemed clear, though, that whatever Jon's peculiar notions might be, he came by them naturally enough.

Not that Sophie saw such evidence before her now. Her experience with Cara and Benjamin Trumbull was quite the contrary. Eastlyn's sister and brother-in-law were possessed of sound judgment so that even when one was given to a flight of fancy, the other could be depended upon to indulge it only as long as it was practical.

A less gracious and accommodating couple would not have welcomed her into their home so readily. It was East's letter that had provided her entree, Sophie knew, and not her own character or circumstances. She did not know what he wrote to his sister, for she had never read the correspondence, nor had she asked Cara to share the content.

Sophie's stay had not yet numbered a score of days, but she acknowledged that the largest part of her discomfort vanished early on. She was taken in with such force of good will that she was made quite breathless by it. Cara Whitney Trumbull clearly loved her brother dearly, and it made no difference what manner of problem the scapegrace had encountered, she told Sophie, but that she would do whatever was required to assist him.

It was impossible not to like Eastlyn's sister, though it might have been better if it were otherwise. Sophie found herself content in the house at Chipping Campden in a way that she had never been on Bowden Street. Cara was not given to lying abed for days on end as Lady Dunsmore had been wont to do. She was often about town, quite happy to have Sophie in tow as she shopped for hats and ribbons. Neither did she seem to have any compunction about intro-

ducing Sophie as one Miss Barbara Hyde-Jones, a cousin
visiting from Stoke-on-Trent. The relation was on her dear
husband's side, she was fond of adding, and she confided to
Sophie the embellishment was necessary as her own family
was well known to the townsfolk.

Sophie evinced no objection to being Miss Hyde-Jones
but privately thought the deception unnecessary. Her cousins
would not look for her in the Cotswold Hills, if they even
roused themselves to look at all. She suspected that the sub-
terfuge was merely Cara's desire to share in her brother's intrigues. Mr. Trumbull indulged his wife's fancy because
Cara was so thoroughly delighted to lend her help, and her
happiness made such indulgences eminently practical.

Sophie noted some resemblance between Cara and her
younger brother, though it was largely confined to mannerisms and disposition. In looks they were not so similar, with
Cara being petite and pleasantly rounded and her coloring
being a good deal more fair than East's. She was possessed
of the same strong-willed nature, though, and was not easily
moved from a course once it was set. She was fair with her
children, doting on them in a fashion that was not given to
excess, even with the youngest of the three who was still in
the nursery.

Benjamin Trumbull was as evenly tempered as his wife.
A handsome, strapping man, he was content to let her have
the run of things as long as she did not forget that he was in
charge. It was that peculiar notion of his that Cara found
practical to indulge. From Sophie's perspective the arrangement seemed to work very well.

Sophie became aware of a lull in the volley of words
served from each end of the table. She looked up from her
plate to see that her hosts were both regarding her as if expecting that she should make a reply. The thing of it was, she
had no idea of the nature of the question they had put to her.
Sophie's eyes darted from one to the other, and when they
came to rest again on Cara's inquiring countenance, she nodded a trifle uncertainly.

"Very well," Cara said, accepting Sophie's response as an affirmation. "I shall read it to you." She picked up the neatly folded paper at the side of her plate, the same paper that had caused her surprised utterance earlier and moved her to excuse her children from the table. "It is very brief."

Benjamin Trumbull cleared his throat, causing his wife's attention to be diverted to him in a way that did not bode well. "Perhaps you will agree that I am not required here since I have already been apprised of the news."

"Yes," Cara said. "And it was very bad of you to say nothing and allow me to read it myself. The decent thing to do would have been to warn me. I might very well have choked, and then wouldn't you have had cause for regrets?"

"Indeed I would, dearest." He was already pushing his chair back from the table and folding his napkin. "I cannot think how I would manage without you managing me."

"A very pretty answer. You may go."

Benjamin rose and skirted the table to stand at his wife's side. He dutifully bent and kissed Cara's proffered cheek. As he passed Sophie on his way to the door, he winked.

"Peculiar man," Cara said affectionately, watching him go. "Our Jon is most definitely his father's son."

"I should count that as a very good thing," Sophie said. "Mr. Trumbull is much to be admired."

Cara smiled. "He is, isn't he?" Her gaze dropped to the paper in her hand. One corner of the *Gazette* was dipping alarming close to her coffee. She gave it a shake to snap it to attention and regarded Sophie again over the top. A more serious mien replaced her easy smile. "You were woolgathering earlier."

Sophie admitted it was true.

"There is something in this London paper that you will want to know," Cara said. "I asked if you would like me to read it to you. I think I should inquire again. Mayhap you will want to read it for yourself."

So that was the question that had been put to her. And whatever Cara had seen in the *Gazette* was of sufficient consequence that her husband had declined to broach the subject himself. Sophie was less certain than Cara that she would want to know the particulars. To that end, the manner in which the news was delivered was scarcely of any import. "Please," she said. "I should be obliged if you would read it to me."

Cara's dark blue eyes narrowed in their study until she was satisfied as to Sophie's sincerity. "As I said, it is very brief. *"The engagement of Lady S____ C____ to G____ W____, Marquess of E____, was made public yesterday evening at the home of Lord Barlough. The announcement was greeted with enthusiasm by those attending the debut vocal performance of soprano Miss Harriet Mathews. Miss Mathews chose a selection of arias, difficult in both their range and phrasing and . . .'* " Cara stopped and put the paper down. "The rest of it does not matter, though it appears Miss Mathews was judged to be a success. I trust you can complete the blanks." She stretched her hand toward Sophie, willing her to take it a moment. When she did, Cara squeezed her fingers gently. "It is a scandal sheet. Nothing more. You must not be overset by what is printed there."

Sophie nodded unconvincingly. She felt compelled to point out, "You announced yourself that you could well have choked on the news."

"Yes, but I am given to fits. I do not possess your singular composure."

"I'm afraid that at the moment I am not in possession of it either."

Cara squeezed Sophie's hand again. "You will find it, just see if you don't." She drew back and pointed to the offending column. "Gabriel may very well have cause to send his solicitor around to the *Gazette*. This is gossip of the worst sort, and one can't help but take exception to it." She glanced at Sophie again and saw the younger woman had paled alarmingly. "I did not mean that I would object to the engagement; never say you thought that was my intent. On the contrary, I would approve of such a match since I cannot help but believe it would be advantageous for both of you. I confess, however, that my hope for such a thing dwindles daily as Gabriel has yet to make his promised visit here."

Cara did not miss the faint quiver of Sophie's chin or the brightening of her eyes. Neither of these things were much improved by Sophie biting on her lower lip or blinking rapidly. Cara sighed. "I am making a muddle of it. You are feeling far worse than when I started, and I am deeply sorry for that, Lady Sophia. I wish I might apologize for my brother as well, but I have no notion why he is being so perfectly disagreeable. I am out of sorts with him, you know, and am of a mind to write to him directly and tell him so."

"Pray, do not apologize to me on any account." Sophie's determined smile was weakened by its watery nature. "I will never be able to repay your many kindnesses. My presence here is proof of the deep affection you bear your brother, and I would not see you even mildly annoyed with him. I am quite certain he is blameless."

"Gabriel is never blamed," Cara said wryly. "And he is always responsible." She saw Sophie's confusion and spoke to ease it. "Never mind. It is unimportant. You only need know that he is horribly indulged by my mother and me and that we are unlikely to change in our attitude, no matter how aggrieved we are made by him." Cara poked her finger at the paper. "This is not his doing, however, and I am depending on your good sense to know that."

"I do," Sophie assured her. Even in light of Eastlyn's insistence that she should marry him, Sophie was able to acquit him of this particular effort. "But how can you be so certain?"

"It is simple, really. A true announcement would not fail to give your names. That is done for the paper's protection. It improves circulation, I suspect, giving rise as it does to indecent speculation among the ton. No one approves of it publicly, of course, but privately this sort of gossip is quite warmly greeted." She scanned the particulars again. "The announcement is attributable to no one, which likely means it was merely the subject of discussion among the guests at this recital rather than a formal statement of intent. Further, my mother would be present at such an announcement, and I know from her correspondence that she has answered no invitations for a musicale. My brother does not care a whit for sopranos and has never counted himself as a friend of Lord Barlough, so it is unlikely that he was present at this recital. More to the point, there is no mention of any altercation or gloves being dropped, and I can assure you that had this engagement been discussed in any gathering save for Gabriel's family and closest friends, someone would have been called upon to make amends for it."

Sophie touched her fingers to her chin, afraid she was gaping at her hostess. She knew of at least one time Eastlyn had settled a dispute with pistols, had even called him a murderer for it; but it had taken place many years ago, and she did not really think of him in that way in spite of her harsh pronouncement to the contrary. "He told me he used to regularly thrash the other boys at Hambrick, but you cannot mean he would serve someone a facer in so public a setting."

Cara gave Sophie a sidelong glance, complete with one perfectly arched eyebrow. She looked so much like her brother in that moment that Sophie felt her insides twist curiously. "He has always been restrained with me," Sophie said. "Even when I have sorely abused his charity."

"Yes," Cara said. "That is very much like him also." Her face softened. "You are right, though. He would not serve someone a facer at a public recital. I am remembering the quickly riled boy he was and forgetting the man he has become. It is more likely that he would make a challenge to join him at that gentlemen's boxing salon that he frequents." Cara picked up the paper and turned it over so it would not give her further offense. "The fact remains he would not permit this rumor to gain support if he was in hearing of it. I hope you will forgive my blunt speaking, but this has Mrs. Sawyer's fine prints all over it."

Sophie frowned. She was so certain of Tremont's or

Harold's hand in the matter it didn't occur that the responsibility might lie elsewhere. "Mrs. Sawyer?" she asked. The name meant nothing to her until she witnessed Cara's discomfort. "Oh. You are speaking of your brother's mistress."

"She is no longer his mistress," Cara said firmly. "And it gives me great pain to speak of her at all. I do not make my opinion known to Gabriel on matters of this nature—he is unmarried and does as many of his set do—but I have had reservations regarding his choice of this paramour. I have never met her, of course, so I am guilty of precisely the same speculation I despise in others. Gabriel is my brother, however, so what am I to do when I hear that she is like a cold not easily shaken?"

When Sophie's eyes brightened this time it was because she was amused, not alarmed. She discovered a measure of her appetite had returned, and she spread a dollop of strawberry jam on her toast as Cara continued.

"I can appreciate that she would not want to be cast aside, but to have the effrontery to think that Gabriel would marry her, that is completely objectionable. That is why she left him, you know, because he would not be brought around to marriage. Oh, I know such things are done on occasion, but they cause such heartache for the families and rarely turn out well for the parties involved. Gabriel would not do it. He would not let his heart become engaged to a woman so well known for her avarice."

"Perhaps he was unaware of her rapacious nature."

"Do you really think my brother is so lacking in intelligence that he could not see such a thing for himself?" She did not give Sophie opportunity to answer what was a strictly rhetorical question. "More likely he was amused by it. He is invariably amused by things the rest of us find distasteful. That is not to say he finds it tolerable, only diverting after a fashion. It is my opinion that he had it set very well in his mind what she was and was going to end their arrangement soon. If Mrs. Sawyer is as shrewd as she is purported to be, she would have sensed this and acted accordingly."

"You are not at all sympathetic toward her?" asked Sophie. "Her situation is unenviable."

"Her situation is of her own making, but it is perhaps a flaw in my character that I cannot be charitable."

No, Sophie thought, it was another measure of how much Cara loved her brother. She would write to Eastlyn herself, she decided, this very afternoon, and let him know he did not have to travel to his sister's home to acquit himself of wrong-doing. Unlike Cara, Sophie was not at all distressed when East had never arrived at Chipping Campden, but had allowed his letter to speak for him.

He had further acquitted himself by sending a timely message by courier that something had occurred requiring his attention in London. In this manner he hoped to put a period to his sister's worry. It did not, however, keep Cara from speculating on the nature of his London business, and she fretted for several days until her husband requested that she cease her musings, or at least make them silent ones. His interference was timely because Sophie had been on the verge of making a full confession for her part in provoking Eastlyn to go. She doubted that Cara would have been so charitable toward her if she knew the truth.

If Cara could understand that Mrs. Sawyer deeply desired marriage to her brother, how would she ever comprehend that Sophie did not?

The colonel rolled his wheelchair around so he no longer faced the fireplace. He tapped his spectacles until they rested low on his nose and treated Eastlyn to a long and level look over the gold rims. "You have nothing else for me?" he asked. "You have spent more months than I care to contemplate on this enterprise."

"Five," East said. "The opposition will not be moved."

The colonel shook his head. "Five months. As long as that? I wish you had not made it so clear."

"You knew." He glanced at the tall clock standing in the

corner of West's study. "You can probably make an accounting of the days and the hours."

"Very nearly." Blackwood was not smiling. "Is this because of Tremont?"

"Yes. He is gaining a considerable following. I had Helmsley's agreement to support the scheme; then he changed his mind. Said he was convinced that Tremont is in the right of things."

"What does Helmsley want?"

"A position in the Foreign Office. A clear path to becoming prime minister."

"The hell you say."

"I do say."

The colonel was silent. It seemed to him that Eastlyn had not been sleeping of late, and if it was true, it could not be entirely blamed on this assignment. Blackwood knew his work had been tireless and that he had been constrained by the need for secrecy, but it was the sort of thing that East usually thrived on. It challenged his thinking, his temper, his arguments, and his abilities. He would not give it up easily, and the colonel debated whether he should even ask. It could not hurt to change the subject. "You have talked to West?"

Eastlyn nodded. "He told me I could find you here."

"I was referring to the particulars about his father's death. Does he seem all of a piece to you?"

"Quite. I expect you will make your own assessment." Eastlyn saw the colonel's faint nod. "We were together at the club last evening. North was also there. And Southerton as well. I suppose it was our own version of a wake, save that there were no tributes made to the late Duke of Westphal. He shall remain unlamented, though I must say that West was more tolerant of his father's shortcomings than the rest of us. He has greater concerns about inheriting the title and property. It surpasses all understanding that the old duke would legitimize West's birth now."

Outside a cold, dreary November rain struck the windows. East turned in the direction of the sound, but there was little that could be seen of the street beyond. Darkness fell very early now, and the street lamps added only the most tenuous light, flickering wildly as though they might be extinguished at any moment.

It was a fitting sort of day to see the Duke of Westphal put to rest. The small gathering of mourners in West's London home were there because they were acquainted with Mr. Evan Marchman, not because they grieved for the passing of the man who had sired him. East's mother and father had come as had Southerton's parents. Even the Dowager Countess of Northam had been present for a time, amusing them by insisting that she was still out of sorts with West for breaking her beautiful son's nose twenty years earlier. No one could convince her her son's countenance was much improved for it.

A smile edged East's mouth. The memory was a good one.

The colonel noted the change in East and was encouraged. "That is something, at least. You are noticeably lacking in humor these days."

"I can rouse myself to it."

"For your friends, I suspect."

East did not deny it.

"Is it Lady Sophia?"

"I'm not sure of your meaning."

"I think that is not true," the colonel said bluntly. "But I will explain nonetheless. I am asking if Lady Sophia has been on your mind of late and if her presence there might explain your lack of humor as well as your lack of success with the Company's proposal."

Eastlyn said carefully, "It is better that we do not discuss Lady Sophia, Colonel. As for the proposal, I shall have to redouble my efforts."

Blackwood removed his spectacles and carefully folded the stems. It was all done in aid of giving himself time to think and form a reply. He might very well lose East if he pressed too hard, yet he might lose him if he did nothing at all. "I have always admired your discretion, East. Indeed, it is a quality that has made you a particular favorite of mine for assignments such as the one I gave you in June. I believe I would trust you with anything. I suppose it has never occurred to me that you would not extend the same trust to me. If it helps, I will tell you that I have learned some things about Lady Sophia on my own. You would not be talking out of school."

East could have shut the door on further conversation at that moment. He did not. "What you know can be of little import. I have not seen Lady Sophia since I was at Tremont Park."

"In September. Late in the month as I recall from your report."

"Yes."

"She has not been in London since then," the colonel said. "Tremont has been back, of course, but she has not."

"That signifies nothing. She has never been one for gadding about in society. She prefers the country."

"Which brings me to one of the rather surprising things I learned. She is not at Tremont Park."

"Then you must be mistaken that she is not in London. I'm certain if you present yourself at Number 14 Bowden Street, you will find her."

The colonel shook his head. "No, I will not. Lady Dunsmore has hired a governess for her children. That is the rather awkward and humbling position previously occupied by Lady Sophia, I believe. They made good use of her as their poor relation. It is not surprising that she would not return there when she made her escape from the Park."

Blackwood was not deterred by East's stubborn silence. "It is no exaggeration to say that she has fled. That is the word the family uses among themselves to describe her absence. You know as well as I that there has been no public disclosure that she is missing."

Eastlyn sat up straighter in his chair. There was only one way the colonel could know particulars about conversations in Sophie's family. "The Dunsmore governess is in your employ."

"Let us say that she has been remunerated for her services." He met East's censure directly. "You left me with no choice. I did nothing at all in the beginning, precisely as you asked. I made no inquiries about Lady Sophia's own health after you met with her and became ill. I kept my own counsel when it seemed to me you were distracted from your purpose with Helmsley and Barlough because you wanted to go to Tremont Park. It did not escape my notice that it was around that time that Lady Sophia was rumored to be the intended of Mr. George Heath, though by all accounts it was a short-lived engagement.

"Soon after you returned from the Park there was that unfortunate business in the *Gazette* to further occupy you. Between your mistress and your fiancée, it seemed to me that you had none of the women in your life in hand. You can take me to task for it, but I have no regrets for doing as I did. These last months I have watched you apply yourself as hard as you ever have to the difficult matter of the settlement. Redoubling your efforts can make no difference when you are merely standing in place. I think you must settle with Lady Sophia, East. It occurs to me that she did not take her leave of Tremont Park without your help. If the same notion has occurred to Tremont, then one begins to comprehend why he thinks he and his followers can make such outrageous demands."

Blackwood regarded Eastlyn pointedly. "Make it right."

East had never been upbraided by the colonel before, but then, he thought, he had never presented him with cause. "The notion that I helped Lady Sophia has occurred to Tremont," he said quietly, "because I informed him of it. I conceived the idea, not Sophie. I cannot even say that I was unaware that my actions would jeopardize my ability to negotiate with Tremont; I can only say that it was of lesser importance than seeing Sophie free of his influence."

"I see." The colonel returned his spectacles to his face. "Then she was being very ill-used by her cousin."

"Yes. That he wanted to arrange an advantageous marriage for her was the least problem. All the advantages must be his. She did very well to hold her own for so long."

Blackwood adopted his most considering pose, cupping his chin and rubbing the underside of his jaw with his thumb. "I admit to some astonishment that you did not make her an offer of marriage. That is what I anticipated you would do. Perhaps you will not credit it, but I made a wager with myself to that effect."

"Then you must reward yourself for your foresight."

The colonel's hand dropped away from his face as his chin came up. "How is that again?"

"I made the offer. She refused me." It was not often that Eastlyn saw Blackwood's features truly bearing the stamp of surprise. That expression was very nearly worth what it cost East in pride to make the admission. "I see you did not anticipate such an end as that."

"No. No, I could not. I recall there was some discussion that she was likely to be more successful making you a pigeon than a happy man, but I thought you were joking. She truly said it in response to your offer?"

"It was indeed her answer, though you will understand that I take no pleasure in being reminded of it. You see that she was most sincere in her refusal."

"Bloody hell."

"Yes, well, it was not as if she hadn't prepared me." Eastlyn hesitated a moment, uncertain that he wanted to say more, then decided that he must. The silence he had imposed on himself was crushing him. "I asked her a second time after she was gone from Tremont Park. She would not have me then either."

Blackwood wrestled with the singular sensation of being offended on Eastlyn's behalf. "She cannot be a woman of sound judgment. What can be her reasons for refusing you?" He waved one hand dismissively when East began to speak. "Oh, and do not tell me that she remains convinced you are a gambler, a sot, and a murderer. Even if it were true, a woman looking to remove herself from Tremont's influence cannot have so many scruples."

"As much as I prefer your defense of me to your reproachment, I do not want you to think poorly of Lady Sophia. She is acting as she believes she must, and in that regard she has never wavered. I have called her unreasonable, but it is an unfair appraisal. It is more true that I cannot comprehend her reasoning."

Blackwood regarded East steadily. When he spoke it was with great conviction. "You have always been the one among your friends to act first in righting some wrong, even when that action was most precipitous. You were well named the tinker, East, and now it seems to me that you must apply yourself to repairing this situation."

East accepted the colonel's assessment, for it was also his own. "I have given it a great deal of thought as to how it can be managed. You might know that Mrs. Sawyer is now in an arrangement with Dunsmore. She would not agree to his protection, even to jab at me, if she did not think he could keep her well. I believe there has been an infusion of money in the Colley family, or at least the expectation of such. I think I must find the source of it. It is key to negotiating with Tremont."

"You are speaking of your assignment."

"Yes."

Blackwood's smile was surprisingly gentle, even a trifle rueful. "I was not. Go to Lady Sophia, East. Speak to her, for it is clear to me that your own feelings are engaged. You cannot do more for me than you already have without first settling matters with her. You are resourceful. Find a way to gain her agreement if that is what you desire." The colonel's voice grew more quiet still, and his final words were offered with some reluctance. "Barring that, you must find a way to forget her."

Eastlyn did not answer immediately. He stood and walked

to the drinks cabinet and poured himself two fingers of whiskey. He sipped once from his tumbler of Dutch courage before he spoke. "There is little chance of either."

The colonel merely lifted a skeptical brow and awaited further explanation.

"A letter from Lady Sophia arrived with yesterday's post. I think I must have suspected the nature of what she would write because I did not allow myself to read it then. I waited until I returned from the club." He raised his glass. "Fortification, don't you know." He shrugged and finished his drink when Blackwood made no reply. "Her correspondence underscores the reasons I can do neither of the things you suggest."

"How is that?" Blackwood asked flatly.

"I do not know where she is any longer," East said, setting his glass down and pouring one for the colonel. "She has left my sister's home, so I cannot speak to her." He crossed the room to Blackwood's side and gave him the drink. "And she is going to be the mother of my child, so I cannot forget her."

The colonel looked at Eastlyn for a long moment; then he drained his glass.

Built against the side of a cliff on the Devon coast, the tiny fishing village of Clovelly had much to recommend itself to Sophie. The people were hardworking and steady and minded their own affairs before prying into the business of others. Conversation was all about the fishing and the tide and the ships and the swells. Every aspect of their lives revolved around the fleet that was kept in the snug and safe harbor below the town. What Sophie knew about fishing would not fill a single page of her journal, but she was a keen observer of what went on around her, and she wrote about that instead.

High Street dipped steeply toward the cove below, and the cobbled street was built in steps and stages so that it might be negotiated more easily. One side of the street had a stream running along its length, so that every house and place of business had to be entered by crossing a little bridge. Sophie liked to entertain the notion of moats and castles and bridges that could be drawn up when there was a siege, and she gladly took possession of a narrow house on that side of High Street when the opportunity came to her.

Her home was far cozier than a castle, she reflected, as she crossed the bridge to the front entrance. And the running stream was more pleasant to her senses than a stagnant moat would be. The bridge did not lift, but that was not entirely unfortunate as her neighbors would surely have grown curious if she set herself from them.

With one hand hovering near the door, Sophie turned and gave a last look down the length of the street toward the ocean. It was a balmy day for so late in December, and a gust of wind pressed her redingote against her legs and stirred the hem of her dress and petticoat. It seemed that the street dropped away suddenly, so steep was its descent, and that the white-capped sea actually rose up to meet it. From where she stood it looked as if it might be possible to drop off the end of the earth.

There were days, though far fewer of them now, that this idea had some appeal.

"So you are come at last."

Sophie's nerveless fingers uncurled around the handle of the basket they were holding. The basket and its contents thudded to the floor. A jar of jam rolled away. A split appeared in the paper that wrapped the fish she meant to have for dinner. The string tying off the pouch of dried beans broke, and a third of the beans spilled into the bottom of the basket.

Sophie ignored the wreckage and concentrated on not letting herself become part of it. To that end she calmly closed the door behind her and began removing her bonnet. "I do not know how I could have been clearer that I mean to ask you for nothing."

"I understood you," East said, coming to his feet. His

caped greatcoat lay on the sofa behind him; his hat rested on top. "It does not follow that I mean to ask nothing of you."

Sophie laid her bonnet on the table beside the door. Her efforts to release the buttons from their tabs on her coat were jerky, and it took her overlong to accomplish the task. "You are going to be unpleasant, are you not? Why is it that you are never stopped for lack of an invitation?" She shrugged out of her coat and placed it on a hook at the bottom of the enclosed stairwell. When she turned back she saw Eastlyn's eyes were on her belly. His face was very pale.

"You have lost the child?"

Sophie looked down at herself, at her abdomen that was still remarkably flat even when she smoothed the muslin walking dress over it, and understood what accounted for his question. It was a reasonable assumption on his part, and she might reasonably be expected to lie, but she never considered it. "No," she said. "I am still carrying the child. It is only that I have not begun to swell. I understand it is like that sometimes. It was true of my mother, I believe, and therefore likely to be the same with me."

He nodded, a measure of color returning to his face. "Wait, don't do that," he said, stepping forward when she bent to pick up the basket. "I will take care of it."

Sophie glanced up at him, amused. "I can manage as simple a thing as this."

Eastlyn hunkered down anyway, scooping up the jam jar and putting it back; then he placed his hand under Sophie's elbow and assisted her in rising. Her thanks was polite, though cool, and she brushed past him to carry her purchases to the kitchen. He decided the better course was not to follow. While her pointed remark about his lack of invitation had not stung, it had been noted.

He returned to the sofa and made his second assessment of his surroundings. It was a comfortable enough place, and he was glad for that. He did not want to find her living in a mean little cottage that stank of fish, though perhaps it would have made her more amenable to that first sight of him.

Sophie's home had pleasant light from a large window at the front, however, and an openness that was unfamiliar to him in a space so small. It was because she had little in the way of furniture, he supposed, and no curios on the mantelpiece or on the table at the door. There was a braided rug in front of the brick fireplace and a copper kettle hanging from the hook inside. A large wicker basket rested beside the sofa filled with an assortment of colorful fabrics and threads and yarns, all of which he imagined were part and parcel of Sophie beginning to build her nest here.

From the kitchen Sophie had a slim view of Eastlyn sitting on the sofa. She stood very still, not placing another thing on the table lest she draw attention to herself and be caught staring at him. He was a pleasure to watch. He always was. She saw his head swivel slightly as he glanced around, and she could tell that he approved. That smile was there on his lips, the one that edged the corners upward so faintly it might easily be missed. The sweet familiarity of it made it difficult for her to breathe.

She watched him lean over the side of the sofa and could not imagine what he was about until he lifted her sewing basket onto his lap. He went through it carefully, examining the threads, then the yarns, even going so far as to hold some spools up to the light to mark their color. It seemed important to him to touch her things, to hold them in his palm for a moment as if he meant to test the shape of them without benefit of eyesight, as if once held against his skin he would know it again anywhere. She felt as though she should look away, that what she was doing was intruding on his privacy, and that she was guilty of the very thing she had accused him of: coming to a place she was not wanted.

Still, she could not look anywhere else. Her vision was filled first with his three-quarter profile, the windblown chestnut hair, the dark lashes that were lowered to half-mast, the faint stubble along the line of his jaw, and then with his beautiful hands as he drew out a length of damask fabric the color of sage. He fingered one corner of the material, rubbing it gently to gauge the texture, then pleated it several times as she was often wont to do when her nervous fingers had no other outlet. He had not the look of a man who was nervous, but of one who was remembering and was caught by the regret of it.

When he pressed the material to his face, Sophie felt her knees give way.

East's head came up. He tossed the fabric from him and shoved Sophie's sewing basket off his lap. The contents were spilling onto the floor as he got to his feet. It required only a few long strides for him to reach the kitchen.

Sophie stood with her hands braced on the top rail of a chair, her knuckles nearly white with the effort she had made to stay upright. The chair was situated at an odd angle more than a foot from the table, dragged there when she first grabbed it for support. She thought that she must have cried out, though she didn't remember doing so; then she cast her glance down and realized it was the chair's sudden movement as she almost toppled it that he'd heard.

"Sophie?" His eyes darted over her, assessing quickly that she was all of a piece. "It sounded as if you were—"

"It is nothing." She offered a quick, apologetic smile. "My hem was caught by the table leg. It was a near thing, but I have averted a fall."

East did not question her story, though he doubted the truth of it. The table looked to be situated as it had been when he entered the house, and the leg of it was too smooth to have snagged her dress. "You are flushed," he said. "Will you not sit down?"

"In a moment. I was going to make tea. Will you have some with me?"

"Yes. Thank you."

Sophie nodded and set about drawing water for the kettle. She was very much aware that he was watching her and wondered that it did not make her clumsy or uncomfortable. Once the kettle was set in the hearth, Sophie stoked the fire.

"It will not be long," she said. "Will you not sit?" She noticed the overturned basket for the first time and realized that he must have thrust it aside very quickly to have made it spill in such a willy-nilly fashion. She felt she had to ask the question because to make no comment would have been suspicious in its own right. "What happened here?"

East was already bending to pick up the basket when she put the question to him. There was the slightest hesitation in his movement, and then he continued about the business of collecting the contents. "I believe I must have kicked it on my way to the kitchen," he said. "I am sorry. I hope nothing has been damaged." The etui had opened, and pins were scattered everywhere. He began the painstaking task of collecting them, cursing softly each time he jabbed himself.

"Let me," Sophie said, kneeling beside him. "You are fast on your way to becoming a pincushion."

"Thank you."

"And I also collect you have not many curse words left."

"Not ones I might say in your company."

She smiled. "I imagine your friends have heard them all."

East did not rise, but sat back instead, leaning against the sofa while Sophie continued to deftly pick up the pins. He noticed she had not pricked herself once and supposed her beautifully tapered fingers must give her the knack of it. "I'd like to think we invented most of the really fine curses ourselves."

"I can well believe that you did." She realized her tone was not even remotely reproving and there was no sense feigning it. "How do your friends fare?" she asked. "They are all well?"

"It is good of you to ask."

She paused in her collecting to glance at him. "I do not do it to make idle conversation," she said. "Or even to avoid what we know we must discuss."

"Did you detect something in my manner that led you to suppose those were my thoughts? Because I assure you, they were not. My thinking was contrary, for it has been my experience that many women of my acquaintance, that is, certain women . . . Well, permit me to say they are not . . ."

It occurred to Sophie that she might let him prick himself on the point he was trying to make or she could go straight to the heart of the matter. The latter was the better choice since she might never acquire an answer to her question in any other manner. "You are speaking of mistresses," she said directly. "I am familiar with the word, you know. And I am supposing you're trying to tell me they find the Compass Club to be rivals for your time and your affections. Am I correct?"

"I am all admiration," he said, meaning it.

"Yes, well, that is neither here nor there." They would arrive at the subject of mistresses in due time, Sophie knew. She would see that they did. "I should still like to hear how your friends are faring."

East drew one knee toward his chest. "South is away from town for parts unknown, at least unknown to me. We do not live in one another's pockets as some are wont to believe, but can be depended upon to come together when there is a need to do so. We were all at the service for West's father last month. Mayhap you knew of the duke's death?"

Sophie shook her head. "Poor Mr. Marchman," she said softly.

"West did not have the same affection for his father that you bore yours, but your sympathies would be appreciated by him for reasons you could not expect. Before his death the old duke recognized Marchman as his own son, making him the legitimate heir to the title and properties and fortune. Our friend is now of considerable consequence, poor fellow, and will be known to others as the Duke of Westphal."

"Oh, my." Sophie's eyes had widened during East's recounting, and finally she blinked. "West. So he has come into his name at last. He is unhappy with this, is he not?"

"Most assuredly."

"He has always stood a bit apart from others, I thought. I do not mean to suggest that he was too high in the instep, but rather that he did not strike me as one entirely comfortable in society. It is perhaps a mere fancy on my part. I do not know him at all well."

"It is no fancy," East said. "West is just as you described. How could you know?"

Sophie dropped the last pin into the etui and closed it carefully. She was looking at the ornamental case, not at East, as she spoke. "Sometimes we are obliged to see in others what we know to be true of ourselves." She did not allow him to comment on this small confession. "And what of Northam? You have not yet told me about him."

Eastlyn let himself be moved to this subject because he could see Sophie's discomfort in her averted glance and busy fingers. She had revealed something more than she meant to when she spoke of West, but there would be nothing gained by pressing her now. "North has had rather a time of it," he said instead. "You will understand that I am depending on your discretion once again when I tell you this."

"Of course. I am not a gossip."

He smiled faintly. "No, I did not think you were." He knew quite well that it had nothing at all to do with the fact that she had been the subject of so much of it. Some people took pleasure in it. Others did not. "It is about Lady Northam, you see. Shortly after West's father died, she disappeared for a time, and North did not know where she had taken herself. Their marriage was something of a hastily arranged affair, and neither was entirely happy, though they did their best to make it seem otherwise. When she left, North thought she might have gone to her father's, but she was not there. He asked for our help, and so I was delayed in London while I lent some assistance."

"She was found?" asked Sophie. "And safe, I hope."

"Yes. On both counts."

"That is good, then."

East nodded. "Indeed. She is a fine lady who has had a difficult time of it. There is much about her character that is admirable. Naturally North's affections are considerably more engaged than my own."

"He loves her."

"No one who knows him has ever thought otherwise."

Sophie folded her arms around her sewing basket and hugged it to her midriff. "You said it was a hasty marriage," she said, staring at the damask fabric Eastlyn had pressed so impulsively to his face. "I suppose I was . . ." Her voice trailed away as she found she could not give sound to the thoughts she had conceived.

"It does not mean North did not marry for love."

He had divined her thought perfectly. Sophie glanced at him, nodded, then looked away again. "As you said, those who knew him understood. I do not know him."

"That could be changed, Sophie."

She did not reply. His meaning was clear, and they had not yet arrived at the moment when she could answer him. She pushed the basket aside and rose. "How did you find me?"

Eastlyn looked up at her. The floor was deuced uncomfortable, but his strategy was to allow her to have what advantage she could. "It was not nearly as difficult as finding Elizabeth, I can tell you, though that is not meant in any way as a slight. You made a splendid job of it."

"Yet here you are." She sighed. "Is it because I mentioned Clovelly to you before we parted?"

"No. I would have come here because of that comment if I had had no other clue, but I did not have to depend upon it." East saw the vertical crease appear between Sophie's eyebrows as she considered how she might have given herself away. "It is perhaps wrong of me to take any pleasure from your confusion, but I am not so generous a person to let this moment pass without noting it. You gave me a time of it, you know. It is not unreasonable that I should want a little of my own back."

"No," she said quietly. "No, it's not."

"It was your writing, Sophie, that led me here. I did not know until very recently that it is more in the way of an occupation than a pastime."

Her frown deepened. "I'm not certain I know what you mean. I keep a journal of my observations. It is largely for my own pleasure."

Eastlyn knew prevarication when he heard it. "But you create stories from your observations."

"Yes, again it is for my pleasure. It can be of no importance to you."

"And you have sold at least one such story. In June, I believe. Around the time I visited you at Bowden Street."

"You cannot possibly know this."

"*At Once Beguiled*," he said, proving that he did indeed know. "A novel. It is an intriguing title, I thought. The author, one Alys Frederick, is credited to have a fine talent and is expected to pen several more. The book will be ready for printing in January and at the booksellers the following month."

Sophie's legs slowly folded, making her glad for the proximity of the sofa.

"Alys and Frederick," East said. "Your mother and father, are they not?"

She nodded, resigned.

"When you submitted the manuscript you gave the publisher your name," East said. "And an address where you could be informed of the decision regarding it."

"Yes. That was when I was still at Bowden Street." Sophie's shoulders slumped as she came to understand the trail he had somehow managed to follow. "I was in expectation of a cheque," she said, looking at her folded hands. "I wrote to the publisher to arrange for it to be sent to me at your sister's. Once I received it, I wrote and told him where the next one must be sent."

"Sophie? Look at me." She did and he continued. "It is important that you know Cara did not read your correspondence. I did that."

"But you could not have seen it. I sent it to my publisher."

"Sir James Winslow."

"Yes."

"My father, Sophie. Sir James is my father."

Chapter Ten

"Your father?" Sophie felt as if she were being pressed back into the corner of the sofa, yet she knew she hadn't moved. "But your father is . . ."

Eastlyn waited a moment to see if she would finish her thought. When she didn't, or couldn't, he explained, "It is more accurate to say Sir James is my stepfather. My father died of scarlet fever when I was four, and my mother remarried after she was out of mourning. Sir James's family has been involved in printing and publishing for almost a century. Ganymede Press was begun by his grandfather."

"Then he is in . . . Why, he is in trade."

East almost laughed at her astonishment and the singular emphasis that she placed on the word *trade*. "A scandal, is it not?"

"Oh, no. No, I didn't mean . . ."

He did chuckle now as yet another sentence was left dangling while Sophie collected her thoughts. "Perhaps some tea will help you swallow it all." East rose to his feet and went to the hearth to remove the kettle. Out of the corner of his eye he saw Sophie finally relax her posture. "My father's involvement is largely confined to reading submissions for publication, but that is by his own choice. He also likes to frequent the booksellers to gauge the success of a particular work. My mother wishes he would do less, I think, but that is only so that she might not lose him for hours on end when he is occupied in his study."

"It is rather a lot to take in," Sophie said softly. She spoke more to herself than to East. "I did not realize . . ."

"Of course you didn't. You would have been a great deal more cautious in your dealings with Ganymede had you known of my connection to it."

Sophie couldn't deny it. "You still have not explained how you came by my correspondence. Is it your habit to read your father's letters?"

"No. I think you know that is not the case at all." He examined the pot of brewing tea and pronounced it fit for consumption. He poured a cup for each of them and handed Sophie hers before he rejoined her on the sofa. "There can be little mystery of how it finally came about. My father always knew that the Lady Sophia Colley to whom I was rumored to be engaged was also the writer Alys Frederick."

Sophie grimaced slightly. "I suppose I would have done better to have used a solicitor or some other third party to make the submission to Ganymede. In hindsight, it is not a thing I should have done on my own."

"If you wanted your name entirely protected, then yes, you are right. Allow me to say, however, that Sir James never revealed what he knew. It was clear to him that I was ignorant of your writing, and without any overture from me, he kept your secret. I must also tell you that neither he nor my mother knew I had helped you leave Tremont Park or that you were a guest in Cara's home. I was most specific with my sister that her correspondence with our mother should be without any mention of your presence there, and most particularly that Cara should not make an invitation to Mother to visit."

"Oh," Sophie said softly. "I wondered at your mother's silence."

"Yes, well, it is not that she cannot be discreet, but that it would chafe her. So much discomfort could only be relieved by descending upon you, and that, I think, would have gone very badly."

"She would not approve of me?"

"She would not approve that you do not approve of me."

"I see." Sophie's slim smile was hidden as she raised her teacup and sipped from it. "And your father? What might he have said?"

"He would have said it was all grist for the mill."

"Meaning that one might find inspiration from it."

"Precisely. Another novel might be born of so much intrigue." Eastlyn turned on the sofa so that he might see Sophie more directly. "Sir James revealed nothing to me until I approached him with your last correspondence." He heard her sharp intake of breath and saw the slight tremor in the cup and saucer. She drew it closer to steady it. "I did not speak to him out of any malice toward you, Sophie, and I did not share anything with him in the expectation that he would solve the problem of your whereabouts. I went to him because he is my father and his advice has always been sound. I hope you will believe me when I say this to you: He did not surrender your secret easily. It was his opinion that you were quite sincere in your wish to be done with me and that I should honor your feelings above all else."

"What caused him to be swayed sufficiently to betray me?"

"I cannot know for certain," Eastlyn told her. "But he said something that made me think he was influenced by the recent death of West's father. It is no kindness, he told me, to raise a child a bastard, then turn his world topsy-turvy with a revelation of legitimacy. He thinks West will have a worse time of it as the new duke, unable to know whom he might trust as members of the ton come forward to embrace him."

"My child would not be a bastard," she said quietly.

"You are referring to this pretense that you are now a widow, I suppose. What is the name again? William Frederick? Wilton? Winston?"

"Wendell."

"Mrs. Wendell Frederick." East's brows lifted slightly. "You are very naive, Sophie, if you think your neighbors will not come to suspect the truth." He looked pointedly at her left hand which bore a slim gold band on its fourth finger. "They might accept your deception in your presence, but our child will not have so easy a time of it. You must apply to West if you doubt me."

Sophie's cup rattled in its saucer, and she was forced to put both down before she spilled the hot contents all over her. She clasped her hands firmly in her lap to still them. "I have heard that pregnancies might sometimes be ended, but I could not do it."

"Bloody hell," he swore softly. "I should hope not."

"And I cannot give the child away."

He reached past Sophie to set his own cup down beside hers. The movement toward her made her flinch, and Eastlyn could not mistake it for anything but what it was. "Do you think I mean to strike you?"

There was only a slight hesitation on her part before Sophie shook her head.

"You do not seem as certain as I might wish." He drew back, putting a more comfortable distance between them. "I am not given to the same behaviors of your cousins, Sophie. I thought I was very clear on that point when I last took your leave. It appears you still doubt it."

"You would not be here if you did not mean to cause me pain, my lord."

Eastlyn required a moment to catch his breath. She was so very good at taking it away from him in ways that were not at all pleasant. "That is singularly selfish," he said quietly. "I could say the very same of you. Never doubt that your disappearance has caused me pain. I will acquit you, however, of purposely setting out for Clovelly with that end in mind, and I hope you will find it in yourself to acquit me of the same. If there is pain, then it is because we are ever at cross-purposes. I should like to see that changed, for there is no reason that we should not be of a single mind on this matter of our child."

Sophie continued to stare at her hands. There was a faint whitening to her knuckles as her clasp tightened.

"You have nothing to say?"

She shook her head.

Eastlyn would not permit himself to be discouraged by her silence. He considered the possibility it was a hopeful sign that she did not have an argument at the ready. "Even after learning where I might find you, I did not come immediately. I told you I was delayed by Elizabeth's disappearance and North's request for my help. That is a partial truth at best. I required time myself, Sophie. It is no simple task to reconcile the knowledge of impending fatherhood with the knowledge that you intended nothing should ever come of it. That you might think I should be relieved by your choice to raise our child alone proved to me how little you know me. But then, I reminded myself that there has been little opportunity for you to know me better. It seemed to me that I was acting as you wanted, taking you at your word when you said you desired to be left alone, and yet I came to wonder if you were not responding to something you suspected to be true of my character."

The brief, crooked smile he flashed was rich with self-mockery. "Nothing good comes of trying to divine the bent of another person's thoughts. That is one of the many reasons I have come to Clovelly. I thought I should make myself plain to you this time, and that you would do me the great favor of speaking as plainly in return."

Sophie's fingers unfolded slowly. She ran them along the length of a crease in her lap, smoothing it out. She opened her mouth to speak, and no words came out. She simply closed it again, drawing in her lower lip this time and worrying it gently between her teeth.

Eastlyn laid one arm across the back of the sofa. His fingertips rested very near Sophie's shoulder, and if he stretched himself even the slightest bit, he might have touched her. He refrained from doing so, choosing to watch her instead and gauge her reaction to his nearness. He was gratified to see that she did not withdraw farther into her corner. "I spoke to my friends of my dilemma," he told her and was unsurprised to see her head jerk in his direction. Her expression was almost accusing. East shrugged lightly, refusing to make too much of it. "It is one of the ways in which our circumstances are different, Sophie. You have no one to whom you may apply for counsel, and I am only that alone if I choose to be. I did not tell them all the particulars, only those—"

"Then they know about the child?"

"No. They know I want to marry you and that you will not have me. I applied to them to find out how such a thing might be accomplished."

"And what advice did they have for you?"

"You will not credit it, Sophie, but they said I should steal your chamber pot."

Sophie had no idea what reply she might make to that. She supposed her astonishment was clear because Eastlyn was moved to tap lightly under her chin with his index finger and nudge her mouth closed. Feeling very much in need of his assistance just then, she did not try to avoid his touch.

"I see I shall have to explain it to you," he said. So he sat back comfortably and gave her the story of how he had made the Hambrick Hall courtyard safe from the Society of Bishops. No tariffs or tolls or tributes. No collection of money or goods or services for use of the common areas. He told her how Lord Barlough had almost been brought to his knees for want of a chamber pot and how the Compass Club had been particular that every detail of the contract be carefully explained before showing the archbishop and his tribunal where they could find their buckets. "So it was done, you see, in aid of striking a balance between what the Bishops would try to do us all and what we would let them. I cannot say how things went on at Hambrick after we left, but I suspect that there are always a few boys willing to make a stand against the Society."

Sophie had listened to all of East's recital without interruption. Now she asked, "And how many do you think still choose to make a stand?"

"You are not speaking of Hambrick Hall."

"No, I am not. I am speaking of those boys turned men who would still stand in opposition to the Bishops. How many are there?"

"I can think of three beyond myself. I am not alone, Sophie."

"Four of you." Her slight smile was humorless. "Four of you against Tremont and all the Bishops before and since. What can you possibly think you can accomplish?"

Eastlyn shook his head. "This is not why I told you what trick I played at Hambrick Hall. We should not be talking about Tremont. You are shifting the subject to avoid—"

"It is relevant."

"I fail to see how."

Sophie regarded him levelly. "Because it is the reason stealing my chamber pot will not work."

"You understood it was a metaphor? I had no intention of—" He broke off because Sophie looked as if she meant to bring that metaphor crashing on his head.

"You will endeavor not to be so patronizing," she said. "Your meaning was perfectly clear. Your friends recommended that you find a method by which I could be coerced into marrying you. I can hardly credit that you did not take that opportunity to tell them you had already got me with child. It must be every bit as good a trick as hoisting those buckets in full view of the courtyard. There was a great deal of snickering from those looking on, I would wager. All those fingers pointing at the buckets as you and your friends reeled them in. The rumor of what you had done passing from one boy to the next. You must have been very satisfied with yourself."

Eastlyn said quietly, "Is that what you think, Sophie? That I forced a child on you so we would come to this pass?"

She stiffened at having her words thrown back at her, sensing the unfairness of them for the first time. "I . . . yes . . ."

Her eyes darted away. "No. No, I do not think even you could determine that I should have a child and make it so, but you cannot deny that you came to my bed hoping I could be convinced to marry you. You would not pass on that opportunity."

"I do not deny it. I am not proud of what I have done, but neither do I regret it. You cannot insist that I should regret it. I would do it again, Sophie. And again."

"The child is—"

"I was not speaking of the child. I was speaking of lying with you, of coming to your room in the dead of night and lying with you. That is what I cannot regret. Do not misunderstand, I find that I very much want this child, but you must know that I wanted its mother first." Eastlyn moved just the fraction necessary to allow his fingertips to graze her shoulder. He felt the slightest pressure there as if she were already leaning into him. "You have every right to punish me, but I would have you be aware that you are doing it. The last letter that you sent me, informing me of your pregnancy and the fact that you were already gone from Cara's . . . It seemed to me that you thought I would be unburdened by your news. I would have you know it had quite the opposite effect. If you send me away again, Sophie, as I suspect you mean to do, then you must also know that it is without any lightness of feeling that I go."

The ache behind Sophie's eyes pressed tears to the rims of her lower lashes. She blinked first, trying to hold them back, then dashed them away with her fingertips. She took a handkerchief from under the long sleeve of her gown and pressed it to each eye in turn. "I am a waterworks of late."

Eastlyn took the linen from her hand and gently wiped the tears that had fallen onto her cheeks. "It is the child, I suspect. You would not admit it is caused by any softening toward me."

The subtle mocking timbre of his voice engaged her watery smile. "No," she said. "I would not admit it." With very little effort on East's part Sophie felt herself being drawn to his side. She fit so naturally into the curve of his arm that she wondered that she was ever comfortable anywhere else. She closed her eyes when she felt his lips against her hair. "I think you mean to wear me down."

"That is my plan precisely," he whispered.

"I see."

Eastlyn merely held her. Her breathing was soft and even; his breath ruffled her hair. The scent of her provoked sweet memories of her mouth under his and her fingers tripping lightly down the length of his spine. The sensation was so real that he nearly shivered with it. She drew her feet onto the sofa, curling them to one side. Her shoulder lay more heavily against him. East counted off the minutes on the clock at ten before he felt her stir again. "You fell asleep."

"Hmm."

He spoke quietly and knew full well he was taking advantage of her weary state of mind. That, after all, was the plan. "I want to stay here, Sophie. A fortnight, if you will permit it. You should know at the outset that I will—"

"Yes."

"—sit on that little bridge at the front and make a nuisance of myself to your—"

"Yes."

"—neighbors and you until you relent. I will—" He stopped this time because he vaguely heard her voice coming to him as though from a distance. "You said yes."

"Twice." She reached behind her and patted him on the arm that was lying across her shoulders. "You are to be congratulated for your plan. It seems to be a very good one."

"Then you approve that it does not involve chamber pots."

"I do."

He nodded. "Good."

"You have thought of some way to explain your presence here, I collect. The good people of Clovelly have not been overly curious about me, but that is bound to change with your arrival. You attract notice, my lord."

"I don't mean to."

"I know. You cannot seem to help it." She turned her head and looked up at him. "Who shall we say you are?"

"Your husband back from the dead?"

She gave him a disapproving look. "Not likely. I told everyone he broke his neck in a fall."

Eastlyn rubbed his nape as if he could feel the bones crunching there. "I don't suppose you mentioned that you pushed him."

Sophie ignored that. "You could be my brother. I have always wanted a brother, and Mrs. Trumbull seems to think you are a good one."

"I suppose that would suit as long as you don't begin feeling sisterly toward me, or worse, acting upon it."

She laughed. "I think that is most unlikely."

"Very well. You must call me Gabriel, then."

"No."

"That is what my sister calls me."

"Your mistress, too, no doubt. I would rather call you East as you invited me to do before. Your friends call you East, and above all things, I should like to be your friend."

The comment about his mistress made one dark eyebrow jump. He regarded her askance and managed to say, "I also desire your friendship, Sophie. I cannot say, though, that I desire it above all things."

"For now, then."

He nodded. "For now."

Sophie settled back once more into the shelter of his arm. "What does your family expect of you?"

East knew this was no idle question. She probably had been wondering at it since he arrived. "They expect me to do what is right."

"That is not always so easy to know, is it?"

"No."

"I regret that I had to take my leave of your sister and her husband so suddenly. They must think I sorely abused their hospitality. I am quite certain that the letter I left behind did little to assuage Mrs. Trumbull's fears. She has every reason to be vexed with me."

"Yes. She does. Your brief acquaintance with Cara should also have assured you that she has a generous heart. She knows that I am the villain of this piece."

"The villain? Hardly that. And she is your sister. She will forgive you anything. She said as much herself when we were speaking—"

Sophie's abrupt end caught East's curiosity. "Yes? You and Cara were speaking of . . .?"

"We were speaking of you, of course."

"There is more. There is always more with you, Sophie. You were not so shy about speaking your mind a moment ago."

"Very well. We were speaking of Mrs. Sawyer. Your sister is not inclined to feel at all charitable toward her. I can't believe that she would be more disposed to me. Mrs. Sawyer has done naught but bedevil you with sly tricks, like those you might have encountered at Hambrick. She has not presented you with a swollen belly and claimed that you are the cause of it."

"I must point out that you have not done that either," he said dryly. His hand hovered over the flat of her abdomen. "May I?"

Sophie nodded and for a moment could not breathe. She watched Eastlyn's palm lower the fraction necessary to cover her belly. "She does not move yet," she told him. "Mayhap it is only my imagination but I feel a heaviness there."

"Is that why you think we will have a daughter?"

"No. I think it because it must not be otherwise."

Eastlyn measured the silence that followed as so complete he knew Sophie would not explain herself. He was not surprised when she trapped his hand under hers and asked him about his former mistress instead. "She has not been under my protection for a very long time. She ended our arrangement before I made my first proposal to you. How did you learn of her?"

"She is the one who began the rumor, isn't she?" When he did not answer, Sophie added, "Tremont says it is so. Your sister also led me to believe it."

"Then there is no point that you should hear it from me as well."

"It is good of you not to want to speak ill of her. You are very kind in that regard." She glanced at him and saw faint color rising in his complexion. It made her smile. "Your sister told me Mrs. Sawyer's name. Before that, long before, I knew you had a mistress. It is only that I had no name to put to her. She is a widow?"

"Yes. Her husband was a soldier. He was killed in fighting in Belgium."

"That is very sad for her," Sophie said, meaning it. "I imagine she was not left well off. It could not have been easy."

Eastlyn kept his tone carefully neutral. "She has managed."

"Your sister said Mrs. Sawyer hoped that you would marry her."

"Cara says a great deal and knows very little." He sighed. "You will not be moved from this, will you?"

"No."

"The truth is, I do not know if Cara is right, though I suspect she is. Mrs. Sawyer was not so straightforward as you, Sophie. If she had been, she would have asked me directly to marry her and not practiced roundaboutation."

"You are usually quite good at comprehending the meaning just below the surface. I wonder that you were not more certain of Mrs. Sawyer's hopes in regard to you."

"Perhaps I did not want to be." East's hand slid away from Sophie's midriff, and he laid it on the arm of the sofa. "It was a comfortable arrangement in many ways, so comfortable that I did not realize how utterly boring it had become. Mrs. Sawyer knew before I did that I was preparing to end it. She found another protector and gave me my walking papers. It was a civil parting. There was not a cross word exchanged."

"It sounds rather cold."

"Yes. Did you think she loved me, perhaps? That was not her way at all. It is likely that I had finer feelings for her than she did for me."

"Then I am sorry for you both. It must be a very bleak sort of bargain that is struck between a gentleman and his mistress."

"There are benefits," he said wryly. "And no, I will not discuss them. Why is it important to you?" He felt her shrug. "That is no answer. Is Mrs. Sawyer the reason you refused me, Sophie? Did you think I meant to keep her as my mistress?"

"It occurred to me. I did not know the arrangement was at an end when you first proposed; however, it did not weigh as anything in my decision to turn you down. Gentlemen have mistresses. It is done all the time. I suppose one comes to find a certain convenience in the arrangement. I have had experience learning to tolerate all manner of intolerable things. A husband's infidelity would scarcely cause me a moment's lost sleep."

"Liar." He said it with the gentleness of an endearment.

"It is not all a lie. I did not refuse you because you had a mistress."

"But you will not permit me to continue such an arrangement when we are married."

Sophie thought he was being overly confident in supposing they would be married, but she was of no mind to have that argument now. He had said it in just that fashion to tweak her. "I do not know if it is the sort of thing a wife can stop, but I doubt I should ever become accustomed to it."

"You will not have to. There will be no mistresses."

She was quietly skeptical.

"I am serious. No matter what you have come to believe, it is not done by everyone. I can name any number of men who do not engage in the practice of setting up a mistress once they are married. My father has never done so. North either. Southerton and West are unattached, and neither has anyone under his protection."

"Paragons, every one of them."

He chuckled. "I do not think I would go so far as to say that."

Sophie felt the rumble of his low laughter against her back and shoulder and knew a sense of such longing that she ached with it. She closed her eyes again, afraid the sudden press of tears would spill over. There was a hard lump at the back of her throat, but she managed to get words around it. "Would you have me as your mistress?"

The question was not entirely unexpected. East had posed it himself several times on his long ride to Clovelly, and in each instance the answer was the same. "No," he said after a moment. "No, I would not. Would you want to be?"

"I never thought so."

"If you are at all uncertain now, it is because of your present situation. You are not Mrs. Wendell Frederick, late of Stoke-on-Trent. You are Lady Sophia Colley, and becoming any man's mistress is not done. A woman like Mrs. Sawyer may place herself in a man's protection and society will accept it, even going so far as to privately admit that she is doing what she must to survive. It would not be like that for you. Among the ton, you would not be my mistress, Sophie. You would be my whore."

In spite of the warmth of his arm about her shoulders, Sophie shivered. His words were as frank as those she had spoken to herself.

East's fingers found the comb that tamed the curling length of Sophie's hair into a twist. He nudged it free and smiled when he heard her soft sigh. The heavy, honey colored strands poured over the back of his hand. He sifted through them and touched her nape, massaging the knot that kept her head so stiffly upright. In time she simply melted against him, and he was not at all sorry for it.

Eastlyn waited until Sophie was asleep before he eased himself away. He laid her carefully on the sofa and covered her with his own greatcoat. Except to pillow her head on her arm, she hardly stirred.

He left the cottage and rode to the inn in nearby Bideford

where Sampson was waiting for him. After arranging for one trunk and a valise to be sent to Sophie's home in Clovelly, East informed his valet that he should return to London for the Christmas holiday. Sampson did not own to being shocked by this, but East suspected that was the case, though whether Sampson disapproved of him taking up residence with Lady Sophia or managing his own wardrobe for a fortnight was unclear.

The carriage and team would remain behind at a livery in Bideford, and Sampson and the driver would avail themselves of the public coach on the return. Eastlyn was generous in the funds he provided for this trip, knowing they both found this mode of transport lowering.

Sophie was awake by the time he returned, and the house was filled with the warm aroma of the meal she was preparing. East stamped his feet just inside the doorway and dropped his hat and gloves onto the table beside Sophie's bonnet. He glimpsed Sophie giving him an over-the-shoulder glance from where she stood at the table.

"You did not wear your coat," she said in disapproving accents as East approached. "It is a mistake for you to think the weather will not turn cold."

"I wore my hat."

Her mouth flattened. "You should have worn the Carrick and not left it with me."

"How else would you know that I meant to return?" He came up behind her and placed his hands on her waist. "In any event, you were sleeping soundly under it when I took my leave. I was of no mind to disturb you."

"Where was your mind when you covered me with it? You might have used something else. There are blankets in the bedrooms."

Grinning, Eastlyn kissed Sophie lightly on the top of her head. "I do believe that living in Clovelly has made you a proper fishwife."

Sophie's mien softened, as did her shrewish tone. "You could have left me a proper note."

"I left my coat."

She released a long breath and nodded slowly. The movement made his chin rub pleasantly against the back of her head. She had refastened her hair in the comb but not as tightly as before. Fine wisps of it tickled her temple and her nape, and for a moment she closed her eyes and allowed herself to lean against him. Her sleep under the caped greatcoat had been deep but not dreamless. It had been like lying under him, the weight and scent so firmly in her mind that she expected to find him with her when she opened her eyes. He would not credit that she had been panicked by his absence, nor that she had been hurt by it. It was not until she took stock of the coat and its meaning that she was able to reason that he intended to return.

"I suppose my disposition was not improved by sleep," she said, slipping out of his hold and skirting the table. She set down the plate in her hand and placed silverware beside it. "Where did you go?"

"Bideford. That is where I left Sampson."

"He is coming here?"

"No. I mean to manage on my own." Eastlyn noticed that the surprise she had shown upon thinking Sampson might join them only deepened when she realized he would not. Her mercurial thinking made him smile. "What? Do you not think I can? If you can be Mrs. Frederick, then of a certainty I can be . . ." His voice trailed off as it occurred to him that he did not have a name.

"Mrs. Frederick's brother?" Sophie said with no intention of being helpful.

"Mr. Tinker."

"Tinker? I don't think I like the sound of that."

"Most definitely Tinker," he said, ignoring her.

Sophie merely shook her head, resigned to his choice. She pointed to the chair where he should sit while she prepared the remainder of their meal. They dined on simple fare, a fish chowder that Sophie made with cod, potatoes, fat salt pork, milk, and pilot bread. Onion, pepper, butter, and a liquor made by boiling the fish bones added savor to the stew.

Eastlyn resisted a third helping when it was offered to him. "I left my hollow leg in London." To forestall temptation, he pushed his bowl away. "I do not think my mother ever cooked a meal in her life. My sister either. How did you come to learn?"

"I spent a great deal of time in the kitchen at Tremont Park. Mrs. Hubbard was the cook then, and she let me sit on a stool beside her while she worked. Sometimes my governess would find me and send me back to my room, but most often they learned not to look too hard for me."

"You did not like the schoolroom?"

Sophie gathered the dishes. "Not nearly as much as I liked the kitchen."

"Or the stable?" He held up his hands, palms out, when she cast him a suspicious glance. "I was not referring to your penchant for spying on grooms and scullery maids. I swear it. I was thinking of your skill on horseback. You must have spent considerable time out-of-doors."

"I did." Sophie filled a basin with hot water from the kettle and set about cleaning the dishes. East offered to assist her, but she turned him down. "Were you offended when you saw me riding astride? It is not at all conventional."

"No, it's not," he said. "But was I offended? No. Did you think I might be?"

"I suppose I did." She looked askance at him. Laughter hovered on his lips and brightened his eyes. "You are a trifle arrogant, you know, and you are accustomed to having your way. It is not unreasonable to suppose that you hold firm to a certain manner of doing things."

"You are confusing me with North," he said. "He will tell you himself that he is a prig."

"I doubt I shall have cause to make the inquiry, my lord."

"East. You promised that you would call me East." His voice deepened to a husky timbre. "You have only done so once."

Sophie's response was to apply more effort to scouring the stew pan.

Watching her, Eastlyn was satisfied that she remembered very well the occasion of it. He wanted her to keep the memory of lying with him in easy reach of her consciousness, just as he did. "I confess, Sophie, that upon making your acquaintance I could not have conceived of you riding in such a fashion."

"Like a hoyden, you mean."

"Yes. Precisely like that."

Sophie opened the back door and stepped out onto the small porch. She threw the dishwater into the garden and shook out the basin. When she returned, she stood for a moment on the threshold, hugging the basin. "When do you think we met?"

East frowned, uncertain of her meaning. It was put before him in plain enough terms, but the prickles at the back of his neck suggested nothing was quite as straightforward as it seemed. "It was at a musicale. A recital of Mozart pieces. You don't remember?"

"The recital to which you are referring was Bach."

"It may have been."

"It was."

"It was in Lady Stafford's salon," he said.

"Lady Stanhope's."

"Dunsmore was there with his wife. I am not mistaken about that."

Her faint smile was a shade regretful. "No. You are not mistaken on that count." Sophie put the basin away and wiped her damp hands on her apron before she removed it. She nudged a chair from under the table and sat at a right angle to Eastlyn. "I was very quiet on that occasion, as I recall. I do not think I spoke more than half a dozen sentences."

"Rather more than six."

"You do not need to be generous. You could not have formed any good opinion of me. I did not set out to give you one."

"Because of Dunsmore?"

She was puzzled for a moment, the small crease appearing between her brows. "Oh, you mean to thwart Harold's plan for me to attract a rich suitor? No, that was not the reason I did not care what you thought of me. Not entirely the reason, in any event. Abigail was there. Lady Dunsmore. Do you remember meeting her?"

"It is a vague recollection. She is a tall woman, I believe. Rather pale in her complexion. Red hair?"

"Yes."

"Is it important that I recall her?"

"No, not really. She was ill that afternoon. I thought you might have been struck by it."

"She could not have been too ill," East said. "Else she would have remained at home."

"It is her nerves," Sophie explained. "She is easily overwrought and is given to megrims. She is often abed. The children test her patience, and she prefers the quiet of her own room."

"I am not certain I understand how her presence at the recital influenced you. Were your thoughts occupied with her health?"

"I was there as her companion, else I would have remained at Bowden Street with Robert and Esme. It was my task to make certain she was comfortable, not to make myself agreeable to the guests. She was most particular that I tread carefully around you." Sophie hesitated as she felt herself the target of Eastlyn's closer study. "She warned me not to make a fool of myself. She had seen it happen before. At Almack's. I was only recently out of mourning clothes, and I had not been in London so very long when Harold and Abigail agreed I should accompany them there. It seemed the very height of gaiety to me and a little silly, I suppose, but I could not help but be transported by the dancing and gowns and the crush."

"Many people are of a similar opinion," East said. "I would rather be transported to Van Diemen's Land."

"Yes," she said softly, not quite looking at him now. "I can imagine that you would find it distressingly tedious. There can be no enjoyment in having to dodge so many determined mothers."

"I manage," he said dryly. "I have the dubious honor of being approved to partner young women in their first waltz. It is a privilege I share with Northam and Southerton. As you might imagine, West was not sanctioned by the patronesses."

"Then perhaps the circumstances of his birth are not entirely unfortunate."

East greeted this suggestion with a sardonic look. "You will not engage me in that argument now." He was resolved that his child would not be born a bastard. "Tell me about your evening at Almack's. If it was after your mourning was at an end, then you must have been considerably older than most of the females being presented."

"Considerably older," she said with a hint of wry humor. "Ancient, really. One-and-twenty."

"Forgive me. I should not—"

Sophie waved his apology aside. "I take no offense. I *was* older, just as you said, though the measure of it was in years, not experience."

East wondered at his blunder. It was precisely the sort of misstep that could bring negotiations to a complete halt. He was too clever to make these mistakes when dealing with ambassadors and foreign consuls. He had indeed lost his balance with Sophie. The feeling that the whole of the world was listing to one side never left him when he was talking to her. He cocked his head in an effort to right things to the perpendicular once more. "You were permitted to waltz?"

Sophie nodded.

"And were you as accomplished as I might expect?" He saw her avert her gaze just for a moment. "Never say you trod upon the poor fellow's toes. Or worse, that he trod upon yours."

"No. He was a practiced partner. I was not his equal, but he was kind and did not draw attention to my lack of skill."

Eastlyn watched her eyes slide away again. The movement was almost imperceptible, but he was seasoned in looking for just such things. The slightest shifting could denote deceit. It might warn of a truth only partially told or mean that a lie had settled unpleasantly on the tip of a tongue. He was not certain what it meant in Sophie's case, only that it did not bode well. He let her go on.

"We did not have more than a few polite exchanges during the waltz," Sophie told him. "It seemed to me that he was not of a mood to talk. For my part . . . Well, for my part I only wanted to look at him. That is what Lady Dunsmore told me afterward, and I cannot say that she was wrong. If it is possible to embarrass someone with adoration, then that is what I did to this poor gentleman. It must have been very uncomfortable for him because he left soon afterward and was careful not to look in my direction."

"I cannot believe anyone would be discomfited by your adoration, Sophie."

"Bored, then. He might not have been as uncomfortable as he was bored. He was only doing his duty, you see. I was naught but an obligation. I do not attach any blame to him for wanting to see the last of me, but I would not want to be his obligation again."

Eastlyn had the feeling return that she was saying rather more than her words would strictly suggest. For all that Sophie thought he was clever at coming to the meaning beneath the surface, he knew himself to be drowning now. "Have you had occasion to meet him since?"

"Yes."

"And?"

"I was careful not to give him disgust of me."

"By saying little or nothing at all?" East asked. "That was her ladyship's suggestion, I take it."

"It seemed a good choice. The proof that I acted improperly on the occasion of our first introduction was borne out when he never mentioned it. For many weeks after that second encounter, I thought he meant only to spare my feelings, so openly had I worn them on my sleeve, but then I became aware that he did not speak of our first meeting because he did not recall it."

Eastlyn frowned. "He did not recall . . . How is that possible?"

"It seems I made that little of an impression upon him." She snapped her fingers to emphasize the insignificance of that initial meeting. "You will admit that it is lowering to arrive at such a conclusion."

"Mayhap you are wrong."

"No. I am quite convinced of it."

"I cannot conceive of such a thing."

"Yes," she said. "I collect that is so."

East merely shook his head. "This experience at Almack's . . . It was the reason you were so reticent to engage in conversation with me at Lady Stafford's?"

"Stanhope."

"Forgive me. At Lady Stanhope's."

"After Almack's, Lady Dunsmore always urged caution. I believe she lived in perpetual dread that I would make a cake of myself with any man who showed the least interest in my company."

"I wish you had not been so agreeable to her ladyship's instruction. I would have been pleased to have even a small measure of your adoration."

Sophie laughed. "No, you would have found it as tedious as my conversation."

"Well, there you have me. My recollection is that our conversation was excessively dull."

"Then I must judge it a success, for that was certainly my intent."

East's mouth twisted wryly as he took measure of the lift of her chin. There was a stubborn sort of pride there in the set of her shoulders and the angle of her head. "You might well judge it otherwise," he said quietly, "when I tell how that dreary conversation set the course of all that followed."

The animation that had brightened Sophie's eyes vanished from her features. Her lush mouth flattened, and her chin fell. "What do you mean?"

So he told her. If he had felt an absence of pride in recounting the story to his mother, he now had self-loathing to fill the void. He chose his words with care, not to make his actions seem less objectionable, but to spare her what he could. He explained how he had spoken unkindly of her to his mistress, all in want of avoiding a discussion of marriage. He only had to provide a few details after that, for Sophie quickly divined how things had proceeded from there.

"I wondered why I was chosen among so many women to have my name linked to yours." She smiled, but the line of it was rueful and a bit mocking. "I came to Mrs. Sawyer's attention for possessing none of the virtues you would find agreeable in a wife. The irony of it makes me a little dizzy. Had I not been so determinedly dull at the Stanhope recital mayhap you would not have come to be so fixed on the idea of marrying me now."

Sophie regarded East steadily. A muscle jumped in his cheek as his jaw tightened, and she realized he was bracing himself as though for a blow. "Do you think I mean to set the blame with you?"

"You should."

"Your sister says that you are never blamed but always responsible." The memory of her conversation with Cara Trumbull made her smile a trifle wistful. "I do not think I understood it then. I do now." She reached across the table and laid her hand over East's. "I am of no mind to blame you. I have some part in this also. However, if we take so much upon ourselves, what is left for Mrs. Sawyer? She certainly deserves some reproof for her actions."

Sophie withdrew her hand and stood, her manner brisk. "I believe I would like some tea. I have a few fingers of whiskey here if you would prefer it."

"Whiskey."

She nodded. "I shall see to it." She began to walk past him and felt her arm caught. East's grip was light at first, so light that she might have pulled away from it easily. She did not. The chair scraped against the floor as he angled it away from the table. Only the slightest tug was necessary to bring her onto his lap.

"In a moment," he said. Her face was very near his, and his eyes made a study of her mouth until her lips parted to draw a small, unsettled breath. He closed the distance between them slowly, giving her ample time to turn her head or scramble to her feet. She did neither.

The kiss was sweetly languorous. The unhurried nature of it reminded Sophie that Eastlyn meant to win her surrender by the slow erosion of her defenses. His only mistake was in thinking it would take so long.

She let her head come to rest in the crook of his neck when he drew back. "There should be certain rules between us," she said softly.

"Rules of conduct, you mean?"

"Rules of warfare."

"I see." He turned his head slightly and kissed her smooth brow. "There are really very few of those, Sophie. It is all about gaining an advantage, you see, and acquitting oneself honorably. Advantages may be achieved in many different ways: the number of men; their positioning; the element of surprise; the swiftness of the dispatches; and the efficacy of the weapons. Will your fears be quieted if I promise not to draw my pistol?"

"I should like it better if you promised not to kiss me."

"I would be very foolish if I were to make that concession."

"Then you should not kiss me so well."

"I must acquit myself honorably, remember?"

Sighing, Sophie raised her head. "It isn't fair that you should have all the advantages."

He grinned. "You only think it because you haven't yet taken stock of your own weapons." East set her from him. "I will take that whiskey now," he said.

A trifle dazed by the abruptness of his dismissal, Sophie went to the front room. She could still feel the pressure of his erection against her hip. It seemed to her that Eastlyn's promise not to draw his pistol had been hastily given.

Chapter Eleven

Eastlyn did not go to Sophie's room that first night in Clovelly, nor she to his. Without a word passing between them they negotiated an agreement to govern how they meant to go on. He slept on a narrow cot in the room where Sophie wrote during the day; she stayed in the room across the hall, her door closed but never locked. There was mutual respect for the privacy of the other, and they were careful not to lapse into casual intimacy abovestairs. He did not play the lady's maid for her, and she did not assist him with his neckcloth. She did not approach him when he was bathing, and he left the house when she drew water for herself.

They stepped carefully at first, conscious of manner and conversation. In those first days following East's arrival, more reserve and restraint was practiced, rather than less. They spoke of things inconsequential and important, but there were subjects that were not broached because the peace between them was too fragile. Over the course of a sennight they fell into a routine that while not entirely comfortable, served them well enough not to be challenged.

Sophie was the first to rise each morning. East would lie abed and wait for the sounds of her being sick to pass before he set his feet to the floor. When he arrived downstairs, he would find her sitting at the kitchen table, drinking tea and nibbling on a cracker, her complexion pale, but her smile firmly in place. He did not mention that he had heard her distress, and she did not share that she had experienced any.

They walked after breakfast, exploring High Street all the way to the cove, sometimes sitting on the stone pier to watch the fleet of fishing boats managing their catch or making their way across the water. East doubted that anyone who saw them together believed they were brother and sister, least of all the woman Sophie had hired to help her with house chores, yet he did not disabuse Sophie of the notion that her stratagem was working. It seemed to him that telling her they were found out was the surest way to get himself ejected from her home. To that end he tolerated the disapproving glances Mrs. Randolph slid in his direction when Sophie was gone from the room, and he answered to the name Mr. Tinker when he was greeted by the grooms at the livery or by the fishermen at the pier.

They went to church together on Christmas Day and exchanged gifts when they returned. East gave Sophie a Paisley shawl that had many of the warm honey hues of her eyes; she presented him with a pair of leather riding gloves. They admired their gifts, pronouncing them the very right thing, and then fell into the first awkward silence they had shared since East's arrival.

It lasted two days.

Sophie did not think she could bear the estrangement, yet she had no idea how to make it right. It had come about so suddenly that at first she couldn't comprehend the truth of it. It was not that they didn't speak, but that there was no ease in it. This was much more than the reticence of those first days when they meant to step cautiously. This was clumsy and tense, not done of a purpose, but because they could not seem to help themselves, and the distance of conversation became a physical separation as well, one that she never felt so keenly as when they were occupying the same room.

Now she watched East set aside the book he was holding

without marking his place and realized he had done very little reading. She followed the movement of his hand as he put three fingers to his left temple and massaged lightly, closing his eyes against the bright, flickering light of the fireplace. "You are unwell?" She frowned when she saw the line of tension around his mouth and the hard set of his jaw. "Is it a megrim?"

Eastlyn opened his eyes, then winced slightly as he was confronted with the firelight. He tried to relax his jaw, working it gently from side to side to relieve the pressure that was building steadily in his head. "Pray, do not concern yourself. It will pass."

Sophie was certain that it would, but not without a great deal of suffering first. "Will you allow me to bring the physician? He does not live far, and I'm certain—" She stopped because East was causing himself considerable distress by shaking his head. "Very well. Then may I prepare you something? Tea?"

"Nothing." He was too nauseated now to eat or drink.

Sophie set her sewing in the basket and stood. "Won't you sit here, then? It will at least remove you from the direct light."

East accepted this proposal, not so far gone into his pain that he could not see the sense of it. He took Sophie's seat, pushing himself into the corner of the sofa so that he could stretch his long legs on a diagonal before him. Tipping his head back slightly, he closed his eyes again. "Do not hover. It is most unpleasant."

Sophie took a step backward, but she didn't sit.

"You're still hovering."

She dropped into the chair he had occupied.

"Now you are staring."

"You can't know that. You haven't opened your eyes."

"I don't have to. Some things I know."

Sighing, Sophie shifted her glance away from his pale and rigid features. "Do you take laudanum?"

"Infrequently. I hope you do not wish to ladle that down my throat."

"No, I do not." She picked up her sewing basket and placed it on her lap. "But I also have no wish to see you suffer."

"Then you may quit this room and go to your own." Even to his own ears his tone was untempered by humor. He roused himself enough to look at Sophie. Her head was bent, and she was searching the contents of her basket, yet the manner of her search was so scattered he knew the effort was a false one. "I apologize. That was badly done of me."

Sophie glanced up. "I took no mind of it."

East found a soft grunt was sufficient to communicate his disbelief.

"Well, it is truer perhaps that I took little mind of it. You are only half as disagreeable as Abigail when she is similarly afflicted."

East might have smiled if the effort would not have cost him dearly. "Dare I hope there is some small compliment there for me?"

"A very small one." She bent to her task again, this time looking with the purpose that had been absent before. She found her needle caught in the fabric of her own gown instead of the one she was repairing. Holding it up to the lamplight, she threaded it, then resumed her work. "Lady Dunsmore takes to her bed immediately," she said, "and has the curtains drawn around it. She cannot bear for there to be any noise." Sophie glimpsed the faint, mocking smile East cast in her direction. "Oh. Of course. I will endeavor to be quiet."

East could not say whether minutes or hours passed before he heard her voice again. This time it came to him as if from a long way off, the timbre of it soft and slightly hollow. It seemed to him that he was at one end of a tunnel or at the bottom of a well, and that she was calling to him from outside that place. He went to her willingly and sensed that he was in the right for doing so because she lavished him with praise and tender ministrations.

It was still dark when he woke, and several long moments passed before he could make sense of his surroundings. The fireplace was on the wrong side of the room, and the curtains were not drawn across the window. His room had only one chair, and now he counted two. There was also a table here, and he had none. Sophie's writing desk was gone, and where he might have expected to find it, he found an armoire instead.

This was not his bed, and he was not alone in it.

Sophie felt East's head stir on her lap. She recognized the transition from a sleepy shifting of his body to full awareness by the return of tension to his shoulders. She let her fingers trail lightly across the back of his neck. "You're awake."

"I seem to be."

"And your megrim?"

East had to concentrate on what he was being asked. He was no longer certain of the proper attachment of his head. "My megrim?"

Sophie's fingers stilled. "You don't remember?"

"I'm not . . . No, I don't remember." He started to sit up, but she pressed him down, placing her palm firmly at the back of his head. "Bloody hell."

Darkness hid Sophie's sympathetic smile. "For the moment you shall have to surrender to me. My strength is superior to yours." Her fingers sifted through the hair at his nape, and she felt his cheek press more heavily against her thigh as he relaxed. "Does it happen often that you cannot recall the attacks?"

"Not often. Usually there are signs when one is imminent, and I can do certain things to forestall it or lessen the impact. The worst of them, like this one, come with no warning, and I count myself fortunate not to drop to my knees." He tried to catch a glimpse of her face. "Or did I?"

"No. I should not have managed you on the stairs if that had been the case. You did look as if you might slide from the sofa, though, and that is why I thought it prudent to make other arrangements. You will have noticed this is not your room."

"I did," he said. "I wondered if you had."

Whatever pain his sore head still caused him, Sophie

thought, he had not entirely lost his wry humor. "It was not entirely for your comfort that I brought you here. I was thinking of my own."

"You did not have to sit with me."

"You asked me not to leave," she told him. "But you mustn't think I was persuaded by that pitiful plea. I hope you know me well enough to comprehend that I make my own choices."

East had no doubt this last was true. "Was I truly pitiful?"

"Oh, yes."

"And you weren't moved?"

"Not in the least."

He smiled. "Does it give you pleasure to pretend your heart is so hardened toward me?"

She ignored the question. "I think you are feeling more the thing."

"I believe I must be." He could not help but notice that she did not move or suggest that he do so. Her fingers continued to sift through his hair, the manner of it so idly done that he was tempted to acquit her of all knowledge of it. "I remember sitting with you belowstairs," he said quietly. "You were sewing."

"Yes. And you were reading."

"Was I?"

"Hmm. *Life of Nelson*."

He could recall the book, though whether he knew it from previous reading or what he had accomplished that evening was unclear. "Did I say anything for which I must beg your forgiveness?"

"You already apologized."

"I see." He had been hoping the answer would be no. "You believe me, don't you, that I don't remember?"

"Yes." She hesitated. "Does it frighten you?"

"Frighten? No, not precisely. It is . . . disconcerting, I suppose you would say."

"I would say it is frightening." She felt East's soft chuckle vibrate against her thigh. "I imagine there is very little that makes you afraid."

"Few things," he said. "But they make me very afraid." Before she could ask him what they were, he asked her.

"It is far simpler to tell you what I'm not afraid of," she said. "I like lightning storms and spiders and jumping Apollo over the largest fence in the field."

He waited for her to go on. When she didn't, he turned on his back and looked up at her. "I have never known a female who likes spiders."

Sophie shrugged.

"Bravery is stepping out to meet the things that frighten you," he said gently. "It doesn't matter how few or how many fears you have; it is what you make of them, or what you allow them to make of you. I would not want to test my courage against yours, Sophie."

She was silent. Her hand cradled the back of his head, and her fingers were still. "I'm afraid of you."

He smiled a trifle crookedly. "No, you're not. I think you'd like to be, but the sad truth for you is that I belong on your short list with the lightning and spiders and riding hell-for-leather. I don't pretend to understand why it should be against your will, but I know that it is so."

"How can you not understand the why of it," she said, more to herself than to him, "when you give voice to the thoughts in my head as if they were your own?" She looked down at him, studying his shadowed, teasing grin. "Do you think it is comfortable having you forever in my mind?"

"I wish I understood you half so well as you think I do." When she made no response, he said, "Concerning that list of all you find darkly fascinating . . . May I flatter myself to suppose that I come before the spiders?"

The sharp tug on East's hair was sufficient answer. Sophie nudged him so that he turned on his side. He lifted his head, and she slid out from under him, not to remove herself from the bed, but to lie fully clothed alongside him.

"Sophie?"

"You should sleep, my lord."

"East."

"Go to sleep, East."

The curious thing, he decided, was that it was so easily accomplished.

Sophie was alone in bed when she woke and not at all comfortable with the twinge of disappointment that accompanied this realization. She rose, stretched languidly, and stripped down to her chemise. She had only put a damp flannel to her face when she was overwhelmed by nausea. Kneeling at the bedside, head bent over the chamber pot, was how East found her a few moments later.

Shaking his head, he set a tray of tea and stale crackers on the table and hunkered beside her. He grabbed a fistful of her hair to keep it from falling forward into the pot and patiently waited for her to empty the contents of her stomach. Sophie tried to wave him aside, but this time it was he who would not be moved. When he was certain she was quite done, he briskly removed the pot, then put Sophie back to bed.

"You are pitiful," he said, placing the tray across her lap.

"Only that? I feel wretched."

"You look wretched."

She smiled wanly. "I think it is an odd sort of diplomat who speaks his mind so frankly."

"I can be politic when I have to be." He sat on the edge of the bed and encouraged her to take some tea. "I do not have to be now. I am concerned for you, Sophie, and I would be negligent if I did not say so. You are sick every morning and sometimes late in the afternoon. It is little wonder you have no belly to show for this child. It cannot be healthy for either of you."

Sophie regarded East over the rim of her teacup. "You know a great deal about it, do you?"

"More than you might suppose. I spent a good many years attached to Wellington's army. One can't avoid the camp followers and the wives who march to the drum. It is impossible not to learn something about how the women managed, and from what I have observed—and heard—since my arrival, I would say you are not managing at all well."

She bristled a little at his assessment but said nothing.

"When Mrs. Randolph arrives, I am sending her for the physician."

"I am perfectly healthy." Sophie bit into a cracker and chewed it determinedly. "He will only complain that you have made demands on his time for no good reason."

"He will be very well compensated and may complain all he likes."

Sophie understood this was a battle she should not wage with him. Still, her surrender was reluctant. "Oh, very well. I suppose you mean to have your way."

"Yes," he said. "I do."

Somewhat to Sophie's surprise, he left her then. She finished her tea and crackers and tried not to think about the niggling ache that owed nothing of its existence to morning sickness. She could not even be properly put out with his high-handedness, owing to the fact that she had been somewhat the same with him the night before. It had been a mistake not to turn him in the direction of his own room. She had thought it even as she was helping him negotiate the path from her door to her bed, but couldn't bring herself to act on it. He would have taken his leave later if she had insisted, but she hadn't had the sense to do that either.

Sophie was still trying to sort it out when he returned to her bedchamber, this time carrying two bowls of porridge. It was not decent, she thought, that he was freshly turned out in buff breeches and a splendid fawn-colored waistcoat, while she was still in her chemise with only her face and teeth cleaned. They had done so very well to avoid these situations for more than a sennight, and within the space of a single evening it was all coming undone. "You might have knocked," she said, pivoting away from the washstand.

"Indeed, I might have," he said. He watched both her eyebrows lift at his pleasant, no-quarter-given tone. "Sit here,

Sophie, and eat some porridge. I promise you will not be sorry."

Sophie considered defying him, but she could think of no good reason why she should. Sighing, she went to the table and sat. "It would be preferable if your demands were unreasonable, I think. I should like to have a good row with you this morning."

"Marry me."

Her mouth curved upward at the readiness with which he obliged her. "You are quick to . . ." Sophie's voice trailed off as she measured his intent and saw that he was perfectly serious. "You think you have worn me down?" she asked.

"No. Not nearly as much as I might have wished, but I am not a man of infinite patience. If I had any doubts on that score, last evening put a period to them. I mean to have you, Sophie." He used his spoon to gesture pointedly toward the bed and watched her eyes widen as she followed the direction of his hand and his thoughts. "I would rather you were my wife."

It stole a little of her breath away to hear him announce his designs so boldly. He was regarding her steadily, pinning her back in her chair so that she could not look away without calling herself a coward. "You are certain that your patience is at an end?"

East merely smiled.

Sophie returned it.

It was East's experience that in a standoff it was always the other fellow who blinked. That was not the way of it now. He set his spoon down and pushed his bowl away. "Sophie?"

"I suppose you think the thread of my patience is longer than yours," she said. "I suspect the truth is that it is far shorter. I have been on a very tight tether these last days if you would have had but the sense to know it." She rose and rounded the small table to stand beside his chair. "Will you lie with me now?"

He wondered at his hesitation when he should have already been closing the distance to her bed; but then she

smiled again, a trifle less confident than a moment ago but
no less willing, and he was not proof against it. When he
stood she was immediately in his arms, her mouth was on
his, and the kiss surged between them.

He lifted her, not sweeping her across his arms, but just
the few inches necessary to remove her feet from the floor.
For the length of the room there was no break in their kiss,
and when they tumbled to the bed their mouths separated
only long enough to draw air.

Neither of them made claim to a side. They rolled into
the middle of the bed, ropes creaking, the mattress nearly
curling around them from the force of their descent. Sophie
welcomed the weight of East on her, and she arched under
him to feel the entire length of his body pressed hard against
her. Almost frantic with need, she helped him raise her
chemise until it was rucked about her waist. She lifted her
knees. His hand slid between their flush bodies and fumbled
with the buttons on his breeches. Her fingers found his erect
penis and curled around it, and then she was taking him into
her.

East's first hard thrust made her moan softly. Her hips
jerked upward, and she dug her heels into the mattress. She
raised her arms around his back and bit off a second cry
when he thrust again. Her head was flung back. She could
feel his hot breath on her throat, at the curve of her shoulder,
then once more just above her mouth as he lifted his head
and surged forward.

The buttons of his waistcoat rubbed the midline of her
abdomen. They made an impression on her flesh through the
thin material of the chemise. The sensation was barely dis-
cernible from every other assault on her senses. She had the
taste of him on the tip of her tongue and his scent in her nostrils. He filled her vision, eclipsing the room and the sunlight. She knew his breathing better than her own, took his
rhythm for hers, understood every curve and angle of her
body in contrast to his.

He came to her with a certain violence that she did not try

to tame. She felt it, too. It was there in the press of her nails in his arms and the way she nipped at his shoulder. She wound her fingers in his hair and tugged hard, making him take her mouth again and take it deeply. She did not so much cradle his body as make it her prisoner.

Sophie drew breath in short measures, each one building on the last, filling her lungs with no release in between. Her breasts rose, aching. She rubbed against him, wanting the touch of him there, his lips, his hands, his chest. He took her with the hot suck of his mouth, dampening the chemise around her nipple and drawing both in, using his teeth and tongue to alternately tease and soothe.

She was hardly aware of what she asked him to do to her, only that he seemed to understand what she wanted. She had told him she was afraid of most everything, but here she knew herself to be fearless, even when he brought her to the point of release and kept her there, just hovering at the edge so that pleasure became as sharp as a finely honed blade.

It could not last forever. In the end it was not that he pushed her, but that she leaped. The intensity of her orgasm forced a cry from her throat, and his mouth was not on hers to capture the sound. She thought he looked for a moment as if he wanted to laugh, and the truest measure of her fearless state of mind was that she didn't care if he did. She would have welcomed his laughter, embraced it in the same way she did his own release, absorbing the shuddering strength of it because it was meant to be shared.

Eastlyn lay on his back, his forearm covering most of his brow. He lifted his arm a fraction, revealing one eye, and looked askance at Sophie. She was also lying on her back, her breathing just steadying. The rise and fall of her breasts became slow and even until he could no longer make out the faint pulse in her throat. "They will have heard you at the harbor," he said.

She sighed. It was not much of an exaggeration, she supposed. She had cried out quite loudly. "Do you suppose it might be mistaken for anything save what it was?"

"No. And if they missed it in the cove, I'm sure Mrs. Randolph did not."

Sophie turned her head. "She's here? You heard her come in?"

"Yes," he said. "To both questions."

She glanced at the door to make certain it was closed, though she recognized it was late to be doing so. "This is rather awkward, is it not? I mean, if she heard us, then she must be thinking the most awful things."

For a moment East did not understand; then when he took her meaning he gave a shout of laughter. "She doesn't think we're really brother and sister, Sophie. I would not be the recipient of so many disapproving stares if that were the case."

Sophie tugged on the neckline of her chemise, smoothing it properly into place as she turned on her side. "She stares at you?"

"Disapprovingly." He saw that Sophie was much struck by this, confirming his belief that she had never once noticed the housekeeper's censure. "And she clucks her tongue."

Sophie made the tsking sound three times with her own tongue. "How that must chafe. I think you are not accustomed to being cast in the role of the scoundrel." She fell on her back again and stared at the ceiling. "I wonder if we might depend upon her discretion?"

"I think we can depend on not depending." East sat up and threw his legs over the side of the bed. He applied some effort to making himself presentable, tucking in the loose tails of his shirt and pressing the creases from his waistcoat with his palms. He removed his hopelessly wrinkled neckcloth and buttoned his breeches. Standing, he leaned over the bed and stamped Sophie's rather bemused smile with his kiss. "I will not be gone long."

Although Sophie took him at his word, she was sitting at the table eating cold porridge when he returned. He glanced from her to the bed and back again, his disappointment not entirely feigned. He dropped into the seat opposite her but let his own bowl of porridge remain where it was. "Mrs. Randolph is gone," he said. "I sent her away."

Sophie nodded. "Not to bring the physician, I hope."

"No. She is gone for the day." Before Sophie's hopes were raised, he added, "I have not changed my thinking entirely. It is only a reprieve of sorts. She will return with the physician tomorrow." He watched her composure falter just a bit as a pale pink tide of color washed over her face. As always, Sophie was not as unaffected as her serene countenance would suggest. Her warm honey-colored eyes darted away from his, then returned uncertainly. She was shy of a sudden, and he realized he liked this look of her as much as he did her bold one.

"You have the most splendid eyes," he told her. The compliment had rather a different effect than the one he intended. East was almost set back in his seat when those splendid eyes narrowed skeptically. "I am not flattering you. I have always thought they were excellent in their coloring and directness." This made them slide away again. "And even when they are not direct, I find they have much to recommend them." He reached across the small table and lifted a heavy lock of hair from her shoulder with his fingertips. "They match this exactly. You must have noticed."

Sophie brushed her hair back so that it slipped from his fingers and fell behind her shoulder. "I do not find it at all singular."

"Perhaps because you are not sitting where I am. The view from here is extraordinary."

Discomfited, Sophie dropped her hands to her lap and began making pleats in the loose folds of her chemise. "I am unused to pretty compliments."

East considered this a moment. What Sophie did not say was that she could not judge the sincerity of them. He suspected this was at the heart of her confusion. "Mr. Heath did not remark on your eyes?"

"No."

"Or your hair?"

"No."

"Your lips?" The line of that lush mouth flattened immediately, forcing a grin to Eastlyn's. "Did he never kiss you?"

"No."

"Perhaps it is because your acquaintance was so brief."

"I think it was because he was in love with Miss Sayers."

"Oh, yes, I had forgotten that."

"I don't believe you. You are teasing me to amuse yourself."

"A little now." His eyes slid toward the bed. "And later, a lot."

Sophie felt a surge of heat, not all of which could be seen properly in her face. The centers of her eyes darkened, and between her thighs she was damp. She drew in her lower lip a fraction, setting the tip of her tongue to it.

Watching her, East thought Sophie knew something about teasing, even when she did not set out to do so. "I would have your answer," he said, his voice pitched low and husky. "It occurs to me that you gave me none before."

She could not pretend ignorance. There was only one question of any import between them. "It was not a request that you put before me earlier. It was in every nuance a command."

"And that makes little or no difference to you. You ignore one as well as the other."

Sophie stared at her folded hands for a long moment before she slowly raised her head and faced Eastlyn. There was no lingering amusement in his eyes; they matched hers for gravity of expression. "I do not know how to say yes," she told him quietly. "I know you do not expect romantic notions to enter into this marriage arrangement, but it is no simple thing for me. Perhaps it could be different if I had never come to love you; I could agree to your proposal as coldbloodedly as I agreed to poor Mr. Heath's. The choice of loving you, though, was removed from me at the outset; indeed, it never felt like an act of conscious will. Rather, it was as if you had tapped a wellspring in my heart and left me without any means to dam it."

She took a small breath then, steadying herself. It seemed to her that East was perhaps paler than he had been when she started her speech, but she did not try to interpret what it meant, only observed that it was so. "I do not blame you for it. I do not think you were careless of my feelings, only unaware of them. I trust that you are not the rogue I named you once; you might be cruel to be kind, but I acquit you of being cruel. I think you make it a point to avoid innocents like me for all the reasons that have come to pass." She was moved to smile faintly, recalling something he had confided to her. "You told me you prefer transportation to Van Diemen's Land to partnering a young woman in her first waltz. It is unfortunate that your sense of duty and obligation means you cannot always have your way in such things. It is easy to imagine that more hearts than my own have been attached to you in the course of those steps."

Sophie saw him frown slightly, and she realized she had said something more than she meant to. To distract the course of his thoughts, she quickly pushed her bowl and spoon aside and rested her clasped hands on the table. She meant the posture to show resolve and firmness, not an attitude of pleading or prayer. "I would not have shared my bed with you outside of marriage if I had not loved you. You could have forced me to that pass, but you did not. That *was* a choice I made, and I can still find no reason to regret it."

Eastlyn said, "But it does not change your opinion of marriage."

"It does not change my opinion of a marriage between us."

He pushed his chair away from the table and stood. He would have used his size to intimidate her if he thought it would have done any good. He was considering using his pistol. "For all your protestations of a fine affection for me, I do not understand the distinction you're making."

"It is not a fine affection," she said sharply. "I love you."

East's fingers plowed hard through his hair. "Bloody hell, but you make no sense."

Sophie's chair scraped the floor as she shot to her feet. Her hands folded into fists at her sides; her knuckles whitened. "I have never been moved so near to throttling someone. I should let them kill you, you know, but then what pleasure would there be left for me?"

Eastlyn held his ground while Sophie gladly gave up hers, putting a good distance between them as if she believed her own threat. He watched her widen the part in the window curtains and lean into the glass, pressing her forehead against the pane.

Her shoulders were hunched forward as she hugged herself. He did not think she was crying; she was too angry yet for tears.

He slowly released a carefully held breath. "You have been afraid for me all this long while?"

She answered with a small, jerky nod.

"You might have told me that at any time."

"I did not want to tell you now. Do you think I don't know how little difference it will make? You will dismiss my fears or make light of them. Or you will try to convince me that you can protect yourself. You have experience with the Society of Bishops, after all." Sophie turned away from the window to face him, surprised to see that he had drawn closer. Her voice lowered, but did not soften. "Tremont cannot be persuaded to any action by the removal of his chamber pot. You would have to remove *him*."

"Before he tries the same with me?"

"Yes." She searched his face, but his dark eyes had become impenetrable, and his expression yielded none of this thoughts. "If I had told you this when you made your proposal, you would have pressed me harder than you did. You would have wanted to remove me from my cousin's influence, and given little thought to your own safety. I left the Park with you because you promised you would not force marriage on me. It occurred to me then that you might lie to

Tremont and tell him we planned to marry, but I know now that you did not."

"How can you be certain?"

"If he thought we were married, he would not wait so very long to make me a widow."

East's gaze dropped to Sophie's flat belly. "Tremont is the reason you want a daughter."

"Yes, of course. Our daughter cannot inherit your entailed estate. But if he learns I have had your son, he will use the child to take whatever he wants from your holdings. It will be a bloodletting. Do not think for a moment that your parents can stop him."

"And if we don't marry?"

"Then my child, daughter or son, will be a bastard, and it matters little who the father is. Tremont cannot take money that is never settled on me or my child."

"Another reason you have asked me for nothing."

She nodded. "Just so."

"Bloody hell."

Sophie nodded again.

"Come here," he said. He knew he could have gone to her—there was enough despair in her eyes to make him want to do so—but he marked the fullness of her trust in the steps it would take to bring her to his side.

There was no hesitation. She went willingly because standing in the circle of his embrace was where she wanted to be. She felt his arms close around her back, his hands resting just above the curve of her bottom, and she turned her head and laid her cheek against his shoulder.

East kissed the top of her head. Her hair was silky against his mouth, and she smelled of lavender. "You were right that telling me everything only makes me more determined." He was prepared for her effort to move away, and he did not let her go. Negotiations often required a show of strength to gain an opponent's attention, and Eastlyn thought he might have been slow in demonstrating his. "I understand why you left this explanation unspoken for so long, and I appreciate that your fears are real and that you have acted at every turn to shield me from harm; but it is unfair that you have given me no opportunity to prove to you that I can manage the thing myself. I do not underestimate your cousin, Sophie, but my sense of him as a man of few scruples has much to do with the fact that he was the Society's archbishop."

East turned his head so that he might better see hers. "Why do you think he is capable of murder?"

Sophie's voice held no inflection; she had been made numb to the truth of it three years past. "Because it is how he came by Tremont Park. He is responsible for my father's death."

"You know this for a fact?"

"You *do* find it difficult to credit." Her faint smile was a trifle sad. "I thought you might. You want to think better of him in spite of your words to the contrary."

"You're wrong, Sophie. I find it surprisingly easy to believe. What I want you to tell me is if you know it for a fact."

"You are asking if there is proof. If I saw him with my father at the end."

"That's right. Did you?"

She shook her head. "No. He was with his congregation the day my father died. It was a Sunday morning in April. Abigail was with me. And Harold. Not in Papa's bedchamber, but in the house. They did not want to leave me because we all knew it would be soon. I did not ask them to stay, or even invite them to the Park; but they were there because ownership would move to their side of the family, and they thought they should show this last measure of respect."

When Sophie tried to step back this time, she found that East permitted it. She did not go far; she did not want to. "What do know about my father, East?"

"Little enough beyond the things you have shared." He saw she did not believe him. "There were people who were willing to tell me what they knew of him. Sometimes I listened; most often I did not. If there were things I should know, I supposed I should hear them from you. The gossip is just what you would expect: gaming and drinking, both to excess. I know there were debts. You are my source of the less well known aspects of his character: that he was given to bouts of melancholy, that he never stopped missing your mother, and that he was perhaps a better friend to you than he was a father. He indulged his grief, Sophie, and left you too often to make your own way, and that is the reason I judge him more harshly than you. I know you nursed him in his final years, but I know little about what put him in his bed. I have heard there was an accident and that he never properly recovered, but the nature of the accident is unknown to me."

Sophie felt as if she had made herself vulnerable to a succession of small blows. She was surprised that she did not waver on her feet or that the breath had not left her body. Her voice was both quiet and steady. "You did not learn, then, that he was addicted to opium."

"No."

She nodded slowly. "I have often wondered if it was widely known. Apparently not. You are aware the use of it is not remarkable. But to become a slave to it? That is another mark of my father's indulgence, is it not?"

East knew he had hurt her with that assessment, but he did not apologize for it. "When did he begin to use the drug?"

"Almost immediately after his accident. He was struck down while hunting. The ball lodged in his back, near the base of his spine. A surgeon removed it but could not repair the damage made by the bullet or his own extraction of it. My father came to know pain that no one should be made to bear. In the beginning the physician suggested laudanum. The doses increased gradually. He complained that it always took more to dampen the pain. Eventually he chose to smoke the opium as well."

Sophie marveled at the acceptance she heard in her voice.

She had not thought she would ever come to this place. "You might not believe that he was in full possession of his faculties, but there were many days when that was true. He read a great deal, played cards, and did not shun conversation or company. There were times, of course, when it was not possible to speak to him if one was in expectation of a reply, and there was always the pain."

"I am sorry," East said. "For his pain and your loss."

Sophie knew it was sincerely meant, and the ache around her heart eased. "I think I was his friend then," she said. "Or more parent to him than child, though I did not enjoy much influence. We were well matched in our stubborn natures, and he did not want to hear that the opium was killing him. I did not want to hear that he could not tolerate his life without it. We came to an impasse early and stayed there for most of the time he had left. I would give him what dose the physician determined I should, and my father would get the rest of what his body demanded elsewhere."

"Tremont?"

"Yes, he made certain the opium was available. I did not pay for more than was recommended, and I never purchased it in any form but the tinctures, yet my father always had what he wanted."

East considered this. "Dunsmore?"

"Harold is an obliging son. He does what his father says." Sophie impatiently brushed back a tendril of hair that was tickling her cheek. "You are perhaps thinking that my father is in many ways responsible for his own death. You are not alone; that is certainly the view held by Tremont and Harold. If I need to assign blame, they tell me I have to look no farther than my own mirror. They are not entirely wrong, East. I could have fought my father harder. I could have taken the drug away."

"If you could have done so, you would have." Eastlyn reached for one of Sophie's hands and took it in his own, squeezing lightly. "Was it an overdose in the end?"

"Yes. In the very end. That was the opinion of the physician."

Eastlyn nodded, his expression grim. "You will not want to hear this from me, but I must tell you that there is no evidence of murder here."

It was what she expected he would say, though he was right that she did not want to hear it. "The murder happened years earlier. When the good reverend shot my father."

East frowned. "Did I misunderstand? I thought you said it was an accident."

"My cousin could not very well admit he had done the thing intentionally, but he has never denied that it was his weapon that fired—"

"Or misfired."

"That *fired* in the direction of my father."

"There were witnesses?"

"My father and Tremont were not alone. It is not precisely the same as saying there were witnesses."

"I take it everyone was of the opinion that it was an accident."

"Yes. But it does not mean they saw precisely what happened, or if they saw it, interpreted it correctly. They cannot see into Tremont's heart and know his intent."

"And you can?"

Sophie regarded him steadily. "Never doubt it." She tugged on her hand, and he let her go. "He is an evil man, East. You must keep that at the forefront of your mind. He conceals his envy and greed and amoral soul with simple misdirection, drawing attention to the sins of others while he does as he pleases. He cultivates a reputation that is the very opposite of the one nurtured by my own father. If my father was society's scapegrace, then Tremont is its saint."

"Not to everyone, Sophie. He is not without considerable influence, but he does not have license to act in any manner he chooses."

"He does if no one stops him."

Eastlyn could not argue the point. As a former archbishop, Tremont would enjoy certain protections. It made him wonder about the friends who were with Sophie's father when he was shot. Perhaps it was a place to begin, he thought, but not at this moment. He was not at all sure he could share what he was considering with Sophie. She was warning him, not asking for his help. If she believed that she had influenced him to take action against Tremont, she would never agree to marry him. Still, there was one point that gave him pause. "Your father survived the accident," he said. "How did he explain what happened?"

Sophie's eyes slid away, and for a moment she stared at a point beyond East's shoulder. Regret shaded her features. "He couldn't," she said finally. "He remembered almost nothing."

It was not what she said that made Eastlyn want to know more, but the way she said it. He knew there was something held back. "Sophie?"

She glanced at him and was caught. "He was foxed."

"Badly?"

"Yes. So deep in his cups, in fact, that when Tremont summoned servants to carry my father back to the manor, they thought he was dead."

"The servants thought that?"

"Everyone thought that. Papa's stupor was so severe that they mistook him for dead." Her short laugh held no humor. "Can you credit it? That is what saved his life. Had my cousin known the truth, he would have waited for my father to bleed to death before calling the servants. I cannot doubt that is what would have transpired. I was witness to Tremont's face when he realized my father was still alive. It does not matter what my cousin has ever said about the shooting, East, because I know what I saw in his unguarded face that day was his confession."

Eastlyn understood then that Sophie required no further proof of Tremont's guilt, that whatever evidence he might gather would be in aid of proving to others what her cousin had done. "With whom have you shared your suspicions?" he asked quietly.

"No one."

"No servant? What about Dunsmore or his wife?"

"No one," she repeated. "If the servants are suspicious of Tremont, then it is because they have observed his true nature in the course of performing their duties. Harold was a witness to what happened. He already knows the truth, whether he says so or not."

"And Lady Dunsmore? What does she know?"

"I cannot say, only that she has heard nothing from me. Her constitution is fragile, and while I have been Abigail's companion these last years, Harold has never allowed me to be her friend."

Eastlyn knew that Sophie had been alone even as she had been surrounded by family, yet the depth of her isolation continued to catch him unaware. She would still be alone with her secrets if he had not provoked her. "Do you regret having told me?"

Sophie did not answer immediately. It was not so simple as saying yes or no. "I suppose that depends on what you make of it."

"And what of the other that you told me?" He saw her eyes reflect her confusion. "Have you forgotten so soon? You said you loved me."

Sophie's features cleared. "You would have me say it again?"

"I would have you say you do not regret telling me."

"I do not regret it," she said. "What I regret is that I cannot feel differently." Her faint smile had an ironic curve. "You did not expect that, I collect, but it is the truth. I do not want to love you. I would choose some other path if such were presented to me."

"I see."

"I doubt that you do, since your feelings are not similarly attached. I can tell you, you would not like it."

"Love is bothersome, then."

"Yes."

"And inconvenient."

"Very."

"It makes little allowance for reason," he said.

"It makes none at all. There is no sense to it."

He went to her this time. Putting his arms loosely about her waist, he drew her closer. "That is my experience also."

Sophie glanced up at him, uncertain.

"Marry me, Sophie."

"But—"

"I love you."

And it was then that Sophie knew he had worn her down.

Chapter Twelve

Sophie's knees sagged a little. She felt the enormity of what she was about to do as a nearly intolerable weight on her shoulders. East's arms tightened immediately so that he was supporting her, and the burden of what she was feeling was shared. Her throat was dry, and her eyes were wet. It was all she could do to nod.

East's smile was gentle. "Are you accepting my proposal, Sophie?"

She nodded again.

"I should like to hear it."

"Yes," she said on a thread of sound. "Yes, I'll marry you."

He thought she seemed more resigned to her decision than certain of it, but he was not going to challenge her answer. He kissed her lightly on the mouth. "You will not regret it," he whispered. "I swear, you will not regret it."

Sophie allowed herself to be led back to the bed where East encouraged her to sit. He did not join her, but drew a glass of water for her instead. She took it gratefully.

"Perhaps something stronger," he said when she drained the glass quickly. "Sherry? I believe I saw some in your cupboards."

"No. Water is sufficient." She let him pluck the glass from her hand and refill it. When it was returned to her she sipped until the ache in her throat passed. She set the glass aside and made a swipe at her damp eyes with her fingertips. When East produced his handkerchief, she accepted it. "This is not at all the usual thing, is it?"

"I cannot say. No one has ever agreed to marry me before."

That raised Sophie's small smile. "Then it can only be because you never asked."

"I asked you," he reminded her. "Several times."

"Yes, well, you thought you were obliged to do so." She dabbed at her eyes. "You would not have liked it if I'd accepted you."

"You are more certain of that than I am." East pocketed his handkerchief when she returned it and sat beside her. "Give me your hand, Sophie." He opened his palm so she could lay her hand across it. His fingers closed gently around hers. "Nothing obligates me," he said. "Except acting on my own judgment. In the garden at Bowden Street I judged that a proposal of marriage was the honorable thing to do. At the inn I judged that a proposal would protect you. Neither of those judgments was wrong, but each was incomplete. I did not know that I loved you then, but I always knew I could. You should never doubt that."

East threaded his fingers through hers. "I lose my balance when I am around you, Sophie, and I find I rather like the perspective it gives me."

"Perhaps you should have a drink instead."

Her wry tone made him chuckle. "A poor substitute. I know it for a fact."

"Then you didn't drink enough."

"There could never be enough," he said quietly. "I love you."

Sophie nodded faintly, accepting it. She stared at their clasped hands for a long moment, then at him. "I wish I were not afraid." She leaned into him, slipping her hand free so that she could place it on his shoulder. It was at her urging that they came to lie on the bed with his mouth but a hairsbreadth from hers. "I don't want to be afraid."

She tilted her head so that her lips brushed his. Once. Twice. Her mouth parted, and she deepened the kiss, touching the tip of her tongue to his upper lip, then engaging his own. She held him close, her hands running the length of his back. There was comfort in the weight of him against her and the way his fingers lay lightly across her breast.

East felt her panic even as she tried to restrain it. The edge of it was there in her voice and in the first wild beating of her heart. She would have had him take her hard and without thought if he had allowed it, but when he held himself back and let her know that he was unafraid, she accepted that, too.

He kissed the corner of her mouth and moved to her throat. She murmured something that might have been his name. He wanted to believe that it was. He liked the idea of it on her lips as he kissed the curve of her neck, then her shoulder, and again as he pushed her chemise down over her arms.

The small of Sophie's back arched when East's mouth found her breast. The first tug of his lips uncurled the knot in her stomach and flooded her with warmth. Heat came later, building slowly as he teased one kind of tension from her body and replaced it with another.

She came to know his touch everywhere. She felt his mouth at the sensitive inner curve of her elbow and at the back of her knee. He lifted her hair and kissed the hollow just below her ear. His mouth drew a line from her waist to her hip. He caught her wrists and held them on either side of her head while he kissed her long and deeply and made her move restlessly under him.

He removed her chemise and studied her with his eyes and then his hands, then again with his mouth, parting her thighs so that he might know her there as well. He watched her darkening eyes and knew she understood his intent. He

pressed his lips to her abdomen first, then caught her glance
again. This time she nodded, and his mouth moved lower
still. He had no difficulty recognizing the sound of his name
as she cried out with this first, most intimate touch.

She was as responsive as he knew she would be. He felt
her fingertips graze his hair, then his shoulder, before finding purchase in the bedclothes. She rocked back, lifting for
him, then gave herself up to the pleasure of it. He made her
mindless of everything but her own need and the fact that he
had aroused it.

Sophie felt the familiar rise of heat and the tension just
beneath the surface of her skin. She absorbed every touch of
his lips and tongue and fingers as a separate sensation, yet
knew them all at once, and when she came she had not
known how close she had hovered to the edge until she
stepped away from it.

He was there to catch her, as he always was. The in-
evitability of it struck her anew, and she wondered that she
had ever resisted it. It occurred to her that there had been a
kind of safety in loving him with no expectation that it might
be returned, and that perhaps she had not been protecting
him at all, but herself.

Sophie's eyes fluttered open. East was watching her,
looking vaguely satisfied. "I think you flatter yourself," she
said.

He grinned. "A little. Am I wrong to do so?"

She could not even pretend to consider her answer. "No.
You have a rather happy talent for . . ."

East waited, enjoying that she was put to a blush as she
searched for the right phrase.

". . . negotiating terms of surrender."

"Indeed."

Sophie looped her arms about his neck and drew his head
down. "I imagine I shall have to do whatever you like now."
She nudged his groin with her hip and felt the heat of his
erection through his breeches. "At least while we are still
abed."

"I never once supposed," East said wryly, "that you would do my bidding out of it."

Laughing, she helped him out of his clothes, all of them this time because she wanted to see him naked. She moved over him with her body in much the same way he had moved over hers. She tempted and teased, sometimes with her hands, sometimes with her mouth. Her exploration was more curious than bold and proceeded with a caution that was a torment in its own right. She asked him what he wanted, and he showed her. Her hair brushed his thighs as she bent her head and took him into her mouth.

Sophie thought perhaps that she should not want him in this way, that it was something only to be done for his pleasure, yet she could not deny that there was pleasure for her as well when he groaned softly or threaded his fingers through her hair. She remembered the hot suck of his mouth on her breast and the heat that spread across her belly and how her skin had felt too tight. She had wondered if she could bear it, and she had because there really had been no choice. Now it was East's turn to know the same and Sophie who reveled in the response of his body and the knowledge that he made himself vulnerable to her.

East caught her arms and drew her up and over him, and for a moment he thought he would come right then, when what he wanted was to be buried deep inside her. Her thighs parted on either side of his, and instinct, not experience, guided her. She mounted him, and when she was settled, she felt herself contract around him. He caught her hips and held her still.

"Don't move." His voice was tight with the effort it took to sustain this moment. "Not even there."

She held her breath.

He found he had the wherewithal to smile, though he suspected it was more of a grimace. "You can breathe, Sophie."

Her lips parted so she could take a shallow sip of air.

East took in her flushed face and the soft tangle of honey hair about her shoulders. "You have a remarkable seat."

Just as if she were guiding Apollo to change his direction, Sophie gave Eastlyn a nudge with her thighs. He was not proof against that and groaned. A muscle worked in his jaw. She leaned forward, lifting her hips slightly before settling on him again. She drew his hands from her hips to her breasts. His thumbs made a pass across her nipples, and she contracted around him again. This time he did not ask her to stop what she could barely control. He let her have the rhythm of the ride and held back as long as he was able, knowing all the while she would break him and that he would have no regrets for it.

When he came he nearly unseated her. She fell back, holding her own, then collapsed on top of him. The shudder that he felt from her was not the same as his own release. Her breathy little gasps were the result of laughter she could not quite restrain. She pressed her cheek against his shoulder, and when he could finally see her face he witnessed that she had abandoned herself not just to him, but to joy.

She was radiant.

He caught her hair and tugged lightly so that her head came up, and then he took her mouth. He kissed her slowly and deeply, the nature of it at once reverent and carnal, a celebration of what was of the soul and of the flesh.

Sophie did not know there were tears until she tasted them on his lips. They were hers to shed, his to take. She drew back, her smile tentative and watery. He gave her one corner of the sheet to dry her eyes. "It seems I am forever crying," she said. "I have no patience for it, so I cannot imagine how you suffer it."

He searched her face. "You are luminous, Sophie. Incandescent."

She squirmed uncomfortably and would have moved away from him if he had not held her close. "I am tolerable to look upon, East."

"More than tolerable, I should say, but I won't because you do not like compliments of that nature. What I mean to say is that you possess a quality that is not so easily defined, one not just of lightness, but of light."

"It is the tears."

"You may believe that if you like."

"I do. The other . . . when you speak of the other . . . I am reminded of a saint. I am not that."

"No," he said with some feeling. "You are not that." Before she could object to his quick agreement, he added, "And neither am I. To that end I wish to arrange for a special license. I cannot be depended upon to stay out of your bed if you make me wait overlong for our wedding."

"It had not occurred to me that you would." She eased off him and sat up, drawing a sheet around her. "I have no intention of asking you to do so. I am already carrying a child, so you cannot give me another. I fail to see the need for haste." When he regarded her as if she had taken complete leave of her senses, Sophie could not maintain the gravity of her expression. "You are surprisingly easy to tease, my lord. I would not have thought that would be the case."

"Which part of your little speech was the tease?" he asked, giving her an arch look. "Inviting me to your bed or failing to see the need for a special license?"

"The latter." Sophie thought he did not look entirely relieved, as if he did not trust her. "You may procure your special license. Even I know I will come to show soon enough."

"That, at least, is something."

"You understand, of course, the necessity of keeping our marriage a secret until that time."

East pushed himself upright, modestly pulling a blanket with him, and leaned back against the headboard. "Sophie, I can honestly tell you that I have been seated across the table from diplomats who spoke languages other than English and found more to comprehend in their speech than I often do in yours. Do me the great favor of telling me this is another tease."

Sophie shook her head. "I cannot. It must be a secret."

"Bloody hell. Did you just not say you know the pregnancy will reveal itself?"

"Yes, but until then, we should not reveal our marriage."

"What is gained by that?"

"Time. A few months perhaps, if I am careful. It might be time enough for me to settle with my cousin."

"Settle with him? I don't like the sound of that, Sophie."

"He is invested in the opium trade, East. I have known it for a long time. He has even made a profit of it on occasion, though he has never had much to show for it. Do you recall the steward at Tremont Park?"

"Your cousin's spy? I do recall the man."

"Mr. Piggins makes some of the investment arrangements for Tremont, but I suspect he also steals from him, else why is my cousin perpetually indebted? I have suggested that Piggins be relieved of his position because he knows nothing about managing the farms or the tenants or the cattle, but Tremont will not hear a word against him."

"Then you never told him Piggins was stealing."

"No. Never. Piggins can have all of Tremont's profits and I would not care. I want no benefit of the opium trade, even to save myself or Tremont Park, but it does mean that I should not confront the whole of it. My cousin continues to take the public position of being against the trade while he tries to profit privately. He might be willing to bargain for my silence on the matter. He would not like to have his true character revealed. People would not think ill of him being in the trade, but they will damn him for the hypocrisy. He can have no power if he is not perceived as a man of his word."

"Why now, Sophie? You have kept your silence for years. Why would—" He stopped because he saw her eyes flinch and knew this as a sure sign that she was holding something back. "You *have* confronted him before, haven't you?"

She gave no other sign for a moment, then jerked her head once.

"When?"

Her fingers began making pleats in the sheet while the line of her mouth remained mutinously flat.

Eastlyn took a stab at the answer to his question. "Not before your father died, I think. As much as you feared your father's use of the opium, I think you accepted that he came to rely on it. He would have been unhappy with you if you had stopped his supply. So it must have been later. Perhaps when you realized Lady Dunsmore had become addicted."

Sophie shot him a sharp look.

"It's true, isn't it? She is as reliant on the tincture of opium as your father was."

"How could you know that? I have never—" She bit her lip, and her eyes slid away from East's. "You did not know until just this moment, did you? It was only a suspicion." Out of the corner of her eye, Sophie saw him nod. "I am afraid you will have the better of me at every turn. It cannot be much sport for you to interrogate me when I give up the answers so easily."

He reached for her, cupping her chin and bringing her round to face him. "I am in earnest, Sophie. Lady Dunsmore has always been a bit of a cipher. You were a companion to her when one would suppose she would have little need for such. She is given to megrims and enjoys the privacy of her own room. She has rather a nervous constitution and only the smallest circle of friends. I believe you acted as governess for the children because it meant one less person being privy to her problem." He let his hand fall when he knew he had her full attention. "But I am not so certain you would have confronted only Tremont on Lady Dunsmore's behalf. For her, it seems to me that you would have also gone to her husband."

Sophie nodded faintly. "Harold is invested in the trade as well. I cannot say how successful he is, only that there is rarely any money for the household. Perhaps his profits only pay his debts from the previous quarter." Her fingers stilled for a moment. "He saw nothing wrong with it, East. Abigail is disappearing before his eyes and the eyes of his children, and he defends his support of the trade as being a sound practice. He would not admit there was any cause for concern. Abigail only takes it for her headaches, he said, and never once owned that now her headaches can last for days at a time."

Eastlyn took this in. The opening was there to tell Sophie that Dunsmore had placed Mrs. Sawyer under his protection, but he judged it would only distract him from his purpose. "Was it at Tremont Park that you confronted the earl?" he asked. "Perhaps while I was there? You asked me about the political matter I was there to discuss with him. Was that when you realized the extent of his scheming?"

Sophie gave him a brief, ironic smile. "I have always understood that my cousin's public opinions and private actions were seldom congruent. What you told me at the Park was merely confirmation of yet another example. Some weeks earlier I overheard Tremont speaking to Piggins about a ship called *Aragon,* and I knew Tremont had a substantial investment in *Aragon*'s cargo. The size of the investment was such that there was little left to manage the Park. It was clear to me that if the ship failed to make port, there could be no recovery without engaging one more creditor. It seemed unlikely that anyone could be found to lend Tremont money. The estate's debt is already crushing."

"So you went to him?"

She nodded. "I told him what I knew. He meant to withhold his support of the Singapore settlement until he had the concessions he wanted. I cannot be certain what demands he intended to make on the prime minister, but I know that he wanted to coerce you into making a second proposal of marriage. I threatened him with telling you everything."

"Is that why you ended up in the chapel?"

"In part. And because I kissed you at the lake. Tremont meant to punish me for that as well."

East's fingers made furrows in his thick hair as he ran his hand through it. "You cannot seriously mean to confront the man a second time, Sophie. I have seen for myself that he is capable of any manner of retribution. He is already nursing wounds from having lost you. It was a considerable blow to his pride when I told him I had helped you leave the Park and that he could not expect that you would return. He did not like having you absent of his control."

"Yet he has not found me."

"He has not sent anyone for you," East said. "It does not mean that he doesn't know where you are. I found you, Sophie. Given time, so can he. Perhaps he already has."

"No. He would force me to return to the Park or Bowden Street."

"There is another explanation separate from him not wanting to give rise to a scandal: Tremont does not need you just at the moment."

She frowned slightly. "I don't understand. Do you mean to say that he has abandoned the idea of marrying me off? How could you know that?"

"I doubt that he has abandoned the idea. It is probably truer that he means to use it as the need arises." East saw that he had merely deepened Sophie's confusion. "It is the *Aragon*, Sophie. The ship has delivered its cargo and returned. It is safe to assume that both of your cousins profited from their investment."

"How long have you known this?"

"All of it? Only since you fit the pieces of this puzzle together. I am familiar with *Aragon* because I have been involved with this government's concern regarding Singapore since June. I am aware of all of our trade with China and a great deal that the Americans and French are doing as well. The East India Company's business is important to the Crown, and the competition for favored status with the Chinese is of particular interest to them. They make certain I know about rogue traders like the *Aragon*'s captain who operate without sanction from either government."

Sophie leaned over the edge of the bed and plucked her chemise from the floor. She held it bunched in front of her while she considered what East told her. "Then there was more risk in Tremont's investment than I suspected. He might well have bankrupted the estate."

"Perhaps." He watched her abandon the sheet in favor of her chemise and knew a measure of regret. "But he is still a Bishop, and he can always apply to the Society for help."

"How fortunate for them that he profited this time."

East thought that if he kissed Sophie just then, he would know the taste of sarcasm. "*Aragon* arrived in Liverpool shortly before I left London to come here. I know this because I was at Lloyd's when news of her arrival was delivered."

Sophie knew that Lloyd's insured merchant ships and their cargo. "Go on. I am familiar with Lloyd's."

"It meant little to me at the time. I had no understanding then that Tremont and Dunsmore were involved in the trade. What I did know, however, was that in recent weeks Dunsmore's spending was in excess of his customary extravagant manner. He might rarely have had money for the household, but it seems to me that he must have very patient creditors, for he spends money as though he has it. It occurred to me that he had already received funds from some source or that he was in expectation of receiving them soon. I knew it was not at the gaming tables where he had achieved success because I witnessed some of his losses there. I left London before discovering the origin of his new wealth. It would have taken some time to trace it all the way back to *Aragon*. I did not imagine I would learn the truth in Clovelly."

Sophie had drawn her hair forward over one shoulder and was absently untangling the ends as she listened. Now her fingers paused, and she regarded Eastlyn with a pensive mien. "How is it that Harold's spending came to your attention? With so many things to occupy you, it seems to me that Harold's habits should have been of little note."

"You are wrong. They are important on two counts: he is Tremont's son and your cousin. The first makes him of political concern; the latter a personal one. I had a vague notion that he might know something more than he was revealing."

"In regard to what?"

"In regard to his father's political ambitions for one. Your whereabouts for another. You had not yet left Cara's, and I had no inkling that you intended to do so. Making certain that I knew Dunsmore's business was but one way of keeping you safe."

Sophie remembered how angry East had been when he left her at the inn. She had been certain that he would not want to see her again, and when he did not arrive at his sister's home to make any explanations, she thought she had been in the right of it. To learn now that he had been acting to protect her from as far away as London set her off balance. As East had said of himself, she found she liked the perspective from this new angle.

"Sophie?"

"Hmm?"

"You are wool-gathering."

She gave him a brief, distracted smile.

"You have some deep thoughts, I collect."

Sophie meant to hug those thoughts to her. Perhaps it had not only been his own sense of honor that prompted him to act as he had in London. Perhaps he had felt something for her even then. It was not possible that he had loved her from the first, as she had him, but it was possible that he had entertained a certain affection for her long before he declared himself, perhaps before he knew it in his own mind. "I'm sorry," she said. "You were telling me about Harold."

East wondered at the route her thoughts had taken but knew he was unlikely to learn of it. "I was done telling you about him."

"No. You have said nothing about his spending except that it was outside the common mode for him. I want to know more of the particulars."

"It cannot be important."

Sophie would not be dissuaded. "You mentioned losses at the gaming tables, but that is in every way a common occurrence. He has no luck with cards or dice. Tell me something I would not suspect."

"Do you remember the night I came to your bedroom at Bowden Street?"

"I am far less likely to forget it than you. I am not the one seized by megrims and odd lapses of memory."

Eastlyn could not fault her for pointing out the truth, but he gave her a quelling look for her saucy retort. She was as unaffected by it as he thought she might be. He went on, "Then you will also recall that Tremont and Dunsmore were gone from the house. I noticed that you were surprised by their absence when I informed you of it."

Sophie nodded. "Tremont had spoken to me earlier that day, and he never mentioned an engagement for that evening. He frequently told me when he was going out. I think he meant to remind me of my own confinement." She smiled crookedly. "As if such were needed. I must have presented myself with more composure than I felt for him to think I was unaffected by my situation."

"You were holding fast to your decision not to marry," East said. "Tremont likely thought another turn of the screw was in order."

"Where was he that night?" asked Sophie. "Was he with Harold?"

"Let us say that he was with his son for some part of the evening. I imagine they did not spend the whole of it together. They went to an establishment called the Flower House, not far from Covent Garden. It is frequented by gentlemen who have certain peculiar tastes in entertainment."

Sophie's fingers began to pleat the fabric of her chemise again. The small, vertical crease appeared between her brows as she considered what East was *not* saying. "This establishment? It is for whores?"

East sighed. He should have known she would come at the thing directly. "Yes, Sophie. It is a brothel."

"And my cousins were there?"

"Yes."

She eyed Eastlyn sharply. "It begs the question how you came by such intelligence. Did you perhaps pass them in a hallway?"

Amused by her querulous tone, East grinned. "I watched them go inside. That is all." He held up his hands, palms out, as if to ward her off. "I was coming from a gaming house not far away when I saw them. It occurred to me that if I knew where they were going and how long they might be occupied, I might take advantage of an opportunity to see you. When I followed them to the Flower House I knew they would not return to Bowden Street much before morning."

Sophie was not entirely satisfied with this explanation. "I think you know rather too much about this place."

"You have accused me of murder, gambling, and an indulgence in drink," East said. "Do you wish to add another vice?"

She said nothing for a moment, examining the crease in her chemise while she considered her apology. "I regret having said those things," she said quietly. "It was all in want of stopping your proposal, but that is a poor enough excuse. I did not know so very much about you then, and I should not have judged your character on the gossip of others, especially when I despised the same being done to me." She glanced at him and could not make out the tenor of his thoughts. "Will you forgive me? It was wrong of me to charge you with such behavior, no matter the provocation."

"Even if it's true?"

"Even then." She hesitated, and her fingers resumed their pleating once more. "Is it true?"

Eastlyn leaned forward and reached for her busy hand. He laid his over hers, quieting it. "There is truth in almost everything one hears," he said. "You must decide for yourself the degree of it." He released her hand and drew his legs up tailor fashion, resting his elbows on his knees. "I have been making wagers with my friends for more than a score of years. At Hambrick we had little money to spare so our wagers were confined to coppers and shillings. Our pockets are deeper now, but the wagers between us have not changed. Even in the betting book at White's it is rare for any one of us to offer up more than a few hundred pounds."

Sophie's mien remained thoughtful. "It is not the usual practice of a gamer."

"No," he said. "It is not. But it is *my* practice." East made a steeple of his fingers and lightly tapped the tips together. "As for drinking, it is certainly true that I have been foxed on occasion, but I can tell you that except for a sore head I have never suffered overmuch. Neither have I forgotten anything. It is not drink that prompts a loss of memory, but the severity of a megrim."

"So you are a temperate drinker."

"With infrequent lapses into excess."

"You are practically a paragon."

East looked pointedly at Sophie's belly. "Hardly that."

She ignored him. "And a murderer? There is something more to the story than the gossip."

"Someone told you about Hagan, I take it." East shook his head, his mouth set grimly for a moment. "It was a very long time ago, Sophie. I was just beginning my diplomatic work, and I was to have a meeting with the Russian consul. Hagan was the one who gave me the assignment. I was supposed to offer some guidelines for an agreement by which we might form an alliance with the Russians against Napoleon. We already knew that Prussia meant to give the French license to cross their land, and it appeared Boney was only in want of an opportunity to do so. He was still in Spain at that time, and a Russian invasion would have to wait; but with his steady annexation of most of the Continent, it seemed clear he would eventually turn to Moscow."

East threaded his fingers together so that his hands made a single fist. "There was another aspect to my assignment, however, of which Hagan was unaware. It was known to the foreign secretary that someone in the corps had compromised an earlier attempt to do much the same thing. I was to discover that man's identity."

Sophie's eyes widened a fraction, and her voice held equal parts astonishment and awe. "Why, you are a spy."

East shook his head. "No. I am the tinker. The one who makes repairs." It was a fine distinction, perhaps, but in the Compass Club, it was West who was the spy. "You might have already concluded that Hagan turned out to be the one I was looking for. I discovered him in a tryst with the wife of a member of the Russian delegation. He would not believe me that she was using him to procure information for her husband. I was frank in my description of the lady's behavior and the lady herself, and Hagan took exception to it. He called me out."

"I was told you had thrown down the glove."

Eastlyn shrugged. "People forget the particulars even if they once knew them. In truth, there was little known factually about what happened. Most of it was supposition."

"Then is it true that you killed him?"

"It is true that I meant to when I set out that morning. Hagan's pistol ball struck me first." Eastlyn showed her a faint, slightly puckered scar on his left arm just below his shoulder. "I had a choice then to delope, and I decided he did not deserve so easy a dismissal; but it was also enough for me that he knew I could kill him. I adopted the middle course and aimed my shot low. He took it in the thigh, close enough to his ballocks that he would forever think twice before he compromised himself with a woman." He regarded Sophie directly. "The reason that you heard he was murdered is because he immediately left the country and has never returned. It is quite possible that he did come to a bad end, but it was not by my hand. I suspect the Russians no longer found him useful."

Sophie thought it was likely East knew more about Hagan's bad end than he could properly tell her. She did not press him. "So you are not a murderer either," she said. "It would seem that you have been poorly judged by many people."

"Perhaps, but they are judgments not often repeated behind my back, and only once to my face."

The realization that he was speaking of her incautious words put color into her cheeks. "I deserved to be called out for it."

"I decided to marry you instead."

She looked at him narrowly, wondering if she could believe him. "You are diabolical."

"Thank you."

"It is not strictly a compliment, you know." She stretched crossways on the bed, raising herself up on one elbow. "You told me rather a lot about your assignment on behalf of the East India Company. It doesn't seem to me that it is much different than what Hagan did. Weren't you concerned that I would say something to Tremont?"

"You gave me your word that you would not."

"You could not have trusted me so completely."

East said nothing.

Sophie saw the whole of it then. "You did *not* trust me. You took me into your confidence in anticipation that I *would* say something."

"No," he said. "Only that it would not matter if you did. It surprised me how very much you knew about the Company's plans, but then I had not realized that you listened to your cousin practicing his speeches from the other side of the door."

"You made everything you told me seem as if it should be an intrigue."

He shrugged. "I thought you were looking for one. I only meant to oblige you."

Sophie's fingers curled around one corner of a nearby pillow, and she hurled it at him. East caught it easily. Her attack was a little more difficult to deflect, but he managed to capture her wrists and pin her back to the bed. The blankets and sheet tangled around them, assisting his efforts to keep her confined. She was breathing hard when he finally subdued her.

"Admit it, Sophie," he said pleasantly. "You are more embarrassed by your gullibility than you are angry with me.

And I did not lie to you about anything except that you should keep it all a secret. It was inevitable that the arguments for and against the settlement proposal were going to be made public."

She glared at him. "I thought you trusted me."

"I do . . . after a fashion." East was forced to shift one of his legs across both of hers when she tried to squirm away. The unmistakable press of his erection against her hip made her go still. He acknowledged this evidence of his desire with the ironic lift of one eyebrow. "I did not know about the *Aragon*, Sophie. If I had suspected Tremont was actually involved in the trade, I would not have told you why I was meeting with him. It did not occur to me that you might use some part of our discussion to blackmail him."

He felt her relax, though the cast of her eyes was not so forgiving. "You threatened to tell him what you knew and put yourself at great risk. You are fortunate that he only made you absolve your sin with prayer. He could easily have done more than set you on a bed of stones. That is why I will not let you confront him a second time. That is for me to do, Sophie. It is all part and parcel of my work, and your interference will only complicate matters." East searched her features. He thought the line of her mouth had softened a little, but he was not so certain that he would risk kissing her.

"I will agree to one of your demands," he told her. "We will be wed here in Clovelly by special license, but the marriage will remain a secret from everyone but my family. I will arrange a house for you in London, and you will let it about that it is part of a settlement from the estate of a distant relative. A settlement that is not subject to entailment, of course."

"Of course," she murmured.

"We will find a suitable companion for you until such time as we make our marriage widely known. With your companion, you will be able to go out in public."

"There is Lady Gilbert," she said softly. "My great-aunt in Berwyn."

"Very well. I shall find her, but companion or no, you will not—under any circumstances—visit Bowden Street, and you will not entertain your family alone in your home."

"Very well." Her voice was not raised much above a whisper.

"I am very glad to hear it. This secrecy cannot last, Sophie, but I concur with your assessment that it will provide time. I can use it to gather evidence of Tremont's involvement in the opium trade. It is a task that would be made more difficult if he knew we were married."

She nodded, though he had not asked for her agreement.

"Then it is settled."

"Yes."

East regarded her closely, gauging her sincerity. She did not look as if she meant to bite him any longer, or rather that if she did, it would be of a kind he would not mind. Her eyes were vaguely slumberous, darkening at the center with her lashes lowered. Her mouth was still parted on her last spoken word, and it no longer seemed that her response was entirely meant as an answer to his question.

Dipping his head, Eastlyn brushed her lips with his. She followed the movement, trying to reach him as he drew back. He came again and touched her just as lightly this time, the contact as fleeting as the first. The breath she caught sounded like a whimper. He saw her eyes dart over his face as she tried to anticipate him. Her wrists were still pinned, her body held taut under his, and when she moved it was only to lift her chin and offer the slender curve of her throat. He put his lips there, at a point above her collarbone, and tasted her. The suck of his mouth left a small bruise. He had not meant to mark her skin, but the sight of it made him feel oddly powerful, as if he had laid claim to her in the most elemental way.

He lowered his head again, taking her mouth hard. His tongue speared her. She kissed him back, equal to his strength, and if there was surrender it was not because he held her body flush to the bed, but because she wanted him in just this manner. When she could stir, her movements had a restless edge and only one purpose: to be closer to him.

She was made breathless by his kisses, and light-headed. When she opened her mouth to draw air, he stole it from her. He whispered her name against her lips and what he meant to do to her against her ear, and then she could not breathe or even think beyond that moment. At the periphery of her vision there was darkness, but at the center was the image he had placed in her mind. She had a view of herself lying under him and his lean frame cleaved to hers, and it was as if she were apart from both of them, watching him move a moment before she felt his lips on her skin. There was his mouth on her breast, at the underside of her arm, then at her throat again. And there was her shift being pushed to her thighs and the blankets unwinding around her legs.

She did whatever he asked. "Raise your knees, Sophie." And when he was settled between her thighs, a second husky command: "Lift your hips." She felt him push inside her and her back arched and then he demanded her mouth. She gave him this, too. Her wrists were released, and his hands slipped around her back. He sat up, carrying her with him. She remained joined to him, her face close to his, and she felt boneless and weightless, unable to move until he told her to put her arms around his neck.

Her breasts rubbed his chest. Their aching fullness was not relieved by the press of his skin against hers. She wanted his hands there, and he teased her by placing his palms on either side of her and running his hands from her waist, along her ribs, and then down again, always stopping short of cupping her breasts. He made her tell him what she wanted, and she hardly recognized her own voice when she found it. The breathy, husky timbre sounded as if it were spoken by another woman, one drugged by desire and shameless in her need.

His thumbs made a pass across her nipples, and she closed her eyes against the intensity of the sensation. Her hips rocked forward, drawing him more deeply inside her. He took her mouth, her breath, her voice. Her body rose and fell in a slow, undulating motion, like a wave washing over him.

The sound of her own heartbeat was a roar in her ears, and for a moment she was deaf to everything but that. The bed creaked, embers popped in the fireplace, there was the rustle of the sheets and the moist suck of their mouths, and she heard none of it.

He was all hard muscle and tension, his need defined in the taut features of his face, in skin that was pulled too tightly. His embrace was too intense to be sheltering, too demanding to be comfortable. It was exactly what she wanted, this raw, naked need of his, and the sense that he could not get close enough to her, or thrust too deeply.

Her teeth caught his lobe. She bit gently, and she told him what she wanted, her breath hot against his skin. The words were ones she had learned from him; but on her lips they were earthy, not rough, and he knew himself to be as helpless as she had been earlier.

They collapsed together, arms flung wide, legs tangled. Sophie's hair hung over the side of the bed, and she thought that if East moved she would simply slide limp and liquid to the floor. When he raised his head she pushed it back to her shoulder, and she thought she heard a small, raspy chuckle, though she could not imagine how he came by the strength to summon it.

They lay in just such an abandoned posture until their breathing eased and their limbs where once again sound enough to lift. East rolled away and pulled Sophie back the few inches necessary to keep her from spilling onto the cold floor. She turned on her stomach and buried her face in a pillow that was filled with the scent of both of them.

"Did you really tell me that you wanted me to—" East stopped, bent close to her head, and whispered the rest of it in her ear. Sophie's short, embarrassed moan was proof that she had said exactly that. Eastlyn lifted part of the heavy curtain of Sophie's hair and brushed it back so that he could make out a measure of her flushed profile. She turned her head just the fraction required to look at him with one accusing eye. "It is to be my fault, then," he said, unconcerned and unrepentant. "You mean to charge me with putting those words in your mouth."

"I mean to charge you with pulling them out of it."

He grinned as she placed her face squarely in the pillow again. "You are going to suffocate." Her muffled reply was unintelligible, and Eastlyn let it pass. Turning on his side, he laid one arm lightly across her back. She fit herself to him without any urging, and for a time they slept.

East woke first and was already preparing a luncheon for them when Sophie arrived in the kitchen. She set the table and added a kettle to the hearth for tea while he stirred the soup pot. When it was time to sit, East did not miss that Sophie placed herself somewhat gingerly in her chair. She intercepted his look of concern and warned him with a quelling glance that he should not inquire. Because he believed she was fully capable of throwing her soup bowl at him, East did not challenge her.

The ache that made Sophie ease herself into her chair was more of a certain awareness of her body than strictly a discomfort. She could still feel the pressure of East's hands on her breasts, at the small of her back, and cupping the rounds of her buttocks, but between her thighs it was the absence of him that she felt most keenly. No matter how uninhibitedly she had expressed herself in their bed, this was not a subject to be discussed over soup.

Later, they walked along High Street almost the entire way to the cove. There was more than a touch of winter in the air this afternoon, but the chill was bracing, and the walk proved more invigorating than tiring. East bought Sophie some threads and ribbons. He would have purchased the milliner's entire supply of bonnets and gewgaws if she had expressed the least interest, but she was wholly satisfied with the ribbons. It occurred to him that her lack of interest in fashion might make her an inexpensive wife. He said as much to her when they passed the dressmaker's shop and she did not glance once at the window.

"It is not difficult to have little interest in such things when your taste is far superior to my own, and I know that you will never permit me to go about shabbily." She gave him a sideways glance and saw he was much struck by her reasoning. "I think you will find it quite expensive to turn me out to your satisfaction."

"You are wrong, Sophie." He tipped his hat and bid a good afternoon to Mrs. Godwin, the harbormaster's wife, who had three of her five children in tow. When the parade had moved on, he added, "It will not cost me a farthing to keep you naked and abed."

Sophie would have stumbled and fallen if East had not had her arm. She glanced over her shoulder to make certain he had not been overheard. The Godwin children were chattering happily, and their mother was making a critical study of the gown in the dressmaker's window. "You should not say such things," she whispered. "Why, Mrs. Godwin—"

One of East's brows kicked up. "I believe that Mrs. Godwin's brood is proof that she has a husband whose thinking is similar to mine."

Sophie realized that if she did not want to suffer more of the same, she would have to distract him. To that end, she led him to the bookseller's shop and proceeded to prove how very expensive she could be.

"You emptied my pockets," he said as they stepped onto the footbridge to the street. "Now I *know* I shall have to keep you—"

She trod upon his foot. "In the library?" she asked sweetly. "That is what you meant to say, is it not?"

East agreed that it probably was, but when they arrived home he put her over his shoulder and carried her straightaway to bed.

* * *

It was after dinner, when they were sitting much as they had the night before in their separate places near the fire, that Eastlyn told her about Dunsmore and his arrangement with Mrs. Sawyer. He watched Sophie's fingers momentarily still in plying her needle when she heard the name of his former mistress.

"That is peculiar, don't you think?" she asked him, attending to her work again. "Did they know each other before your name was linked to mine?"

"I don't think so."

That was Sophie's suspicion as well. "I suppose Harold has kept a mistress before. Abigail has never mentioned it, though. Perhaps she was as unaware as I was." She glanced at him. "What do you suppose it means?"

"I don't know. It might have no significance."

"You do not believe that. How long was Mrs. Sawyer your mistress?"

East had resigned himself to discussing this frankly when he broached the subject; however, it did not mean he was in any way comfortable with it. "Six months, I think. It could have been longer. There was the obvious purpose to our liaison, Sophie, but nothing beyond it."

"Not on your part, mayhap," she said. "But Mrs. Sawyer wanted a husband. Do you suppose she wants the same of Harold?"

"Your cousin is married."

Sophie regarded East directly and made sure her tone was carefully neutral. "And my father was the Earl of Tremont and now he is dead. I have learned that when people decide what they want, there are any number of ways they might achieve their ends."

Chapter Thirteen

Sir James Winslow handed a glass of sherry to his wife. It seemed to him that she clutched the stem of the glass rather more tightly than she ought to. Outwardly she was composed, but this tight grip of hers was the real expression of her confusion.

He decided not to join her on the upholstered bench and stood just slightly behind her instead. In this position she could sense his nearness and rely on his ability to catch her if she simply keeled over.

It was a shock, of course. There was no getting around that Gabriel had served them something more than was easily taken in at one sitting. As difficult as it was for him to digest the particulars, dear Franny looked as if she could not yet swallow.

Sir James allowed his glance to shift from his son to his new daughter-in-law. Like Franny, she appeared perfectly composed, but he sensed in her a desire to flee the room. It was not that she held too tightly to a glass of sherry, but that her hands held too tightly to each other. The clasp was nearly bloodless. Sir James found he still had enough good sense to smile as Gabriel absently reached out and covered both of

Sophie's hands. Beside him, he felt some of the tension seep from Franny's shoulders. She had observed her son's gesture and knew it for the protective, loving expression that it was.

"You are quite certain your marriage must be kept secret," Sir James said, directing his comment to his son.

"Yes," East said. "But for as little time as possible."

Franny sipped her sherry and was grateful for the immediate calming influence that spirits had on her. "I don't believe I comprehend the necessity. You will have to explain it to me again."

East smiled. "Again? That sort of trickery is beneath you, Mother. I did not explain it even once. I asked that you trust me that it must be so." He tilted his head toward Sophie and spoke in feigned confidential tones. "You would do well to guard your tongue around her, for she is very good at eliciting information. Growing up, Cara and I confessed to all manner of things we had vowed to keep to ourselves."

Sophie's eyes widened faintly.

"He is impudent, is he not?" Franny asked.

East squeezed Sophie's hands lightly. "That is strictly rhetorical. Mother knows the answer."

Sir James chuckled as Sophie's glance darted between Gabriel and Franny, as though trying to determine if offense was taken on either side. "You must not mind them," he said. "They are each quite able to hold their own, but then I suspect you recognize that. I imagine the same can be said of you."

Sophie lifted her eyes to Sir James's kind face. He was not a tall man, nor particularly broad of shoulder, but he was solid and steady with a patient, considering air about him that Sophie found comforting. This was the man, she remembered, who read her manuscript, who knew the bent of her mind perhaps better than her own husband. He had dark, intelligent eyes and a way of holding his head slightly to one side that gave the impression of perpetual thoughtfulness. A faint smile hovered about his mouth even in this pensive mode. He wore spectacles to read, and they rested below the bridge of his nose so he could look over the top of the thin gold frames.

Sophie felt those keen eyes on her now as he awaited her reply. "I cannot say that I hold my own any longer, or indeed, that I have anything left to hold."

"Worn you down, has he?" Sir James asked.

Straightening, Eastlyn cleared his throat. "She would like me to think that." The shadow of his smile passed, and he regarded his parents gravely. "I regret that so much has been done without your knowledge. You should know that Sophie wanted me to write to you so that you might be forewarned of our arrival and the circumstances surrounding it. Perhaps if I could have persuaded her to pen the thing herself, you would have received such a missive, for she is infinitely more capable of expressing herself in the written word than I am."

Out of the corner of his eye he saw Sophie's head swivel in his direction. Until that moment he doubted she'd had any idea of how much of her work he had read. "I elected to tell you such things as I can in this manner because I wish to make myself understood. I wanted you to meet Sophie here, with me, and observe for yourself that I am fully content with the decisions I have made."

"That is perfectly apparent," Franny said. "I wonder, though, if your wife is of a similar mind, or if she has simply surrendered her judgment to yours."

East removed his hand from Sophie's lap. "Such a thing is not possible, Mother."

Sophie felt the full force of Lady Winslow's skeptical gaze. "I was in every way agreeable to my husband's plans. I wanted to be married in Clovelly with the same dispatch as he, even knowing as I did that it might give you reason to hold me in little esteem. Eastlyn would take a great deal upon his own shoulders and have me be blameless in your eyes, but we know, even if he does not, that I bear at least equal responsibility. In my defense, I can only offer up the fact that I love your son, and that I will do whatever is in accord with my feelings for him as long as I am not asked to compromise what I know to be right."

Franny glanced at Sophie's abdomen, then met her gaze squarely. "You seem to have rather broadly defined what is right. If Gabriel had not found you, you would have brought my grandchild into the world a bastard."

"Mother!"

"Franny."

Sophie paled a little, but her chin came up, and she set her shoulders. "You are right to have disgust of me, and I would never fault you for it. I cannot ask you to feel differently when there is so little I can explain to you now. I also know that an explanation might not suffice. I would only ask that you do whatever is in accord with your feelings for your son and not compromise your conscience. I can accept that."

Lady Winslow cocked one eyebrow, subjecting Sophie to her cool scrutiny for several long moments. "You and I will deal well together, I think," she said at last. "Which may be in every manner as important as how you and Gabriel get on."

"More important," Sophie said softly.

"Just so." Franny's eyes slid away from Sophie's and darted between her son and her husband. She did not miss the knowing glances they exchanged. "You must not be fooled by them," she told Sophie. "They look as if they comprehend what happened here, but it is only a pretense. They haven't the least idea."

Eastlyn chuckled as his father rolled his eyes. This earned him a stern glance from his mother while Sir James escaped notice. Holding his hands up, palms out, East warded off Franny's censure as much as surrendered to it. "It is always a lesson to me how the female sex can go at a thing without drawing pistols."

Franny merely smiled, this time in concert with Sophie. "Tell me about the house he has found you. If you must needs pretend there is no marriage, I hope he has at least arranged a decent home. I suppose I shall not be allowed to visit and see for myself."

East heard the wistfulness in his mother's voice and interrupted Sophie's reply. "You cannot, Mother. For the time being, no one must suspect that Sophie has a connection to my family."

"Surely you don't expect that I should give her the cut direct in public."

"Not at all. At social functions you must treat her no differently than you would anyone. To do otherwise would cause comment. I would not have hired a hack for her this evening, or brought her here under cover of darkness, if I did not think it was important that we not be seen together save at a public function."

Sir James folded his arms across his chest and regarded East with a measure of skepticism. "You will have to tread more carefully than the rest of us in public, Gabriel. You have only to look at your wife and everyone around will know you have deep feelings for her. You might be able to school your features when you're negotiating terms, but that inscrutability is notably lacking when you glance at your lady wife."

Franny nodded, a half smile playing about her lips. "He's right, you know. It has never been in doubt, at least to my mind, that you love Sophia. With so many other precautions already in place, perhaps it would be wise for you to not see her in any public venue."

East shook his head. "That isn't possible. The French ambassador's winter ball is next week. I have already given North my word that I will be there. There is an invitation for Sophie as well."

"But you do not mean to escort her, do you?" Sir James asked.

"No. She will be accompanied by Lady Gilbert. Her ladyship is actually a distant relation on Sophie's mother's side. Lady Gilbert has traveled all the way from the Lake District to join Sophie and will lend her countenance so that she may go about in public without comment. They will be companions to each other, though Lady Gilbert knows nothing of the marriage. It remains a very small circle that know we are wed."

Sir James's mouth curled to one side as he considered this. "Colonel Blackwood?"

"Yes."

"North and the others?"

This time Eastlyn shook his head. "I haven't said anything to them. North has much to occupy him at the moment, and South is still away from London."

Franny released a sigh. "I do not know what tricks Northam is up to since Elizabeth returned, but I suspect South has taken up with that actress one hears so much about." She glanced at her husband. "What is her name again? I can never—"

"Miss India Parr."

"Yes, that's it. And Lady Redding is beside herself with the notion that her son may be besotted with an opera dancer." She eyed Sophie again. "That is something, at least," she said. "You are not an opera dancer."

"No," Sophie said. Then with preternatural self-possession, she added, "But I should like to be."

East gave her a wry, sideways look. "You will give her an attack of the vapors, Sophie."

Franny tapped the rim of her glass with her forefinger. "If I did not faint at the news that you are married, or that there is to be a child, then I think I deserve a modicum of respect for the state of my nerves." She sipped her sherry. "What of West? Why have you said nothing to him?"

"West is still coming to terms with his inheritance."

"I think you are underestimating your friends. You have always made time for one another. *North. South. East. West. Friends for life, we have confessed. All other truths, we'll deny. For we are soldier, sailor, tinker, spy.* Is that not your club charter?"

"Yes, and at the moment it is North who has asked for, and will receive, our assistance."

"It is that Gentleman Thief business, isn't it?" Franny asked, resigned. "That is why you must be at the ambassador's ball."

East said nothing and allowed his mother to draw her own conclusions. He was not surprised when she took his silence as a confession.

"Oh, it is," she said. "Never say you mean to allow Sophie to be part of that intrigue."

Sir James laid a cautionary hand on Franny's shoulder. "Gabriel knows what he is doing, Franny. He would not place Sophie or his child in the least danger."

"Thank you for that," East said. He felt Sophie's hand slip into his and give his fingers a gentle squeeze. "If you have any lingering doubts, Mother, you must respond favorably to your own invitation and see for yourself that nothing untoward is happening."

"You may depend upon it."

"Thank you for that," Sir James said with a touch of irony. "You know how I enjoy these affairs. Rather be reading."

Sophie was immediately sympathetic. "So would I, though this ball seems as if it might have something to recommend it. Perhaps, Sir James, you would like to accompany me to the ambassador's library and—"

"No," East said firmly. "That is the one room where neither of you will go, under any circumstances." He ignored the startled looks that came at him from every direction. "Tell Mother about the house, Sophie."

A heavy fog crept up from the Thames and moved stealthily through the streets and alleys, blurring the architecture of homes and cathedrals alike until they were indistinguishable from the meanest brothels and warehouses. The hack moved slowly, horse and driver picking their way carefully along the cobbled streets, wise enough to know that their sense of direction could fail them when the city was as fogbound as it was tonight.

Eastlyn did not mind the slow going. Sophie was curled

beside him on the bench seat, and her head rested on his shoulder. She had allowed him to wrap her in part of his Carrick coat until she was fairly cocooned by it. He did not doubt that she could be made more comfortable in his own carriage, but it was hard to see how at the moment. She was quiet, though not sleeping, and he supposed it was too much to hope that she would fall into that dreamless state before they reached her home.

"I think it did not go too badly for either one of us," she said. "Though your mother gave me a start now and again."

"Only a start?" he asked dryly. "I thought she meant to box my ears."

Sophie smiled lightly. "Has she ever?"

"No. She threatens it often enough, but she can never bring herself to do the deed, not when I was yet a boy, and certainly not now. She remembers the scarlet fever, I think, and how the tips of my ears were cherry red and tender, and it stays her hand even when I have given her cause to use it."

"I like her enormously. She spoke her mind and did not soften her words. We hurt her by not waiting to say our vows, no matter that we had our reasons for doing so. I am glad she did not pretend it was otherwise." Sophie snuggled closer as a gust of cold air found its way under the door and slipped under her gown. "Are you certain we cannot tell your parents more about my cousins?"

"Did you not hear my mother? She knows more than she should about North and the Gentleman Thief. That intelligence she has directly from North's mother. And Southerton's mother is her source for every bit of knowledge that she has about Miss Parr. I am depending on my father to keep her from confiding in her friends about our marriage. He may well have to take her to the country to secure her silence."

"But she is not a gossip, East. She would only speak of it to ease her own mind."

"I know that, but no matter her motive, the end is the same. She will have to content herself with ruminating over the particulars with my father."

"Poor Sir James."

"He would concur."

Sophie pushed at the hem of her gown and prevented another chilling slip of wind from reaching as high as her knees. "Is there really to be an intrigue at the ambassador's ball?"

"I suppose that is a fair statement."

"And I am to have a part in it?"

"A small part. A very small part."

"There is something to happen in the library, I collect."

East sighed. "Yes. A trap is being laid, and I am to have the unremarkable task of making certain no one enters the library who is not supposed to be there—and that most certainly includes you and my father."

"Well, now we shan't. Is the trap meant to catch the Gentleman Thief? This is exactly the sort of affair where he would show himself, isn't it? There will be jewels in such plenty that his most difficult task will be choosing what he means to take."

East thought Sophie had rather too much enthusiasm for intrigue. "Then have a care what you wear."

"That is no worry to me. What remains of my jewelry is paste. Except for the ring my father gave my mother, there is nothing that has not been sold or passed on to Abigail." She turned her head so that she might see East's profile in the dim lamplight. "You mustn't blame it entirely on Tremont. I sold a great many things myself when Papa was lying abed. It would have gone for opium otherwise, and I needed it for seed and necessities for the tenants."

He marveled that she dealt so fairly with her cousin. If she had laid the whole of it at Tremont's door, it would have been understandable. He did not comment because she would have only shrugged it off. Instead, his arm slipped around her back, and he laid his palm against her hip.

"Who is Colonel Blackwood?" Sophie asked. She thought she felt East stiffen momentarily, but it was so quick a reaction, then so effortlessly controlled, that she believed she might have imagined it. "Your father asked you if Colonel Blackwood knew about our child, and you said yes. I should like to know who he is."

"He directs my work," East said simply.

Sophie considered what it was that Eastlyn didn't say. "You and your friends are something more than you seem, I think. I have not a complete understanding, but I am coming to it directly."

"Is there anything I can do to set you on another course?"

"I don't believe so, no. Soldier. Sailor. Tinker. Spy. That is what your mother said, is it not?"

"She said a great many things."

Sophie lifted her head and kissed East's cheek. "I don't mind that you mean to be uncooperative. I shall ask your mother. She will be appalled that you have not told me as much as you should. Now that it is arranged that she and your father will be at the ambassador's ball, I will have my opportunity."

Eastlyn merely grunted.

Chuckling, Sophie resettled her head against his shoulder. "I think your father might tell me also. He is possessed of a most amiable disposition, and I suspect he is the calm to your mother's storm."

She was right in her assessment, but East did not tell her so. "My father likes you, Sophie. I could tell that he was pleased with himself for having the good sense to buy your novel. When the two of you put your heads together after dinner, Mother despaired that she would ever get you away from him. Watching you with Sir James, I confess to some envy. You were undeniably animated in your conversation. Were you discussing your writing?"

Sophie was glad that East could not easily see her blush. "No," she said. "We spoke very little of that. Mostly we spoke of you."

"Me?"

"Yes. I was telling him of our first encounter."

"Really? You were more expressive in the telling of it than you were on that occasion."

"I suppose it must have seemed that way." She fell quiet for a moment. Except for the horse's steady clopping, there was hardly any sound from the street. It was as if the fog had not only distorted the appearance of the nightscape, but muted the usual cacophony as well. "Will Tremont attend the ambassador's ball?"

"He was on the invitation list. Dunsmore also. They both responded that they would attend."

Sophie did not ask how he had come by this information, but she was certain she could rely on it. She knew she was correct that her husband was something more than he seemed. *Tinker.* He had been honest with her about his work as a repairer of things; she was the one who had not understood the extent to which he meant it.

"It troubles you?" he asked when Sophie made no reply.

"No. Not at all." She realized of a sudden that she was not serving up a lie to ease his own mind, but that she spoke the truth of hers. "It is because you will be there, I think. Even if we can spend little time together at the ball, I will know that you are observing me from the corner of your eye. You don't mind that I depend on you for that?"

"No. Is it your intention to dance with a great many young bucks?"

"Oh, yes. But it will all be in aid of softening the rumors that might attach themselves to us."

"Of course."

Sophie's agreeably sleepy smile became a wide yawn. She stifled it with her fingertips and closed her eyes when East encouraged her to do so. It was surprisingly easy to fall asleep under East's heavy greatcoat and the equally heavy blanket of fog.

* * *

The house that Eastlyn had secured for Sophie was in a respectable neighborhood on the verge of being only tolerably so. It was impossible to find her better lodging without giving rise to comment as to the means of her support. Sophie's distant connection to Lady Harriet Gilbert of Berwyn in the Lake District, and the consequence she lent by coming forward to chaperone Sophie's return to London, provided suitable companionship, but Lady Gilbert was known to have been living in genteel poverty and could not have provided more in the way of creature comforts for her great-niece-once-removed.

They agreed on the tale Eastlyn had woven in Clovelly, namely that Sophie had come by a small settlement upon the death of a relative even more obscure than Lady Gilbert. East wished that he could have created a dead relative with deeper pockets, but that would surely have brought Tremont and Dunsmore around to her home, demanding to know the particulars and demanding a share.

Lady Gilbert was asleep in a chair in the drawing room when East brought Sophie in; nevertheless, she roused instantly to take command of the situation, directing the servants to make certain Sophie's bed was turned down and that her room was suitably warm. She would not hear of East accompanying Sophie to her bedchamber and insisted that he set her on her feet at the bottom of the stairs.

Although their acquaintance was short, East learned quickly that it was better to follow Lady Gilbert's directions than to go his own way. Her ladyship's slight frame and lack of height did not diminish her strength. She wielded an ivory-knobbed cane with considerable force when she thought she was being crossed, and East was in no mood to feel that tip being jabbed at his ribs.

He put Sophie down and steadied her. She gave him a sleepy smile, but it was her aunt's proffered cheek that she kissed. East placed his hands on Sophie's shoulders and turned her toward the stairs, then watched her mount them. It was only when she disappeared into the hallway that he relaxed his vigilance.

Lady Gilbert rapped East lightly on the shin with her cane. He immediately gave her his full attention, which was what she hadn't had when she said his name only seconds earlier. Being in love, she thought, was as near to being dotty as a young person got. She made no apology for using her cane. "May I have a word with your lordship?"

East could not imagine that she would accept any answer but his assent. He nodded and gestured her to proceed him to the drawing room. The hall clock began to chime the midnight hour as they passed, and for East it was a reminder of how late he had kept Sophie out. He should have been more considerate, he thought, but it had been a full fortnight since he had been in her company. He had left Clovelly soon after their marriage ceremony and had immediately set about arranging for Sophie's safe return to London. It was with a mixture of relief and anticipation that he greeted the news that she had finally arrived. That was three long days ago, and it chafed that he had to share her with his parents this evening and with Lady Gilbert at almost every other turn.

East closed the pocket doors behind him as soon as he entered the drawing room and waited for Lady Gilbert to choose a chair. He wanted to remain well outside of the sweep of her cane.

Lady Gilbert ignored every one of the room's fine appointments and chose to stand with her back to the fireplace instead. She tugged on the ends of her shawl and drew it more closely about her shoulders. "Tremont was here this evening," she said without preamble. "His son also. Sophia was gone no longer than half an hour when they arrived."

East had not thought they would learn of Sophie's return so quickly. He was uncertain that it could be kept secret until the ambassador's ball, but he had allowed himself to hope she would have a few more days of peace. "Did they say what they wanted?"

"To see Sophia, of course. They were rather surprised

that she was gone from home when I was yet about. Oh, do not concern yourself that I said anything more than I ought. Tremont in particular was easily convinced that I am not all of a piece."

"Did you have cause to wallop them with your weapon?"

"I gave Dunsmore a good poke with it."

Eastlyn almost felt a sympathy for Harold. "How did you explain Sophie's absence?"

"I did not. I simply spoke all around it. I find that it is the best of diversions, and since neither of them knew of my connection to Sophia through her mother, I recounted the family history for them in great detail over tea. They cannot possibly deny that such a connection exists now, and I satisfied their curiosity about Sophia's inheritance. They were disappointed it was not a larger sum."

East had no difficulty believing that. "Did they say they would return?"

"No. And I did not invite them to do so." She tapped her cane against the fireplace's marble apron. "I am not yet in my dotage, though perhaps you would prefer that it was otherwise. You and Sophia have told me little enough, but I am not without eyes in my head. I also hear well enough when I set my mind to it. You would have me believe that Tremont presents some threat to my niece, but it occurs to me that the real threat may be you." Lady Gilbert's large, arthritic knuckles turned white as she gripped the knob of her cane more tightly. "Is it your intention to marry the gel or do you mean for her to give birth to your bastard?"

Two evenings following his reluctant explanation to Lady Gilbert, East stood outside the darkened house at No. 14 Bowden Street. Eastlyn observed it from the front, rear, and sides before determining how best to make his entrance. Tremont was now staying in his own town residence, but Dunsmore was at home tonight and was unlikely to sleep as soundly as his drugged wife.

East found a window on the ground floor that had not been properly latched. He pulled it open and soundlessly boosted himself onto the sill. Swiveling around, he dropped to the floor, the toes of his boots tapping lightly on the wood. He listened and heard nothing. When Sophie had shared stories with him about Dunsmore's children, she couldn't have suspected how he would use the information. Robert and Esme were, in fact, his largest concern. Children were unpredictable, and a nightmare could rouse the house. There was also young Robert's penchant for setting traps for the servants, and East did not want to be caught by one of those. In retrospect, he knew that on his first nocturnal visit to this house, he had been extremely fortunate to have escaped unscathed by anything but the sharp edge of Sophie's tongue.

East lighted a candle and cupped his hand around the flame to hide the glow and protect it from a draft. He was not yet where he wanted to be. The rear parlor was not likely to give up any secrets. He paused at the door, pressing his ear to the wood. Greeted only by silence, he eased the door open and stepped into the hall. He knew from his previous visit, as well as Sophie's descriptions, that Dunsmore's study was on the opposite side. He was prepared for it to be locked and almost did not test the handle to prove that this was so. When the door opened easily, he nearly stumbled into the room, half expecting to confront Dunsmore sitting behind his desk in the dark.

The study was unoccupied, however, and East released the breath he had been holding so carefully that the candle flame did not flicker. He crossed the room to Dunsmore's desk and set the candle in a dish. He glanced around, taking in the study's appointments before he sat at the chair behind the desk. Experience had taught him there was usually a way to find something that did not require upending an entire room. Leaving evidence of his presence behind had never been an option for him; the colonel required discretion in all things.

Now, faced with the task of finding proof of Dunsmore's

participation in the opium trade, East placed himself squarely in the viscount's seat and began a slow, thoughtful examination of the room. Private papers, by their very nature, demanded that they be kept away from prying eyes. The door to the study had been left unlocked, though, so East had to wonder if Dunsmore was merely careless or was so confident of his hiding place that he could permit an open invitation to the room. With small children living underfoot, it seemed to East that it must be the latter.

He gave the desk a cursory inspection, first with his eyes, then his hands. There were no hidden drawers that he could detect and no false bottom. East moved his attention to the paintings on the far wall, studying their arrangement and whether something might be hidden behind them. Books lined the shelves at his back and to his right. On his left, a fireplace with an ornately carved mantel took up most of the wall space. East left his chair so that he could examine the fireplace more closely. The scrollwork was intricate, the design embellished with roses in full bloom and many more that were only buds. He ran his fingertips along the carving, just beneath the mantelpiece. There were no protrusions or indentations that might have indicated a spring or a catch. He retrieved the candle and studied the carving with benefit of the light. It required two careful examinations before a fine line in the wood extending vertically from the apron to just above the top of the right andiron caught his eye. It could easily have been mistaken for a crack of the aging wood except that it did not follow the grain and was split so precisely that it likely had been made deliberately.

Eastlyn found the opening for the cleverly concealed door by pushing at each individual rosebud until he found one that could be turned. The slender door sprung open, and East rocked back on his heels as more than a score of tin soldiers tumbled onto the apron. He could not have been more surprised if a hand had reached out from inside the cupboard and pulled the door closed.

Chuckling under his breath at what he had found, as well

as his reaction to it, East pushed the soldiers out of the way and knelt on the apron. He saw the ledger immediately. It was unlikely that Dunsmore knew his children used the cubby-hole to quarter their soldiers, else he would not have left his ledger there.

The discovery presented a dilemma for East. If he took the ledger and left the soldiers, Dunsmore would accuse Robert and Esme of stealing. If he left all as it was, then Dunsmore would make the same discovery he had and move the ledger to another hiding place. East decided the best course was to take Dunsmore's book of accounts and return the soldiers to the nursery. If the children were as wise as Sophie had led him to believe, then they would not go to their father to raise the question of how their troops had managed to break camp.

He held up the candle while he leafed through Dunsmore's accounts. Some of the entries were cryptic, but there were others that East had no difficulty understanding. His knowl-edge of the ships and captains involved in the trade made some connections obvious. He could see at a glance that Dunsmore had had the misfortune to invest in the *Nineveh* and *Minerva*, neither of which made it to Chinese ports. *Nineveh* was reported lost in a storm around the Cape of Good Hope and *Minerva* was taken by pirates in the Indian Ocean. Whatever debts Sophie's father had left, East could not imagine they were as damaging to the estate as those of Dunsmore. If Tremont's own investments were as badly con-ceived as his son's, it was little wonder that they had pinned so much hope on a good marriage for Sophie.

And it gave greater credence to Sophie's fears that his own life would be forfeit if he gave her a male heir. Tremont and Dunsmore would find a way to manage both Sophie and his son's inheritance. The income from his estates would never support the ill-considered gambling that Tremont and Dunsmore were doing under the guise of investing.

East shut the ledger, closed the cupboard, and began gath-ering the soldiers. He stuffed them in his pockets until they poked him uncomfortably with their tiny bayonets and drawn swords and carried what remained in his hands. Securing the ledger under his arm, East returned first to the drawing room and dropped the ledger outside the window where he could retrieve it later.

The stairs did not creak overmuch as he mounted them, and the door to the nursery swung noiselessly on well-oiled hinges. East moved cautiously in the room, afraid he might stumble on neglected dolls or wooden horses. He found the toy chest, opened the lid with the toe of his boot, and then emptied his hands and pockets. He was about to close the chest when the unmarked leather spine of a book caught his eye. Curious, he plucked it out and quickly thumbed through the pages. Here was something Sophie had left behind, and something she would be happy to have again in her own possession.

"I say, are you the Gentleman Thief?"

Eastlyn carefully tucked the journal under his coat and turned slowly in the direction of the youthful, inquiring voice. He extended his arm, holding his candle steady until the circle of light encompassed the small figure on the threshold of an adjoining room. East squatted so that he would not appear so threatening to the boy and beckoned him closer, saying his name softly.

"How'd you know who I am?"

East shrugged. "Your sister is Esme."

Robert's barefooted approach was quiet. He was still wary, but infinitely curious. "Have you come to take my toys? I shall scream, you know. And my father will come and shoot you."

"That would be unfortunate then, because I have only come to make an inventory. You have a great many toys here. They were not all put away, I noticed." He picked up a nearby ball and dropped it into the chest. "You've been told to return things to their proper place, haven't you?"

Robert's dark eyes grew almost impossibly wide, and he

nodded slowly. "Cousin Fia told me someone might come, but I thought she was having me on," he whispered in awed accents.

"I knew your cousin when she was your age. If memory serves, she was a very serious young girl with hair the color of honey. She left quite a few things lying about until I warned her that she shouldn't."

Robert was a believer now, and as he considered this information, he became more hopeful than he had been. "This is to be my warning, then?"

"Yes. Hand me that doll, will you?"

"It isn't mine," Robert said quickly, giving it over. "But I'll tell Esme what you said."

"Very good." East closed the chest and straightened. "I don't expect that you'll know when I've come to look in on you again. If you're missing a toy that was left discarded and unwanted on the floor, you will know I've been here." He managed to keep his smile in check as Robert nodded solemnly. "Go on. Back to bed."

Robert tore out of the room, and East winced as the door was slammed closed. He waited, listening for signs that the governess had been roused or that Robert had awakened Esme to tell her of his odd encounter. Across the hall, there were no noises from the parents' bedchamber.

East left the house by the same route he had entered. He retrieved Dunsmore's ledger, brushed it off, and tucked it under his arm. All things considered, including Robert Colley stumbling upon him in the nursery, he had not managed the thing too clumsily. And more importantly, he had his first chamber pot.

Mr. Sampson regarded his employer with a considering eye. "Your lordship is unaccountably restive this evening. I cannot fathom if you are looking forward to the ambassador's gala or dreading it."

"What if I told you it was both?"

"Then I would say it is a most peculiar state for you." Sampson adjusted Eastlyn's jabot and cravat and pulled on his satin frock coat to improve the line over his shoulders. "You will endeavor to remain still a moment. There is a loose thread on the waistcoat."

Eastlyn allowed Sampson to cut the silk thread and fuss over him for another few seconds before he had had enough. Never one to examine himself in front of a glass, East did not change his habits now. The edge and cuffs of his navy frock coat were heavily embroidered with metallic gold thread, and he felt the weight of the garment on his shoulders. The collar points were so stiffly starched that Eastlyn was cautious of turning his head lest he draw blood. He brushed at his white satin breeches and adjusted the fit at the knee. Straightening, he presented himself for his valet's dark scrutiny a second time. "Your verdict, Sampson. I await your verdict."

"Your lordship is most handsomely turned out," Sampson said dryly.

East accepted this, not because he particularly believed it, but because Sampson did. "I depend on the pride you take in your duties to make it so."

Sampson acknowledged this with a slight bow of his head. "All is in readiness, my lord. The carriage is outside."

"Good."

The valet held out East's felt tricorne hat. "It is to be hoped that Lady Sophia will enjoy herself this evening."

There was an almost imperceptible hesitation in Eastlyn's reach for his hat. He regarded Sampson with a faint air of wariness. "Why do you suppose she will be there?"

Sampson merely responded with a wry look.

"I am so obvious?" asked East.

"I am afraid so, my lord."

East nodded slowly, taking Sampson's observation as a very good thing. He carefully schooled his features until they reflected nothing so much as boredom and knew that he would have to manage it the entire evening. "Your verdict, Sampson," he drawled. "I await your verdict."

Sampson favored East with a slight smile that often served in place of a generously spoken compliment. "Your carriage," he repeated, opening the door. "It will not do to keep her ladyship waiting."

East decided that was sound advice as well.

A light snow covered the grounds outside the ambassador's residence. Carriages lined the street in front of the gated residence and filled the drive leading to the main entrance. Drivers, footmen, and young tigers, all splendidly turned out in their livery, waited stoically in the cold January night to be of service again. More than one hundred torches lighted the entrance and drive, lending the illusion of twilight to a night with no moon's silver grace.

The ballroom was already a crush of guests when Sophie and Lady Gilbert were announced. Sophie's discomfort was immediate and nearly paralyzing. If not for her great-aunt's insistence that she find a chair, Sophie knew she might have stood in just that spot, an expression of perfect terror fixed on her face.

"You look like death, my dear," Lady Gilbert whispered. "Pinch your cheeks. Your features are bloodless. And do endeavor to breathe. You cannot expect to enjoy yourself if you do not breathe."

Smile still in place, Sophie took a deep breath through her nose and let it out slowly. She hoped that satisfied her aunt, because she was not going to pinch her cheeks.

"That is better," Lady Gilbert said. "You do know it must continue, do you not? In and out. In and—" She stopped, encouraged by what she saw. "Yes, I can see that you have the way of it now."

Sophie nodded faintly. Her eyes wandered over the guests, taking note of no one specifically, but of the glittering whole. Satin and silk in a rainbow of colors was the order of the evening, and the men were often as extravagantly turned out as the women they partnered. Lavender silk and pale pink satin mingled on the ballroom floor as lines were drawn for the next set. Ivory fans fluttered with abandon, but seldom because their owners were overheated. It was Sophie's observation that the fan was the finest tool of a seasoned flirt and could be used to great effect when wielded properly.

Through the narrow opening between the guests around her, Sophie caught flashes of diamonds as the dancers began to move to the music. There was the occasional striking glimpse of rubies and emeralds, but this evening, perhaps in a nod to the winter season, most of the women wore icy diamonds at their throats.

Lady Gilbert leaned toward Sophie. She lifted her cane a few inches off the floor and used it to point to a couple not far away. "Do you know them?"

"They are the Baron and Baroness of Battenburn."

"I am observing they seem to be acquainted with a good number of the ambassador's guests. They must be in the popular set. Odd, that. They are barely of any rank."

Sophie tempered her smile. Lady Gilbert, she had learned, was something of a snob. It mattered little to her that she was practically penniless; her late husband had been a viscount, which she considered vastly superior to a baron. "They are considered to be most amiable and enjoy a great circle of friends." As she watched, the baron took his wife by the arm, and they began a slow turn around the perimeter of the room. In every instance they were greeted warmly. "Everyone is not so particular of rank as you, dear aunt."

Lady Gilbert merely sniffed.

Sophie was grateful for the distraction provided by an acquaintance of her aunt's who was purposefully making her way toward them. After introductions were made and amenities exchanged, Sophie was excused from active participation in the conversation as the two childhood friends filled in details of their lives since last they parted.

The light strains of a waltz came to Sophie over the insistent murmurings of the crowd. She excused herself from her aunt's side and slipped through the crush so that she might better hear the music and view the dancing. She nodded politely to the guests who caught her eye and offered the usual pleasantries when she was greeted, but knew herself to be perfectly content to stand at the edge of the ballroom and observe the graceful sweep of the dancers in concert to the three-quarter time.

"You are looking well this evening."

Sophie stiffened, but she did not turn. She wondered that she had not spied him earlier. "Thank you." Nothing in her response invited further conversation.

Tremont stepped closer so that he was standing at Sophie's side. "I confess I had not thought to see you here this evening. I never supposed that your name would appear on the ambassador's guest list."

"I cannot fathom it myself, but if it was a mistake, then I am glad for it. It is likely to be an affair without equal, and it is fortunate for me that I have been invited to witness it."

"But not participate, eh? I notice that you have had no partners."

It disturbed Sophie that Tremont might have been watching her since her arrival, but she would as soon cut off her nose as permit him to see it. She made no reply.

"You missed Prinny," Tremont said pleasantly. "He arrived just as the music began and left shortly after the first set."

"I suppose he felt it was necessary to make an appearance."

"It is just the sort of thing he does to placate the Frogs."

"If that is all the Prince Regent must do to keep the peace, then I hope he responds as favorably to all his invitations."

Sophie pivoted slightly on her heel so that she was no longer shoulder to shoulder with her cousin, but positioned to leave him. The ribboned hem of her ice-blue silk gown did not shift with her movement, and she caught a measure of the fabric in her gloved fingers and lifted it so that she would not trip.

"You dare!" Tremont hissed close to her ear. "I have not given you leave to go."

Sophie could barely draw air. His breath was hot on her skin, and there was no part of her that was warmed by his attention. She felt herself grow cold, then numb.

"You cannot keep running from me, Sophia. Do you think I don't know that you are in league with him? You would do well to encourage a change of course. Neither of you has the least idea what you are confronting."

Sophie was certain he meant to say more, so she was surprised when his tight grip on her elbow eased and his hand fell away. Out of the corner of her eye she caught the approach of Lord and Lady Redding, the Viscount Southerton's parents. She had only ever met them once before, and she could not imagine why they were moving so purposefully in her direction until they were upon her, greeting her warmly, and engaging Tremont in conversation.

Rescue came from the most unexpected sources, Sophie discovered. Lord Redding skillfully drew Tremont to the side while Lady Redding began an animated conversation, most of it cleverly hidden behind her fan.

"It is to be the gallery, my dear, and that is all I know," the countess said, interjecting these words into her discourse on Prinny's brief visit and the stir it caused. "Will you be able to find it?"

"I am sure of it."

Lady Redding nodded and laughed as if Sophie had said something witty. "Go on. I will sit with your aunt for the nonce and make excuses for your absence." She guided Sophie a few steps away from her husband and Tremont. "He is a most disagreeable sort, is he not?" Her fan fluttered, giving her words an odd warbling sound. "Yes, I am speaking of your cousin, and when you know me better you will learn that it is not in my nature to speak ill of others. However, it seems I must make an exception. I thought you might faint before we would reach you." She snapped her fan closed and tapped Sophie lightly on the forearm. "Quickly, my dear. Before you cannot make your escape."

Sophie offered Lady Redding a fleeting, grateful smile

and hurried away. She paused only once, and that was to watch the Earl of Northam and his countess step onto the floor as the strains of another waltz began to play. She knew a stab of envy for the couple's easy grace and open affection. Whatever problems had existed in that marriage, Sophie doubted they remained unresolved. It did not seem possible that what she observed passing between them was feigned for this public setting. They moved as one, beautifully paired, matched in their movement and effortless elegance.

It was North who had asked for Eastlyn's help tonight, she remembered, and Eastlyn who had asked for hers. The moment of envy passed, and she felt small of spirit for having experienced it. She turned away from the dancing and threaded her way through the crowd until she reached the grand hall. Large gilt-framed mirrors mounted on the walls multiplied the throng, and for a moment she thought she would never find her way through to the gallery.

Helpful servants were in abundance, however, and Sophie was shown directly to the room she sought. She did not ask for escort into the long gallery, but requested privacy. The liveried footman obligingly closed the doors behind her.

Sophie glanced to her right and left. Candelabra set ablaze on the tables lighted the room sufficiently for her to see that she was alone. She took several steps into the gallery, turning slowly so that she might have the paintings revealed to her in circular splendor. It was only when she returned to her starting point that she saw him. He had been there all the time, of course, standing against the wall as if he were the subject of one of the full-length portraits. When he stepped away, it was as if he had moved outside a frame, his vitality and essence of life too powerful to be restrained by oils and a two-dimensional canvas.

East's smile made him recklessly handsome. "Can you hear the music?" he asked softly. "Come, Sophie, let us have another waltz."

Chapter Fourteen

Sophie's feet were buoyed by the lilting measures of the waltz. She found herself standing in front of Eastlyn without memory of the journey. She lifted her face as he slipped one hand into hers and another at the small of her back. Her smile was wondrous; her eyes bright. It was in every way like the first time he had asked her to dance.

"You remember," she said softly. "I did not think you would."

"You should shoot me for a fool," he said quietly. "It would be a kindness."

Sophie did not think so. Her ice-blue gown shimmered as East turned her in a wide arc with his first sure steps. She followed his lead, her body lithe and light in his arms. She was aware of the distant music, but it was not what guided her through the intricacies of the dance. Her body responded to the subtle prompts of his: the signals of his hand and wrist, the gentle pressure of his fingers on her back, the slight tilting of his head. This rhythm was different from the one they shared in bed, but no less intimate in its communications. His eyes held hers, the regard profoundly knowing. Her flushed, radiant features could not be entirely explained by her execution of the steps.

The gilt frames of the French ambassador's paintings created a kind of golden glow at the periphery of their vision. The portraits passed in a blur and might easily have been confused for the crush of interested guests on the perimeter of the ballroom. Sophie and East circled the long gallery twice before their steps finally slowed. It came to them only afterward that the music had long since faded away.

East led Sophie to the couch that faced the large fireplace. He turned slightly sideways as he sat so that he might not have his back completely to the gallery's doors. His arm lay protectively across the curved back, close enough to Sophie's bare shoulders that he could feel her warmth.

Sophie turned also. At the far end of the gallery she could see a set of double doors that she knew did not lead into the hall. "Is the ambassador's library beyond there?"

Eastlyn nodded.

"Is the Gentleman Thief in there now?"

"I think you are rather enamored of that fellow," he said. It was no answer to the question she had asked, and he had to hope Sophie would not press him. "If you find his exploits romantic, you might have said something. I am not such a poor sneaksman myself, you know."

Sophie's eyes strayed from the library doors as she gave East her full attention. "I know how clever you are," she said. "And it is much more romantic to steal kisses than jewelry." To prove her point, she leaned toward him and brushed his lips with hers. "There. Do you see? That was—"

What Eastlyn did next simply robbed her of speech. His mouth slanted across hers, and the steady pressure of it pushed her back into the curve of the couch. Her arms slipped around his neck, and she drew him down on top of her. Her fingers threaded in his thick chestnut hair, tugging lightly. She arched under him, stirring restlessly as the kiss deepened. He sucked on her tongue and lips, and she felt her breasts swell above the empire waist of her gown. The weight of him was like a tender tether, securing her when she thought she might simply float away.

It was the opening of the doors to the gallery that parted them. East's head came up over the edge of the couch, and he spied Lady Northam stepping into the room. Sophie's flushed features appeared over the same curve a moment later. She was grateful when Elizabeth politely averted her eyes as she passed them on her way to the library, though she doubted North's wife missed East's devilish grin or her own squeal of surprise and protest as she was pushed back onto the cushion.

The line of Sophie's mouth flattened stubbornly when East tried to nudge another kiss from her. Barely moving her lips, she whispered, "It hardly seems fair that Lady Northam is allowed to assist in catching a thief and I am relegated to kissing one."

"How do you know that is what she is about?"

"Because you let her pass, and you told me your unremarkable task this evening was to keep anyone from the library who should not be there."

"So I did." Sighing, he sat up and helped Sophie do the same. He made his cravat presentable again while she tucked several wayward strands of hair behind her ears and straightened the low-cut neckline of her gown. "Did you mind lending your lips in the service of your country?"

The glance Sophie darted in East's direction was patently suspicious. "In the service of my country? That is puffing the thing up a bit, don't you think?"

East shrugged, his features neutrally set.

Sophie wondered what she could believe, then decided it did not matter. "I would lend my lips to you in service of the very devil." She expected that he would give her his disarming, reckless smile, but he did not. Instead, his eyes darkened, and the cast of his features became serious. "Why did you never tell me, Sophie? There were so many opportunities when you might have said something."

They were no longer talking about Lady Northam, the Gentleman Thief, or Sophie's service to the Crown. The change in subject gave her a small start, and she blinked widely at East before she found her voice. "You are speaking of our introduction, are you not?"

He nodded. "It was not at the Stanhope recital."

"No."

"I was your partner in the waltz at Almack's. Your first waltz."

"Yes. It was a favor to one of the patronesses, I believe, for there was no reason for you to seek me out otherwise, and certainly there was no reason that you should remember me. I could not have attracted your notice without someone prompting you, nor held your notice much beyond the moment."

East wished he could have said she was wrong, but the truth was he didn't know. Even now, his recollection of that evening was vague. "My head ached abominably," he said quietly. "I know I was almost desperate to leave the assembly, but I was reminded quite forcefully of promises I had made to partner several young ladies in their first waltz."

Sophie nodded. "You danced with Miss Caruthers and both of the Miss Vincents."

"The twins?"

"Yes."

"Aah. So that is why it was interminable. There were two of them."

Sophie's smile was faint, even a bit rueful. "It must have seemed so to you, but I cannot help thinking that they might have wished it had gone on far longer. I know it was that way for me."

"Was I unkind just now, Sophie? I did not mean to be."

"No. It is just that for you it was a duty, and for us it was a pleasure. I suppose I am feeling a little sorry for all of us who trip so easily over our hearts, even when we manage not to do the same with our feet."

"It was a pleasure to dance with you," he said. "Never think it was otherwise. My memory may be indistinct, but it is rarely false. I watched you arrive this evening, saw you enter the ballroom on the arm of your aunt, and something about that moment struck me as familiar. It was as if the scene had been played out before me at some other time. You arrived at Almack's with Lady Dunsmore, didn't you?"

"Yes. Harold followed later."

"And you stood a moment at the entrance to the hall, almost on the brink of retreat."

"I wished that I might have run," she said. "I was paralyzed, though, and Abigail pulled me along, much as my aunt did tonight."

East nodded. "You wore a similar color."

"Yes." A small crease appeared between her eyebrows. When she had chosen her gown for this evening, she had not consciously given thought to her encounter with East at Almack's. Now she had to wonder if it were not at the back of her mind all along. Had she done it to provoke him to arrive at this memory? "I did not wittingly set out to make you remember," she said. "But perhaps it was more important to me than I realized."

"You might have simply told me."

"The awkwardness of saying the whole of it stayed my tongue."

"You must have thought me cruel to have made no mention of that meeting."

"Not cruel," she said. "Never that. It did not occur to me in the beginning that you had truly forgotten it, but I thought you were guilty of nothing save trying to spare my feelings. I am certain I behaved foolishly."

He studied her solemnly set features. "You might have acquitted me of being purposely cruel," he said, "but I can recall several times that you made a good effort to get a little of your own back."

Sophie's heart-shaped face was all angelic innocence. "Oh?"

"You told me in the garden at Bowden Street that I was outside your notice."

"Oh."

"I believe I wondered if you would come to the park if

you knew I would be there. You were quite firm in your dismissal of that notion, even when I tempted you with the fact that I might be driving a new barouche."

Sophie's laughter was cut short as the door to the gallery opened suddenly and Northam stepped inside. He did not spare a glance for her, but gave his direct attention to East.

"Is she there?" he asked. At Eastlyn's affirmative nod, some of the tension seeped from North's rigid stance. "And her friend?"

"I most sincerely hope so."

Northam thanked East, smiled politely at Sophie, then strode off in the direction of the library.

Sophie watched him go, sighing as he disappeared into the ambassador's inner sanctum. "The Gentleman Thief is wretchedly unlucky this evening if he means to go in there."

East caught Sophie's chin with his fingertip and directed her eyes back to his. "I do not care so much as this"—he snapped his fingers—"for the Gentleman. I am more curious about the tale you wove for me at Clovelly. You asked me frankly when I thought we had first met. It must have given you considerable pause when I said it was at Lady Stanhope's."

"Actually," Sophie said dryly, "you said it was at Lady Stafford's. I was left with the rather sad fact that you did not even recollect the particulars of our second introduction. Perhaps it is the fault of my pride, but I could not bring myself to tell you about that other time."

"When you told me Lady Dunsmore had cautioned you to behave circumspectly at the recital, was that true?"

"Yes. She did not want me to repeat my pathetic performance at Almack's."

"But that was so long in the past."

She shrugged lightly. "She remembered it well enough. As I did."

East slowly released a measured breath. "It seems impossible to me that I could have forgotten."

"Perhaps it is just as well. It could have been no more favorable an impression than the one I made with you at the recital."

East took Sophie's hands in his. "Do you know what I did *not* tell Mrs. Sawyer about that encounter?"

Sophie was not at all certain she wanted to hear. He had been rather blunt in cataloguing her deficiencies to his mistress. What manner of things had he considered too appalling to share even with her? "I am not sure that—"

East did not allow her to finish. "I did not tell her about your splendid eyes," he said gently. "Or that your innocence was rather more responsibility than I wanted. I said nothing to her about the radiance of your smile each time you cast it about in any direction but mine. I did not mention that your mouth looked perfectly delicious when it was guarding your tongue, or that even the most insipid conversation could not conceal the intelligence in your expression."

He briefly touched one finger to her lips when she would have spoken. "You might think it is because she was a jealous woman that I did not say any of these things, and there would be some truth to that; yet it does not explain the whole. There are some things a man cannot properly admit to himself, even if he would be vastly improved by the knowledge. In this particular case, I was perhaps guilty of looking rather too hard to find something disagreeable."

Sophie took East's hand in hers. "Too hard?" she asked. "I doubt that. There was much that was disagreeable, and I should consider you foolish indeed if you had ignored all of it for a pair of splendid eyes. Your life would be made hell if you wed me because you thought you could tolerate an impoverished wit in exchange for a radiant smile. You would be bored in a sennight." She paused a beat and added slyly, "Even sooner if I were not possessed of a perfectly delicious mouth."

She offered that mouth now, and East was not proof against it. The kiss lingered sweetly, and gradually they found themselves once more stretched out on the narrow couch. When the doors to the library opened sometime later, and Northam and Elizabeth emerged, East merely raised one hand above the back of the couch and waved them on.

Lady Gilbert gave Sophie the benefit of her careful appraisal, looking pointedly for anything that was not just as it should be. "He took some pains not to muss your gown, I see," she said sternly. "You must not let his effort be in vain. You would do well not to look so satisfied. It cannot help but make people think there was more to your absence than a hem in need of repairing."

"I doubt I was missed at all," Sophie said. Still, she accepted her aunt's censure and schooled her features into an expression of polite interest that was wholly lacking the animation of a moment ago. There was little she could do, however, about her warmly flushed cheeks except to hide them behind her fan.

She knew what her aunt thought had taken place elsewhere in the ambassador's residence, and Sophie did not discourage her from thinking it. Lady Gilbert would have been decidedly disappointed if she knew that except for some long, passionately felt kisses, Eastlyn had behaved with singular propriety. Sophie had tried to tempt him with more, but he had led her from the couch to the center of the gallery, and at the first measures of another waltz he had taken her into his arms and swept her across the floor.

She had fallen in love with him again, this time with the clarity of knowing that his confidence was earned, that his smile was never misplaced, and that his character was as fine and strong as tempered steel. He danced with her as if he were making love, guiding her with a touch, holding her steady with the strength of his glance. She was made breathless by a succession of turns in just the same manner as when he kissed her. He teased the tension from her so that she was no longer mindful of the steps she took. She gave herself over to feeling the music until the lilting melodies were as much inside her as out.

She had not wanted it to end.

"Your cousins are watching you," Lady Gilbert said, tapping Sophie lightly on the knee with the tip of her fan. "Heavens! Do not look at them. They will take great delight in having rattled you. Odious toads. I cannot say that I like them above half."

Sophie's reverie was successfully banished by this reminder that there were at least two among the ambassador's guests who had an interest in her. "Is Lady Dunsmore here?" she asked.

"I do not know. I have never had any occasion to meet her. You must look around and determine her presence for yourself."

Sophie did. Her eyes alighted once on Eastlyn in conversation with the ambassador, but she did not permit her gaze to linger there. Neither did she allow her gaze to rest on Tremont or Harold standing resplendent among a cadre of friends. She recognized Helmsley, Prinny's most vocal detractor in Parliament, and Lord Pendrake, the sycophant who was so often in the company of Lord Harte that he looked vaguely uneasy to be part of a group that did not include his matching bookend. As her glance moved on, she saw Lords Barlough and Harte approaching the others. That this particular group had formed in plain sight of her could be no accident. Sophie suppressed a shiver as she acknowledged the truth of it and forced her attention in another direction. "Abigail is not here." She snapped her fan shut. "I hoped that I might see her. She cannot be at all well if she is yet at home."

Lady Gilbert sniffed. "You are too kind. You were ill-used by her."

Sophie made no reply. She could not make her aunt understand that she had not minded the place she had been given in the family after her father's death. Robert and Esme were more often a joy than a hardship. Abigail was inevitably demanding, and in no way able to be a true friend, but she was not by her very nature unkind. Had her need for the laudanum not held sway over her mood and shaded her good judgment, Abigail could have been a temperate voice in the household, perhaps standing up to her husband as Sophie had been wont to do in those early days of living under one roof.

Sophie glanced around again and this time saw that Eastlyn was gone from the ambassador's side. She thought he had left, but it was far worse than that. He was bowing slightly to Lady Powell, preparing to partner her in the next dance. Sophie considered several things she might do to the widow, all of them painful. When she saw Lord Edymon coming determinedly through the crowd toward her, Sophie flashed him her brightest smile.

She accepted his hand with an alacrity that surprised him. She had, after all, turned down his proposal of marriage three years earlier, and he had expected a gracious, but not effusive greeting. Evidently, he thought, the long separation had made her more kindly disposed toward him and softened her opinion of the country dances.

Lady Gilbert was long asleep by the time Eastlyn let himself into Sophie's residence. Still, he made a quiet ascent of the stairs. In deference to her aunt's sensibilities, Sophie had been reluctant to allow him to spend a single night in her bed since she had arrived in London. Even when Eastlyn informed her that Lady Gilbert had used extraordinary tortures to wrest the truth of their marriage from him, Sophie would not relent.

Until tonight.

He suspected it was the waltz that had calmed her fears. The waltz, and the undeniable need she had for him on the sofa in the ambassador's gallery. He almost wished he had taken her there, but some modicum of sense prevailed. The realization that any of the ambassador's four hundred guests might come upon them also gave him pause, but it was a narrow thing. Sophie had used her perfectly delicious mouth to make a convincing argument for reckless abandon.

Eastlyn reached the landing and cocked his head, listening for any signs of stirring. Candlelight slipped out from under Sophie's door, but he noticed that she had not left it open for him. Hefting the journal and ledgers he carried under his arm to better secure them, East started down the hall. Sophie's door opened while his hand was merely hovering over the knob.

"Quickly," Sophie said, pulling him into her bedchamber. "Else my aunt will hear you."

The chuckle that rose in East's throat was smothered by Sophie's urgent kiss. He nearly lost his grip on the books as she flung her arms around him and drew his head down. He managed to get to her bedside before he dropped them. One started to slip over the edge, but he caught it with his knee and kept it there until Sophie released him long enough for him to let it slide gently to the floor.

"What are those?" she asked. Her mouth was still against his. Her lips and warm, sweet breath tickled him.

"Later." He did not want to explain now how so many sleepless nights strung end to end had afforded him the opportunity to refine his sneaksman skills. She would quite correctly point out that he might have been mistaken for the Gentleman Thief had he been caught. This moment, then, would be lost, and just now that was of more import to East than all the evidence he had gathered this past week.

Sophie tried to glimpse what East pushed to the bottom of the bed by standing on tiptoe and straining to see over his shoulder. Her tenuous balance made it easy for him to topple her. Her protest came to nothing as he followed her down.

Candlelight flickered over them, lending its glow to Sophie's upturned face and East's profile. She fell silent, her lips parting a fraction as he studied them. She had the sensation of his mouth on hers moments before he lowered his head and touched her in fact.

It was as if they had never parted in the gallery. Every one of Sophie's nerve endings was charged with anticipation. The first contact of East's mouth fired them all off in quick succession, and she felt her flesh tingle with the press of a thousand tiny darts. Tension immediately replaced that swift explosion, and Sophie arched under him, finding purchase in the quilt and bunching it between her fingers.

The thin fabric of her shift was rent by East's impatience. Sophie wondered only that it did not happen sooner. She moaned softly as his mouth worked its way down from the curve of her neck to the puckered tip of her breast. He took the nub between his lips and tugged gently, laving it with the damp edge of his tongue until her short gasp became a whimper.

She showed the same disregard for his clothes that he had shown for her shift. It was not so simple, though, to tear a frock coat or a finely made linen shirt, and Sophie had to be satisfied with the one button she left dangling from his embroidered waistcoat.

He reveled in her frantic desire for him, not minding in the least when she managed to remove his tails, waistcoat, cravat, jabot, shirt, shoes, stockings, breeches, and drawers, and he had yet to eliminate the remnant of her shift. When he finally wrested it from her, he waved it not like a man claiming victory, but one offering his surrender.

Laughing, Sophie bore down on him. He cautioned her to quiet with a finger to her lips. She bit it.

"Ow!" He drew it back quickly.

"Shhh." She murmured this against his lips. "You will wake the house."

East suspected none of the servants would be brave enough to venture forth, and Lady Gilbert would be too polite to interfere. "Everyone will return to their slumber soon enough," he whispered huskily. "Sooner if you do not bite me again."

She found his hand and brought it to her mouth, kissing his fingertip this time. "That is better, is it not?"

"Infinitely."

She smiled because he did. It was a sly and wicked look that they mirrored to each other. Heat was raised anew and sensation stirred again. East caught Sophie's shoulders suddenly and twisted her around so that she was facedown on the bed. Surprise kept her from struggling. She laid one cheek against the sheet and eyed him with a mixture of interest and wariness.

East ran his thumb down the length of her spine and back up again. On his next pass he went lower. His palm moved over the curve of her bottom, and he felt her lift her hips in reaction to the touch. He dipped his head and brought his mouth close to her ear. Even before he spoke a single word, she responded to the anticipation of it, and a delicious sort of shiver made every part of her body sensitive to his touch. With only the slightest urging, Sophie drew her knees under her as East moved to kneel behind her. He stared at the elegant curve of her back as she raised her buttocks. His hands caught her hips, and he pulled her close until she was pressed hard and intimately against his erection.

Sophie's eyes closed, and her fingers curled in the sheet. Her mouth parted on a silent O as she felt East's measured entry. He moved with exquisite slowness so that it was in every way the wicked, pleasing torture his eyes had promised earlier. It required all of her control not to rear back and force her own need on him. She waited him out, knowing that she would be sweetly rewarded for her patience.

His penetration was deep. His hands on her hips kept her bottom in full contact with his groin. Before he began to move in earnest, she was already contracting around him. He did not have to see the small siren's smile curving her lips to know that it was there. His appreciative chuckle ended in a soft groan as she raised herself on her elbows and gave him more freedom of movement. Holding her hips still, East withdrew slightly and thrust again. Sophie's unbound hair fell forward over her right shoulder. She bit off the small cry that came to her lips.

One of East's hands fell away from her hips, and when she felt it again, it was between her parted thighs. This time she did not catch her own cry and could not summon the least embarrassment for even one of her responses to him. When she felt his rhythm change so that the movement of his hips was quick and shallow, she gave herself up to the same quickening of his fingers. Every part of her body pulsed under him, and when he came it was as if he had set off a second round of charges. He had laid all of them with such care that she had only been aware of his caress. Now she felt the sparks of heat and light skitter across her skin wherever he had touched her: at the back of her knee, in the hollow of her throat, along the sweeping curve of her back. Her tender breasts knew the separate trails his fingers had made from peak to valley, and her flesh held the memory of the hot suck of his mouth.

It came to Sophie as something of a shock to realize that East was now stretched out beside her, and that no part of his body was touching hers. The light press of his fingertips still lingered at the base of her spine and her hips. She felt the sensation of his mouth on hers. She offered up a sleepy, sated smile and was warmed by the chuckle that rumbled deeply in his chest.

"I think you should have asked me to dance much, much earlier," she whispered.

"Had I known you could be tumbled for a waltz, I would have." East turned more fully on his side and propped himself on an elbow. "Could I have had you so long ago at Almack's, I wonder?"

Sophie eyed him carefully, trying to gauge the seriousness of his question against the teasing she hoped it was.

"You might have claimed a kiss that night, for I was truly smitten, but I would have been able to keep my petticoat firmly in place. In any event, you would not have suggested anything so improper as a tumble."

"You think I am such a gentleman, then?"

She smiled because he sounded a little disappointed that it might be her estimation of him. "I think you are a rogue with the manners of a gentleman. It makes you quite dangerous, you know. You might be anything you like in aid of serving your purpose—or that of Colonel Blackwood's." She leaned over and kissed him lightly on the mouth. "But I do not believe you would sacrifice your principles or your honor on anyone's account, and certainly not to fondle an innocent like myself in the heady throes of her first passion. You would have defended me against such an overture, not made one yourself."

"It occurred to me that you would require such a zealous defense this evening," he said wryly. "Edymon's eyes strayed quite often from your face, I thought."

"He was particularly admiring of my gown."

"He was admiring of your particulars."

Sophie could not quite keep her laughter in check. It came out as a delicate, expressive snort. Ignoring East's devilish grin, she said, "I noticed Lady Powell was attached to your side after your first set with her."

"A barnacle would have been easier to remove. She had no interest in me, but was full of questions about South."

Sophie was skeptical. "I was a witness to the coy manner in which she wielded her fan. It is a wonder you were not bruised by so much playful tapping and batting." She gave East's forearms a cursory glance to assure herself this was not the case. "I have noticed that she has a proprietary nature. What did she want to know about Lord Southerton?"

"His whereabouts. He has come and gone from London again."

"He has?"

"Hmm."

Sophie frowned. "Is there nothing at all you can say to me? Is it your colonel's work again?"

East considered what he could say. This was not a matter of his trust in Sophie, but rather of the trust that had been placed in him by others. "South's absence from town is in some way connected to his work for the colonel, but that does not explain it entirely. He is gone now to Merrimont near Devon to search for Miss Parr."

"She has been absent from the London stage for quite some time."

"Yes, but South used to know where she was. Now he does not. The circumstances of her disappearance are unlike yours or Elizabeth's. She did not voluntarily leave him."

"Then why are you abed with me? You must help him find her."

Before Sophie unwrapped him from the warm cocoon of blankets and forcibly removed him from her bed, he caught her wrist and pressed her splayed fingers to his chest. "The offer has already been made and rejected," he told her. "West. North. We have all gone to him. He thinks I am unsympathetic to the swirl of gossip that surrounds his connection to the actress. I suppose because he knows our engagement put me squarely in the eye of a storm of rumors, he believes I am more than a little relieved to share in the ton's attention."

"You might have told him we were married," she said gently. "He would have seen it a little differently."

East shook his head. "It was not the time. I could not express my own happiness when he is so miserable."

Sophie nodded, understanding. "His parents were my rescuers this evening. Did you set them on that course?"

"Your rescuers? How do you mean?"

"I left my aunt's side to better view the dancing, and Tremont slipped so easily to my side that he must have been lying in wait. At the moment I suspected he meant to be most difficult, Lord and Lady Redding arrived. Lord Redding engaged him in conversation, and her ladyship took me under her wing. She is the one who told me I would find you in the gallery. She seemed not at all alarmed to be part of an intrigue, but I suppose that is because she has had naught else to do of late but worry about her son."

East's cheeks puffed a little as he released a slow, measured breath. "It is my mother who is responsible for that timely intervention. I asked her to tell you where I could be found. I do not doubt that when she saw Tremont at your side she considered it would be better for Lady Redding to direct you. Your cousin would have hung on my mother's every word if she had engaged you in conversation."

"Then Lady Winslow was clever to have acted as she did."

"Yes, well, you should have little doubt that South's mother now knows more than I intended." He held up his hand when Sophie would have interrupted. "It is unimportant, and too late to change it if it were not. What did Tremont say to you?"

She hesitated and realized that it was a mistake to have done so. East was immediately suspicious that she meant to prevaricate. She was forced by her own brief pause to tell him the truth now. "He tried pleasantries at first," she said. "But I did not warm to them, nor to his discourse about the Prince Regent's brief appearance at the ball. I made to leave, and he took exception to it."

East's eyes narrowed a fraction. "How?"

"He took my arm."

"He grabbed you, you mean." East moved aside the blanket and examined both of Sophie's arms above and below the elbow. "It is only because you were wearing gloves that you are not bruised."

Sophie drew the blanket up again. "Then congratulate me on my foresight for having done so," she said, "and leave off blaming Tremont for rising no higher than our low expectations."

East offered a small grunt in appreciation of her point. "Go on. I am certain there is more."

"Only that he told me I could not keep running from him. He imagines that I am in league with you, though in what manner he meant that I cannot say. He said I would do well to encourage you in a change of course."

"That is all?"

"There was one more thing. He told me that neither of us had the least idea what we were confronting."

Eastlyn wondered if that was true. Did Tremont know something more than he and Sophie, or was it merely the bluff of a man who felt the wall was ever closer to his back? "That is when Lord and Lady Redding arrived?"

"Yes. I have no idea what else he might have been prepared to say. In any event, he would not have remained at my side much longer because I meant to trod hard upon his toes."

"A singular plan."

"You think it would not have worked?" she asked. "I can assure you, he would have taken his leave with a limp that was noticeable to all. He did not consider that I would draw attention to us or give public expression to my disgust of him. He is used to fawning and flattery and being surrounded by people like Lord Pendrake who offer a surfeit of both."

"You remember Pendrake well, then."

"Of course. He was one of those in the hunting party when my father was shot. The man is a toady." Sophie stopped suddenly and regarded East with some surprise. "I never spoke of him to you before," she said slowly, trying to recall any reference to him. "How did you—"

"I know the name of every man who was in that hunting party, Sophie. I began making inquiries during the same time I was making arrangements for your return to London."

"You could have asked me. I am not likely to have forgotten who they were."

"I did not think you would be forthcoming. The truth now: would you have told me if I had put the question to you?"

"No."

"Just so."

"That is because I would not have trusted you to let it lie. Indeed, you have proved me right. Tonight I thought Tremont was making reference to the opium trade, but he was not, was he? At least, not entirely. That is why they all gathered at the ball. You must have seen them. It is a certainty we were meant to. He has come to learn that you are raising questions about the shooting. That is unlikely to put him at his ease with either one of us."

"Do you care whether Tremont is at his ease?"

"Never doubt it. He is considerably more dangerous when he is pacing. One never knows precisely in what direction he will pounce."

"I predict it will be east."

Sophie was unamused. "You do not take him as seriously as you must. If you will not show some greater care, I will apply to your friends myself and ask them to help you see reason."

"They are more likely to encourage me, rather than the opposite."

"Then all of you are lacking in your upperworks."

That pronouncement, delivered as it was in unambiguous accents, raised East's grin. "North is a deep thinker," he said. "And by many accounts, South is considered brilliant. West has only to read a thing once before he knows the whole of it."

"Intelligence is not the same as good sense."

"Well, there you have me."

Sophie knew that she had not altered his thinking in the least. There were no arguments to dissuade this man from doing what he thought was right. She had not tried to shift him from his course because of Tremont's warning; rather she had done it for her own sake.

She did not soften immediately under East's first kiss, but neither did she have the intention of holding herself from him. If he knew that, he pretended otherwise, and applied himself to winning her over with singular purpose. As an exercise in carnal persuasion, it offered much in the way of satisfying argument. It was the only time that Sophie was convinced that in surrender there was more to be gained than lost.

When East woke, he saw the lighted candle at the bedside had been moved to the escritoire. Sophie was sitting in a high-backed chair, one leg pulled under her to give her height. Her shoulders were hunched over the small desk. Several quills stood in the inkstand, and occasionally she would pick one up and twirl it between her fingertips or tap the feathered end lightly against her chin. For the few minutes that he observed her, she never once dipped a pen into the ink pot.

Her purpose at the desk was reading, not writing. The slim volumes that he had carried to the room were stacked precariously at her elbow. Each time she turned a page she came close to shifting the pile and scattering all of it to the floor.

East leaned over the edge of the bed and found his shirt and breeches. He knew Sophie had to have heard him stirring and then dressing, but she did not glance in his direction. The long sleeves of her robe fell loosely about her elbows, and she propped her head in her hands and continued to read.

East tucked his shirttail into his breeches as he crossed the room to join Sophie. He stood at her side a moment before pulling over a wing chair from the fireplace. He sat on the curve of one arm, stretching his legs casually in front of him. His bare toes nudged Sophie's under the desk.

"You are determined to disturb me," she said without looking up.

"That is my intent, yes."

Sighing, Sophie lifted her head from the cup of her palms and gave East a sideways glance. There was no coyness here, only an accusation. "I understand why you left the discussing of these until later. I do not doubt they were meant to be private accounts. How did you come by them?"

"I had supposed that would be obvious."

"You stole them."

"Yes."

"You have been extremely busy of late. I count six books."

East frowned slightly. "Not seven? I meant to carry that many. Have you looked through all of them?"

"No. This is but the second." She pushed the stack of ledgers toward him. "You can count them for yourself."

East saw at a glance that she was correct. "These are all the account books. The journal is missing. It is the only volume bound in green leather."

"A journal? Whose?"

"Yours."

"You stole one of my diaries? Why in the—" Sophie stopped because he was shaking his head and looking at her as if she were the one who had taken leave of her senses. The leg she was sitting on was beginning to fall asleep. She rose a bit and pulled it out from under her. Pins and needles jabbed at her foot so that she was forced to stand and hobble about to relieve it. "Perhaps you better explain what you've done," she said, turning on East. "Else you are certain to grow weary of my questions, and I am just as certain to lose all patience with your answers."

East followed Sophie's limping progress to the fireplace where she poked at the embers before adding more coals. "It was never my intention to keep you in ignorance," he said. "That I brought these ledgers with me tonight is proof of that. I am in need of your help, Sophie. I understand most of what I've read here, but you are more familiar with the financial straights of your cousins. I thought you might be able to unravel some of the accounting."

Sophie pointed to the book that lay open on the escritoire. "That one belongs to neither Tremont nor Harold. I do not recognize the writing, but it is not theirs. The first ledger I examined did not belong to them either, but the handwriting in that one is not the same as this."

East held up one hand and ticked off a finger for each

name he mentioned. "Tremont. Dunsmore. Harte. Pendrake. Helmsley." He tapped his thumb and index finger a second time. "And Barlough."

For a moment Sophie did not breathe. It was as if an invisible fist had driven hard between her ribs and forced every bit of air from her lungs. "That is all of them," she said finally. "They were all there."

East nodded once, satisfied. "The clubs," he told her. "That is where I came by the information. It is not difficult. You find someone who knows someone who remembers. You sort through the stories, the poor recollections as well as the more reliable ones, and finally you have enough commonalities to form an opinion as to what the truth might be."

He gestured to the chair Sophie had vacated, inviting her to sit again. She was still holding the poker in her hands and seemed to have no idea that her bloodless grip did nothing to still her trembling fingers. "It was my intent to learn the names of every member of Tremont's hunting party. I thought it would be a good beginning. When Harte's name came to my attention, it was not a great leap to suppose that Pendrake might have been there as well. It was easy enough to confirm."

Sophie replaced the poker. "You have noticed they are often in each other's company."

"I could not fail to notice. It has been that way for as long as I have known them." He saw her puzzlement and spoke to ease it. "They were only a few years ahead of me at Hambrick Hall."

"The Society of Bishops." Sophie sank into her chair. "Is that it?" she asked, her voice reed thin. "Were they members of the Society?"

"Not were. *Are*. Once inducted, one is always a member."

"Friends for life, we have confessed? That is what your mother said about the Compass Club, is it not? *North. South. East. West. Friends for life, we have confessed. All other truths, we'll deny. For we are soldier, sailor, tinker, spy.* I am not certain I comprehend the difference between you and the Bishops any longer." Sophie briefly picked up the ledger she

had been studying and used it to make her point. "If theft is an acceptable course of action, then it seems one does not have to stray far to commit murder. Surely you must see the irony of assisting Northam in laying a trap for a thief this evening."

East actually reared back a fraction. Sophie might as well have struck him with the flat of her hand as thrown those words at him. "Perhaps it was a mistake," he said quietly, "to bring these here."

"Perhaps it was."

Nodding, East leaned into the space separating them and collected all the account books. Out of the corner of his eye he saw that Sophie had raised her hand as though she meant to stay him. It hovered a moment, then fell back to her lap.

Eastlyn rose and placed the books on the mantelpiece. He began gathering his clothes. "I mentioned Barlough's name to you before," he said, "when we were discussing the Society at Tremont Park. I told you he was archbishop when I was at Hambrick."

"I remember." Sophie's response was stiff. Her eyes followed East's progress as he collected his clothes.

"You expressed a certain curiosity about the Bishops the following afternoon at the lake."

"And I heartily regret it." The timbre of Sophie's voice deepened, lending weight to her next words. "*Sworn as enemies of the Bishops.*" Her slight smile held no humor. "By your own admission, little has changed since you and your friends made that oath. I would never willingly say or do anything to provoke you into confronting them again."

East's voice was not much above a whisper. "I imagined that you would trust me to make it right."

Sophie fell silent a moment, slowly shaking her head. "At what risk to yourself?" she asked finally. "Should I want justice for my father when your own life might be forfeit?"

Eastlyn sat on the edge of the bed, his cravat dangling between his fingertips. "There is more here than justice for your father, Sophie. More even than the fact that these men are profiting from the opium trade they publicly oppose." He dropped the cravat and took up his stockings, ignoring the patent curiosity he glimpsed in Sophie's features. He continued dressing, pulling on the stockings and buttoning his breeches at the knee. He was smoothing his shirt, adding the cravat and positioning the stiff collar points, when Sophie could no longer restrain herself.

"What more can there be?" she asked.

"Offering favors for profit. Selling secrets. Blackmail." East's dark glance pinned her back in her chair. "Slavery."

Sophie's mouth opened, then closed again.

East buttoned his waistcoat. "I am not saying that any one of them is worse than another. It is the whole of it that must be stopped." He ran a hand through his hair. "I did not wed you with the intention of turning you out in widow's weeds. I freely confess that I am rather fond of this life and have no wish to hurry it toward an end. I cannot promise you that I will not take risks—it would be tantamount to promising that I will not draw another breath—but I swear I will exercise my best judgment in every matter that is put before me."

The ache in Sophie's throat made it difficult to speak. Swallowing did not ease it. She watched East shrug into his frock coat, then collect the ledgers and place them in the crook of his arm. Her eyes stung but remained dry.

Eastlyn's long stride took him to the door quickly. He had already given the glass knob a quarter turn when he heard Sophie coming up behind him. Her bare feet padded lightly on the floor. She stood just inches at his back, close enough for him to feel the heat of her body. He imagined that her fingers were pleating the sash of her robe and that her lower lip was drawn in just the narrowest fraction as she worried it.

"Leave the ledgers here," she said quietly.

East pivoted slowly on his heel and leaned back against the door. Sophie was precisely where he had imagined her to be, fingers and lip engaged in the activity he had seen in his mind's eye. He took the books from under his arm and held them out to her.

Sophie's hands trembled slightly as she accepted them. "There is one ledger for each of the gentlemen you mentioned?"

"Yes."

She nodded. "Tremont. Harold. Pendrake. Harte. Barlough."

"And Helmsley."

"Another Bishop?"

"Yes. He was at Hambrick before Tremont. Dunsmore is the only one who was never a member of the Society."

"Yet he is part of their circle."

Eastlyn did not answer immediately. He pointed to the ledgers instead, his eyes on Sophie. "Read them," he said. "Then tell me if you think he is part of it or apart from it."

Chapter Fifteen

Colonel John Blackwood's angular features were set thoughtfully as he tapped the bowl of his pipe against his palm. He regarded his visitor over the rim of his spectacles and wondered at her calm demeanor. He could not imagine that she came by it easily. If it was meant to impress him, it did. According to East, this angel's face concealed a steely spine. "Will it offend you if I smoke?" he asked.

"No. I enjoy the fragrance." Sophie's eyes darted to the leather pouch on the table at the colonel's side. "I sometimes packed my father's pipe for him."

The colonel smiled; it seemed to him that her memory was a fond one. "And lighted it on more than one occasion, I suspect."

Sophie nodded. "My father must have thought it a very good lesson to indulge me. I coughed wretchedly, of course, and I believe the color in my face was an alarming shade of gray. Still, I am nothing if not stubborn. Papa stopped allowing me to light his pipe when it no longer made me ill to do so."

Blackwood opened the leather pouch and withdrew some tobacco. "When I was a boy I used to climb to the attic to partake in the secret ritual. Where did you go?"

"The stable loft. Not at all sensible, I know." Sophie was not strictly speaking of the risk of fire, but she did not explain that to the colonel. There was no proper way to relate the story of her first glimpse of a young man's bare arse as he tumbled a scullery maid. If the colonel wondered at her blush, he would not have the answer for it from her.

The colonel lightly tamped the tobacco in his pipe bowl. "We have exchanged pleasantries," he said. "Shared anecdotes. Perhaps it is time that we come to the purpose of your visit. Eastlyn would not countenance it, so it is left to me to suppose that he knows nothing of it, or that you are here in opposition to his wishes."

"He is unaware. We have not spoken for nearly a fortnight."

One of the colonel's graying eyebrows lifted slightly. It was his only indication of surprise. "Is that at your insistence or his desire?" He lighted his pipe and puffed. A blue-gray halo of smoke encircled his head.

"A little of both," she said. "I have not wished to see him, and he has not forced me to. I know very well that he has certain skills that allow him to come and go as he pleases. I am unaware of any locked door that presents a challenge to him." Sophie's fingers absently smoothed a wrinkle that had appeared at her knee. The hem of her lavender silk gown fell softly into place at her feet. "Do not misunderstand. I have not barred him from my home. I have only asked that he not press me."

"Not press you? In what manner do you mean that? He is your husband."

Sophie did not miss the colonel's disapproving accents. "Can you appreciate that I wish him to remain so? He has had a certain course of action set in his mind for some time. I am only trying to come to terms with it. Quite frankly, Colonel Blackwood, East is rather more convincing than I wish he might be." Her smile was faint. "But I suspect you already know that. You have depended upon his talent for persuading others, perhaps even nurtured it."

"He is an effective negotiator."

"It is not only words that serve him," Sophie said. "Eastlyn studies his opponents as if they were pieces on a chessboard. He understands all the ways they can be moved. He knows their strengths and their vulnerabilities. If the soundness of his argument does not persuade, he is quite willing to bring other pressures to bear."

"It is a good strategy," the colonel said.

"It is dangerous."

"It is not without risk."

"You think there is some difference," Sophie said. "I do not. I was at the French Ambassador's ball a fortnight ago. I have some idea of the risk that Lord Northam took that night in his attempt to catch the Gentleman Thief. If there were no danger in that enterprise, how do you explain that he was shot but a few days later?"

Blackwood removed the pipe from his mouth and expelled a long breath. "So you know about that."

"The gossip circulated more quickly than the rumors of my engagement," she said. "I would have had to have been on the Continent not to have heard of it—the North American Continent."

The colonel tipped his pipe to her in the manner of a salute. His slight smile was not without humor. "Then you also know that he is recovering."

She nodded. "I have it from Lady Northam herself."

"Elizabeth came to see you?"

"Yes. It was at Eastlyn's request, I think, though she did not tell me that. It was all accomplished quite smoothly in the guise of a social call, yet the timing of it made me suspect there was more purpose than was revealed. I suppose he meant her presence to allay my fears."

Blackwood nodded thoughtfully. "Perhaps he reasoned that if you could see how Elizabeth was doing in the wake of her husband's shooting, you would know it could all be managed."

"That occurred to me. Of course, Lady Northam did not

know there was this other aspect to her call. I believe East told her only that she should try to persuade me as to his fine character."

"It seems that he very much wants to be in your good graces again," the colonel said, "if he sent in Elizabeth. You must allow that it has a certain desperation to it."

Sophie nodded, her brief smile faintly rueful. She moved closer to the edge of the chair, but did not stand. Her folded hands were leached of color at the knuckles. "I am desperate also, Colonel," she said quietly. "I would not have come otherwise. I do not fully understand how you are involved in the activities of the Compass Club, but I know each man has great respect for you. If you were to tell East that he must—" She stopped because Blackwood was holding up one hand, already shaking his head.

"There are some things I can never tell any one of them," he said. "You would be sadly mistaking their independence or resolve if you thought it was otherwise. They are not horses that can be reined in."

"But you command them."

"Command?" He shook his head. "You are in the wrong of it there. I assign them certain duties. That is all. East tells me you know about the proposed settlement in Singapore and what he was asked to accomplish on behalf of the Crown. It should have been an unexceptional assignment. It has been vastly complicated, perhaps even compromised, by the actions he has taken on your behalf."

Sophie did not shrink from the colonel's dark, appraising glance. It was as if all the strength that had been drawn from his limbs was now focused in his eyes. "Had I known it would come to this, I would not have left Tremont Park so willingly. Has he told you about the ledgers?"

"Of course. Are they still in your possession?"

"Yes. I thought he would come for them when I was not at home, but he left them with me."

"Can you not suppose why?"

"He wants my approval."

The colonel's slight smile mocked her. "Your approval? You mistake him very much if you think that is what he wants. Tell me, Lady Sophia, what did you find when you examined the accounts? Eastlyn says you have some experience with managing the finances of Tremont Park."

"I saw there were certain commonalties in the accounts. Money associated with the same investments. Many losses or gains in the same ventures."

"Could you identify the ventures?"

She shook her head. "It seemed to me that much of it was in shipping, but Eastlyn mentioned other things." The colonel waited her out, and she went on. "The selling of secrets. Blackmail. Favors for profit." Her voice dropped to a mere whisper. "Slavery."

"That's right. The one that disturbs you most is the only one for which there is no penalty. Slavery, like the opium trade, has produced a great deal of debate on its financial merits and moral poverty. What it has not produced is a law prohibiting it. What else did you understand from your review of the ledgers?"

"There was a considerable amount of money exchanging hands."

"What did it mean to you?"

Sophie hesitated. "I attached no particular meaning to it."

Blackwood let that pass, though he suspected she understood more than she was willing to tell him. "Do you recall Eastlyn's first meeting with you at your Bowden Street address?"

Although bewildered by this change in subject, Sophie nodded. "Yes. Of course."

Finished with his pipe, the colonel placed it on a silver tray at his side. He said casually, "I believe he proposed to you on that occasion. And you refused him."

"Yes."

"You softened the refusal with some refreshment, I think. Lemonade, perhaps. I seem to remember that it was lemonade."

Sophie frowned. "It may have been. I don't understand what that—"

The colonel interrupted her with a glance. "East came here afterward. In a short time he was unwell. I believed then, and I continue to believe it now, that he was drugged. Given the dealings of your cousins and the dependency of Lady Dunsmore, a tincture of opium is most likely to have been used. What I do not understand is the why of it. Can you explain it to me, Lady Sophia? Who was desirous of drugging him, perhaps seeing him made the fool, or exposing him to foul play when he had not all of his wits about him?"

For a moment, Sophie could not move. Shock held her still and drained her face of color. She could not think, let alone think clearly. What she was hearing the colonel say made no sense, and yet she had a memory of Eastlyn's long fingers curled around a glass of lemonade and her own voice inquiring if the taste of it was to his liking.

She forced herself to work backward from that moment and return to a few minutes earlier when she was in the house with Harold. He had pressed her to tell him what answer she meant to give to Eastlyn, and she would have none of it. He had paused long enough in his harangue to permit her to request refreshment, then had at her again. Sophie recalled the maid arrived very quickly with the service. Too quickly? But what did that signify except—

Sophie's handclasp broke apart as she stood. "I must go," she said. "Will you send word around to my husband that I must see him?"

The colonel realized that whatever conclusion Sophie had drawn, she was not going to make him privy to it. He counted it as a good sign that she had determined she must see Eastlyn. "Of course, I will send someone to his home. You may depend upon it." He wheeled his chair to Sophie's side and escorted her to the door of his study. "Tell me, Lady Sophia, have you come to realize what it is East wants from you?"

She looked down at the colonel's raised face and nodded

faintly. "My understanding," she said softly. "It is all he ever needed."

Lady Gilbert excused herself from the sitting room soon after East's late evening arrival. She made a show of yawning widely and leaning on her cane heavily to indicate her deeply felt fatigue, but refused both Sophie and East when they offered her assistance to her bedchamber.

"She's a peculiar piece of work," East said. "Did she give you a wink and a nod?"

"Yes."

"I suppose she believes it is an improved state of affairs that I am here tonight. I am wondering if she is correct."

Sophie poured two fingers of whiskey at the sideboard and carried the tumbler to Eastlyn. "I hope she is." She handed him the drink. Her fingers brushed his. There was no mistaking the current that ran through them at this brief contact. His eyes darkened, and that same change was apparent in her own. "I have missed you."

"I required only your invitation."

She nodded. "I know. You will think me perverse, but there were times I wished you would storm the gates. When I heard North was injured . . . I thought that it might easily be—"

Eastlyn shook his head. "I wasn't there."

"It was kind of you to ask Lady Northam to call on me. She thinks very well of you." Sophie was not fooled by East's pretense of ignorance. "I believe she meant to persuade me that you might even make a fine husband."

"I did not ask her to do that," he said quickly. "I had only hoped that she would get me out of Dutch, since I seemed wholly incapable of managing the thing myself."

This confession raised Sophie's faint smile. She sat on an upholstered bench situated at a right angle to East's wing chair. She faced the fireplace while he enjoyed direct benefit of the heat only where his long legs were stretched before him. "The ledgers are here," she said, pointing to the table just inside the room.

East did not follow the direction of her gesture. His eyes remained on her face, on the curve of cheek and jaw that were bathed in firelight. "I saw them when I came in. Do you mean for me to have them, Sophie? To do with them what I want?"

"Yes." She drew in a breath and released it slowly. "It is not because I wish you to do anything, but because I understand you must. I love the man that you are, East. I do not think I fully understood the consequence of those words until this afternoon. It is unfair of me to say I love you and then demand that you act in every way contrary to what you believe. I know you tried to tell me the very same, but I couldn't hear you then. If it is true that rage can blind a person to his actions, then it is no less true that fear can make one deaf to reason."

Sophie's glance shifted sideways, and she saw no censure in his regard, no hurt or regret. "You cannot know how I wish I had arrived at this pass a fortnight ago," she said quietly. "If you mean to stand against the Bishops, I should not have made you stand against me as well."

"Never doubt that you are the more formidable opponent."

"You do not mean that."

"I do."

Sophie was silent a moment. It was because he had cared so fiercely about the outcome that he could say such a thing; it still had the capacity to make her heartbeat trip over itself. "You love me so much?"

"Sophie." East's smile was gentle. "Is it so difficult to believe?"

"Sometimes." Her eyes darted toward the fireplace where the flames curled and flickered in slender ribbons of yellow and orange. "It is not for you to convince me, I think, but for me to convince myself. I cannot quite trust my good fortune." She placed her hand on her abdomen. There was barely any roundness yet, but the flesh was firm, and the cup of her palm exaggerated the curve that would come to her belly soon enough. "It is not only because of the child?"

"No." East put down his drink and moved from his chair to kneel on the floor beside Sophie's bench. He placed his hand over hers. "Do you think I cannot love you for your own sake?"

Her smile wobbled a bit. "I am stubborn," she said. "And too serious by half. It is not so easy for me to laugh at myself or admit when I am in the wrong. I would rather be at home with a book than attend any affair with more than ten people present. I am impatient. Of late I have been a waterworks, and I do not expect it to pass until I am delivered of our child, perhaps not even then. I am confounded by mean-spiritedness, and I do not suffer fools."

"God's truth," Eastlyn said. "You are no saint."

"I am serious, East."

"I know."

Sophie was not proof against the amusement in his eyes. "You shall make me laugh at myself after all. I think you must be very good for me."

"I am."

She lifted her hand from under his so that he could lay his palm against her belly. "It will not be so very long before my state will be obvious. Can you feel how I've swollen?"

East thought she sounded more hopeful than certain. "Your belly will soon precede your feet into a room," he said. He raised himself to the bench and sat beside her. "Will you like that?"

Sophie nodded. "Yes. I expect I shall." Her smile faded as she considered what her obviously pregnant state would mean. "Have you considered what you intend to do about my cousins?"

"Oh, yes."

She waited for him to elaborate, but he did not. "You will not get yourself shot, will you? Do not think I will accept it with the same aplomb as Lady Northam."

"I have no intention of getting shot."

Which was not the same as saying he wouldn't, Sophie thought. "When I was with Colonel Blackwood today . . ." She glanced at East, a frown puckering her brow. "You knew that, didn't you? Did he explain it in his note?"

"He did. Go on."

"He told me a surprising thing that you have never once mentioned to me. I do not think it can be because you have forgotten it." At East's puzzlement, Sophie explained, "The refreshment I served you in the garden at Bowden Street . . . I understand it was something rather more than it should have been."

"Aah, yes." His expression cleared. He should have known the colonel would press this point with Sophie. "Laudanum and lemonade."

"Why did you never tell me?"

East shrugged. "At first I believed the colonel was mistaken. It seemed to me that I should have been able to taste something. I have since learned, depending on the amount of laudanum and the tartness of the drink, that it is not necessarily so."

"You have experimented?"

"The way you are regarding me now is precisely why I've never mentioned it. It was not recklessly done, Sophie. I had a chemist prepare each dose of the laudenade."

"Laudenade?" she asked weakly. "You are quite mad, East. I have always wondered, but now I am certain of it."

He merely grinned as if a compliment had been paid. "I did not suspect for even a moment that you were responsible. It made no sense. I had already proposed when you went inside to request the refreshment, and you knew then that you meant to refuse my offer."

"Colonel Blackwood is not so certain."

"He has a suspicious nature, and I could not recall whether you had taken any of the lemonade for yourself."

"I did not."

"It is just as well that I did not remember that aspect. It

would have raised the colonel's sensitive hackles. You will have noted that he is considerably protective. He wanted to make immediate inquiries about your health that evening. I would not allow him. As far as I was concerned, whether or not you had been unwell proved nothing, and I did not want the colonel wading too deeply into my personal affairs."

"Thank you for that."

"He was not entirely accepting of my decision, Sophie. After you left for Tremont Park, Blackwood arranged for the new governess at Bowden Street to provide him with certain intelligence."

She nodded slowly, worrying her lower lip as she considered this. "That is how you learned that Abigail depended upon her laudanum."

"Yes. And that led me to the rather vague notion that perhaps the lemonade that was served was not meant for us."

"That occurred to me also, but only this afternoon."

"It appears that Lady Dunsmore was taking more laudanum than even you suspected. It begs the question: was she doing so on purpose?" East watched Sophie's hands for the answer and found it in the white-knuckled fists she made in her lap. "I thought that might not be the case. You suspect that it was something being done to her."

Sophie closed her eyes briefly and answered on a thread of sound. "God help me, but I do."

Eastlyn took one of her hands in his and eased her fingers open. In spite of the proximity of the fire, her skin was cold to the touch. "I believe we can acquit the children," he said quietly. "And the servants—unless you tell me that Lady Dunsmore was a tyrant nonpareil. Was she?"

"No." Sophie's gaze remained focused on the flames. "Demanding. Peckish. Often unreasonable. But she was no tyrant. She hadn't the strength of will to be."

"Then there is only one person remaining. Perhaps the idea had not fully formed in your mind until today, but I think you have had some inkling of it for weeks."

"I don't know what you mean."

"When we yet were in Clovelly I told you that Mrs. Sawyer had accepted your cousin's protection. You asked me if she had designs for a marriage with Dunsmore, and I reminded you, rather naively as it turns out, that Dunsmore was already married. Do you recall your response then, Sophie? It cannot have been far from the front of your mind for all this time."

It was not. Each time she thought she had pushed it back, there were reminders that moved her suspicions front and center. "I told you that I have learned that when people decide what they want, there are any number of ways they might achieve their ends."

He nodded. "You were referring to your father's death," he said, "but perhaps not only that. Lady Dunsmore's habit of taking daily doses of laudanum must have stirred all manner of memories for you."

Sophie's gaze fell to her lap. She looked at Eastlyn's fingers threaded through hers and felt the strength and warmth of his clasp finally penetrate. "I did not believe he would attempt to kill her. Not really. I hate him for the part he took in my father's death, but his actions made some sense to me. As vile as they were, I could understand that it is sometimes in the nature of men—and women—to covet what another has. If Mrs. Sawyer was trying to poison Abigail, that would at least be understandable, but this began long before she was in any way part of Harold's life."

"How long before?"

Sophie carefully considered the question before she spoke. "It would have to have been after Esme was born. I cannot recall her complaining of headaches or using any powders before that time, but then you must remember that I was only infrequently in her company. Still, I think she was not suffering then."

"Esme is four?"

"Yes."

"Then she was born not long before your father died."

"Seven months." She frowned slightly. "What are you thinking, East?"

He did not answer immediately, letting the idea take shape first in his own mind. His fingers squeezed Sophie's gently, imparting his warmth again to flesh that had suddenly grown cold. "I am thinking that perhaps Lady Dunsmore has certain knowledge of things you and I have only suspected."

"She was not at Tremont Park when my father was shot."

"She did not have to witness the shooting to learn what happened there. Someone could have told her directly, though that is unlikely, or she might have overheard a conversation she was not meant to. It has been your own experience to hear Tremont practicing his speeches from the other side of a door."

Sophie could very easily imagine Abigail coming upon a discussion between Harold and Tremont that she should not have paused to listen to. "She might know a good deal more than the truth about the shooting." Her eyes strayed to the ledgers. "It is possible she has some understanding of what those mean."

East nodded. "I think that's likely."

"Do you suppose she confronted Harold? He must be aware that she knows something, else he would have no reason to harm her."

It was a question in his own mind, and another for which he did not have an answer. He had not considered the possibility that his plans for Dunsmore and the Society of Bishops might place the viscountess at risk. Her life would be forever changed by what he intended, but his concern had been only that she should survive the scandal. Now it seemed he must assure that she *survived*. He would have to remove her and the children from Bowden Street before he could challenge Dunsmore or the Society.

East removed his hand from Sophie's and stood. He retrieved the stack of ledgers and placed them on the floor beside the bench. He chose the one on top to give to Sophie and took the second for himself. "You have reviewed them all?"

"Yes."

"And what is your answer to the question I put to you? Is Dunsmore part of the Society's circle or apart from it?"

"Your question is a trick one. He is both those things at once."

"Tell me."

"Harold does not stand with the others to form the circle, so he is not part of it in that way, yet they all look to him because he is at the center of it."

Eastlyn nodded approvingly. "How did you determine that?"

"I arrived at it slowly," she admitted, "because even with your parting words in my head, I could not get my mind past the idea that the Society of Bishops was in the service of Tremont. Then I considered that mayhap it was Helmsley who led them around by the nose. He has had a long political career, and his position in government is more powerful than any of the others. When I could not make sense of it, I looked carefully at Barlough's ledger because you told me that he had been an archbishop as well. It was then that I chose Harold's book and finally saw the pattern of withdrawals and payments."

"You came to the thing more quickly than I," he told her. "Dunsmore's book was the first one I had in my possession. By the time I looked at all the others I no longer had a good grasp of what had been in his."

"But you came to the same conclusion."

"Yes."

"Harold is demanding money from all of them."

Eastlyn nodded. "It is blackmail, Sophie. It serves no purpose to shy from the word. Dunsmore is blackmailing all of them, including his own father." He pointed to an entry at random on the open ledger in her lap. "One hundred pounds to *Gilhead*." He found a similar entry in the book he held open. "One hundred fifty pounds invested in the same ship the following day. I have Harte's ledger. Whose do you have?"

"This is Tremont's."

Eastlyn used the toe of his boot to topple the stack of accounts on the floor. He found Dunsmore's book at the bottom and picked it up. It required only a few moments for him to find the pertinent entries. "Here is a record of one hundred pounds deposited. *T. Gilhead*. And another for one hundred fifty pounds marked *H. A. Gilhead*. I think we can assume that H. A. is so that Dunsmore could distinguish between payments made by Harte and those made by Helmsley."

"Why *Gilhead*?" she asked.

"It's a ship trading in goods to India. Many of the entries refer to merchant vessels. It is merely a way for Dunsmore to keep an accurate record of what he is being paid. It provides a reference for the others in dealing with him. Some of the investments made by the Society are in reality just that, but I believe they were expected to share some fraction of their profits with your cousin. He made the same investments, so he knew which voyages were successful and which were not."

"Some of the ships transport slaves?"

"Yes." East thumbed through several pages of Harte's ledger. "Here. *Crusader* and *Valencia*. Their captains are known slavers. It appears the Society made investments to both and later paid Dunsmore with some of the profits."

"Bloody hell," Sophie whispered. She closed the ledger and looked up, catching Eastlyn's surprise before he could mask it. "You say it often enough. I cannot think of a single reason it should be the exclusive province of the male gender." Sophie's eyes were a shade defiant. "Bloody, *bloody* hell."

East did not take issue with the vulgarity, choosing to kiss her delicious mouth instead. It was a brief kiss, but the swiftness of it was part of what set Sophie so nicely off balance.

"What was that in aid of?" Her tone was not as sharp as she wished it might be. When Eastlyn merely grinned at her, she found her bearings. She lightly jabbed one corner of the ledger she held at his ribs, then dropped it hard on top of the others in his lap.

"Bloody hell, Sophie." He moved the books so they were out of her easy reach, including pushing those on the floor aside. "God's truth, but you are dangerous."

"Apparently it is a family trait," she said, more serious than not. It was sufficient to sober them both. "What is it that Harold holds over all of their heads? Is it really my father's shooting?"

"I suspect it began there. It is impossible to know the particulars without having been a member of the hunting party, but perhaps Harold was not meant to know the shooting was deliberate. It might be that he observed the whole of it, but had nothing to do with its planning."

"He became part of it when he kept his silence."

"I agree. He is no less culpable in my eyes, though his guilt is not so clear as a matter of law. I think that while it began with your father, it did not end there. His leverage with them has increased over the years. The more they paid, the more they had to pay. He used their money to learn about their business, their perversions, their secrets. It is possible that Dunsmore knows more about the Society of Bishops than any other person outside of it."

"I don't understand why they haven't killed him."

"I have considered that. If I were in Dunsmore's position, I would put a detailed account of all that I knew in a safe place."

Sophie shook her head and gestured to the stolen ledgers. "I have learned that such a thing does not exist. You came by all of these easily enough."

East did not disabuse her of the notion that it had been a simple thing. She would not want to know how often the colonel's work had engaged him in similar activities. Neither would it ease her mind for him to confirm that none of it was without considerable risk. "Private things are rarely kept safely in one's own home," he said. "A better solution is to give them to someone else. In Dunsmore's place I would give my documents to a solicitor, with instructions to make them public upon my death—in the event that it was untimely. Because this is the Society, and one can never be certain who may be counted among their members, I might give copies of the documents to several solicitors."

"I am not certain Harold is so clever. Does he seem so to you?"

"He is alive, Sophie. His solution to the problem may be different than mine, but the fact that he is still blackmailing members of the Society is proof enough that he has given the matter thought and arrived at some plan."

"They all know their ledgers are missing, East. Why has no one come for them?"

"Because they do not know *all* the ledgers are missing. I doubt that they have spoken to one another about it. Would you? You must keep in mind that Dunsmore's book is the key to all the others. Without it, their accounts are harmless enough. Some of them may not be overly concerned. Pendrake kept his ledger quite openly with the household accounts. He was not worried that someone would understand the import of it. And no one save for your cousins has any reason to suspect that I might have taken their books."

Sophie could no longer remain seated. She rose and crossed to the fireplace, choosing to stab at the fire with a poker rather than do nothing at all. "I cannot reconcile that it is Harold, and not his father, who is the puppeteer. It seems to me that he is always in Tremont's shadow."

"Perhaps because it is a good place to hide."

Sophie smiled faintly. "I had not considered that." She glanced over her shoulder at East. "I better understand Tremont's desperation to have me make a good marriage. He must have wondered how he would secure the funds to keep paying his own son."

"I am certain that is so. Dunsmore put none of his money into the estate."

"How that must have galled Tremont. After all, he shot

my father with an eye toward not only acquiring the title and estate for himself, but an inheritance for his son." Sophie replaced the poker and stepped to the edge of the marble apron. "Do you suppose Tremont knows what Harold is doing to Abigail?"

"It's more likely that he believes as we did, that Lady Dunsmore is doing the thing to herself."

"What will happen to her, East? And the children? If you expose Harold, he could very well believe that it was Abigail who betrayed him. Whatever he might do to her, I do not want it on my conscience."

"I have already decided that I must get her away from Bowden Street."

"Robert and Esme, also."

"Of course."

"Where will they go?"

"A safe place. Trust me."

"I do." She hesitated. "I could help you."

"I think not."

"The children trust *me*. You don't know them."

Eastlyn supposed the time had come to tell her about his encounter with young Robert Colley. "That is not precisely true. I expect Robert will not have forgotten me." Before she could insert a question, East told her the whole of it. He thought Sophie would be unhappy with him for disturbing the nursery, but he was not prepared for the sharp regret that made her teary. "I didn't mean to wake him," he said quickly, "but you must see that I had to return his soldiers. He would have been blamed for the missing ledger otherwise."

She nodded and gave him a watery smile, blinking back the tears. "You mustn't mind me. I expect it is because I miss them. You cannot know what it was like to be shut away from them for an entire month. I could hear them whispering in the hall. Sometimes Esme would slip drawings under my door. They did not understand any of it, of course, but I imagine they thought I had done something terrible to be locked in my room for so long. I was glad when Tremont made me accompany him to the Park. It was far better than being a prisoner at Bowden Street."

East stood and went to her. She stepped into his embrace and laid her head on his shoulder. His chin nudged her hair. It was no less a sweet comfort for him than it was for her. "Robert will be happy to see you again," he said. "His sister, also, I expect." He heard Sophie sniffle once, then felt her searching the pockets of his frock coat for a handkerchief. He set her away from him as she blew her nose, then led her back to the bench. She sat while he stacked the ledgers again and carried them to the table.

"I was never able to find your journal," he said, setting the books down. "I searched for it in the carriage and later, in my home. It doesn't seem that I left it behind, so I must have carried it here with these. Did you come across it?"

"No. Where did you find it in the first place?"

"At Number 14."

"That's not possible. If you had taken it from Tremont Park, that would be understandable, but not from Bowden Street. I left none behind when I left for the country."

"You are certain?"

"Quite. They are all accounted for. Why did you think it was mine? Did you read it?"

"No. That is, I only glanced at it. I found it when I was returning Robert's soldiers to the toy chest. I thought you would want it back, so I took it."

"If you found it there, it was probably one of Abigail's."

"She kept a diary?"

"She used to. I do not think she writes often now. Sometimes she wrote stories for the children. I expect it was one of those that you found."

East said nothing. He ran a hand through his hair, furrowing it deeply as he contemplated a point beyond Sophie's shoulder. The line of his mouth was flattened, and his eyes were narrowed.

"What is it?" She was becoming familiar with this particular expression of East's and knew it was nothing behind her that had captured his attention. "East?"

"I'm not certain," he said.

"Perhaps if you say it aloud . . ."

A crease appeared between his brows, and he took a short, impatient breath before he spoke. "What if the journal was originally with Dunsmore's ledger? And what if Robert found it when he hid his soldiers there?"

"He cannot read her script," Sophie said. "He would have mistaken it for one of his mother's storybooks."

"Yes. And carried it back to his room."

"Why is that important?"

"It's not. What is important is why Dunsmore would have kept one of Abigail's journals in the same hiding place as his ledger." Now East focused his eyes sharply on Sophie and saw that she understood. "We have to find the journal."

Sophie was already rising to her feet. "If you truly carried it into the house, then it must still be here." She swept through the door as he opened it and felt him closely at her back as she hurried up the stairs. On the threshold to her bedchamber, she paused. "Wait here a moment. We must pretend everything is as it was on the night of the ambassador's ball." She did not wait to confirm that he was in agreement, but slipped inside her room and closed the door.

Sighing, East hooked his left arm as if he were hefting the books he had carried in that night. He placed his right hand on the doorknob and gave it a small twist. Sophie flung the door open and pulled him into the room. Her kiss was not as urgent as the one she had offered a fortnight earlier; but she threw her arms around him just as fiercely, and he had to tighten his grip on the imaginary pile of ledgers under his arm.

Sophie broke the kiss suddenly and whispered against his mouth, "What happened next?"

"I believe you demonstrated considerable eagerness to have me in your bed."

That was how Sophie remembered it also. She pulled him toward the bed, more impatient now than persuasive, her lips but a hairsbreadth from his. "It is awkward, is it not? Did it seem so at the time?"

"If it did, I didn't mind." He looked down at himself and realized his arm was no longer in a position to hold the books. "I dropped them here."

Sophie eased her arms from around his neck, but stayed close. "Here? At the foot of the bed?"

"Yes . . . and one started to fall . . . and—" East hunkered down and began sweeping under the bed with his hand. "I remember pressing it against the bed with my knee, trying to keep it from dropping to the floor and waking your aunt."

Sophie joined him, lowering herself until she was prostrate with a clear view of under the bed. "Will you give me the candle, please?"

East took it from her bedside table and put it in her hand before he stretched out on the floor as well. The tiny flame was all that was necessary to reveal the location of a book far under the bed. The green leather spine was dulled by a few dust motes, but it was recognizable to East as the journal he'd found.

Dropping his shoulder, East stretched his arm far enough to catch the book with his fingertips. "I must have kicked it under here." He pulled it out and sat up, leaning back against the bed frame. Sophie joined him, drawing her legs up, careless that her silk gown was stretched tautly from knee to knee. She peered over East's lap as he opened the book.

"It is most definitely Abigail's," she said. "Though I can see why, at a glance, you would have mistaken it for mine. There is a great similarity in our copperplate script."

East nodded absently and continued to thumb through the pages, skimming the neat handwriting for particulars. "There appear to be no stories here for the children."

Sophie held up the candle to provide better light. Individual words leaped out at her as East paged through the journal, but she had no sense of the whole. "What are you looking for?" she asked. "What will make you stop long enough to read carefully?"

"Names. Dunsmore. Tremont. Your own." Although there were dated entries, they were of little help. Neither he nor Sophie had more than a vague idea when Abigail might have learned something that placed her life in jeopardy.

"Abigail called Harold 'Dearest,'" Sophie said. "She always did. I doubt she would refer to him in her diary in any other manner. Tremont has been 'Father' since she married Harold. I am 'Fia.' It is Esme's way of saying my name, and Abigail adopted it."

East gave Sophie the journal and took the candle. "You will find what we are looking for more quickly than I."

"Assuming there is something to find."

He acknowledged the truth of that, but could not bring himself to believe otherwise. "Go on," he said. His tone was both gentle and encouraging. If Sophie found nothing at all, it would be hard for her, he realized, but finding something would be harder.

Sophie started at the beginning, running her finger quickly along the edge of each page as she read. Her features remained expressionless save for intense concentration. Occasionally her lips parted, changing shape around words she gave no sound. For slightly more than a quarter of an hour there was only the sound of the pages being turned and the soft hiss of the candle flame.

"What is it?" East asked when he saw her finger slow. In the stillness of the room, her sharp intake of air also caught his attention. "Read it to me, Sophie."

She nodded faintly, holding the journal with a sure grip to steady her hands. *"It has occurred to me that no woman can truly know the heart of the man she loves until he has become her husband. The ardency of courtship is no predictor of what may follow, indeed, courtship itself seems a cruel convention that serves to prepare no one for the realities of marriage. I do not know what I might say to him as I am no longer confident of the bent of his mind. He argues so fiercely that he frightens me, and I find myself wondering what manner of retribution there would be were I to speak my thoughts aloud."*

Sophie softly cleared her throat. "That is a single entry. What follows was made sometime later, perhaps after a few hours of contemplation, perhaps after days of it. Her hand is heavier here, and the strokes are broad. Even the ink has a different appearance. I suspect she was drawing it from a different bottle." Sophie continued, her voice grave, *"I have determined that the children are best served if I keep my own counsel, for I realize now that I comprehend little of the ways of their father and grandfather. How fervently I wish that I might have remained in ignorance, for sometimes it seems that the stain of another generation has been visited upon my children. Can they be innocent when their blood is also his blood? It seems there is but one innocent here, and I find it increasingly difficult to look upon her. There are moments when I think she suspects the truth and remains here to punish them, mayhap punish us all. When there is a calm upon me I doubt thoughts such as these, and can understand they are but a fancy. What demands might she make on my family if she was as certain of the truth as I? She rarely speaks of her own father, and never of the accident that confined him to his bed. Perhaps it is because she would find no sympathetic ear or comfort in false platitudes. How can Father offer consolation when he acknowledges openly that he shot his cousin, and admits privately that he was acting according to his own conscience? What manner of conscience excuses murder?"*

Sophie lowered the journal onto her lap. "I cannot read more."

Eastlyn did not take the book from her, slipping his arm around her shoulders instead. She turned into the shelter of his embrace and remained there, unmoving and quiet. There were no tears now, but a terrible ache of acceptance that closed her throat.

"It's enough, Sophie," East said gently. "You have done enough."

Sophie closed Abigail's diary. "Will it serve as proof, do you think?"

East remained silent for a long moment, thoughtful of his response. "Archimedes said that with a fulcrum and a lever that was long enough, he might move the world. The stack of ledgers belowstairs is our fulcrum." He took the journal from her lap and held it up. "And this is our lever."

Suspicious of his intentions, Sophie looked at him askance. "What is it that you mean to do?"

His smile held cold resolve, not humor. "Publish them, Sophie. Books are meant to be published."

Chapter Sixteen

"What's wrong with calling the lot of them out and shooting them?" Lord Northam chose a card from his hand and tossed it on the table. "Your restraint is admirable, East, but what is the good of being a crack shot if you don't mean to take aim and fire?"

West made his play and took the trick. "I'm for shooting them."

"It has much to recommend it," Southerton said. He followed West's lead. "Although with so many of them to dispatch, you'd have to start deuced early in the morning. I'm afraid you couldn't count on me in that event. Like to sleep in." He felt three pairs of eyes regarding him with considerable interest and not a little knowing humor. He remained unmoved by their regard. If they wanted to see him before the noon hour, they should not have been so eager to help him find Miss Parr. What man would want to leave his bed while she was still in it? "Make your play, East. And have a care not to renege."

East made his selection and laid it carefully on top of the others. He gave South his pointed attention. "It may still come to shooting someone."

Chuckling, North played trump and took the trick. "Can't

say that you'd enjoy that, South. Hurts like the very devil." He tapped the edge of his collected cards on the table, squaring off the trick. "There's also a great deal of fussing by women, one of whom is certain to be your mother. You should think about that before you take another jab at East."

South pretended to consider this sound advice. He darted a glance at Eastlyn. "You'd be cruel enough to allow me to live, wouldn't you?"

East let his faintly ironic smile speak for him.

"Bloody hell, man, but you are without a conscience." While the others were laughing, South gestured to a footman to bring drinks to their table. The play resumed until they were served; then they simply folded their cards and tossed them into the middle of the table.

The club was crowded this evening, but the conversation all around them did not impede their own. As was their manner when things of import were to be discussed, they did not invite the attention of others by behaving with unexpected gravity. Individually regarded by society as careful, considerate men, their reputation when they were in one another's company was something else entirely. No one in the club gave them the slightest heed when rich, rolling laughter fairly erupted from their table.

"Chamber pots," South said as the laughter subsided. "Damn me, if East's not talking about chamber pots again. Messy business, that. You all can't have forgotten what it was like."

"Still," West said, "it was an inspired stroke. And it brought the Bishops to heel. These account books could do the same thing, especially if East makes them available for public inspection."

North regarded East over the rim of his glass. "Do you really mean to publish the ledgers?"

Eastlyn nodded. "It is already being done."

"What about making them public?" asked South. He gathered the cards and began idly shuffling them. "There is considerably more at risk here than one of the Bishops dirtying his pants. They will not be merely made a laughingstock, East. They will be ruined."

"Are you trying to talk me out of it?" East asked.

South shook his head. "Simply advocating for shooting them."

West rolled his tumbler of Scotch between his palms. "You are inviting us rather late to the table." There was no censure in his voice; it was only a statement of fact. "But it is better than not being invited at all, I suppose." He said this last while darting a mildly critical glance at Southerton. It served to remind that worthy that he had never asked them to come to his aid. Friendships being what they were, they elected to mount a rescue anyway, as much for South's sake as to see the delectable Miss India Parr again.

East smiled as South squirmed uncomfortably under West's cool regard, then spoke to save him when he considered it had gone on long enough. "I would have spoken sooner, but I had to consider Sophie's wishes."

"You are a deep one, East." North sipped his drink. "Married for so long, and none of us with any inkling of it." He glanced at South and Westphal and saw by their expressions that, indeed, he had spoken for them as well. "She really was so fearful for you?"

Eastlyn nodded. "She still is. These weeks since the ambassador's ball have been difficult. First, there was the matter of the Gentleman Thief. That bit of intrigue did nothing to ease her mind. I think she suspected me of those thefts until you had the good sense to get yourself shot during the apprehension. Even though Sophie was entirely put out with me at the time, she could still acquit me of shooting you."

This raised North's chuckle. "So you were in her good graces again, though I doubt it lasted overlong."

"How could it when South immediately got himself into a fix? Sophie was not yet settled with what Lady Dunsmore had revealed in her journal, nor with my plan to publish the whole of it, when I learned that I must leave London."

"Didn't say you must," South said, somewhat defensively.

"Lady Northam said you must. Women always think they know what it is we should do, and I think it is badly done of them to be right so often."

This gave them all pause. Eastlyn finished his drink, then broke the silence. "There is more," he said quietly. "Sophie is carrying my child."

That news effectively put the others back in their chairs as they considered the likely order of events. "God's truth," West said feelingly, "it is a good thing that you married her." A muscle jumped in his jaw. "Society has no use for bastards."

Because East understood the very personal nature of this remark, he let it pass. "I want to live with my wife," he said. "I want to be able to escort her on my arm as my marchioness. Whatever scandal attaches itself to us, it will be short lived. I would prefer that none of it touches our child. To that end, gentlemen, it is better that I confront the Bishops now."

"What about Dunsmore?" North said. "You have been clear in the telling of this that he is no member of the Society."

"And he will be dealt with apart from them." They did not ask East to explain himself, and he did not offer.

"What do you require of us?" South asked.

East pointed to the cards in South's hands. "Deal," he said. "And I shall explain all."

The invitations went out two days following. Each was sent in an elegant envelope that had been made with linen fibers and flecked with gold. The carefully set seal was that of the Prince Regent. The fine copperplate engraving on the card inside couched the command for the presence of each man as a request. It was to be a sennight hence that the prince would dine with company at Windsor Castle. No one who received this invitation considered declining it. It would not be politic to do so, no matter what personal opinion was harbored for the prince. There always existed the possibility that an opportunity would present itself to encourage Prinny on a different course of thinking, one that would parallel one's own and win favor with like minds in Parliament.

The Earl of Tremont prepared for the evening with reasoned care. He was suspicious of the Prince Regent's attention, but cautiously hopeful that it might portend a change in his own fortunes. So little had gone well for him of late, and much of the reason for it could be laid at Sophie's door. He wondered that he had been so lenient with her and not forced a marriage, even if it was an arrangement of only middling potential for wealth. It had been a mistake to pin so many of his hopes to her match with Eastlyn, but he had been convinced that she would recognize her duty to marry well and acquit herself honorably. Sadly, that had not been the way of it. She was impudent and incorrigible, and these flaws of character had not diminished when she abandoned childhood. The indulgence that she was shown by her own father had made her headstrong to a fault.

He could well remember the accusation in her eyes when she learned her father would not walk again. Somehow she had known that the accident was not that her father had been shot, but that he had lived. Each farthing that his own son extracted from him was as nothing when measured against what it had cost him to look upon Sophie's accusing eyes.

It gave Tremont great satisfaction to arrive at the castle and put all thoughts of Sophie to rest. That he had been invited to dine with the prince was proof that Sophie did not comprehend the influence he now enjoyed. His warning at the ambassador's ball had been most sincerely meant. Neither she nor East had the least idea of what they were confronting.

Tremont was shown directly to a receiving room in the Round Tower and announced. He might have staggered back if the doors had not been pulled so quickly closed behind him. He found his bearings, offered a faint smile in the way of greeting the others, and took his first steps into the room with more assurance than he felt.

They were all standing, not one of them surprised by his

entry. Indeed, they had been discussing that very thing, since it occurred to them he was the only one missing from their party. No one among them counted it likely that Dunsmore would appear.

Barlough separated himself from the others and stepped forward. "Tremont. Helmsley has only just said that you would be the next to arrive. There was no time to make a wager on it, but I do not think any of us would have challenged him. It does seem that you complete our little group."

"You are here at the prince's express wishes?" asked Tremont.

"The same as you." Barlough's tone narrowly missed being contemptuous. "It was certainly not the Princess Caroline who extended the invitation."

Tremont's coolly-colored eyes narrowed briefly as he surveyed the group that had been brought together. "Helmsley. Pendrake. Harte." He nodded to each in turn, and they acknowledged him in kind. "It is an interesting assemblage, is it not? Old friends, well met." No one made any reply to that, and Tremont was struck by the notion that he was not alone in his unease. Seeing them here, as the only guests of the Prince Regent, had a far different import than being part of the crush at the ambassador's ball. He thrust his chin out between the starched points of his collar. "Have you been told when we might expect Prinny?"

Lord Helmsley was a solidly framed man, with the stature of one who might have been hewn from the stump rather than the entire tree. When he stepped to one side, a small table was revealed. He pointed to the neat stack of ledgers upon it. "We have not been told anything," he said. "But we believe that was by intention, not oversight. It seems to us that we have been encouraged to study these instead. You will have already recognized your own, I think. There is one for each of us. The question, Tremont, is what the bloody hell has your son done now?"

Tremont went immediately to the table. His book of accounts was on top, the placement suggesting it had been the last ledger they had examined. It was not prescience that led them to conclude he would arrive. Indeed, the presence of his own ledger made it a certainty. He would have wondered at their intelligence if they had not expected him.

His ledger was distinguished from the others by the gilt initials on the black leather spine. Still, he picked it up and briefly examined the contents. There was no mistaking that the writing was his own. "This was taken from my London residence before the ambassador's ball. Was it so long ago for you?"

Barlough nodded. "We are fairly certain the thefts were accomplished within a few days of one another. Pendrake did not miss his until recently, owing to the fact that he leaves the thing lying about as if it were of no more importance than a Gothic novel." Pendrake's narrow face flushed with this rebuke, but he accepted it without comment. The edges of Barlough's mouth tightened as he regarded Tremont. "I will say again, Tremont, what has your son done?"

There was a thinly disguised implication, Tremont knew, in Barlough referring to Harold as his son, instead of calling him Dunsmore. Implicit in that statement was Barlough's belief that he should have exercised more control over his son. They had always thought he had been negligent in bringing Harold to heel. By the time they voiced their opinion, it was too late. They all paid because he had not acted to stop Harold, and now everything they did was compromised by the fact that someone outside the Society was privy to its workings. "Harold is not responsible for the thefts," he said. "I am certain of it."

This did not calm the waters. Harte, standing at Barlough's shoulder, said, "Then why is his book not here? We know he keeps one. We have all seen him record our payments."

"I don't know where his book is." He set his ledger back on the stack. "How do I know one or all of you is not responsible?"

Barlough began to deny it, but Helmsley stayed him as

the doors to the receiving room were parted. They fell quiet, all turning at once. To a man their features were set without expression.

Colonel John Blackwood took his time surveying the group. It did not matter what manner of face they showed him; he could smell their fear. Nodding once, he indicated that he was ready to be wheeled into the room.

Standing at the back of the colonel's chair, the Prince Regent was pleased to oblige.

At No. 14 Bowden Street the front door was opened in response to an impatient, rather imperious knocking. Without announcing the purpose of her visit, Sophie swept past the butler. She was followed by her three escorts, none of whom responded to the man's queries or protests.

They mounted the stairs quickly. In the upper hall, Sophie pointed out Lady Dunsmore's bedchamber to her companions, then went on in the direction of the children's rooms. Abigail's shriek did not cause her even a single misstep, though she imagined it had given Northam, Southerton, and Westphal a good start. It had occurred to her to warn them of Abigail's penchant for high-pitched hysterics, but the abundance of confidence they had displayed kept her silent. Hysterics or no, Sophie thought, they would make short work of Lady Dunsmore's abduction.

Neither Robert nor Esme stirred when she entered their room. Standing between their beds, she watched them sleep for a moment. Like bookends, they faced opposite sides of the room, but were perfectly matched in posture. Sophie sat carefully on the edge of Robert's bed and lightly placed a hand on his shoulder. As was his habit, he woke almost immediately and sat straight up. Experience had taught her that although he looked for all the world as if he were alert, his brain would need a minute or more to catch up with the rest of him.

"So you've come," he said with pitch perfect aplomb. "I expected you would. Told Esme you could not forget us so easily."

Sophie bent and kissed his forehead. "How right you were," she whispered. "Up with you now. We are to have an adventure." She helped Robert push back the blankets and get his legs over the side of the bed. He began to shiver, and Sophie realized for the first time how cold the children's room was. She found his slippers and put them on his feet before she stirred the fire to life. "Go warm yourself, then find something you can wear over your nightshirt."

Robert shuffled toward the hearth, holding out his hands as he went. He swayed slightly in front of the fire, for all intents and purposes asleep on his feet.

In the event he required rescuing from a fall into the fire, Sophie watched him out of the corner of her eye while she packed a valise with clothes for both children. He was upright, but still only dressed in his nightshirt and slippers, when she scooped up Esme. The little girl never opened her eyes, but simply burrowed into Sophie's arms. "Come, Robert, we are away."

He pivoted on his heel, the coordination of the movement indicating he was almost completely awake. "I say, Cousin Fia. Is Mama to come with us?"

"Certainly. I shouldn't be surprised if she is waiting for us now."

"And Father?"

Sophie wished she had prepared herself for Robert's questions. It was something she could have anticipated and planned for. Now she found herself hesitating, wondering what she could say that would satisfy him sufficiently to engage his cooperation. Her pause, though, proved to be her saving grace as Robert's impatience prompted him to answer his own question.

"He will be with Artemis, I think." His brow puckered, but he regarded Sophie directly. "I wasn't sure that he would allow us to go with him."

Distracted by Esme's soft cry for her mama, Sophie only listened to Robert with half an ear. She shushed the little girl, pressing her cheek against Esme's downy hair. "Robert. We must go. Will you take the valise?"

Robert needed two hands to heft the bag, but he was game for it. Sophie opened the door and let him precede her into the hallway. She urged him forward, one hand at the nape of his neck. Northam was waiting for them at the foot of the stairs and would have started up to help them if Sophie had not shaken her head. The valise thumped hard on every step, straining Robert's grip, but Northam's assistance would have been unwelcome.

Several servants besides the butler were now gathered at the entrance. Confused by the goings-on, they looked to Sophie for direction. The bolder among them were desirous of an explanation.

"Your concern speaks well of you," Sophie told them. "Lady Dunsmore and the children will return in due course, and her ladyship will want everything to be kept in readiness for her. If his lordship returns, you may tell him whatever you like. There is no secret to be kept, not even the fact that I was here." She felt Northam's palm pressing at the small of her back, a sure indication that she must finish quickly. "Take no risk upon yourself in order to protect me. That is the very last thing I would wish."

She moved quickly past the murmured farewells and quiet weeping. How much had they all known? she wondered. Without a doubt, their collective knowledge was far more than her own. It occurred to her that one of those weeping now might have been made to help Dunsmore drug Abigail. She would not be surprised to learn of it.

Northam's fine carriage was waiting for them. Southerton took Esme from Sophie's arms until West had assisted her inside. When he was assured she was comfortably settled, he handed the sleeping child back to her. Northam gave young Robert and the valise a boost up the carriage steps. When Robert saw his mother curled in the far corner, her head lolling weakly against the leather squabs, he hurled himself onto the seat beside her to lend his support and protection.

North spread a rug across Robert's thin legs, tucking him in. "Your mother will be grateful for your care," he said gently. "When she is better, she will thank you for it." Stepping back so that only his head and shoulders were visible in the doorway, Northam offered Sophie a wry smile. "Lady Dunsmore is all of a piece, though she was somewhat more excitable than we anticipated."

"She fainted?"

"Yes," he said after a moment. "I suppose it was rather like that." He closed the door before Sophie could raise the obvious question, and gave his driver Eastlyn's Everly Square address. The carriage rolled forward, followed by South and West on horseback. He mounted his own animal just as the door to No. 14 was closing.

All in all, Northam reflected, it had gone surprisingly well. He had had some doubts about taking Lady Sophia into the fray, but saw there was wisdom in it because of her affection for the children. She had proved herself to be a good soldier, doing precisely as she was instructed from beginning to end. Even Lady Dunsmore's shrieking had not deviated her from her purpose, though perhaps she had been more prepared for her ladyship's response than the rest of them. He chuckled at the thought that Sophie had let them walk into that bedchamber, knowing full well that a banshee awaited them. It was a proper comeuppance for their surfeit of confidence.

It was the sort of thing that East himself might do, though generally not to his friends. North considered it could only behoove him to become a friend to Lady Sophia, for she was in every way able to hold her own.

Mrs. Sawyer's home was quiet as Eastlyn let himself in using the side door. This tradesmen's entrance took him into the deserted kitchen. He paused on the threshold until he had his bearings, then navigated the darkened room without serious mishap. He was unfamiliar with the house Dunsmore had found for Annette, but careful study of the outside had given him some idea of how its rooms might flow from one to another. East negotiated the servants' stairs without benefit of a candle. His movement along the upper corridor was made easier by a window at the far end that framed a three-quarter moon.

He quietly opened and closed the doors to three rooms, none of which revealed his former mistress or her new lover. It was when he stood facing the fourth and final door that he allowed himself to think the end was in sight.

And it was upon opening it that he realized such thought was premature.

The stays in Prinny's corset creaked as he lowered himself into a chair. The fashion of the day had always proved to be his most steady challenge. As long as Brummel dictated that svelte figures and trim waists were *de rigueur*, he was forced to pare his own substantial silhouette with a stiff whalebone corset. He pretended not to notice the sound and dared anyone else to make even the slightest note of it. Though these men—with the exception of the colonel—numbered themselves among his most ardent opposition, not one of them smirked.

"Go on," the Prince Regent said. "It is all very fascinating. The ledgers tell their own story, but it is vastly entertaining to hear it from you. You were saying, Tremont?"

The earl glanced at the account book in Colonel Blackwood's hands. It was opened to the page detailing monies paid to his son through a scheme to defraud Lloyd's. "I am certain I was at an end," Tremont said.

"Oh, that is too bad of you. And here I was, set to inquire about the attempt on my life last year. You recall it, perhaps? At the opening of Parliament? It occurs to me that in light of this conspiracy, another investigation is warranted. What say you to that, Colonel? It is possible to believe anything of them now. Even that they would kill their sovereign."

There was a general murmur of protest from the Bishops, but the colonel quelled it before it had gone very far. "Have a care what you say, gentlemen, for I have it on good authority that one of your own acted in that regard. It remains to be seen if he acted entirely alone, or with your approval." The colonel lowered his spectacles so that he might more clearly see the writing in the ledger before him. "Now, about your investments in the opium trade, it has occurred to me that—"

He was interrupted by a knock at the door and the entry of one of Prinny's secretaries. The man bowed, made his apologies for disobeying orders forbidding exactly this sort of interruption, and presented the Prince Regent with a note that he was certain would excuse him.

Prinny dismissed him, read the brief correspondence, and passed it to the colonel. The Prince Regent gave Blackwood full marks for his unchanging expression; the man's frustration must have been enormous.

The colonel folded the note and used it to mark his place in the ledger as he closed it. "It appears we are all guilty of underestimating your son, Tremont," he said without inflection. "He has fled, and has had the good sense to leave his mistress behind, though not sense enough to leave her alive."

Eastlyn found his friends gathered in his drawing room, keeping company with his wife. None of them took pains to hide their surprise that he had returned before the two o'clock hour—and alone. They all knew it meant that something was not as it should be.

Sophie started to rise in her chair, but sat down again when East bid her do so. "What has happened?" she asked, voicing the question for all of them.

East had his own questions first. "Lady Dunsmore is here? And the children?"

"Yes. Yes, they are all abovestairs sleeping. Lady Gilbert also. Lord Southerton escorted her here himself."

West jumped to his feet. "You look as if you could use a drink, East. Brandy?"

"Whiskey." East went to the hearth, stripped off his coat and riding gloves, and warmed his hands. "Leave us, Sophie."

"I will not, my lord." She felt the room grow silent. Even West halted in his tracks to the drinks cabinet. "It is not my intention to embarrass you in front of your friends. It is no pleasure to oppose you in this, but I will remind you that Harold and Tremont are still my family. I may despise the fact of it, but it *is* a fact. I want to know what has happened."

East turned. He knew he could expect no interference from any quarter of the room. "Very well," he said. There would be no argument from him; there was no time for it. "Dunsmore was not at Mrs. Sawyer's. When he left Bowden Street this evening, he went to her home straightaway, but he was not there when I returned from delivering the colonel to Windsor Castle."

"The Bishops?" asked North. "They were at the castle?"

"Yes. All of them. Every invitation accepted, precisely as we hoped. I did not stay long. Prinny was anxious to put the whole of it before them, and the colonel was having difficulty containing him."

West put a tumbler of whiskey in East's hand. "What of Mrs. Sawyer? Did she say where Dunsmore had gone?"

Eastlyn's eyes darted to Sophie, then back to West. "Mrs. Sawyer is dead. Murdered. It seems likely that it was by Dunsmore's hand, though what might have been his motive is not clear. I cannot be certain if he fled because he killed her or if he killed her because he meant to flee. I sent for the runners, then delivered a message to the colonel that gave him the particulars." He knocked back half of his whiskey. "There was a trunk in Mrs. Sawyer's dressing room that was partially packed. I could find no evidence of a specific destination. She might have been intending to leave him."

"Or leave with him," South said. "What do you think, East? Did it seem the packing was done in haste or with some care?"

East considered what he had seen in Annette's dressing room. "It was done carefully, though not with the economy of space that one expects from a servant. I believe she must have been doing the thing herself." That seemed to indicate Annette had not wanted anyone in the household to know she meant to leave. The runners would question the servants, but Eastlyn wished he had taken the time to do the thing himself. Something of his frustration must have shown on his face, for the others were quick to remind him of what had already been accomplished.

"You put the Bishops in one room," said North. "That was no small feat."

West nodded and pushed back a lock of hair that had fallen across his forehead. "The colonel will get everything he wants to know from them. Prinny's presence will be a pure torture for them, East. Bloody brilliant of you to think of including him."

"Lady Dunsmore is safe," South said. "Given what happened to Mrs. Sawyer this evening, you may well have saved her ladyship's life."

East did not dismiss their statements out of hand, yet they rang a trifle hollow. He did not have Dunsmore, and the viscount ultimately had been his responsibility.

Sophie rose from her seat and went to her husband. "I am sorry for your loss," she said quietly. "I cannot imagine how terrible it must have been for you to find her."

East was made speechless by her sincere concern. He drew her close, at once mindful of his audience and uncaring of it, and rested his chin against the crown of her head. He breathed deeply of her scent and absorbed her hard-won calm. It was easy to forget that Dunsmore was her cousin, and that she might harbor fears that his blood stain would attach itself to her.

He raised her face and kissed her smooth brow before he

set her from him. "Some sherry, West, if you please." He led Sophie back to the couch and joined her. He looked to the others for suggestions of what could be done next. "Desperation will dictate if Dunsmore will come here for his ledger and his wife's journal. It can be planned for, but not predicted. I thought I would be escorting him here tonight."

"No one could have known he would be moved to kill Mrs. Sawyer," West said. The gravity of their situation kept him from pointing out that there were times he could have cheerfully done the thing himself. He handed Sophie a small glass of sherry and encouraged her to drink. "Does Dunsmore have a favorite haunt?"

"Only the usual places all gentlemen are wont to go," she said. "The clubs and gaming hells. The theater." She glanced at Eastlyn. "What about the Flower House? Would he go there?"

"No," he said, ignoring the startled expressions of his friends. "He would not go there tonight."

South rested his chin on his fist; his brow was creased with thought. "If he got some sniff of what was in the air tonight, he would go to ground. It is the only thing that makes sense. It is possible that he learned something from Mrs. Sawyer. She was remarkably well connected, East. You know that."

"It is one thing to know the fox has gone to earth," North said, "and quite another to find the den. It required considerable good fortune to find Elizabeth when she did not want to be found, and you know the effort that was made to return Miss Parr to London. How much more difficult will it be to hunt someone we do not know nearly as well?"

"Infinitely more difficult," South said. "Perhaps all of a week. Are you in?"

"Of course." North reached in his pocket and extracted two shillings and placed them on the arm of his chair. "I make it to be ten days before we find him. West?"

"Six and one-half days. I'm an optimist." He found two shillings and placed them beside North's. "South?"

"Seven full days." He tossed his money to North. "East? What chance do you give Dunsmore when we are all in the hunt?"

Sophie stayed East's hand when he would have gone searching for his coins. She remembered him regaling her with tales of these wagers, but had never thought to witness one. To hear someone else tell her of this one, she would have wondered at the absurdity of it, perhaps judging it to be crass given all that had come before. Yet being a party to it, she saw it differently. The wager bonded them to a single cause and strengthened their resolve. For all that the thing was made with a certain black humor, it was also made in earnest. "Do you have enough for me?" she asked East. "I should like to be included."

"Of course." He looked to his friends for approval. "If there is no objection?"

They all agreed there was none and watched East show coin enough for himself and Sophie.

"I will be heartily glad if we find him in a sennight," he said, "but I think it will take twice as long to put him in the Tower. Sophie?"

"I suspect that if you are good at what you do, you shall find him before the night is out." She took a sip of her sherry as they exchanged puzzled glances.

"Perhaps you did not follow the conversation," East said.

"No. I followed it exactly. It was what Lord Southerton said about the hunt that made me think of it. Robert told me tonight that his father had gone to Artemis. She is the Greek goddess of the hunt, is she not? Might Artemis not also be the name of a ship?"

All four men surged to their feet at the same time. North dropped the collection of coins in Sophie's lap on his way to the door. "Your winnings," he told her. "Artemis is no ship, but a ship's captain."

East dropped a kiss on Sophie's cheek. "He is master of the *Raleigh*. It is a packet ship on the Black Ball Line, one that makes regular voyages to Boston from Liverpool."

"Liverpool? But you will never catch him tonight if he has gone to—" She stopped because Eastlyn had already picked up his coat and gloves and was following the rest of the Compass Club out the door.

Sophie dismissed the maid who was sitting with Lady Dunsmore and took up the position herself. Although she had prepared herself for bed, she knew there was almost no possibility that she would sleep for what remained of the night. There was some measure of comfort in being companion once again to Abigail.

It was difficult to reconcile the fragile figure in the bed with the one who had credibly resisted the efforts of Northam, Southerton, and West to remove her from her home. Her shrieking aside, South reported a number of injuries to his person, most of them the result of well-placed kicks below the knee. Northam had taken a blow to his midsection, and West—who had been the one to finally subdue her—had sported several red marks along his jaw. Had Lady Dunsmore not chewed her nails to the quick, she would have drawn blood.

Sophie brushed aside damp tendrils of hair from Abigail's cheek and forehead. "Poor Abigail," she said softly. "What a secret you have required yourself to keep." There was no change in the cadence of Lady Dunsmore's even breathing, nor any alteration of her pale, drawn features. It was impossible not to note that she was considerably thinner than she had been this past summer, and Sophie could only suspect that her own absence from Bowden Street had contributed to the decline. Harold had been free to act against his wife without fear of reprisal from any quarter.

Sophie refilled a glass of water at Abigail's bedside before she sat down. To make the interminable waiting more bearable, she worked on an embroidery piece that required almost no thought and very little in the way of a fine hand. She occupied herself in this manner for the better part of an hour before she fell into a light doze.

"He's here."

Those two words pushed Sophie into wakefulness. The embroidery hoop slid from her nerveless fingers and dropped to the floor. Blinking, she sat upright, only to find that Abigail had already done the same. It was only then that Sophie realized the urgent whisper had not been part of a dream already forgotten, but a cry from the wraithlike figure in the bed.

"Abby?" Rising, Sophie went immediately to her side and blocked her from easily leaving the bed. "What is it? What can I do for you?"

"He's here."

There was such insistency in the words that Sophie found herself glancing over her shoulder. "No one is here," she said. "It is naught but a dream." She remembered how often she had been required to soothe her father in just such a fashion, knowing all the while that dreaming hardly described the visions that had plagued him. Looking at Abigail's features, Sophie saw the same vacancy of expression she had seen in her father. There could be terror, sorrow, or worry expressed in the voice, but the countenance remained oddly calm.

She sat on the edge of the bed and offered Abigail a drink of water. The offer was not acknowledged, and when Sophie pressed the glass to Abby's lips, there was no attempt to sip or swallow. "Will you not lie down?" Sophie asked. She placed one hand on Abigail's shoulder and pressed lightly. When she was met with resistance, she stopped and allowed her hand to fall away. "Very well. But you must remain abed."

Sophie could see no indication that she was heard, but she took it as a good sign that Abigail's restlessness subsided. She plumped the pillow at Abby's back, replaced the water glass, and stood. "Shall I go to the children?" she asked. "Will it give you peace to know they are both well?"

Except for a faint fluttering of her lashes, there was no response from Lady Dunsmore.

Sighing softly, Sophie made her decision. "I'll only be a moment." Until she was out of the room, Sophie did not realize how much she had desired to have some excuse to be so. No good memories were stirred by seeing Abigail in the same state as her father; the feelings of helplessness were as uncomfortable as they were unwelcome. Recognizing the need she had to do something, and understanding that she did it as much for herself as for Abigail, Sophie hurried down the hall toward the children's room.

The door opened even before she touched the knob. Sophie did not have time to register either surprise or dismay. She was pulled into the room so quickly that there was no sense of how the thing came about. What she recognized was the fierce grip just above her elbow. Harold had always known exactly how to place his thumb and fingers to make her light-headed with pain. Quite against her will, Sophie felt her knees begin to buckle. Harold's shadowed features filled the center of her vision, while darkness clouded all of the periphery. She would have sagged all the way to the carpet if he had not pressed her back to the door.

"Do not alarm the children," Harold said quietly. "Do you understand?"

Sophie nodded because it was expected of her, not because she understood anything that was said. Harold blocked her view of the large bed. She could not see if Robert and Esme were still sleeping or if Harold had already roused them.

Harold eased his grip and helped Sophie regain her balance. "I watched Eastlyn and his friends leave," he said. "You can expect no help from them, Sophie, and you cannot expect to fool me into thinking otherwise. I have come for my wife's diary and my ledger. I have it on good authority that Eastlyn took them."

Sophie did not answer. She strained to see past Harold, raising herself on tiptoe.

"Robert and Esme are fine," Harold told her, pulling her attention toward him again. "And will remain so. I know you have no good opinion of me, but I am not such a monster that I would hurt my own children."

"Then let us leave this room," Sophie said. When he didn't move, she added, "What you want is not here."

He hesitated, then nodded once.

When he stepped back, Sophie had a glimpse of the children sitting on the edge of the bed. It was enough for her to see that they both were more sleepy than frightened. "Let me tuck them in. It will only take a moment."

"A moment," he said.

Sophie went to the bedside and helped the children back under the covers. Esme curled against her brother and closed her eyes at once. Robert was less confident that all was as it should be.

"He told me to let him in," Robert whispered.

Sophie recognized that it was at once an explanation and a question. The boy needed reassurance that he had done nothing wrong. "Of course you should have done so. I would have done exactly the same thing if I had heard him. You must have very good ears, indeed."

Robert smiled sleepily. "I think I must. He told me he was not scratching at my window very long."

Behind her, Sophie felt Harold's approach. She bent and kissed Robert's forehead, then rose. "He wanted to say his prayers," she told Harold. Giving him no opportunity to challenge her, Sophie turned her back on him and quickly left the room. He had no choice but to follow her into the hallway. She had gone only a few steps before he brought her up short. Sophie closed her eyes briefly against the pain. The placement of his fingers was precise. She knew there would not be more bruises, only deeper ones.

"You are mistaken if you think I am intent on running from you," she said tightly. "I am only of a mind to give you what you came for and then to see the last of you."

Harold studied Sophie's face for a moment in the candlelight and wondered if he could believe her. He permitted his grip to relax a fraction. "Show me."

Sophie didn't take a forward step until he released her. When his hand dropped away she led him downstairs, glancing once toward the front door as they passed through the entrance hall.

Harold merely shook his head when he saw the direction of her gaze. "I suppose you think it would have been better if I had not come at all."

Sophie shrugged. "I cannot say if it would have been better. It only seems to me that you are taking a great risk by doing so."

He had only half an ear for her words. Her steps had slowed, and it was this that caught his attention. "What is it?"

"I am uncertain of the location of Eastlyn's library," she said. "I have not been in his home before this evening, Harold. I do not yet know my way through the rooms, or even if we will find what you want there."

Harold eyed her narrowly, trying to discern if there was a lie. He gave her full marks for not denying that she knew of the existence of Abigail's journal and his account book, or that Eastlyn had taken them, but this hesitation of hers now made him suspicious. "I have little in the way of patience remaining, Sophie. You would do well to begin searching."

Her chin came up. "And if I don't, Harold? What is it you will do? Can I expect the same as Mrs. Sawyer?" She saw his mouth tighten whitely at the corners. "Though I suppose you would prefer to poison me as you did my father and your own wife, there is insufficient time for such methods. It shall have to be a quicker end for me. East would give no details regarding your mistress's death. Did you strangle her?" She glanced down at her arm, then back at Dunsmore. "It is easy for me to imagine. I think there were many times when you took me by the arm that you wished it was my neck."

Harold did not respond. He reached past Sophie and opened the door behind her, then motioned to her to step inside. After removing a lighted candle from one of the sconces in the hallway, he followed. Even without the candle he would have known he was in Eastlyn's private study. He recognized the fragrances distinctive to leather bindings and rare books, the hint of tobacco smoke and port. "You have brought me to it straightaway," he said.

"It seems I have. I did not realize there would be so many. I do not know how you will take them all."

At first he did not understand what she meant, for it seemed odd to him that she would remark on the number of volumes Eastlyn had collected for his town library. It was only when he turned slightly and followed her gaze that he realized she had not been surveying the floor-to-ceiling shelves lining the room. Her attention was on the pyramid of wooden crates stacked beside the fireplace; at the apex they towered above the marble mantel.

Harold brushed past Sophie and held out his candle. The crates were stamped with Eastlyn's Everly Square address, the contents clearly marked as books. He asked the question, not because he did not know the answer, but because he required hearing the answer to believe it. "What books are these, Sophie?"

"The ones you came for," she said with perfect calm. "Abigail's journal and your ledger of accounts. The Society's ledgers as well, though you did not ask for them. Scores and scores of each, I imagine. I shall leave you to them, Harold."

Dunsmore spun around and made to lunge at Sophie. She eluded him, in part because she was prepared for just such a predictable end, but also because Eastlyn's presence on the threshold of the library made Harold falter, then go rigid with surprise.

East held out his hand to Sophie, pulling her toward him quickly when she accepted it. He moved to one side in the doorway, allowing her to pass, then pressing her to stay just behind him. He noticed she had some objection to this position, perhaps because she was thinking he was arriving rather late to the rescue. "Did you believe for even a moment that I was not nearby?" he asked.

"Robert told me he let you in," she said. "Could you not use the front door? You might have frightened the children."

"Your cousin was watching the front of the house."

"I saw you leave." It was Dunsmore who spoke, not Sophie.

Eastlyn shrugged. "I know. West glimpsed you as he was mounting his animal. One can be too furtive, you know, and that was your mistake. West has a remarkable eye for what is out of place. You should have fled to Liverpool, Dunsmore. There would have been a few hours reprieve in it for you. It occurred to me that you might come for your books, but I could not depend upon it. Mrs. Sawyer told you I had them?"

Dunsmore nodded vaguely as he tried to take in what Eastlyn was telling him. Light flickered across his features as the candle in his hand wavered.

"She also told you about the invitations that Prinny extended to certain members of the Society," East said.

This time Dunsmore found his voice. "Yes."

East wished it had been otherwise, and something of his regret showed on his face. "I intended that she should know about your ledger," he said. "And Lady Dunsmore's journal, of course. Then, if she chose to remain under your protection, she would at least know the nature of the man who was keeping her."

"You knew that she would tell me," Dunsmore said. "You wanted her to."

"I hoped she would," East admitted. "But I did not consider that she would learn about the invitations to Windsor Castle. I knew the danger of giving her too much information. Was she cuckolding you, Dunsmore? Is that how she came to know about the Prince Regent's invitations?"

Dunsmore's expression turned scornful. "She had Barlough in her bed. And Pendrake. Both of them while she was under my protection. It never occurred to her that I would realize the truth when she told me about their invitations. Her protestations aside, I knew immediately how she had come by this latest *on dit*." His short bark of laughter held no humor. "Poor Annette. It was impossible for her to suspect that she was being manipulated. Barlough and Pendrake went to her bed to take a pound of *my* flesh, not hers. She was so naive."

In that one regard, perhaps she was, East thought. "Was she leaving you for one of them?" he asked.

"For Barlough or Pendrake? No. She was leaving me, though you should not imagine I was made jealous by that. She was a whore, after all. No better than she ought to be."

"The bargain you struck with her was for her protection. She did not deserve to die."

"She wanted more of everything. Money. Power. Standing. There was no reasoning with her. I did not know about these books then, Eastlyn, and obviously, neither did she. I might have spared her had I understood that silencing her would accomplish nothing. I still thought if I could collect my books and go, things might once again be turned in my favor." Raising his candle, he gestured toward the pyramid of crates. "A pity they cannot easily be burned. There are more elsewhere, I collect."

"Many more."

He nodded. "A pity. It is not your intention to exact a fortune from me, then."

"No. Nor from anyone in the Society."

"I see." Harold looked past Eastlyn to where Sophie stood. Though her complexion was pale, she remained maddeningly composed. "I am still your family, Sophie. Have you considered that? Robert. Esme. Even Abigail. All of them will come to hate you when they learn of your part in this. They will be stained forever if these books become fodder for the public."

"If they come to bear me ill will," she said evenly, "then I hope that in time they will also come to forgive me. I can ask no more of them than that."

"And what of me, Sophie? What is to become of me?"

Eastlyn shook his head, drawing Dunsmore's eyes to him. "She has no part in that decision."

"Then it is to be you? What satisfaction will you demand? Pistols? I have heard it remarked upon that you have quite a steady hand."

"No. I am of no mind to shoot you, though there would be

some pleasure in it. But as you said, you are still Sophie's family, and she is my wife." East noted that Dunsmore did credibly well masking his surprise; it was only the rapid blinking of his eyes that gave him away. "That makes you a member of my family as well," East said. "Therefore, you are quite free to go. There is satisfaction enough for me in knowing how popular these books will become."

For a moment Dunsmore could not believe his good fortune; the pressure in his chest actually eased. It was when he caught the cutting edge of East's tempered smile that the full impact of what had been planned was borne home. As quickly as that, he could no longer draw a complete breath. "They will kill me," he whispered hoarsely. "The Bishops will kill me. You cannot make me leave. Where will I go?"

"I cannot say what they will do, or where you will go, or even how far you will get, but I *can* make you leave. My friends are prepared to help if called upon to do so. I would be remiss if I did not mention they were in favor of shooting you." He gave Sophie a sideways glance. "Will you open the front door?"

Nodding, she ducked from under Eastlyn's protective arm and slipped away.

Panicked now, Dunsmore actually stumbled backward as Eastlyn made to seize him. A plump dollop of hot candle wax fell on the ball of his thumb. Unprepared for the flash of pain, he reflexively jerked his hand toward his chest. The movement extinguished the flame. Darkness gave him a moment's respite, and he dived for cover behind where he imagined the crates to be. He missed his mark by only a few inches, but it was enough to throw his shoulder into one of the sharp corners. The pyramid groaned, shifted, and the hasty construction of this monument to his avarice did not hold. The crates were pushed wildly askew by his weight and momentum.

Dunsmore threw up his arms to protect his head as the whole of his life crashed in upon him.

Epilogue

Eastlyn turned Sophie in a graceful arc as they reached
the edge of the ballroom. The hem of her lavender silk gown
lifted, swirled, and settled modestly back into place as she
followed his lead. Her face was raised to his, and he guided
her as much with his glance as the pressure of his hand at her
back. The eddy of silk that brushed his legs was only a mild
distraction. It was the promise in her eyes that made it difficult to concentrate on the three-quarter strains of the waltz.

"Have a care, Sophie," he whispered, narrowly avoiding a
collision with the prime minister and Lady Powell. "Unless
it is your desire to leave the assembly early, you must exercise a modicum of restraint."

Nothing about Sophie's expression changed in the least.

Eastlyn raised an eyebrow. "I see you mean to test me."

Her smile merely deepened.

"I believe I saw a cupboard under the stairs that might
suit," he said dryly. "Do you fancy a turn with the linens and
dusters?"

"It would be a squeeze."

"Overcrowded, is it?"

She nodded.

East sighed. "I should have thought of it sooner." His eyes darted around the large room. Crystal chandeliers split the candlelight into rainbows that were no less bright than the spinning, shimmering crowd. He noted that his friends and their ladies were all accounted for and that the widow Powell was still in the arms of the prime minister. The Dowager Countess of Northam was engaged in deep conversation with Lord and Lady Redding, most likely over the particulars of a wager, he suspected. Colonel Blackwood had the ear of Wellington and two representatives of the East India Company, while a number of distinguished guests sidled closer. At first glance, Eastlyn could find no one obviously missing. It was only when he glimpsed his sister being led onto the floor by her husband that he realized who had absented themselves from the ballroom. "Devil a bit, never say it is my own parents."

Sophie's smile widened a fraction. "It is my most fervent wish, my lord, that when we have enjoyed a like number of years together, you will still want to fondle me under the stairs."

"You may depend upon it."

It was the resolve in Eastlyn's voice that put Sophie to a blush. She was glad for the turn that set her back to the guests. By the time Eastlyn brought her around, she was once again composed. Only she knew how her heart tripped over itself; if not for East's steady lead, her feet might have done the same.

The glitter and color and candlelight of the assembly was magnified in the large gilt-framed mirror angled above the entrance to the ballroom. Sophie glanced over East's shoulder to observe their reflection as they passed. When her eyes shifted back to him, she saw that he had caught her out and was amused by her lapse into self-absorption.

"I cannot help it," she said without apology. "I have not the same measure of confidence that you possess. I must look in a mirror from time to time and assure myself I am all of a piece."

"Is that what you think, Sophie? That it is confidence that keeps me from turning my head?"

A small crease puckered her brow. "Isn't it?"

His slight smile was enigmatic.

Sophie's steps faltered a bit, and the miscue set her off balance almost as much as his smile. Had she misjudged him so profoundly? "Your presence in any room is invariably noted, East. Surely you are aware of that."

"I should be the greatest of fools if I were not."

"Then you take my point."

"Only if you insist that I should."

"I am of a mind to trod upon your toes, my lord, but we should be made sadly awkward by it. You are being perfectly obtuse, you know."

"Perfectly? There is some comfort in perfection." Before Sophie could manage a retort, East guided her through the open French doors at the end of the ballroom and onto the wide portico. The night was cool and clear, and as many stars shone in the blue-black sky as diamonds flashed among the dancers. Eastlyn led Sophie away from the circle of candlelight. As soon as they were safely ensconced in shadow, he pressed her against the marble balustrade and kissed her soundly.

Sophie did not discourage the kiss; rather she looped her arms around his neck for better purchase and stood on tiptoe to greet it. The brisk air prickled her skin, but the shelter of Eastlyn's shoulders warmed her again. "It is a good distraction," she whispered when he drew back. "But I think you know that."

Eastlyn raised Sophie's cashmere shawl around her upper arms and knotted the ends just below her breasts. "If it were a better distraction, you would not note it at all." He brushed his lips to hers once more. "I want to take you home. The cupboard there will not be so crowded."

Sophie's smile was sweetly regretful. "It is unfortunate, then, that this evening is in your honor."

"It is in the colonel's honor."

"Only officially. The East India Company is in your debt, even if you will not allow them to properly say so. Their settlement will be firmly established before the year is out, and it is in no small part because of your effort."

Eastlyn fell quiet as he reflected on the consequences of that effort. "I am not entirely proud of it," he said at last. "There will be a military presence in Singapore, a hundredfold increase in the opium trade, and more ill will toward the Crown than we can fully appreciate. We have not yet reckoned with the cost of success, Sophie." He raised his hand and laid it against her cheek. His thumb brushed the line of her lower lip. "And what of the price that was yours to pay? What I accomplished required that you surrender something at every turn."

Sophie shook her head. Her cheek rubbed against the cup of his palm. "My good name?" she asked with ironic inflection. "I loved my father very much, but the family name was already in a state of disrepair before his death. It was no sacrifice to accept yours."

"That is not precisely how I remember it. No man has been turned down more often than I in offering his name."

Her breathy little chuckle vibrated against his hand. "That still rankles, does it?"

"A tad."

Sophie took his hand and placed her lips in the heart of his palm. "If there is a wound, I would heal it." Her smile faded as she laced her fingers through his and lowered their clasped hands. "I have no regrets, East. None. Perhaps it is wrong of me to harden my heart against Tremont, but I can rouse no pity for him. Transportation is a fitting punishment, perhaps more exacting in its toll on his spirit than hanging would have been. That his good friends will be his companions on the voyage is also fitting, for they might have expected hanging as well. They have you to thank for their lives."

"Or curse for them," East said.

"Or curse," she repeated.

"Dunsmore?"

Sophie shut her eyes briefly against the vision of Harold lying so still beneath the toppled pyramid. When the crates had been cleared, there had been almost no blood to signify death, only an awkwardly positioned head on the broken stem of his neck. Two months had passed since that night, but the sight was still called too easily to mind. "It was a kinder fate than the Bishops would have shown him, kinder still to Robert and Esme to know their father's death was an accident and not murder. The Prince Regent showed great compassion in not confiscating the estate. Tremont Park will be Robert's now, as it should be, and I know that has come to pass because you interceded on his behalf."

"It was the colonel."

"It was *you*. It is no good denying it. I shall always recognize a tinker's work."

"Lady Dunsmore has suffered enough," East said quietly. "And the children do not deserve the sins of their father."

Sophie drew his hand to the swell of her stomach, still barely noticeable beneath her open silk tunic. "What of a father's goodness?" she asked. "I wish our child might have your compassion and kindness, your strength of character, your sense of what is right and the resolve to pursue it."

Eastlyn bent his head and kissed Sophie's smooth brow as she blinked back tears. "Dull stuff, all of that," he whispered. "Better that she will have your stubborn streak and bedevil us by being up to every trick." He lifted Sophie's chin. "She should also have your eyes."

They both gave a small start as their child kicked hard.

"There is proof of strength," Sophie said.

Chuckling, Eastlyn smoothed the tunic over her belly. "And character." He stepped back, taking Sophie's elbow as he recognized familiar voices approaching from the ballroom.

"Said they were out here, didn't I?" South announced. "That's a shilling each you owe me, and I'm not accepting markers. You shall have to part with the whole of it at once."

He held out his hand, and North and West dutifully placed a shilling in his palm.

"Where did you think we'd gone?" East asked Northam.

"The cupboard under the stairs."

Sophie and East traded glances. Hers was filled with humor, his with something more akin to horror.

West observed this exchange and said, "We made our apologies to your parents, East, so all is right with the world. They were extraordinarily gracious, considering."

East held up one hand. "You will spare me the details, West, else I will want to know the name of your seconds."

Laughing, West shook his head. "You will hear none of it from me."

To assure that secrecy was kept, East pointedly regarded the other two. "North? South?"

"East?" Southerton asked wryly.

Sophie glanced at the only direction left. "West?"

He grinned boyishly. "Very well, my lady. The whole of it is this: Friends for life, we have confessed."

South took up the rhyme. "All other truths, we'll deny."

North added, "For we are soldier."

"Sailor," said South.

East drew Sophie closer. "Tinker."

"Spy." West made a slight bow.

Delighted with their impromptu recital, Sophie applauded. "Bad verse can have no greater champion. I am awed."

"Do not encourage South," North said. "He will be moved to write a second stanza, and the man is no Byron."

"Byron is no Southerton," South said.

No one argued with this pithy observation.

West gestured toward the open doors. "The colonel wishes to escort your wife to supper, East. That is, if you will permit him."

"Sophie?" East asked.

She nodded. "The colonel flatters me." She stood on tiptoe and kissed Eastlyn's cheek. "Tonight is in his honor, after all."

With varying degrees of admiration and amusement, the Compass Club watched Sophie gracefully exit the portico and disappear into the crowded ballroom.

It was after midnight when Sophie and East arrived at Everly Square. They were met at the door by the butler and relieved of their outerwear. Eastlyn's eyes went immediately to the stairs in anticipation of seeing young Robert peering around the landing. Sophie saw the direction of his gaze and knew the purpose of it. It had been nine days since Abigail and the children had moved to Tremont Park, but Sophie still thought the house seemed inordinately quiet without them. Throughout Abigail's recovery, Lady Gilbert had been her constant companion, so Sophie was not surprised when her aunt chose to leave London for the Park. What Sophie could not have anticipated was that she would miss the sound of Lady Gilbert pounding the floors and stairs with her cane.

Sophie touched East's hand. "This respite will be short lived, my lord. Perhaps we should determine to enjoy it."

"I can think of several ways."

Sophie watched East's eyes stray to the upper floor a second time, and she recognized the glint in them for what it was. "I would race you to the top, but I am hampered by these skirts."

"And your enormous belly." He noticed she was not at all displeased by this description. He scooped her up as she critically examined the swell of her abdomen. "You are still as slim as a virgin."

"Hardly that, but your mother says I am unlikely to show overmuch until my eighth month."

Eastlyn started up the stairs. "You will refrain from mentioning my mother. It is bound to put me off my stride."

Knowing the importance of stride, Sophie pressed her lips together tightly. Sampson was waiting for them when they reached the bedchamber. The valet accepted his dismissal with his usual neutral demeanor and blandly offered to keep Sophie's maid from disturbing them as well.

"Now you have done it, Sophie." East dropped her on the bed. "Sampson will not forgive you if you ruin my stock."

Sophie raised herself on her elbows and crooked a finger at him. When he bent, she pulled on it, then him. As soon as he was sprawled beside her, she turned and kissed him full on the mouth. His arms would have come around her, but she drew back and shook her head. "I have had it in my mind all evening that I should undress you," she whispered. "You have no objections, I hope."

"None."

"Good." She sat up and took his hand, urging him to follow her when she left the bed. "Come, my lord. Some things are best accomplished in the dressing room." Sophie felt some initial reluctance, but she overcame it with an over-the-shoulder glance that promised much in return for his co-operation.

The dressing room they shared was crowded with two armoires, a vanity, three padded stools, a washstand, commode, and a large cheval glass. Sophie guided East across the small Persian rug and directly to the mirror, softening his discomfort by stepping in front of him. Reaching behind her, she found his wrists and pulled his arms around her until they were crossed under her breasts. She caught his eyes in the mirror.

"What do you see, East?"

"All I ever needed."

Sophie's eyes brightened with unshed tears, and her smile was watery. She had to work her words past the ache in her throat. "I love you for saying so," she said quietly, "but I know you hope I will be put from my purpose. Will you not lift your eyes, my lord, and tell me what you see."

Eastlyn glanced at his reflection. "An extraordinarily fortunate man."

"An uncommonly handsome one," she said. "But I have

never known you to acknowledge it. I have always supposed you cared little for what society makes of your fine looks and your manner, but I think now that perhaps you have cared too much. It is still the roly-poly young boy you see, is it not? The one with a fondness for sweets who eagerly thrashed anyone who remarked on his size. You have not been that boy for a very long time, though I wonder if you are not afraid you will glimpse him when you look upon your reflection. I mean for you to be done thrashing yourself, my lord, and see what I see."

Sophie turned in East's arms and began to unbutton his frock coat. She felt his breath catch when he realized her intent, but he did not stop her, not when she discarded his coat, nor when she loosened his stock. He watched her delicate, deliberate movements as though from a distance at first, then came to see them more clearly as he reconciled the vision in the mirror with the one he had harbored in his mind's eye.

Sophie ran her hands across his broad shoulders, then down his arms, smoothing the fine linen fabric of his shirt before she removed it. She laid her lips at the curve of his bare throat and settled her palms on either side of his trim waist. She knelt slowly, her mouth making a damp line of kisses along his taut flesh. His skin retracted where her fingertips trailed. She applied herself to his shoes and stockings, then finally his satin breeches and drawers, and when he was naked she made love to him with her mouth and hands, every kiss a perfectly nuanced expression of carnal passion and depth of feeling.

She brought him to his knees, and he played the lady's maid, stripping her of silk and cashmere, satin and batiste, until it was only her flesh beneath his hands, soft and pliant, warm and achingly responsive. The glass was forgotten; voyeuristic pleasures paled in the wake of absorbing the heat of each new caress. They learned to see themselves through the eyes of the other, and that vision was at once distorted by love and made unflinchingly honest by it.

In the aftermath of lovemaking, he took her to bed, and

they settled there, deep in the downy comforter, fitted like spoons in a drawer. Sophie stared out the window and silently counted the stars framed by the sash. "There are eleven tonight," she told him.

East raised his head and followed the direction of her gaze. "So there are." He propped himself on an elbow and studied Sophie's features in profile. "Do you find your peace there?"

"Sometimes," she said. She welcomed the arm that slipped around her waist. "I am not so alone as I used to be, but there is always comfort in what is familiar." She stroked the back of his hand with her fingertips. "Is it the same for you?"

He nodded. "It used to be a package that arrived at Hambrick Hall every Thursday. Scones. Biscuits. Tarts. Little iced cakes. I was partial to those cakes, you know."

Sophie turned on her back and looked up at him. "And now?"

Eastlyn bent his head and brushed her mouth with his own. "Don't you know, Sophie? It is this sweetness that I crave, and the woman who has courage enough to give me my just desserts."

About the Author

JO GOODMAN lives with her family in Colliers, West Virginia. She is currently working on her newest Zebra historical romance, the fourth book of her Compass Club series set during the Regency period. Look for West's story in August 2004. Jo loves hearing from readers, and you may write to her c/o Zebra Books. Please include a self-addressed stamped envelope if you would like a response. Or you can visit her website at www.jogoodman.com